FAMILIES
AT WAR

Ken Scott

and

Dave Rowland

OAK TREE PRESS

This edition published in 2013 by
Oak Tree Press
www.oaktreepress.co.uk

Oak Tree Press is an imprint of
Andrews UK Limited
The Hat Factory
Bute Street
Luton, LU1 2EY

This book is based on a true story, the characters depicted
therein are real but all names have been changed to protect the
privacy of families still living in the Valencian Community,
including that of Felipe Albero Gomez. The tragic events during
the Spanish Civil War described in this book are historically
accurate, to the best of both authors knowledge

Cover photograph of Felipe Albero Gomez aged 19
He is alive and well and living in Altea aged 96
Photographer is unknown

Dedicated to Felipe Albero Gomez and the ordinary working man of Spain who had no choice but to fight in a war orchestrated by others

Key Characters

Juan Francisco Cortes – The stolen, abandoned child

Maria Bejerano Aznar – Mother of Juan Francisco Cortes

Felipe Albero Gomez – Father of Juan Francisco Cortes

Inmaculada Aznar Masanet – Maria's Mother

Miguel Orts Bejerano – Marias Father

Jose and Bertomeu – Maria's brothers

Father Pascual Bautista Cano – The priest.

Vicente Cortes Ortuño – Adoptive father of Juan Francisco Cortes

Fatima Ausina Devesa – Adoptive mother of Juan Francisco Cortes

Mayor – Nicolas Barber Lloret.

FAMILIES
AT WAR

Prologue

Sunday was an altogether perfect day for Maria Bejerano Aznar.

"No work today," her Mother announced with a smile as she woke Maria from her slumber with a cool cup of orange juice freshly squeezed that morning. Oranges were always in plentiful supply in the tiny mountain village of Abdet in the province of Alicante, one of the few things that were.

Her parents took great pride in tending their small plot of land on which they grew oranges, lemons, olives, almonds and even a lone avocado tree that yielded nearly two hundred fruit each year. They grew tomatoes and peppers and potatoes too and her mother was regarded as a bit of a specialist in tending a small herb garden at the rear of the house. Although an idyllic and peaceful existence it was heavy, backbreaking work tending the land which provided them with barely enough food to sustain the family through the winter and Maria recalled many an evening when she and her brothers and sisters were sent to bed hungry.

But Sundays were different. Her mother would be singing the hymns they'd sing over and over again at church and without fail as Maria climbed down the stairs to the small room on the ground floor her mother and father would be sat at the laden table with smiles on their faces.

She'd look at the fresh bread and eggs and a little ham, tomatoes and oranges, a pot of milk and always, always, always a jug of steaming hot coffee. It was a delightfully pleasant change from the usual crude breakfast of day old bread and olive oil which occasionally, as a midweek treat, had a sprinkling of salt.

They'd say grace and then begin as if they'd fasted for a month, the children continuously scolded for eating too fast.

It mattered not if the family went without for the rest of the week. Sunday was different... Sunday was perfect.

"It is the day of the Lord," her mother would say. "We must eat drink and be merry for today we show our appreciation to our Holy Father."

After breakfast the whole family would wash. The children would strip down to their underclothes while father hauled

1

bucket after bucket of ice cold water from the well that was fed by a mountain stream and poured it over them. They'd shriek and scream as the freezing water enveloped their bodies but if the truth be told Maria enjoyed the weekly ritual even if it did take her breath away. Even as her mother scrubbed at her finger nails with a harsh, well-worn scrubbing brush and raked a toothless comb painfully through her long dark hair Maria enjoyed the feeling of being clean and recalled the priest's words that cleanliness was next to Godliness.

Afterwards the Sunday best clothes would be set out on the chairs and boxes that stood around the eating table but on no account were they to be worn until the church bell struck the half hour mark before midday mass.

The children would yell and cheer as the bell chimes seemed to fill the entire room and they ran to the chairs in a competition to see who could get ready first. Outside they'd be inspected as mother made them line up, armed with a clean white handkerchief which she used to remove the dirt and grime from the faces and hands that the water had failed to shift.

Señora Inmaculada would walk up and down the line like a soldier overseeing her troops and only when she was absolutely one hundred per cent sure that the family had passed muster would she disappear inside the house to shout for her husband.

Maria heard the raised voices again. It was the same every Sunday.

"What are they arguing about?" her young brother asked.

"Money" she replied. "Always money on a Sunday, money that we don't have."

Her young brother frowned. "Then why are they arguing if we do not have any?" he asked with a puzzled look on his face.

Maria shrugged her shoulders. "We must give it to the church."

"But how can we give it if we don't have it?"

Her brother's reply was logical and she answered as she always did.

"It doesn't matter Jose, we still must give. The Church is poor; the Lord needs it more than we do."

It was a nonsense answer but somehow it made sense to her and as always she backed it up with the same answer that the family had eaten well that day with eggs and ham and fresh bread and it was the Lord who had provided for them.

They'd walk through the dusty, shady streets of the village weaving their way through the small and dilapidated ramshackle houses. The houses were whitewashed and baked by the hot sun; they had hardly altered since the Moors had lived there in the 1200s.

A hundred metres before the church Felipe Albero Gomez would be waiting for Maria.

Felipe and Maria had known each other all their lives. They were very close and plainly very fond of each other. It was hardly surprising as they were born just a week apart and since they were a few days old, their mothers had carried them to the fields, where they were placed together on the same rough straw mats in the shade of the olive trees.

It was underneath the olive trees that their inseparable bond had started.

As they grew older, they walked with their families to the fields taking an active part in the work as they grew stronger and wiser. When they reached their teenage years they were working as hard and as long as their parents. The winters were cold in the mountains and the work unpleasant but mercifully the days were short. In the spring and summer months they worked their fingers to the bone, they started work before daybreak in an attempt to avoid the worst of the heat. The atmosphere was stifling, the sun unrelenting and in the village the sun was hot enough to make the stones and earth in the rough roads too hot to walk on. Maria looked on in envy at the only girl in the village whose parents had been able to afford a pair of sandals. Isabel Morales walked tall and proud, she walked without looking where she placed her feet. Perhaps one day Maria would do the same.

The village church was elegant, pristine, clean looking and shiny. It stood out like a diamond in a rough stone quarry. Its imposing structure towered over the rest of the crumbling houses, reinforcing the idea in Maria's mind that God was indeed the superior being, the church all powerful.

The church was full, save for the sick and infirm, every single person in the village who could walk the short journey to the place of worship attended the Sunday service. Maria sat with Felipe and their respective families and she enjoyed every minute of the service delivered from under the shadow of the figure of the Virgin Mary which occupied pride of place in the church.

She loved the singing that echoed around the ancient stone building as the sun streamed through the beautiful ornate stained glass windows picking at the dust particles that lingered in the air. Even when Father Cano delivered his sermon and he grew rather animated and shouted at the villagers whom he occasionally called sinners Maria took on board what it was he was saying and convinced herself as long as she behaved and prayed every night she had nothing to fear and the wrath of God would not come tumbling down upon her.

What Maria didn't enjoy was the school after church, especially when the weather was warm outside. The Church was the sole educator in the village, Father Cano the only teacher. To the smaller children the priest was a fearsome figure, and although Maria enjoyed some of the lessons, Father Cano always seemed to drift off on an angry rant at least two or three times ferociously warning the children of what would happen to them if they dared to stray from the strict rules of the Catholic Church and the ten commandments of Moses. He'd tell the children about a place called hell where if they sinned they'd be sent for eternity.

He painted a fearsome picture of this terrible place where it was hot and smoky and fires burned constantly, where God would send you to suffer and choke and to be punished and tortured forever until the end of time. But Father Cano always reminded them that God loved his little children.

During these lessons Maria would look out of the huge polished windows and long to be out in the sunshine playing with Felipe.

After church Maria and Felipe made the most of the Sabbath. They enjoyed the open air and often spent the evenings with the other village children laughing and playing in the deep cool pools of crystal clear water that the River Algar had carved out over the centuries. There was never a shortage of playmates but from the moment that Maria and Felipe were put together, their parents noticed that they were immensely comfortable in each other's company.

No one else seemed to exist and there was never much doubt amongst the more astute villagers and elders that the children would end up married to each other once they grew into young adults.

One day in Sunday school when Maria and Felipe were aged thirteen, Father Cano decided that their friendship was somehow unhealthy and made them sit on opposite sides of the class. Afterwards he lectured Maria in the evils of participating in the sins of the flesh. Try as she might she couldn't understand what Father Cano was talking about.

Maria and Felipe were older now and in the company of the other young teenagers. Their parents announced one day after church that they were now old enough to be trusted to take the mules laden with almonds and olives down to the coast to sell at the markets around the fishing village of Altea. The trip would take all day, Maria's father announced. It was a major expedition and although Abdet was only 18km from the coast it was at an altitude of 700 metres and it was a long trek down to the coast and a tiresome return journey.

Maria could hardly sleep with excitement the night before the trip. She had watched the older children returning from their ventures for many years and listened while they had described their escapades, the sea and the beaches and the boisterous nature of the market place. She longed to make the journey and to dip her toes in the cool Mediterranean Sea, something she had never set eyes on.

They left at 4am. Felipe and Maria shared a mule and there were two other mules and four older children from the village. They had a pack on the back of each mule with clay jugs of water, some bread, cheese and some dried figs.

The trip down to Altea took over five hours. They followed the carefully maintained tracks first carved out by their Arab forefathers. The idea was to sell the almonds and olives in Altea and buy some dried fish and beans to return with but only if the prices were right. Their parents had given them strict instructions on how much to sell their produce for and how much to pay in return. If they couldn't get what they needed at the right price they were to bring the money home and return another day.

The trip down was uneventful, the air was still cool and they were altogether excited about their new adventure and they talked of nothing but reaching the beach and putting their feet into the sea.

Eventually they arrived at Altea and bartered with the locals as if they'd been doing the markets for years. There were many men who tried to take advantage of their inexperience but they stuck to their guns and managed to get a good price for their produce. Later they purchased beans and dried fish and had a little money left over to enjoy a little lunch from a roadside vendor.

The cool seawater beckoned. It was tantalisingly close to the market and the thought of washing the dust and grime from their filthy bodies was more than they could resist. The youngsters tied the mules to an old palm tree on the beach and walked tentatively into the water. For Maria it was the most magical day of her life. Felipe took off his shirt and plunged head first into the water. As he surfaced he pleaded with Maria to join him. He watched as Maria removed her dress and walked towards him in only a light undergarment. She bent down and splashed water at him before immersing herself in the salty water. As she stood up Felipe became aware of the material clinging to her perfectly formed young body. It was the first time he had noticed the beautiful shape of her breasts and the dark mysterious triangle between her legs. Felipe became aware of a strange but pleasant sensation that he had never experienced before. A little embarrassed, he plunged back into the water.

All too soon it was time to start the return journey home, they had a long trip back and there were ominous clouds building on the horizon. By the time they had reached the tiny hamlet of Xirles an electrical storm had started and the rain was coming down in torrents.

Felipe turned to the oldest boy. "How far back?"

Carlos had been on the market journey many times and was by far the most experienced among the group.

"At least another three hours," he said. "I say we press on, this rain won't last forever."

As soon as Carlos spoke Maria gripped Felipe's hand. Ever since she was a child she'd hated the thunder and lightning but always had a shelter to run to.

"What is it?" he asked.

Maria explained.

The group were already debating whether to move on or seek shelter. The majority of them favoured continuing.

Carlos pointed ahead of him. "There are some old goat herders caves dug into the base of the hills about half a kilometre up that track in the forest. You can take shelter there if you want and catch us up when it stops."

Maria jumped as a streak of lightning forked across the sky. A few seconds later a brattle of thunder almost deafened them.

Felipe gazed into his friend's frightened eyes. "I think that might be a good idea Maria," he said.

They almost ran to the caves as the rain came down harder and the thunder grew louder and at more frequent intervals. They located the small caves quite easily, tied the mule and their precious cargo to a tree root and wedged themselves tightly into the smallest of the caves. By this time the air was full of electricity and they huddled closely together watching the spectacular natural pyrotechnics display. As Maria squeezed up tightly to him and he placed his arms around her he became aware of the same feelings he had experienced on the beach. He glanced at Maria, she turned her face to his and for the first time they kissed. It was the most natural reaction in the world.

The storm raged on but for Felipe and Maria, it didn't exist. It was natural that they cast off their wet clothes and natural that they were wrapped in each other's arms and it was simply Mother Nature taking over when they began to explore each other's bodies and eventually joined in an exquisite act of union and love.

Afterwards they lay together for what seemed like hours.

It was 2am when they eventually reached Abdet. They'd held hands the entire length of the journey. They had talked about love and life and marriage and of the feelings of passion and lust they had awoken in each other. They'd talked about the priests words about the sins of the flesh but both agreed that what they had experienced with each other was no sin. Something that beautiful had to be a gift from the Lord.

It was some months later that Maria noticed her body was changing. She was listless and quite often sick during the mornings and Felipe had commented on several occasions that her breasts looked swollen and painful. She had seen her mother getting fatter like this. She knew what it meant. How had it happened?

She took to wearing loose fitting clothes and carried an old shawl around with her constantly which she used to hide her embarrassment. It was colder now, people were wearing more clothes so no one noticed or at least they never commented.

Eventually her mother came to her room one evening and made her undress. As Maria lifted her shirt over her head her mother fell to the floor and screamed and wailed like a banshee.

Felipe's family were summoned the next day. Felipe and Maria were chastised and abused and at one point Felipe's father struck him across the face and he fell to the floor. His father talked about the shame and disgrace he had brought to the family. Maria rushed to him and wiped the small smattering of blood from his mouth.

"Leave him," she cried, "leave him. He has done nothing wrong it is me who is with child."

As she lifted Felipe from the floor the tears welled up in his eyes. He looked confused and shocked at his father's reaction.

Maria's mother ordered the men from the room and took her daughter's hand as the tears fell. Felipe's mother and eldest sister looked on as Inmaculada explained the facts behind Maria's condition. Meanwhile, outside, the men agreed the only possible course of action.

They would seek a solution from Father Cano.

Despite the drama of the day Maria felt as if a huge weight had been lifted from her shoulders. She hated lying to her parents, covering herself up and sneaking around the house and as she looked into the sad eyes of everyone in the room she confessed to being more than a little confused. She accepted they were a little young to be having a baby but surely this was a wonderful event. It was an unexpected gift from God she explained to her mother.

"Felipe and I will be married in church and raise our very own family and they will go to church and Felipe is a good boy he works hard and he loves me. We'll get our very own house and—"

"Stop you stupid little girl." Felipe's mother interrupted.

She was shaking her head as she stood and walked over to where Maria sat.

"Ha! The Church," she said. "Don't you realise what it is you have done and how angry father Cano will be? Don't you realise that if the village find out about your condition our families will be disgraced forever?"

Maria was shaking her head. "But I love Felipe and he loves me and—"

Felipe's mother slapped her hard across the face. "Shut up, shut up you idiot and listen to me."

The force of the blow jolted Maria hard into the back of the chair. As her bottom lip trembled and the first of the tears began to fall onto her cheeks she looked at her mother for some sort of support.

Her mother sat motionless holding her head in her hands.

～

Over the course of the next two days Father Cano had made his decision, arrangements had been made and his word was final. No one dared to question it.

～

Maria was in torment, the love of her life had not been seen in the village for many days.

"Where is he?" Maria pleaded to her mother. "It's been over a week now and Felipe is nowhere to be seen. He doesn't work anymore; he didn't even go to church on Sunday."

Maria's mother shook her head.

"Tell me Mama, I beg you, is he ill is there something wrong with him? His family do not talk to me anymore they will not even open the door to the house and when they see me coming they turn away and walk in the other direction as if I were a leper."

Maria turned to her father. "Please Papa just tell me what's wrong with him."

Maria's father sighed, withdrew the cigarette from his mouth and cleared his throat. He spoke in a whisper, the words so very difficult to release. "He is not ill Maria. Felipe is well," he said.

Maria breathed a sigh of relief. "Thank you Papa thank you so much, please tell me where he is?"

Maria's father stood took another draw on his limp cigarette.

He shook his head. "I cannot tell you where he is Maria."

Maria stood too and walked over to her father. "Please tell me father, please tell me where he is I must know."

Her father was still shaking his head and Maria fought to contain the tears as she begged her father for more information.

He took his daughter by the shoulder and walked her backwards to one of the chairs. He sat her forcibly on the seat and spoke. "I cannot tell you Maria because I do not know."

A mild panic welled up inside her.

"He is gone Maria... gone."

"But when is he coming back?"

"He isn't coming back Maria, he is gone forever, he will never set foot in Abdet again. He is well and will be looked after but he won't be coming back."

Maria fought for words but they wouldn't form in her mouth. The magnitude of her father's words slowly sank in and the meaning of them was a fate worse than death. She couldn't bear the thought of not seeing Felipe again, couldn't contemplate life without him and still wondered what was so bad about what they done together.

As Miguel picked up his coat and made his way towards the door his daughter collapsed on the cold stone floor and cried like a baby. No one came to comfort her.

As her father reached the door he turned and spoke. "It is the will of God Maria... it is the will of God."

At midnight Maria's father returned with two more men from the village.

"Come Maria," he said. "We must go. We have a long journey ahead of us."

Her mother explained that she must make the trip to Alcoy to a distant Aunt that she had never met. She could return once the baby was born. She had packed a bag for Maria and helped her onto the back of a mule. It was a cool night, the sky black and windowless and the wind whistled through the village as they set off in the pitch darkness. Maria was numb with shock, unable to offer the slightest effort of resistance.

"It's for the best," her mother said as she waved her daughter goodbye.

~

The baby boy was taken from Maria at three days old. She knew nothing about it, waking one morning to find the tiny crib empty. She ran to her aunt in hysterics convinced the infant had been stolen in the middle of the night. Her aunt simply reassured her that the child would be taken care of.

One

Vicente Cortes Ortuño was a lucky man. Whilst four and a half million of his fellow countrymen were scraping a bare existence from the land, working all day for sometimes a bowl of thin soup and a piece of bread, he had a position at the local town hall.

It was not the best of jobs, helping and overseeing any public works that needed to be carried out, but he sat most of the time at a desk and only worked six days a week. When he did take part in any manual work he always delegated the toughest and most dangerous jobs to the labourers under his control. It didn't yield a fortune but he was paid most weeks which meant regular food on the table for his wife and family.

It was Sunday June 11th 1904. Vincent was awake early as always as the sun streamed through his window disturbing his slumber. He sighed as he hung his feet over the bed. He didn't have to get up early but now he was awake he knew it was pointless trying to get back to sleep. The heat in the bedroom seemed to have increased significantly even in the short time he had been dozing half asleep, half awake.

It was going to be a hot one that was for sure. What would he do first, this on his day of rest? He laughed to himself, day of rest, *that's a laugh.* He wandered down to the small kitchen area of his house and took a cup of water from the clay jug that stood on the bench top. He would love a coffee but it was just too hot to even think about lighting the stove. He'd call in at Roberto's bar a little later on, take a coffee and perhaps a *bocadillo de salchicha*, a large homemade sausage in a fresh crusty bread roll. Roberto made the best breakfast in the village for only a few pesetas. It was his only extravagance of the week, and afterwards perhaps a glass of wine or two with the other men of the village.

Without waking his wife, he left the house and walked down to his smallholding just outside the village of Xirles. He had inherited the piece of land from his father, it wasn't big, but it had good earth and most important a share of water from the *acequia,* the water channel that had been first constructed by the Arabs centuries before. The water channels were treated with almost religious reverence, as without them all crops would fail. As he walked the two kilometres to his land, it was obvious that it was going to be one of the hottest days of the year. The fresh oranges he would pick from his trees would be most welcome.

That's when he heard the noise.

The countryside was always alive, the sound of birds singing, crickets and bees. Occasionally he even heard an odd rat scavenging after a rotten almond or the rustle of a startled snake slipping away through the undergrowth.

But this was different, more of a weak cry than anything else. He looked over towards the trees where he thought he heard the noise coming from. He stopped and took a deep breath, scoured the land with a well trained eye and he heard the muffled cry again. Something was hanging from the branch of an almond tree just at the entrance to his land. As he got closer he could see it was a basket made from interwoven palm fibres swaying gently in the light breeze. He walked towards it cautiously not knowing what to expect. He stretched out a hand and stopped the rocking motion. He couldn't explain why but for some strange reason his heart beat had increased beating like a drum so loudly he could hear it himself. Cautiously peeking inside he moved some of the loose fitting scraps of cloth to one side.

His caught his breath. It was a baby boy. The child cried again but broke out into a big beaming smile as if it somehow felt familiar with the stranger peering inside.

Vincent Cortes removed his hat. "Sweet Mary, Holy Mother of God," he exclaimed out loud as his jaw dropped and he made the sign of the cross on his chest. "Well I'll be..."

His natural reaction was to look around as if the child's mother would appear at any minute.

There was nobody around.

He scratched his head, tried to recall if any of the women in the village had been in the family way. No, he couldn't think of anyone, nobody in his village had had a child recently. It must be that of a *forestero* – a stranger.

Vincent Cortes could understand why the mother had hung the basket in the tree. She wanted to protect it from the animals foraging on the floor, but didn't the stupid woman realise the dangers posed by snakes who were just at home raking through the branches of a tree, not to mention the feral cats.

He lifted the basket down as he eased his creaking body to the floor beneath the shaded tree and placed it in his lap. He waited with the basket and the child for nearly an hour hoping, praying, that the child's mother would reappear. He busied himself picking a few bags of oranges every so often checking the child to see that it wasn't getting over hot. He called out again and again and listened for a reply. He heard nothing but the child gurgling out a happy tune.

He shouted out one last time. "*Hola...*" And then he listened for several minutes. It was clear the child was alone. As he took the basket down the baby began to cry.

"I think you must be hungry by now little person," he said. "And a little hot. Let's get you somewhere cooler."

He hooked the basket onto his arm and made his way back to his house to Fatima his wife. She would know what to do, she always did.

It wasn't an altogether unusual event to abandon a baby. While it wasn't an everyday occurrence, a peasant family sometimes took the heartbreaking decision if they thought a child had a disability. Nobody could afford to bring up a child that was never going to be able to work. Vicente gazed towards the heavens several times saying a silent prayer to the almighty thanking him he had been blessed with two fit and healthy sons.

Jose and Bertomeu were sitting at the table with their mother when Vincent walked through the door. Fatima looked at the basket and the strange smile on her husband's face as she spoke.

"What mischief have you been up to today you silly old man?" She said.

~

The Mayor of Xirles was not happy. It was Sunday and still only 9am and somebody was banging on his door.

He thrust his head out the small unbarred window upstairs.

"Who is it?" his wife called out to him from the bed.

He glanced over his shoulder. "It's that fool Vincent Cortes and he looks as if he is carrying a baby."

"*Que pasa Vicente?*" He shouted down. "Don't you know it is Sunday? I have no work today I hope this is important."

Vicente shouted up that he had found a baby and asked what should be done with it.

"What is it for God's sake?" his wife grumbled from the bed.

"An abandoned child." said the mayor as he pulled on a shirt and a pair of trousers and left the room. He opened the door to the house and ushered Vincent through the door mumbling his displeasure.

"So what is this house these days Vincent, the bloody children's home?" He said angrily. He was swearing and cursing his luck as he directed Vincent to the table. "One damned day of rest I get, one bloody day and they bring me bloody children before the sun has come up."

"It's a little boy," Vincent said to the mayor's wife as she too entered the room.

Vincent explained where he had found the child and said how he'd waited for over an hour for the mother to reappear.

"I think it has been abandoned," said Vincent.

The mayor looked up. "Your powers of deduction amaze me Vicente," he said. "But why have you brought it to me."

"You are the mayor Nicolas," he exclaimed. "You must decide what's to be done with it, that's your job."

The mayor stood up and walked towards the sink as he picked up a jug of water and prepared to light the stove. He turned round and spoke. "Keep it if you want Vicente. I have six children of my own and really have no desire to take on anything so young."

Vincent was shaking his head.

The mayor continued. "You have a good job and only two children, feeding another should present no problems."

Vicente at first objected but as he sat in the room with the mayor and his wife the boy kept smiling every time he set eyes on him.

"He likes you Vicente," said the mayor's wife. "Take him home, he's fit and healthy and will take care of you in your old age."

"I will give you the necessary papers tomorrow," was the Mayors parting words as Vicente was unceremoniously dispatched from the house. As he walked home along the hot dusty road he wondered how he was going to break the news to his wife.

Alcoy

The relationship between Maria and her aunt had broken down completely and she was desperate to get back to Abdet. She had had enough of this strange large town and longed for the familiarity of her small village. Her Aunt had barely spoken to her since the disappearance of her baby. Maria had asked her about her son and of course Felipe but the aunt had told her nothing. She was desperate to get back to see if Felipe had returned. He would know how to get their son back.

Maria had planned her escape the previous afternoon, questioning the villagers on which road it was she needed to take to get back to Abdet. The original journey to Alcoy from Abdet had been made during the hours of darkness and she'd wished she taken a little more notice. However, a kindly old lady had pointed her on the right road to Beniloba early that afternoon. In the village of Beniloba she'd ask the road to Benissau and then onto Confrides and eventually home.

She lay awake for hours until she finally heard her aunt turn in for the night. A little while later she could hear the snoring reverberating through the tiny house and it was time to make her escape. She crept downstairs and tiptoed through the house, out into the small courtyard to the mule she'd secretly prepared a few hours earlier. The mule had been well fed and watered for the long journey and she placed a pack in a saddle bag containing water, some bread and a handful of olives. She'd pick oranges on the way as and when she needed them.

The journey back took many hours and she spent the whole time planning what it was she was going to say to her parents, and how she was going to look for Felipe and the baby. Part of her hoped Felipe would be back home where he belonged but something nagged away at her that this would not be the case.

It was breaking daylight as she approached Abdet. As she set eyes on the huge church at the top of the hill she could not feel the presence of her lover. It didn't make any sense but somehow she knew. She felt that Felipe had not returned.

The entrance to the house looked somewhat different as Maria tied the mule to the tree and walked towards the house. She stopped a couple of metres from the stone step and listened. It was still early; the only sound was the high pitched tone of the cicadas. There was no sign of life from the house. She stepped forward and pushed the rough door open. She walked in and sat at the table patiently.

It was twenty minutes before her mother climbed down the wooden stairs. They groaned out a tune in time with each step. Maria sat silently, blending in with the shadows.

She spoke to her mother in barely a whisper. "Where is my child mother?"

The clay jug her mother was carrying fell from her hands as she jumped with a start. It smashed onto the cool stone floor. The sound was almost deafening in the still early morning silence of the old house. Maria never moved a muscle.

"Maria," her mother said breaking into a smile. "You're back. Oh my darling, you have returned."

Maria repeated the question. "Donde esta mi hijo?"

Maria's mother rushed forward and threw her hands around her daughter. "My child my child it is so good to see you."

Maria did not reciprocate her embrace. "Is it good to see me again Mama?"

"Yes, yes my little one," she said. "So good to see you, I have missed you so much."

Maria smiled and gave her a small kiss on the cheek. "A mother's love for her child, its special isn't it? It doesn't get any stronger than that."

She took her mother's hand. "Donde esta mi hijo?"

Her mother ignored the question again. Instead she looked up to the ceiling and pointed. The noise from the broken pot had awoken the whole house. Maria's two brothers were next down the stairs and they hugged and kissed her as if she'd been away for many years. Her brothers had changed, grown a little. They looked like young men now and Maria found it hard to believe she had only been away a few months.

"Look at you both, how you've grown." She said.

Maria's mother had lit the stove and busied around the kitchen lifting oranges and bread and olives onto the table. She was preparing a Sunday feast only it wasn't Sunday.

Maria's father walked slowly down the stairs and Maria stood to greet him. An uncomfortable silence ensued and then he spoke. "You're not welcome here. You must go back to your Aunt."

He walked through the small room, opened the door and disappeared into the street.

Maria's father returned from work just after six that evening. The wrath of his wife was waiting for him. He tried to defend his corner, give rational answers to the questions but it was always an argument he was destined to lose. Inmaculada was not going to send her daughter back to Alcoy again.

"We will be cast out like lepers in our own village," he reasoned.

"Then we will leave this pathetic little village, our daughter is more important to us than any damned villager."

She shot him down in flames each time.

Inmaculada turned to her son. "Jose, go and fetch your sister now. Tell her papa wants to see her."

Jose leapt from his seat and ran out into the street and before Miguel could say another word his wife spoke. "You keep your mouth shut old man or you won't only lose a daughter you'll lose two sons and a wife too."

Maria had walked out of the family home earlier that day not long after her father had left for work. She sat in the small copse half a kilometre from the village. Her brother Bertomeu had brought her a little lunch and she'd slept in the pleasantly warm shade of the olive trees in an attempt to renew her energy levels. She woke and felt strangely refreshed and invigorated. She knew it wouldn't be easy returning home or reintegrating back into village life but this was her home, her village and she'd fight to stay, this was the home of her father, his father too and many generations before them and she vowed she'd find Felipe and their child too. She'd fight any prejudices or preconceived moral issues. She was not ashamed of herself or her child and she could be as feisty as her mother and just as loud. Their son had been created from a wonderful act of love. She accepted she may have been a little young but the only difference between her and the other young mothers in the village was a scrap of paper issued by the church. It was stupid she thought to herself stupid stupid stupid.

Her father stood to embrace her as she walked into the room. She drew strength from him as she felt the tears well up in her eyes. She had her old family back, now she needed to find her new one and their life would be complete again.

The following day was Sunday and it was as if everything had returned to normal. The feast was on the table the coffee brewing on the hob and her brothers, mother and father greeted her as she walked down the stairs.

"You have over slept little one, you must have been tired."

Maria smiled and nodded. "It's not easy making the trip from Alcoy on a donkey that wants to sleep all the way. I had to kick him awake every hundred metres."

As she joined her family and began to eat she noticed there was only one thing missing from the usual Sunday Morning. Her mother was smiling and happy but there were no sweet lyrics emanating from her lips.

Maria was more than a little puzzled. It was fast approaching noon and the Sunday best clothes had not been positioned on the seats. Her father and brothers had gone out hunting and had not yet returned.

"Aren't we going to church today mama?" she asked.

Inmaculada looked a little uncomfortable as she replied. "Not today Maria." She stumbled a little. "Papa thought it best to stay at home today, just the four of us, we've all missed you."

Her mother's reply was insincere.

Maria read her like a book. "Mama, you've never missed church on a Sunday for as long as I can recall. You went to church when I was in Alcoy I assume?"

Inmaculada nodded.

"Then go to church as normal." She said. "If you are ashamed of me then I'll stay at home."

Inmaculada stepped forward and took her daughters hand.

"No Maria I am not ashamed of you, I could never be ashamed of any of my children."

"Then go to church and stop being so silly."

She was shaking her head.

"What is it mama, tell me why you aren't going to church?"

At that moment the door to the room crashed open and Maria's father walked in. He held up two dead rabbits.

"We will feast again this evening," he said. "I've a bottle of wine I've been keeping in the cellar for a special occasion we can open that too."

He threw the rabbits on the table top. "I'll skin these Inma', you peel some potatoes and bake some fresh bread."

"Why aren't we going to church papa?" Maria asked.

Her father sighed, flopped down into the seat and removed his hat. "We are going to church Maria."

Maria looked at her mother then back to her father again. "But we aren't ready, you're all dirty, the boys—"

Her father held up a hand as he interrupted her.

"We are going to church Maria, just you and I... after mass. We have a meeting with Father Cano."

Maria's father was convincing as he walked hand in hand with his daughter through the village streets.

"Everything will be fine Maria; Father Cano will know what to do. He's asked me to bring you to him. He's an educated man and takes his wisdom from God."

It felt good again to be walking the familiar streets, good to feel her father's hand in hers like when she was a child. He walked too fast, he always did and she struggled to keep up with him.

Maria was a little puzzled at the reaction of the villagers they passed. They greeted her like a long lost soul. They hugged and kissed her and their progress was slow. This was strange she thought to herself, her aunt had convinced her she was evil; the talk of the village and people would cross over the street to avoid talking to her. This wasn't the case. And as her old school friend

Nieves, ran into her arms smothering her with kisses the truth dawned on her.

"I've missed you I've missed you," Nieves cried out, "Where have you been, why didn't you tell me you were going away?"

Maria squeezed Nieves tightly as she realised that no one in the village knew the real reason she'd left. No one knew about her child.

Father Cano kept them waiting in the entrance of the church for over an hour. It was hot and Maria wanted a drink. Her father stood with his hat in his hand dressed in his best suit, the one he'd worn for his own wedding sixteen years before. He was nervous; he paced the width of the church every few minutes until at last they spotted the priest striding purposefully down the aisle.

Father Cano was a tall man with a neat well-trimmed dark moustache. He was dressed in black with a large gold crucifix hanging from his neck. His head was bare which surprised Maria a little. She'd never seen his head bare before. He paused for a second or two while he looked Maria up and down.

"Come." He commanded as he beckoned with his hand. Maria and her father followed on behind as he led them to a room and instructed them to sit. They waited patiently for the priest to speak.

His voice was soft and his manner surprisingly pleasant. "How are you my child?" He asked.

Maria nodded nervously. "Well Father, very well indeed.

"Good." he said. He looked at Miguel "And you Miguel are you well too?"

Miguel answered. "Yes father, and all the better for having my wonderful daughter back."

The priest reached across and took his hand. "It was for the better Miguel... you do understand that don't you?"

Miguel didn't even hesitate as he answered. "Yes father of course, whatever you say. We would not question your wisdom or the authority of the Lord."

The priest smiled. It was a sickly smile. Maria turned to her father in amazement as she pointed to the priest. She spoke in a whisper, barely able to utter the words such was her state of shock. She pointed to the priest as she stared at her father.

"It was his decision to send me away? His decision to take my child from me?"

She turned to the priest and in an instant loathed him with all her heart.

"It was your decision to send Felipe away too?"

"It was for the best my child." He replied.

Maria stood. She desperately tried to control the anger and fury that welled up inside her.

She raised her voice slightly. "Better for who father, better for me, better for my child? I don't think so father. Better for Felipe? Let's ask him father. Go and fetch Felipe so that we can ask him if it was better that his son has been stolen from him."

Maria's father apologised profusely to the priest and took Maria by the hand.

"Sit down Maria and be quiet, listen to the father, you are in the house of God, be quiet now," he said, tugging forcefully at her sleeve.

As Maria thought about her son and Felipe and wondered where on earth they were and how she would ever go about finding them she began to tremble with rage.

"You've ruined my life father," she said. "How do you justify that to the Lord?"

The priest stood up and bit back as the saliva sprayed from his lips.

"You ruined your own life," he shouted. "You ruined your own life when you lay down with that stupid peasant boy and let him have his evil way."

Maria wanted to shout and scream at the man standing in front of her but the words wouldn't form in her mouth.

Cano seized the opportunity as Maria stood rooted to the spot in shock. "I warned you about the evils of the flesh week in week out but still you took your gratification like the animal that you are. The church has acted as it sees fit to protect the honour of both families, he continued. He gazed at her father. "Isn't that so Miguel?"

"Yes father. Indeed sir." He said apologetically.

By now the tears of agony and hurt were falling freely. "Tell me where my child is father, that's all I ask," she sobbed. "Tell me where my son is and Felipe too and I promise I will leave the village and never set foot on these streets again."

The priest sat back down at the table and picked up a pen and began to write. Maria threw herself forward and grabbed at the priests robes.

"Please father, please," She cried. "I'll do anything just tell me... tell me."

The priest sat bolt upright as he freed himself from her delicate grip. "Compose yourself girl and remember where you are."

He continued to write. After a few minutes he spoke to Miguel. "She must be punished Miguel she must be punished and pay a penance."

Miguel nodded.

"I've written what she needs to do. Her penance will last six months. If I'm fully satisfied that she has complied with my wishes and repented I may allow her to return to church." He folded up the paper and pushed it across the desk to Miguel. "You yourself will be unable to return to church for four weeks. Perhaps it will give you some time to reflect on how to control your daughter." The priest stood. "You may go now and take that worthless article with you."

Miguel reached down and lifted his still sobbing daughter from the table.

As they reached the door the priest spoke. "You may bring your weekly offering to me first thing on a Monday morning for the next four weeks is that clear?"

Miguel nodded.

"I don't see why the church should suffer financially." The priest mumbled as Miguel closed the door behind him.

Two

This was different from working and tilling the fields back in Abdet. *He is homesick* the other men called out as Felipe lay on his rough straw bed night after night looking at the dirty wooden ceiling while his co-workers played dominoes from small carvings of wood with painted spots.

"He misses his sleeping partner back home in the sticks," one of them called out to him.

"She must play a wicked game on her back," another shouted out, laughing as the rest of the men joined in. "He won't even look at another woman. They are not good enough for a classy boy like him."

The teasing was relentless but what could he do, a mere youth amongst all these men.

"That cock of his has got him into trouble and now he keeps it in his trousers on a permanent basis."

The hut was filled with laughter.

Felipe had regretted taking one of his work colleagues into his confidence. During a siesta period in the fields when everyone else was sleeping he explained the very reason why he'd been removed from his village in the beautiful mountains inland from Altea. He told the man all about his pretty girl back home and how it had taken many days to reach Valencia.

They'd always moved during the hours of darkness. Felipe knew the reason. His two uncles who had accompanied him did not want him to recognise the route back home. His father's brothers had stayed with him two nights in the hustling, bustling city of Valencia and as they left he begged them to take him back with them but they refused. They said they would be back soon and told him his adventure was all part of his journey into manhood.

It was hard to believe that was five years ago.

Felipe was working twelve hours a day, six days a week. It was back breaking work that gave him his food and lodging but little else. In five years he had managed to save just a few hundred pesetas.

It was Saturday night. It should have been the one night a week where he could sleep knowing that he didn't have to get up at dawn the following day. Not even the gang-master would have the nerve to go against the will of the church and make them work on the Sabbath. No one questioned the doctrine of the church. But for Felipe Saturday night was without doubt the worst night of the week. The girls would arrive not long after the men returned from the fields. It was the same ritual each week. The men would bathe in the cool refreshing waters of the river Turia and Felipe would reluctantly join them. Afterwards they'd sit down to eat with the girls and the business transactions would take place but not before the gang-master had taken his preferred choice of girl into his private cabin. Strangely enough no money appeared to change hands on that particular coupling. The girls and the men would sit around the dying embers of the cooking fire and laugh and cavort with each other as the cheap wine flowed and eventually pesetas would change hands.

Felipe would turn in early and pray that he'd be asleep before the nocturnal activity commenced. Inevitably though, it never happened. His fellow workers didn't seem to even care where they performed their sexual rituals and the grunts and groans of their not so secret trysts carried on a few feet from where Felipe laid his head. The girls were rough and nasty; they had no morals and no pride. Felipe questioned the Lord above during his evening prayers. Why it was him who had been banished from his home town because of one beautiful act of consenting love and yet these girls went about their sordid business whenever and wherever they wanted.

It was impossible to sleep this night in particular, the stifling heat of a particularly warm night causing him to perspire and dampen the already filthy bed. The stillness of the night seemed to amplify the animalistic sounds around him even more. He could eventually stand it no more, rose from his makeshift bed as he decided to take a walk outside. He stepped over the heaving sweating naked bodies, some sleeping some still copulating.

As he walked over to the orange grove he noticed the figure of a young woman leaning against a tree. He recognised her as the young prostitute Pilar. The girl had caught his eye on more than one occasion. She was very young and never appeared to smile too often. Up to that point he'd never spoken to her but as she looked up and met his gaze conversation was unavoidable.

Pilar spoke. "It's Felipe isn't it?"

Felipe nodded. The full moon cast a swathe of light on the girl which accentuated her delicate beauty even more. Felipe couldn't help wondering how the poor girl had stooped to this level trying to earn a living. Then he laughed to himself. Was her life as bad as his? At least she had her family, perhaps even a husband and children living in Valencia and one thing was for sure she wouldn't be toiling in the fields for twelve hours a day in the raging heat.

"Can't you sleep?" She asked.

He shook his head. "No I... errr they..."

She laughed. "Yes, we make a lot of noise don't we? They say that's the way men like it."

"Men like you to make noise when you make love?" He asked with a puzzled frown.

Pilar laughed. "Make love Felipe?" She laughed sarcastically. "Make love. Oh no my poor boy we don't make love in there. We screw and fuck. Nothing else my friend, we fuck for money."

Felipe was momentarily lost for words. He attempted to scold her for her bad language but she laughed it off.

"It's the language of the gutter and that's where we are." She pointed at him. "You too Felipe, you are in the gutter, you are a slave to the gang-master as am I. He has his way with me whenever the fancy takes him. You are no different; he screws you by making you work for a pittance while he sits on his fat arse growing rich."

Felipe was speechless, lost for words but the girl had struck a raw nerve. It was true and he knew it.

"They say you have a girl back home Felipe is that true?"

"Yes," Felipe replied. "I will be back there with her soon."

Pilar seemed to suppress a smile. It was a look not lost on Felipe as if she was taunting him in some way.

"Why aren't you in there?" He pointed to the hut.

Pilar flicked a hand across her cheek. "Pah... why would I want to go in there? It stinks. The men are animals... foul... they make me want to vomit."

"Then why do you do it?"

Pilar's mouth gaped open. "You truly are stupid Felipe aren't you? Why do you think I do it? I do it for the money so I can eat and put a roof over my parents head, my brothers and sisters too." She reached out for his hand. "Come, let us walk."

Felipe followed but quickly broke the grip. It somehow didn't feel right but nonetheless it was a pleasant sensation and one he hadn't experienced for so long. He craved human touch again, a hug from his mother an embrace or a kiss from Maria. They walked some distance and within a few minutes he reached for Pilar's hand again.

"Sorry," he said, "it felt good... I miss..."

"You miss the touch of your girlfriend I know. Don't worry we have noticed, all the girls respect you for you are the only man not to take up our offers of business." Pilar laughed out loud. "But if all the men were like you we'd surely starve."

They walked and talked for over an hour.

The women liked to gossip about the latest happenings in Valencia, Pilar explained. The talk had been about the unrest there.

"It's not the city I once knew," she said.

Unrest wasn't new by any means; the peasants had rebelled against their landlord employers many times.

"The bastards treat them worse than their livestock," Pilar said, shrugging her shoulders with a look of disgust on her face. The wealthy landowners knew what to do. They simply called in the Guardia Civil who would do their bidding without question. A few pesetas here and there placed in the right hands and the beatings and killings soon stifled dissent.

Pilar looked animated as she spoke. "This was more than a little different."

Felipe listened as Pilar said the unrest wasn't so much about working conditions or the lack of them, it was about workers being forced to join the army. Felipe's ears pricked back as he listened to Pilar's news of how soldiers were fighting across the sea in a place called Africa. He knew little more than the area around his home village of Abdet and the fields around the farm where he worked in Valencia but Pilar described vast oceans and foreign lands and men with different coloured skin.

"I slept with a soldier only last week," she said. "He'd returned to Valencia wounded. He told me stories of the slaughter of the poor Spanish troops and how the officers had sold most of their ammunition because they needed food and water. Hordes of young Spanish men had been taken from the streets of Valencia and Barcelona, and sent across the sea to die in that strange land."

She spat onto the ground. "The bastards. It all stinks to high heaven, where are the Spanish men with balls? Why do they let them walk all over us and treat us like dogs?"

Pilar's stories were an insight into a different world. Felipe could not help but admire this pretty, fiery prostitute. Increasingly Felipe would look forward to Pilar's visits. She'd finish with her business early as the other girls worked through the night. She'd stand by the same tree and they'd walk hand in hand and he would listen eagerly to the latest installments of her stories that became more astonishing by the week. Pilar would draw small maps and write names of places and explain where the cities of Spain were positioned and where Africa was and how huge the Mediterranean sea was and how long it took the ships to get there.

Felipe wished he could read and write. He could recognise his own name, he had been taught by Father Cano back in Abdet, and he could write Maria too. He recalled how he'd stood in the caves near Xirles with Maria one day and they'd studied and practiced writing each other's names over and over again so that when eventually they'd walked outside into the sunshine Felipe managed to scrawl the correct spelling of Maria's name in the dust outside.

How he wished he'd listened to Father Cano more, how he wished he was back in Abdet.

One week Pilar returned with news that she was clearly excited about. He had to take her by the arms and tell her to slow down.

"The army in Barcelona has swept through a poor working class district," she said. "They took any man they thought was able to fight. They took boys as young as fourteen years, their brothers and fathers too. The only men left were the cripples and infirm and those who managed to hide."

There were tears in her eyes as she explained their families were left without men to provide for them and they faced a future of certain starvation. She explained how it was possible to buy yourself out of the conscripted service, but it cost the equivalent of almost a year's wages, far out of the reach of normal working people. The result of all this was an explosion of street violence never seen before in Spain. It was known as La Semana Tragica.

Tragic Week. (July 25 – August 2, 1909) is the name used for a series of bloody confrontations between the Spanish army and the working classes of Barcelona and other cities of Spain, backed by anarchists, socialists and republicans, during the last week of July 1909. It was caused by the calling-up of reserve troops by Prime Minister Antonio Maura to be sent as reinforcements when Spain renewed military-colonial activity in Morocco on July 9, in what is known as the Second Rif War.

Minister of War Arsenio Linares y Pombo called up the Third Mixed Brigade of Chasseurs, which was composed of both active and reserve units in Catalonia. Among these were 520 men who had completed active duty six years earlier and who had not anticipated further service. Substitutes could be hired if one did not wish to fight – but this cost 6,000 reales, which was beyond the means of most laborers. (Workers did not receive more than 20 reales or 5 pesetas a day.) The flashpoint occurred when a party of conscripts boarded ships owned by the Marques de Comillas, a noted Catholic industrialist, en route for Morocco. The soldiers were accompanied by patriotic addresses, the Royal March and religious medals distributed by pious well-dressed ladies. Spain's narrow social construction was thus on display for all to see, an affluent Catholic oligarchy impervious to the rise of secular mass politics. As the crowd jeered and whistled, emblems of the Sacred Heart were thrown into the sea.

These actions, coupled with anarchist, anti-militarist, and anti-colonial philosophies shared by many in the city (Barcelona would later become a stronghold for the anarchists during the Spanish

Civil War), led to the union Solidaridad Obrera, led by a committee of anarchists and socialists, calling a general strike against Maura's call-up of the reservists on July 26, 1909, a Monday. Despite the civil governor, Ángel Ossorio y Gallardo, receiving ample warning of the growing discontent, acts of vandalism were provoked by elements called the jóvenes bárbaros (Young Barbarians), who were associated with the Radical Republican Party of Alejandro Lerroux. By Tuesday, workers took over Barcelona, halting troop trains and overturning trams. By Thursday, there was street fighting, with a general eruption of riots, strikes, and the burnings of convents.

Many of the rioters were antimilitarist, anticolonial and anticlerical. The rioters considered the Roman Catholic Church to form part of the corrupt bourgeois structure whose sons did not have to go to war, and the flames had been fanned against the Church by anarchist elements within the city. Thus, not only convents were burned, but sepulchers were profaned and graves were emptied.

After disturbances in downtown Barcelona, security forces shot at demonstrators in Las Ramblas, resulting in the construction of barricades in the streets and the proclamation of martial law. The government, declaring a state of war, sent the army to crush the revolt. Barcelonan troops, many of whom had working class roots, stationed in the city refused to shoot workers and troops were brought in from Valencia, Zaragoza, Pamplona and Burgos, who finally crushed the revolt, causing dozens of deaths.

Pilar beamed with pride as she relayed further details. She told of running battles between the army and ordinary men and women.

"The children were fighting too, some of them fought with their bare hands, others used sticks and stones."

Felipe sat on the dusty ground. They faced each other and he held her two hands tightly and begged her to continue.

"They vented their frustrations and violence on the army at first but then turned on the Church."

Felipe instinctively made the sign of the cross. "Surely no. Good God tell me that didn't happen."

Pilar continued. "Churches are being burned and tombs of religious leaders long gone, desecrated." She told Felipe that additional troops had to be sent up from Valencia, to help reinforce the soldiers from Barcelona. She gripped Felipe hard. "I am not telling lies Felipe, it is the truth. There is revolt in the air and I sense the Spanish working man is about to have his day once again."

That's when they heard the noise behind them. The shocking truth dawned on Felipe that they weren't alone and someone had been listening in to their conversation.

The gang-master's reaction was swift and unexpected. He knocked Pilar clean off her feet with a heavy blow to the side of her face. Felipe scurried away and hid behind a tree as he watched in terror. The gang-master was a big man but surprisingly quick and lashed out hard with a kick in the ribs as Pilar curled up in a ball like a startled hedgehog.

"I've warned you before about your big mouth you dangerous little whore." He reached for the huge buckle on his belt and began to unloosen it. "There's only one language you sort understand."

Pilar groaned in the dust as she fought to stay conscious. He tugged hard at the buckle and the belt jerked free. "I let you come here every week to ply your wares and this is the thanks I get, trying to goad my men against me."

He lifted it high above his head and brought the buckle end crashing down on Pilar's back. She winced in pain as the sharp buckle bit into her flesh. Felipe squeezed his eyes tight shut and covered his ears with his hand in a vain attempt to shut out the violence. It was no good. Again and again he felt the vibration of the belt buckle connecting with the soft flesh of Pilar's body. He wanted it to end now, he prayed to God it would end now. He uncovered his eyes.

"Please God, please God help her," he whispered to himself.

Pilar lay motionless as the gang-master stood over her breathing heavily, he raised the belt above his head again.

"Please sir leave her alone, you'll kill her."

The gang-master looked over to Felipe and smiled. His teeth were rotten and black and reminded Felipe of an abandoned graveyard.

"Quite fond of this little whore aren't you?" he grinned. "Don't think I haven't noticed how she looks at you. Don't think for one minute I don't know that you've been fucking her on the quiet."

Felipe shook his head. "No sir, you are wrong I haven't—"

In one swift movement the gang-master covered the short distance from where Pilar lay to the tree that Felipe hid behind. He aimed his kick well catching Felipe a glancing blow to the side of his head.

"Don't lie to me boy, she's not worth it. I could dispatch this whore to God's earth if I so desired and no one would even question me." He knelt down and grabbed Felipe's chin roughly, twisting his head to face him. "Do you hear me boy? I could strangle her with my bare hands if I wanted to."

He released his grip and Felipe slumped to the floor of the forest as the world spun around him.

The gang-master stood and looked over towards Pilar's broken body as she began to groan. "Ahh," he said. "There's life in the young bitch yet." He turned towards Felipe. "Now watch carefully boy, I'm about to show you the only language this whore understands."

He reached down and grabbed a handful of Pilar's dress as he pulled it violently above her hips exposing her nakedness. He bent over her and thrust a hand between her legs. She let out an involuntary moan.

"You see Felipe, she responds. The bitch responds to my touch." He stood once again and pulled at the buttons on his trousers as he let them fall to the floor. He wrapped a hand round his erect penis as he waved it at Felipe. "Let's see how she responds to this."

It was more than Felipe could stand. The pent up frustration of five years released itself in an instant as Felipe rushed the gang-master. He approached him at speed as he instinctively tucked his head into his chest. His hard skull connected with the delicate area at the bottom of the gang-masters ribcage as the air burst from his lungs. The force of the blow spilled them both onto the dusty earth and as Felipe gained momentum he pounced on his prey and rained down punches around his face and head as the man begged for mercy. Felipe punched until he was exhausted, he punched until his knuckles bled and the prone body of the man who had treated them like slaves lay lifeless.

The damage was done.

The crooked body of the gang-master lay in a bloody heap still breathing but only just. Felipe covered his face and cried as the reality of the situation sunk in. He was in huge trouble. The gang-master had always boasted of his brother who was a captain in the army in Valencia. He was sure to inform him, or perhaps the Guardia Civil who had a fearsome reputation. It was rumoured they'd put a bullet through a man's head without a second thought. Their barracks were outside the next town a mere 5 km away. He had no choice, he had to run. He looked down at the battered body of Pilar. What was to become of her? Dear God what an impossible situation he thought to himself. He couldn't leave her there, the gang-master would surely punish her. At that moment her eyes flickered open and a trace of a smile drew across her face.

"Felipe," she said, "what has happened? I hurt so much."

"Be quiet... lie still. I fear I am in trouble and I must flee.

A look of disappointment crept over her. "But why, what have you done?"

Felipe pointed to the crumpled body of the gang-master.

"I'm afraid I lost my temper. God forgive me but I have beaten him senseless."

Pilar smiled. "I told you... the Spanish working man has rebellion in his blood. The bastard has treated us like animals for too long. Don't blame yourself. You did what was right."

Felipe shrugged his shoulders. "That may be the case and I have indeed won the first battle but he has the power the influence and the money to wage war against me." He sighed and looked forlorn. "And I'm not going to hang around to see what sort of temper he is in when he awakes."

Pilar eased herself to her knees wincing and cursing the gang-master as the pain of her broken body registered. "You must take me with you," she said. "If I stay he will kill me."

Felipe was already shaking his head more in confusion than anything else. "No I cannot."

"Yes you will, how else are you going to find your way home you stupid peasant boy. I have made the trip to the fishing village of Benidorm many times as a small girl. I have a grandmother there we can stay with for a while. The road up to Abdet is close by."

Without giving Felipe the opportunity to object Pilar took control. She limped over to where the mules were and a few minutes later reappeared. She'd loaded the mule with water and stolen provisions."We have more than enough to last us. I have taken ham and cheese from the gang-masters cabin and have bread and olives too. Look," she said as she held up a bottle. "We have wine too and we will celebrate tomorrow night when we are far away from this place of shit and rats."

"But what about your family?" Felipe asked.

Pilar bowed her head as she bit her lip. The tears formed in her eyes as she spoke. "They will manage. I will miss them especially my little brother but I have enough sisters to take care of him and my mother and that's all that matters."

They trekked throughout the hours of darkness. At first light Felipe studied the bloody, torn shape of Pilar. Her dress was in tatters, stained with blood, her scalp matted and encrusted and yet still she smiled each time their eyes met. Felipe was confused. He fought the feelings Pilar had awoken within him and remembered the teaching of Father Cano and his lectures on the sins of the flesh. He'd fight his urges and concentrate hard on the image of the beautiful Maria. Just a few days now and he would be in her arms again. They had a child... he or she would be nearly five years old by now. The child would meet his father very soon.

As the sun crept above the hills and warmed their bodies Pilar spoke. "If I remember right there's a small stream not far from here we can wash and replenish our water." She smiled. "It's a nice spot; we can take a little food and rest."

Within a kilometre Pilar had stopped the mule and began unloading the saddle bags. She tied the mule to a tree and led Felipe through a forest glade towards the stream. The canopy of the forest appeared to open up as they walked and Felipe listened as he caught the sound of running water.

"There," she said as she pointed ahead. "I suggest we bathe, it will make us feel better."

Without saying another word she walked forward and placed her feet in the stream, bent down and lifted her torn dress over her head and waded into the water. Felipe stood rooted to the spot. It was more than five years since he'd witnessed the beautiful delicate shape of a young naked woman. Despite his best intentions he couldn't tear his eyes away from her as she turned to face him squealing and frolicking in the waist high water. Father Cano's words came back to fill his thoughts. *Jezebels, harlots and whores.* He talked so bad about the women that made their living that way and yet the beautiful girl who stood naked before him was without a doubt one of God's greatest creations. At that precise moment in time he realized that his feelings for her were like the feelings he remembered having for Maria.

"Aren't you coming in? She called from the water. "It's beautiful and we are free people."

Felipe summoned up some courage from deep within and took a few tentative steps towards the water.

"Come on in and take off those filthy clothes. When was the last time they were washed you dirty scoundrel."

Felipe pulled his dirty shirt from over his head and loosened the buttons on the front of his trousers as he let them fall."

"My my," called Pilar. "Your girl is indeed one lucky lady."

Felipe shook his head unsure of what she meant as he walked in the water towards her.

Pilar reached out for his hands and pulled him into deeper water. They swam for a while then washed the dirt and blood from their clothes. Pilar stretched the washing over a tree branch as Felipe lay down in the sun on a grassy bank.

"They will be dry soon," she said. "The sun's rays are very hot today."

How many days until we reach Benidorm? Felipe asked.

"It depends how quickly our progress is." she answered. "Nine, ten days I think. You will have to put up with me for quite a while yet."

Felipe nodded. "I think that will be fairly easy for me."

Pilar rolled towards him and raised her eyebrows. "And why is that peasant boy?"

Felipe leaned forward and brushed his lips with hers. "Because dear lady of the night, I fear I am falling in love with you."

Three

Their progress was slow as Pilar's body still ached from the beating she'd taken from the gang master. After a few hours he helped her up onto the mule and walked alongside and they kept going. Felipe's bare feet ached too but the fear of the Guardia Civil catching up with them was greater than his pain. They tried to keep to the banks of the river where it was shallow enough to walk comfortably in the river itself. They reasoned that they would leave no footprints and whoever it was who may try to follow would soon give up. Felipe placed himself in the gang masters head and thought that the obvious place to go would be back to Abdet. The gang master knew where it was he came from, but then again would he sacrifice more than a week's trip just to seek a little revenge? Felipe couldn't take that chance. Not for some time anyway. It would be many months before he could return to Abdet. He looked up at Pilar who smiled at him and for a fleeting moment he wondered if he truly wanted to return to his home village. It had been five years and time had moved on. What of Maria? Perhaps she had found someone else, even married and had other children. His child... their child. The child he'd never even set eyes on.

He was amazed how the pain of his loss still registered so powerfully. He would never forgive those who had interfered in his life. No matter that the good book preached forgiveness, he simply couldn't find it in his heart.

They walked from dawn to dusk day after day. At night they lay down together and slept under the stars. It was four days into the journey when the provisions Pilar had stolen ran out and they lived on oranges and figs from the trees.

"We'll need to think about buying some food Felipe, I have a little money so we won't starve." Pilar said. "Fruit is good but a swear I'll murder the next man I see carrying a loaf of bread."

They'd avoided the villages on route up until now but Felipe was beginning to relax a little. There was simply no way could anyone have followed their trail. They were safe. They'd stop at the next village and stock up on food. Pilar reckoned it was only another three or four days to Benidorm.

They stopped at a village called Orba around noon the following day. Pilar insisted they dropped into a small roadside inn where they feasted on a Valencian stew and some local wine. Before they left they purchased some bread and ham. Felipe was feeling quite light headed as he walked back into the sunshine. He stumbled and fell as he approached the donkey and Pilar could not help laughing. "Not used to the local brew are you peasant boy?"

Felipe grinned. "Wine isn't something I've been used to I confess. It's made me feel all strange."

Pilar lifted him from the dusty road. "Come we must walk some more, at least until its dark."

Felipe frowned and held out his hands. "And when we get to Benidorm Pilar what then? We can't eat fresh air and if we keep stealing from the fruit orchards and olive groves we will surely be caught and sent to jail."

He asked a further question. It was something that had preyed on his mind as soon as he'd discovered he had feelings for Pilar. He hadn't wanted to bring the subject up but the wine had loosened his tongue. He was more than a little despondent and feeling sorry from himself.

"And what about us Pilar?" he said. "What do we do? I have told you of my feelings for you but there is no hope for us. I have a duty to my child and to its mother. I must try and make it back home sooner or later I owe it to them both."

Pilar was tending to the donkey making secure the side of ham they'd purchased from the inn.

She turned to face him. "And I must survive peasant boy. With or without you it makes no difference to me but one thing is for sure I can't go back to Valencia. The gang master has the Guardia in his pay and they will surely have a description of me. She pulled tightly on the rope and tied it in a secure knot around the middle of the animal. She stood with her hands on her hips. "The gods have thrown us together for a little while anyway and we should enjoy the time we have, for tomorrow we may be dead. Tonight we will rest and tomorrow continue our journey. I will find work in Benidorm and make a new life for myself." She laughed. "There is always an opportunity for a lady of the night to turn over a few pesetas. You do what you think fit."

She reached for the rope tethering the donkey to the tree and untied it and walked off into the distance. He sighed, looked up into the deepening twilight and cursed the amount of wine he'd drank. He hurried after her.

That night they lay side by side once again, a harsh woolen blanket protecting them from the night air. They were high up in the mountains and it was noticeably cooler.

"I nearly forgot," Pilar said. "We still have that bottle of wine I stole from el gordo. It will warm us up."

"You drink a lot of wine Pilar," he said as she took the bottle from a pocket on the mule's back and placed the neck to her lips. As she drank he watched her slender throat pulse as the wine flowed freely. She was beautiful, her skin like satin and more feelings of confusion welled up inside him. It is not possible to love more than one women he thought to himself. He recalled Father Cano's words from many a sermon about unity and love and marriage. It was clear from the scriptures that a man could only take one woman. He placed the thought firmly into the back of his mind telling himself that the Lord above would sort his little problem out. He had faith and God always answered his prayers. He admitted to himself that the Lord had taken his time to answer him this time but nevertheless here he was free of the gang-master and in a few short months he would be either back home with Maria in Abdet or as man and wife with Pilar. God would decide. It was as simple as that.

She took the bottle, belched loudly and handed it back to him. "It helps me to forget," she said, "forget the wretched life I have." Pilar's words broke up his thoughts.

Felipe spoke. "The life you had Pilar not have. You are free again, you can start a new life, a good life, the Lord will protect you, he will make it good and make up for those dark days you once knew."

Pilar threw him a strange grin then shook her head.

"What Pilar? What is it?"

She reached for the wine again, drained the bottle. "I fear you are a dreamer Felipe. You have not looked at the situation I am in. It will be many years before I can return to my family, I am a wanted woman. The Guardia Civil will be looking out for me of that there is no doubt. I have little money, no job and no roof over my head." She laughed. "I am a whore and now a thief. Pah! and you ask me why I look for solutions in the bottom of a bottle." She wiped her lips and threw the empty bottle into the undergrowth. "You stick to the good Lord peasant boy and I'll keep trying to forget."

Felipe had a restless night. Although exhausted and slightly drunk, sleep wouldn't come. He spent most of the night praying, praying harder than he could ever remember.

"Give me an answer or a sign," he whispered over and over again.

When he awoke Pilar was nowhere to be seen. He searched the forest for some time and eventually made his way towards the sound of running water. He found her clothes on the bankside of a mountain stream. Just then she emerged from the water with a burst of energy. She yelled out to him as the cool, icy water cascaded over her naked body.

"Yes we are indeed free peasant boy. We have the sun and water and we can drink and bathe and its free just like you and me."

Felipe smiled and found himself drawn to her naked breasts as she stood without making any attempt to cover herself. He forced himself to look down at the grass as he spoke.

"You are in a better mood this morning."

Pilar waded slowly from the water. Felipe looked up. She stood on the bank-side, hands on hips as the bright morning sun silhouetted her body. Tiny droplets ran over her hard nipples down to her flat stomach and onto the soft downy hair between her legs. He turned his back on her.

"Get dressed," he called over his shoulder. "We have a long day ahead and must be on our way."

He became aware of her presence close to him. She pressed herself into his back and her arms clasped around his waist. She whispered in his ear. "Why do you not make love to me peasant boy? Why do you tell me you are falling in love with me and then resist me so?"

She nibbled gently on his ear lope and drew a wet tongue down the line of his jaw.

"I see the way you look at me Felipe. You want to take me of that I'm sure."

Felipe broke her grip. "Come, we must get going."He turned to face her.

"Cover yourself up its not decent." He reached down for her clothes and threw them to her. Pilar stood stubbornly, with her hands on her hips. Anger was written across her face now.

"What is wrong with me? Am I not pretty? You haven't even kissed me since you declared your love for me some days back. What is it?"

The tears were beginning to well up in her sad eyes. She reached down for her dress and pulled it over her head. She spat at his feet. "You are all bastards, I should have known better than to let my feelings run free. I thought you were different," she continued, "but you are all the same."

"Please Lord," Felipe whispered under his breath, "please help me."

Pilar burst into tears and ran deep into the forest. Felipe slumped to his knees and his tears flowed too. He clasped his hands together and prayed.

It was an hour before he found Pilar again. It was the longest hour of his life. Surely this was the sign he had been waiting for. He thought he'd lost her, thought she was gone for good and the pain he'd experienced was intense. She sat by an almond tree her eyes red from crying. He knelt beside her. He felt an energy and a passion he hadn't ever known. He leaned forward to kiss her but she pulled her face away. More determined than ever he gripped her face with his strong hand and forced his mouth on hers. She beat at his back with her fists for a few seconds but he held her tight and then she relented. Her tongue slid gently back and forth into his mouth and as he reciprocated he felt the blood rushing to his groin. As she fell gently to the side and lay on the forest floor he grasped her dress roughly and bunched it around her waist. As he stood he let his trousers fall and she slowly parted her legs. He lay down alongside her and kissed her again before easing himself slowly upon her. He bent down and took a hard nipple between his teeth as she moaned with pleasure. He released her, smiled, and as gently as he could pushed his erect penis deep inside her as her eyes clenched in pleasure leaving tiny dark shadows in the lines in the corner of her eyes.

Pilar knew at last she was finally making love. From the first time her uncle had thrown her on her back at thirteen years of age, men had used and abused her for their own selfish pleasure. This was different. Their passion was as one as her nails bit into the small of his back gasping as he thrust ever deeper inside her. What was happening to her body? She sensed that something incredible was occuring and she begged him to continue. Her hips raised to meet him in perfect unity and motion as his actions grew faster. She was panting now as she felt the strange but beautiful sensation building deep inside her. And then it happened. She noticed the change in Felipe's entire body as he tensed up and swelled inside her. Instinctively she arched her back and held it there as Felipe cried out with pleasure. At the same time her whole body seemed to tremble as a wave of exquisite pleasure swept over her.

As they lay together bathed in perspiration panting gently Felipe spoke. He said he wanted to spend the rest of his life with her.

They spent the next few days experimenting and enjoying one other. The weather was hot and sticky and they made love on the river bank time and time again without a care in the world. It somehow accentuated the act. They explored every inch of each others bodies and afterwards they cleansed themselves in the crystal clear mountain stream. They kissed and hugged as they poured water over their bodies with the large clay jug they had taken from Valencia. It became a kind of ritual and when they had rekindled their energy they would start all over again.

Pilar spoke as they lay exhausted side by side. "We can't do this for ever Felipe, as nice as it is."

Felipe turned and grinned. "And why not? What better things have we to do?"

Pilar sat up, reached for her dress and threw it over her head. "We must eat peasant boy and we must find work. We are as man and wife now and you must take care of me. The way we are carrying on there may well be another mouth to feed some time in the future."

She stood up smoothing her dress around her thighs. "Come lover boy its time to get practical. I fear I have released enough seed from you to last a lifetime. There will be no more fun until I've found you a job."

Pilar explained about a railway being constructed between the small fishing villages of Gandia and Benidorm. Some of her younger customers from Valencia had told her that they were going to work on its construction. It was dangerous work but paid well in comparison to the rate of pay in Valencia. The terrain was mountainous and there were large sections that had to be cut out of the limestone rock. Sometimes explosives were used to create the tunnels, but the majority of the work was completed manually.

It all made sense. They were fugitives, of that there was no doubt and it would be easy to hide amongst the thousands of other young people. The Guardia may well have descriptions of the two lovers on the run but it would be like looking for a needle in a haystack and there were far more serious crimes for the Guardia to worry about than the beating of a man everyone disliked.

It was another three days before they came to the first of the works south of Benissa. Huge piles of coarse stone lay at the side of the roads. They had come from the quarries of Villalonga to the north, the bedding stones for the steel tracks.

Felipe sought out the '*Jefe*', the boss, to ask for work. The man was tall and stocky and said nothing at first. He looked Felipe up and down and felt for his muscles on his arms and legs. He seemed suitably impressed. He coughed up a huge ball of phlegm and spat it onto the floor as he pointed to a table and some sheets of paper.

"Leave your name and mark. Two pesetas a day take it or leave it."

Felipe had no choice.

The work was uncomplicated but tedious and hard, he was breaking up and moving rock which had been loosened by the explosive charges. The men that set the dynamite were from Asturias, tough and experienced campaigners who had grown up in the coal mining areas. Even the gang-masters had respect for them; they were paid 10 pesetas a day, five times as much as everyone else.

Pilar had been busy too. They'd both agreed she would never return to her previous profession and they'd made their home in a disused goat herders hut high up on the hills that overlooked the Mediterranean Sea. Pilar had repaired the roof with twine and the branches from nearby pine trees. She'd swept and cleaned while Felipe worked and even constructed a rough bed, and a table and two chairs from broken orange boxes she'd found dumped in the forest. As she sat overlooking the clear blue sea waiting for Felipe to return from work she swore to herself it was the most beautiful place on God's earth.

In time she too began to earn money in her own right, she would cook up huge potfulls of *tombet* a slow cooked, goat and vegetable stew that her mother had made every weekend when she was a child. She'd load the mule with the meat and vegetables and walk down to where the workers were. The railway labourers had to endure its alluring aroma for hours before they finished for the day, it ensured a queue of willing customers.

The cuts and bruises from her beating had all but healed and since Felipe had told his fellow workers that they were man and wife they had been left in peace. He figured they would not arouse any suspicion and began to frequent Calpe more and more. On Sundays they would go to church in the centre of town then spend the rest of the day on the beach where they'd have a special lunch with the luxury of a cup of wine and frolic in the sea together. It was idyllic, those six days of back breaking toil were worth it for this one special day. Life, thought Felipe, was almost perfect.

That Sunday had started like any other. It was hot in church and the sermon seemed to drag on and on. The priest was on a bit of a mission thought Felipe scolding the parishioners for their evil ways, ostracising them for their sins and offending God. Felipe and Pilar were more than happy when Mass ended, depositing a few hard earned coins in the collection box as they left. It was blistering hot and the paved roads burned at the soles of their feet as they made their way to the beach.

The four Guardia Civil were bored. They sat at the top of the beach in the shade of a palm tree, their horses tethered and their heavy Mauser rifles by their sides. One of them had been idly watching the pretty young girls on the beach.

One of them pointed. "Hey Enrique," he called out to his colleague. "That's a pretty young specimen. Can't we find an excuse to bring her in? I'm sure she would be more than accommodating should we get her away from her protector."

Another of the guardia looked over and spoke. He cupped his hand onto his testicles and squeezed making sure his friends were looking on. "Oh my God, I feel my big cock springing into life just looking at her fine arse."

Enrigue laughed. "Big cock Paco, don't make me laugh I've seen more meat on a day old frog."

Enrique stood. He studied the girl a short distance away. "Nevertheless I think we should at least bring her in for interrogation."

"On what grounds?"

Enrique shrugged his shoulders and laughed. "Does it matter...? who will dare to question us?"

Felipe had cast a wary eye over the Guardia Civil men as soon as they had arrived at the beach and he was more than a little uncomfortable now that they appeared to be walking towards them. He took Pilar's arm and explained they needed to be getting back. At first Pilar had resisted but soon realised the change that had materialised in her lover. She followed his line of vision and almost stopped breathing as she watched the menacing looking faces strolling casually towards them. She looked around, wanted to see other people near them, other people that they could have been watching, focussing their attention on. Her blood had almost turned to ice as she realised there was no one.

Felipe gathered up their things. "Come Pilar, let us walk. It's probably nothing but I don't think its wise that we give them a chance to talk to us."

Felipe and Pilar began walking in the direction of the main street. Pilar could feel her heart beating, pounding in her chest, her mouth was dry. Felipe had his hand on her arm trying to reassure her. "Relax Pilar, we have done nothing wrong, there is no way could they have followed us this far."

They had got as far as the track along the top of the beach when Pilar's panic gained the upper hand and she started to run.

"No stop Pilar," he cried out. "Stop right now."

It was a natural reaction to chase after her. The narrow streets of old Calpe were a maze of narrow twists, turns and dead ends, of which Pilar and Felipe were unfamiliar. They could hear the voices of the guards calling after them ordering them to stop.

The first warning shot took a chunk of masonry out of a wall a few metres above their heads.

"Run Pilar run," he shouted. The guardia were older and fatter than they were and they had a start on them. He could see the start of countryside with the cover of scattered scrub and trees just fifty metres away now. If they could make it there they would have a chance.

The next shot struck a tree, just a half metre away, level with Felipe's head. The third shot pitched Pilar straight onto her face. It had hit her square in the centre of the back. She was dead before she hit the ground.

As soon as he turned her over he knew.

Her eyes were closed, the blood already seeping from her mouth and her neck lay limp. He heard the clumping beat of the guardia's boots echoing through the cobbled streets as they grew ever nearer. He sank to his knees wanting to curl up in a ball and die with her. He didn't care.

He looked up to the heavens. "Why Father?" he cried. "Why in heavens name have you allowed this to happen? Why have you taken her from me?"

His tears fell onto her lifeless body as he collapsed upon her. The rough hands grabbed him dragging him from the body of his lover. He wanted to fight them, to kick and punch until one of the bastards put him out of his torment. And then he relaxed. He'd wait. Bide his time. He'd get his revenge. And then before he could gather any more thoughts a blow to the head stunned him as his world started spinning out of control, another blow and he plunged into darkness.

He hadn't been out too long, of that he was sure. He lay on a bed with pristine white sheets and an elderly lady bent over him mopping at his brow with a cool damp cloth. Where was he? Not the underground interrogation room of a Guardia Civil barrack room that was for sure.

Before he asked the question the old lady spoke.

"Relax boy, you've took a couple of nasty blows to the head."

"But- what—"

The woman placed a finger on his lips. "Shhh boy." She paused for a second, tears filled her eyes. "Your girl has gone to heaven. She didn't make it. She's in the arms of the Lord now but the Guardia are still looking for you."

It wasn't a dream. Felipe wanted to curl up in a ball and sleep for ever as the dramatic events registered with him again.

"She can't be... she is so young... she must—"

The old lady nodded. "My boy I am sorry but she is dead and you must keep your voice down or you will be next."

Felipe was aware of shouts from outside the building, footsteps running back and forth.

The lady explained that it had been her two sons who had rescued him and hauled him away before the Guardia had reached him.

She pointed to the outside wall. "That's them looking for you now. They can't understand where you've disappeared to." She grinned a toothless grin. "I'm afraid my son Pedro had to give you a bit of a clout. He sensed you were a stubborn one and feared you'd try and take those bastards on all by yourself."

The lady took his hand. "Nothing I can say will bring your girl back but you must recover your strength and live to fight another day."

Felipe was confused. "What do you mean live to fight another day? I am sure you are strange in the head old lady, anyone would think we were at war."

The old lady grasped at his hand as she leaned forward. Her breath smelled of stale coffee and spices from another world. Trails of white saliva hung in the corner of her mouth.

"We are at war you stupid boy can't you see that? Why do you think we saved you from them"

Felipe shook his head. "We are not at war old lady, I can assure you of that."

The lady stood and walked slowly across the room. "Then we should be." She stood proud, puffed out her chest. Felipe could now make out the shape of her two sons who sat quietly in a darkened recess of the large room.

"I am luckier than most, my boys are strong and work hard and they look after me but take a look at the people around you." She turned to face him. "They starve while the landowners and the church grow ever richer."

He'd heard about the workers in Valencia rebelling against the gang masters and the overseers, the privileged and the men of wealth. And he recalled the time when Pilar had told the tale of the uprising in Barcelona when the people had vented their rage against the church. What was happening to his country? His girl lay dead on the cobbles of a fishing village. What right did the soldiers have to do that? She'd done nothing wrong except flee a life of abject misery.

The lady tried to protest as he raised himself gingerly from the bed. His head throbbed, his whole body ached but he made it over to the small window. Rough wooden slats blocked out the street below but he prised them apart slightly making just enough of a gap to take stock of what was happening.

He caught his breath as his eyes settled on Pilar's dead body. He sunk his teeth into his bottom lip as it started to tremble. Why Lord, he asked again and again, why Lord, why have you punished me a second time. His eyes filled with tears as he looked to the heavens.

He whispered. "Two beautiful people you have stolen from me now. Please tell me the reason... please."

The old lady's ears were sharp as she questioned him. "Two people?"

Felipe nodded as he continued to study the scene unfolding outside.

"Two, old lady."

She shook her head as she made the sign of the cross on her chest.

Outside one of the Guardia slapped a colleague on the shoulder. "That was some shot Jose, you've been practising on the mountain again haven't you."

The man basked in the adulation of his colleagues. He turned towards the window of the house and removed his cap. He was tall and roughly shaven with an oversized bushy moustache. He had a cold penetrating stare. It was a face that would haunt Felipe to the grave.

He lay back on the bed as his head sank into the soft pillow. He sighed deeply. The last few months had been good. His eyes closed and he fell into deep sleep. He dreamt of Pilar, he dreamt of cool mountain streams and the moon and the stars and soft moist green grass and the gifts that he felt the Lord had bestowed upon them in the short time they had been together.

Four

It was six days before Felipe left the old ladies house. By now his rough stubble had grown into a beard and he wore a floppy straw hat to disguise him even further. He had swapped his clothing with one of the old ladies sons and promised her that he would leave Calpe and never come back. The lady walked with him to the perimeter of the village handed him some bread and tomatoes and a leather container filled with wine which he strung over his shoulder.

She kissed him on each cheek and pointed to the road up ahead. "Go home boy, back to where you belong. There are many Guardia here in Calpe and every one of them will be looking for you."

As he started walking away she called after him. "Hey Felipe, you never did tell me what it was you were running from."

Felipe stopped, turned around and spoke. "I don't know old lady. I don't know myself."

He'd walked no more than a kilometre when he stopped and sat by the side of the road. He uncorked the leather pouch and took a large mouthful of wine, wiping a drip from the corner of his mouth. He hadn't liked lying to the old lady but he had to go back to Calpe. The words of the scriptures were on his lips. *But life shall go for life, eye for eye, tooth for tooth, hand for hand, foot for foot.*

He would take revenge for Pilar.

It took only two nights before he located the bar where the Guardia Civil spent their free time. The local fishermen mixed with them in apparent harmony in the bar overlooking the bay, a few metres from the Peñon, the huge limestone outcrop rising three hundred metres into the sky.

Felipe sat in a corner nursing a cup of orange juice while the four men he watched sat at the table and went through at least half a dozen bottles of wine. The Guard known as Jose grew more and more drunk and on his final visit to the toilet bounced off the walls of the narrow passageway that led to the courtyard outside. Felipe wondered how hard it was to kill a man, a drunken defenceless man. Then he memorised the broken body of Pilar lying in a pool of her own blood. It would be easy he convinced himself as he struggled to control the seething anger that threatened to explode inside him.

Felipe thought they would never leave the bar but at midnight one of the older men stood up to leave.

"Come amigos," he called. "Seven hours and we must be at work again. We must be off." He picked up his jacket and placed his hat on his head. "You too Jose, I fear you have drank more than the rest of us put together."

"Just one more drink Juan Antonio," he said, "and I'll be right."

The older man shook his head. "Youngsters," he muttered under his breath as he made his way outside.

Jose was the last to leave. He threw a few pesetas at the bar keeper and bid him *buenas noches* and as he stepped out into the street outside Felipe waited a few minutes drained his glass and left. He spotted the drunken wretch as he urinated in an alleyway leading towards the port. Felipe was trembling with fear now as he felt for the cheese wire in his pocket, the cheese wire he'd taken from the old ladies kitchen.

His hands were bathed in sweat and he began to doubt if he could maintain a strong enough grip on the two wooden handles to carry out the job he'd set out to complete. Doubts began to creep into his head. Dishing out a beating to a violent gang-master was one thing but killing a member of the Guardia Civil was in a whole different league. He would be hunted down tortured and killed. And all of sudden it didn't seem such a wise thing to do.

"Hey you."

The voice of the Guardia had startled him, broke his train of thought and brought him back to the present. He had lost the element of surprise that was so vital to his plan.

"You, peasant boy, take yourself home before I give you a good beating. What are you doing anyway watching men pissing in the dark?"

Felipe doffed his hat in an apologetic gesture.

"Yes sir I'm going home now, sorry sir I'll be on my way."

As he turned to walk away the Guardia called again. "Hey you, wait, haven't I seen you somewhere before?"

Felipe pulled his hat further over his face and started walking away.

"I don't think so, I'm new to the town," he called back over his shoulder.

The Guardia reached for his holster and pulled out his gun. Felipe's blood turned to ice as he heard the unmistakable cock of the pistol, the same sound he had heard seconds before Pilar's death.

"Stop and turn around to face me or I'll shoot you in the back like the dog that you are."

Felipe tried desperately hard to control the trembling that had taken over his whole body as he turned to face the man.

"Take off that stupid hat so that I can see your face."

Felipe raised his hand and felt for the straw hat. He removed it slowly and held it in front of his chest in an almost apologetic gesture, taking care to bow his head so that the guardia could not see him. The hard soled boots of the man who had killed Pilar echoed off the cobbles as he took half a dozen confident steps towards him. A rough hand reached out and grabbed Felipe's chin as he forced his face upwards.

"Look me in the eyes peasant. Be a man for once in your pathetic life."

Their eyes met. Felipe locked on to the cold penetrating stare once again. The eyes registered immediate recognition and the Guardia's face changed from a drunken relaxed swagger to a sobering frown.

"I know you now," he yelled. "You're the—"

Before he could utter another word Felipe had flicked the cheese wire from his pocket with his right hand, swiftly grasping for the wooden handle with his left and with all his strength brought the makeshift weapon into contact with the man's throat. His head slammed into the stone wall and his legs buckled. He tried to cry out, tried to muster enough strength to fight back but already the cheese wire had begun to rasp into the soft flesh drawing blood and cutting off his air supply. Felipe inched closer.

He could smell the foul breath of the man who had casually shot the woman he loved in the back.

"For Pilar," he whispered. "Life shall go for life, an eye for an eye tooth for tooth."

A surge of strength came from nowhere as he lifted the guardia from the floor and his tortured feet danced like a show girl. The thin wire bit into his neck as the blood poured from his throat and the life drained from him. Felipe held him there until the last breath escaped from his lungs and then released him. The blood soaked body slumped to the floor.

Felipe fell to his knees and cried. A different quotation from the Bible had come to him now, one of the Ten Commandments. *"Thou shalt not kill."*

"Forgive me Lord," he wailed up into the night sky, "forgive me."

"Be quiet down there," a voice called out from a window above his head.

"Be off with you," another screamed out. "We are trying to rest."

Felipe knelt down and removed the dead man's gun from the ground. He checked his pockets and took the few coins that were left over from the raucous night of drinking, picked up his straw hat gripped it tightly in his hand and ran for his life.

Five

Vicente Cortes Ortuño felt rightly proud as he watched the boy playing in the courtyard of his home in the village of Xirles. Juan Francisco Cortes was five years old now and at times his legal guardian couldn't help forgetting that he was not of the Ortuño line. He was as much a son as his other two boys and Vicente had almost shed a tear the first time he had uttered the word *Papa*. He'd never really thought about what the boy should call him but it was as if someone somewhere had simply made it happen... it was meant to be.

Vicente looked up to the heavens made the sign of the cross and said a silent prayer of thanks.

"Juan, my boy," he called out. "Don't you be getting too dirty before church or your mother will warm your backside for you."

The little boy looked up forlornly and brushed a patch of dust from his Sunday best clothes.

"Sorry Papa he said apologetically, "I am forgetting it is the day of our Lord."

Vicente grinned. "Exactly right, Juan Francisco, don't ever forget the Lord's day?"

"I won't Papa."

The boy reached out for Vicente's hand and the man raised himself from the stone step. His knees creaked as he stood and he wondered for a second or two if he was just a little too old to be raising such a young child.

As he walked hand in hand with the boy the thought was soon forgotten as the deep tones of the church bells proclaimed the hour of prayer. For Juan Francisco Cortes Sunday truly was a special day. He was the luckiest boy in the world because he had three fathers. Father Vicente was his father at home and of course there was the Father with the beard who lived in the sky and took care of everyone in the whole world and answered your prayers if you were a good Catholic boy. As he sat in the small room at the back of the church he looked up in awe at father number three.

Father Ismael was a young priest who only recently had been sent from Granada to preach in the village of Xirles. Juan Cortes harboured a secret. He knew that Father Ismael had been sent to look over him. Father Ismael said he was his special one and that Juan was destined for the priesthood, to follow in his footsteps. Father Ismael said that the Lord had told him so.

Juan loved the way that Father Ismael held the Bible open as he read from it, carefully balanced on one hand. It truly was a miracle that he never dropped it, not once, not ever. And he spoke with such a passion as he told the stories from the Bible, parables and miracles and described the man called Jesus who was the son of God and of course his mother, the Virgin Mary.

Father Ismael would always pat the head of his young friend Inmaculada, the immaculate one when he spoke of the Virgin Mary and said that young Inma had been named in her honour.

Lucky Inma.

He wished he had been named after someone in the great book and when he was able to read quickly as Father Ismael had promised he would, he would search the bible for a boy called Juan. It was a huge book after all, surely there would be one person in there called Juan.

Father Ismael's story was simply beautiful. More and more people had heard of the word of Jesus and his teachings. At first he had tried to go somewhere quiet to rest, to a place called Bethsaida but they had followed him. Five thousand people had come to hear Jesus talk, said Father Ismael.

Juan raised his hand. Father Ismael nodded, indicating permission to speak. Juan cleared his throat and coughed.

"How many people is five thousand Father Ismael, I cannot count that high."

The rest of the children sniggered. Inma frowned and shook her head as if to say you stupid boy but Father Ismael simply smiled.

He spoke. "My child, their numbers were great. Everyone wanted to appreciate the teachings of Jesus."

Juan wished he had kept quiet now. He was interrupting the story. Father Ismael thought for a moment then continued.

"Imagine all the people of Xirles crowded into the village square."

Juan nodded as he thought about the last fiesta for Easter when the entire village had joined in the festivities and the huge procession wound its way through the village streets and up to the steps of the church.

"Can you imagine that my child?"

"Yes Father Ismael."

"And think of six or seven villages the size of Xirles and imagine... think hard now."

Juan closed his eyes and bit his lip in a demonstration of concentration.

"Can you imagine all of the people in all of those villages, can you picture the scene?"

Juan built up the picture in his head. His mouth fell open the instant it came to him.

"I can Father, I truly can."

Father Ismael smiled. "Then I can continue with the story."

Juan nodded.

"It was approaching nightfall and the disciples of Jesus urged him to send the people back to their towns and villages for they were cold and hungry. Jesus told the disciples that he would feed them." Father Ismael puffed out his chest and looked at the high beamed ceiling of the room. "And then a small boy appeared offering five small barley loaves and two fishes. Jesus took the bread and fish and broke it into baskets giving them to each of the disciples to share among the people."

Father Ismael looked towards Inmaculada, pointed and asked a question of her. "And do you know what happened next young Inma?"

The girl shook her head.

"And you Pepe?" he asked pointing to the boy sitting alongside her.

Pepe shook his head too.

Slowly his eyes fixed on Juan who by now sat bolt upright with his hand in the air positively itching to answer Father Ismael's question.

"Juan?"

"Yes Father."

"Continue my son."

Juan took a deep breath, a little unsure now of the answer he was about to give. It was impossible to simply guess what happened next but nevertheless somehow he felt he knew the answer.

"Jesus fed all of the people Father."

The priest furrowed his brow. "All of them Juan? Why surely that is impossible."

"Yes father, all five thousand of them. Jesus made it happen."

Father Ismael threw his hands in the air. "The boy has been blessed by the Lord for he knows that Jesus performs miracles, that Jesus is truly the son of God."

Father Ismael walked forward and took a hold of the boy's cheeks as he planted a delicate kiss on his forehead. "Bless you my son, bless you."

Father Ismael finished the lesson and asked Juan to stay behind. Father Ismael told him he was a very special boy indeed and if he studied hard and conformed to the laws of the church he truly was destined for the priesthood.

"Your life has been mapped out," he told the boy, "It's written in the stars."

Juan ran home and couldn't wait to tell his parents what the priest had said. He sat down with his mother Fatima who was one of the few people in the village who was able to read and begged her to continue with his lessons. This was the best day of his life. The next great day would be when he could pick up the good book and read it from cover to cover.

Six

Felipe was more than familiar with the terrain, even in the dark, but nevertheless he thanked the Lord for a full moon that helped him on his way. He found a suitable spot on the river bank and quietly lowered himself into the water washing the wet blood from his clothes and afterwards he ran again.

It would only be a matter of time before the body of the Guardia was found and he hurried on trying to put as much distance as possible between him and Calpe. He'd made it look like a robbery by taking the man's money. Hopefully that would be the conclusion his Guardia Civil colleagues would arrive at. Or would they? It was only days since the bastard had gunned down Pilar. Would they put two and two together? Perhaps, he thought to himself, but then again Pilar carried no paperwork and there was nothing to link her with him or indeed the village of Abdet.

He sat down for a while and rested. The tears flowed once again. He had killed a man and the enormity of what he'd done gradually sank in.

He was exhausted but sat for no more than a few minutes and then started to run again. He continued through the thick scrub that covered the Oltá Mountain above Calpe and from there he dipped down to follow the east slope of the Sierra Bernia ridge until it led down to the hamlet of Callosa d én Sarria. He reasoned he could follow the river valley that cut past Callosa d én Sarria, and then it was a familiar climb to Abdet. Something was telling him to run in the opposite direction and yet an overpowering almost magical magnetic force pulled him towards the area he knew so well. He was a fugitive and would need to run, he knew that, but he wanted to see his village just one more time. Was it too much to ask the Holy Father for a glimpse of Maria too?

When he came to Callosa d én Sarria he rested again. His feet were painful now, the skin torn in several places. He cursed his luck and lack of footwear but thanked his lucky stars that he had not disturbed a scorpion or worse, a snake. This was not the sort of terrain to be walking over in the dark.

He dipped his feet in the cold water of the River Algar and held them there until his feet were almost numb. How can this river be so cold he asked himself? He cupped his hands in the river and drank voraciously. He wiped his mouth and gazed up into the night sky. It was as black as pitch but a million stars cried out to him, they told him to go no further. He must press on he told them. Just one look and then he'd turn tail and run again. As he continued he realised he was treading in the same footsteps as he had with Maria all those years ago when they'd made their first trip to the markets of Altea. It was then that he had first discovered the delights of her young body. He frowned. His life had never been the same again.

It was a long trip back to Abdet and he spent the dangerous daylight hours wedged in the thick reeds that hugged the course of the river that ran from Callosa d én Sarria. He ate fruit from the trees and drank from the pure waters of the Algar.

He reached the outskirts of Abdet an hour before dawn on the third morning. His heart pounded loudly in his chest as he watched the sun come up casting a blanket of light over the old familiar village and he fought back tears of emotion. Why had they taken him away, why had they stolen his child and forced him apart from the girl he loved?

As the village came slowly to life and the villagers went about their daily routine his feelings for Maria returned and his whole being ached. It was as if he could almost feel her presence, as if her arms were somehow reaching out to him, as if something or someone sensed he was near.

He fought desperately hard to control his emotions, convincing himself that he would not disrespect the memory of Pilar and yet something so strong, gradually enveloped him. How could this happen he asked himself, he had not set eyes on her for five long years and only a few days ago was grief stricken at the violent death of his soul mate.

As the voices of the villagers carried towards him on the wind he decided it was time to hide. He had grown up in the village and knew every nook and cranny that existed. He remembered a tiny cutaway in the river bank where he would sit for long hours with Maria, watching the tiny fish busy up and down the pool. He would spend the day there and work out exactly what it was he would do.

Felipe fell into a deep sleep. He was home at last.

The hot rays of the early afternoon sun had bathed his body in perspiration when eventually he woke. Once again he had dreamed, dreamed of life and freedom and his family, his village, Maria and his child, the beautiful peaceful church and Father Cano. The images had seemed all so easy, so colourful and the life of his dream so tranquil and so peaceful... so right. Why couldn't life be like dreams, all so uncomplicated? He sighed as he rubbed the sleep from his eyes. He looked around. There was no one to be seen. He plunged into the crystal clear water without removing his clothes and prayed that the last remaining spots of blood would be washed away as he swam.

He lifted himself onto the river bank and basked in the hot sun. Soon the steam was rising from his body and he laughed to himself. If anyone was looking on they would surely think he was on fire. He prayed. He asked the Almighty for answers. He'd seen his beloved village. Was it time to run again or was it time to stop running? If he could just see Maria again perhaps he would have all of the answers to his questions. If Maria was married and had other children then surely there was his answer and it was more than he could bear to live in the village day in day out seeing Maria hand in hand with another man.

The hot flat stones of the path he used to run down every day seemed to make each footstep echo around the countryside as he crept ever nearer. He had to make his way past the area known as the *lavadero*, a line of sloping stones that flanked the ancient Moorish water channel that flowed past the village. The women of the village spent hours there washing clothes by pounding them against the smooth stones, worn shiny by centuries of use.

Maria's house was just a short distance from the *lavadero*. He cursed the heat that radiated from the stones taking care to place his feet away from the darker ones that absorbed the heat of the hot sun. He looked up as he heard voices a short distance ahead of him. The back of a young woman came into view.

It had been more than five years, but it was impossible to not recognise the curves of his childhood sweetheart. He was still frozen mid-step; when for some reason she turned a fraction and looked in his direction and for the first time in what seemed like an eternity their eyes met. He was unaware of anything around him as he ran towards her. He swept her in his arms and they embraced as first Maria and then Felipe burst into tears. It was as if he had been rendered speechless as he held her at arm's length taking in the beautiful vision before him. He convinced himself he was no longer dreaming.

Maria was the first to speak. "It is you my love. It is truly you. You have returned at last."

He took Maria around the back of the ramshackle building next to the *lavadero* and threw his arms around her again. He could not control himself he did not want to let her go. Not now not ever.

The cutaway in the river bank was the obvious place to go. They sat for many hours and talked. Felipe was full of questions and Maria could not get her words out quick enough. He was stunned into silence by Maria's account of what happened to their baby, and the deeds of the Priest Father Cano. He slumped in silence beside her and eventually he asked the question that had been on his lips for many years.

"We have a son Felipe, a beautiful baby boy just as handsome as his father." She disclosed.

Felipe was awestruck, Maria continued. "There is no one else in my heart but you Felipe," she disclosed. "There were days I sincerely believed my heart would simply give out and I would crawl away into the forest and never see the light of day again but I was prepared and I wasn't scared because life without you was a mere existence."

Towards the end of the afternoon Felipe told Maria about Pilar and her death and his love for her and even though her eyes filled with tears she never once released his hands from hers. Maria listened in horror as he gave the account of the murder of the Guardia Civil in Calpe and explained that he must run far away.

"Don't be silly," she said, "How could they possibly guess it was a man who has not lived anywhere near here for five years."

"I can't take that chance Maria. If I lived here I would be putting you and our family in grave danger. Whatever you say will not convince me to stay."

Maria sat back and smiled. "Then my mind is made up. I will come with you."

Felipe was shaking his head. "No, no. You can't. I have no money and I-"

Maria reached over and held his two lips with her thumb and forefinger. "You listen to me Felipe. I've lost you once and I will not lose you again. Now that you're here I will not let you out of my sight so there is no use trying to run off. If you run I'll follow you to the ends of the earth." She leaned forward and kissed him gently on the lips. "You have restarted my heart again, a heart that has been broken for five years. I knew you'd come back eventually and I waited patiently and you have returned. I won't let you do this to me again. You can run if you think that's wise but I tell you this, wherever you run to you will have me running alongside."

This was not the outcome Felipe had envisaged.

"But your family Maria, our son what will-"

"Don't mention my family to me," she interrupted. "For five years they have refused to tell me where our son is and yet I'm convinced they know of his whereabouts." She paused a while drawing breath. "He is nearby, I sense it and one day we will find him."

Felipe took her in his arms again and they kissed. He had not forgotten her taste, the delicate smell of her body. It was as if nothing had changed.

It was some hours later when Maria suggested a drastic but fool proof plan, a place they could run to and never be caught. They would leave for Algeria.

Maria explained there had been an almost continuous stream of people leaving the Valencian region of Spain owing to the lack of work.

"The rich are getting richer," she said, "and the poor grow ever poorer. Felipe, there is no future in Spain. The boats leaving from Alicante to Oran lately have been almost full."

"But this is our country Maria, he reasoned lamely, "our land, our language our families."

Maria stood. She raised her voice as she spoke. "Your country Felipe? She questioned. "Your country? Don't make me laugh. From what you tell me, your fellow countrymen are hunting you down like a dog. Our own families have almost disowned us and your beloved church stabbed you in the back five years ago. We must go to Algeria. There is nothing left for us here."

Maria's words hurt him but he knew they rang true and he could not offer a counter argument... except one.

"Our son Maria. We have our son. He is here in Spain."

Maria nodded. "That much is true and one day we will return to find him." She sat back down on the river bank and her two arms encircled his waist. "I don't know how but we will. You must always believe that Felipe. One day we will return."

Soon after they made love on the banks of the river, their long journey now complete.

Maria returned to her house and brought Felipe some cheese and ham and bread which he devoured voraciously.

"You eat like a pig Felipe, she laughed. "When was the last time you took decent food?"

Felipe shook his head. "I cannot recall. My appetite has not been healthy of late. But now," he smiled, "I am content once again. I am a happy man."

They walked some distance from the village across the fields through a sea of orchids and poppies and enjoyed an idyllic day in a secluded forest far from the beaten track. As night fall closed in, the practicalities of their planned adventure became apparent.

They needed money for the boat fares and a place to rent once they reached Algiers. They both looked at each other and almost telepathically realised there was only one person in the village that had that in abundance. Father Cano.

Maria told Felipe that she was still required to go around to the church every Sunday after mass to clean and scrub the floors. Father Cano by then was usually sleeping off the effects of the wine he had taken with his huge lunch.

Maria laughed. "The Church is always pleading poverty but there is more money hidden in that church and in Father Cano's house than the whole village put together."

Felipe was shaking his head. "No you are mistaken, that cannot be."

Maria took hold of him by the shoulders and shook him. "Listen to me Felipe. The church is not the organisation you believe it to be and Father Cano took our son from us. He is as corrupt as the day is long and richer than the King. He has a wooden chest he keeps locked by the side of his bed. One day as I cleaned the passage outside his room I peered through the gap in the door and saw him counting the money inside. The Bishop and his entourage come to visit Cano once a month and he hands over what they think he has collected leaving him a little left over for food and drink. The rest he keeps in his fat trouser pocket."

Felipe could not take in the gravity of what Maria was telling him. He recalled the repetitive sermons week after week as a child in which Father Cano pleaded with the villagers to give as much as they could. And give they did. He recalled going hungry, how his parents could never afford to buy him shoes or new clothes. He recalled a hunger that chewed at him like a starving dog.

"It can't be true Maria. You are mistaken."

Maria reached into her pocket and pulled out a key. "Then see for yourself Felipe. This is the key to his house. See for yourself and make your choice. Either I am lying or your beloved church had lied to you since the day you were born."

He'd watched from the bow of a tree overlooking Father Cano's garden as the fat bloated priest munched on pickled olives and opened a second bottle of wine. A short while after the bottle fell to the floor empty and Father Cano stood, steadying himself on the heavy wrought iron table. He staggered through the well-kept garden and placed two hands on the frame of the door breathing heavily. A few minutes later he disappeared through the doorway, closed the door and turned the key. Felipe watched as the downstairs lights dimmed and then a few minutes later the light to Cano's bedroom on the third floor of the large house flickered into life.

Felipe sat patiently in the tree until the priests snoring could be heard through the open window of his bedroom. Felipe took the key from his pocket and walked towards the door of the house.

∾

Father Cano woke at first light. He'd slept well but cursed those last two or three glasses of wine as a piercing pain stabbed through his brain. He coughed and spluttered as he threw his legs over the side of the bed and broke wind loudly as he eased himself to his feet.

"You truly are a revolting pig aren't you Father Cano."

The priest fell back onto the bed in shock, unaware of where the voice had come from.

"Who is it? Who is there?" he cried out desperately, rubbing at his eyes trying to grow accustomed to the light of the day.

"I have no money. Please, I have no money just go in the name of the Lord."

Felipe laughed as Father Cano focussed on the darkened figure who sat at the foot of his bed.

"Oh you have money Father Cano, of that there's no doubt."

The voice was familiar. A voice from the past.

"You have more than your fair share of money. See here."

Father Cano gasped as he set eyes on the empty box that lay on its side in the corner of the room.

"Or rather you did have. Today Father Cano, you are a poor man. You have nothing."

At last the voice came to him. "Felipe?"

That's right father, Felipe Albero Gomez. Remember me now? You stole my son and sent me away to Valencia."

Father Cano wanted to reply, wanted to defend himself. He wanted to tell the boy the same thing he'd told Maria that it was God's work and the family honour had to be protected. But at that juncture in time he had noticed the gun that hung loosely in Felipe's right hand and suddenly it was as if his voice had been taken from him.

"I've been a busy man throughout the night Father Cano. Every house in the village will find a little bundle of money when they wake up this morning. Redistribution of wealth I think it's called. I've returned the money that you've stole from them over the last twenty years."

Cano was shaking his head furiously as the perspiration built up on his brow. Felipe stood and cocked the weapon, pointed it at the terrified man of God.

"I believed in you Father Cano, I believed in the Lord." Felipe swallowed as tears of emotion and betrayal welled up in his eyes. "You deceived me Cano." He walked towards the priest slowly. "The people believe in you too because you and your church control them with fear. They give you their last peseta and while they starve you and your church grow fat and wealthy."

"No Felipe my son, you have it wrong the Lord is good and—"

Felipe whipped the pistol across the priests face and as he fell back onto the bed with a squeal Felipe was upon him. He forced the point of the pistol into Cano's mouth. "Give me one good reason why I shouldn't kill you now you stinking greedy bastard?"

Cano was crying now, whimpering like a stricken dog.

"You have raped and pillaged my people for two decades, admit it."

Slowly but reluctantly the priest nodded his agreement. Felipe removed the barrel from his mouth and stood up composing himself. He trained the sights of the gun back on the priest and spoke.

"Here's what we are going to do Father."

Cano nodded. "Anything Felipe, anything you say," he whimpered as his tears mixed with the congealing blood and mucus oozing from his nose.

"Later this evening you will call a meeting in the church. Leave the villagers in no doubt that they must attend."

"Yes Felipe yes."

"You will tell them that this morning's little surprise was a gift from God."

The priest continued to nod.

"And tomorrow you will leave the village for ever and never return."

Felipe waived the weapon in the air. "I haven't figured out how you will manage that one yet but then again that's your little problem not mine."

Father Cano at last voiced his disapproval, a token resistance. "But I cannot Felipe, I belong here, I will have nowhere to go."

Felipe shrugged his shoulders and spoke. "Then you must die Father."

He reached for a pillow and threw it towards the priest. "You can cover your head with this; it lessens the noise of the shot and stems the blood flow too."

Felipe stepped forward and pushed the pillow into his face placed the gun deep into the pillow and pulled the trigger. There was a muffled dull popping sound then a scream as the bullet embedded itself into the plaster wall at the head of the bed. Father Cano could no longer control the muscles of his anal cavity and the smell of faeces filled the room. Felipe pinched his nose as he spoke.

"Oh dear Father I seem to have missed. Never mind I have plenty of bullets left."

Father Cano pleaded for his life as he wallowed in his own mess, mixed with mucus, blood and tears. He begged and he promised and he pleaded until eventually Felipe agreed to spare his life.

"I will run Father but I won't run far. Soon you will hear news from Calpe and will realise exactly what I am capable of. If you are still here by the time the sun rises tomorrow then I will kill you and your God will not be there to help you. If you do not do as I say I will hunt you down like a mountain pig."

Felipe left the house and Father Cano shed tears of fear and shame for the rest of the morning. In the early afternoon he called on the elders of the church and told them to summon the villagers to a special seven o'clock mass where they would all give thanks to God. Before mass he packed a leather bag with his personal possessions and prepared the mule for the long journey that lay ahead.

And in his head the seeds of doubt crept in. Why had the good Lord not intervened, why had the Holy Father deserted him in his hour of need?

Seven

The dockside at Alicante was a hustling, bustling heaving mass of people looking for a better life. As was the way of the world, money talked and Felipe secured their passage on a Spanish registered steam boat the *Ignacio Roca*. Felipe and Maria stood with their arms wrapped around each other as they stood at the back of the rusting hulk taking them to their new life in Africa.

They had left the dockside in Alicante at six in the afternoon and watched from the back of the boat as Spain slipped slowly over the horizon.

"It is my country Maria, we shouldn't be doing this," Felipe said to her as a tear rolled the length of his cheek. "We are leaving everyone behind, our family and our son too."

Maria squeezed him tightly. "We will return soon my love. We have enough money to set ourselves up in business and we will buy a plot of land and work it well employing only the strongest men."

His heart felt rock heavy as he craved his family, his beloved family he'd missed so much. And he had been only a short distance from his family when he'd had to turn tail and run... again.

They settled down and talked in whispers for many hours and Felipe had pushed her sanity to the limit with his doubts, his questions, the doom and gloom that they would almost certainly encounter when the boat docked in Oran. He was in the depths of despair and he knew it and he knew the reason why.

And there was one question that remained unasked and unanswered and it was time for Felipe to get it off his chest. This was the reason he had fought the woman he loved since they had set out from Abdet on a stubborn old mule.

"Why are we deserting our son Maria? Why do we leave his land behind?"

A feint trace of a smile crossed Maria's face as she wiped the tears from his cheeks with a dirty handkerchief. She sat bolt upright as if a sudden burst of energy had somehow entered her tired bones. "Listen to me you idiot and listen well."

Felipe sensed the lecture that was about to be delivered as he made himself a little more comfortable against the wooden hull of the boat.

"We had to run. Of that there was no doubt. We have the Guardia Civil and now the church chasing our tails but we have money and hope and of course we are still young and we have time on our side."

Maria pulled herself up then sank to her knees in front of him. Her face was only inches away from Felipe's and for the first time since they'd left the village he had an urge to draw her towards him to kiss her as passionately as he once had.

"We will find our son Felipe, we both know that. One day we will find our son but if we go and try to find him now we may end up dead." Maria shrugged her shoulders. "And what good are corpses to him I ask you that?" She gripped him hard and stared into his eyes. "He who fights and runs away lives to fight another day."

Felipe was nodding. These were the answers he wanted to hear. Maria was strong and wise beyond her years and of course she was right. They would be back... soon. But they'd write to their friends and family and make sure that Cano had done as he was told, make sure the Guardia weren't crawling all over the countryside.

It all made sense. And in the meantime they'd work and save and invest wisely so when they did return they'd have enough money to settle down again, buy a piece of land and be a whole family once again.

And still Maria spoke about their plans and her strategies. She'd thought things through carefully that was for sure.

Felipe placed a finger to her soft lips. "Enough, he said." Let us get a little sleep for we have much work to do when we arrive in Oran. He rested his head against the side of the boat as Maria leaned in against him and they tried to catch a little sleep.

The trip was over eighteen hours, the boat stank, a pathetic bunch of people with small cloth bundles containing their worldly belongings. Felipe and Maria were carrying little, but the money they had taken from Cano that they had hidden on them, made them probably the richest people on the boat.

The early morning sun woke them and they pushed their way towards the bow, excited now to see who could catch the first glimpse of this strange new land that was to be their home for a short time. It was another few hours before they saw a dark line between the crystal blue sea and the hazy morning sky.

It was just after midday when the boat bumped against the wooden tree trunks that made up the dock wall of Oran. As they boarded the quayside and strolled in the stifling early morning heat their senses were overdriven with new smells and sights of the new country where they were to call home. The language was strange but occasionally Felipe picked out a word or two that sounded familiar.

"This is strange," he said to Maria. "It sounds very similar to our language of Valenciano."

Maria was smiling. "It is meant to be Felipe, I tell you. She cocked an ear towards two street vendors who were haggling over the price of an orange. She pointed to them. "I swear I know exactly what it is they are talking about."

"Me too," said Felipe with a smile, it sounds like French."

All of a sudden he felt a little more at home in Africa.

"Why are they speaking French?" he asked.

Maria pointed to a flag fluttering above what looked like an important building on the far side of the port. The flag was in three parts, red, white and blue. "The same reason our regional language is littered with French words. Invaders Felipe, the French see fit to sail in and conquer our lands. Our forefathers did the same in the America's. I've heard it said that the tongue of the America's is Spanish."

Felipe shook his head. "Surely not?"

They had learnt from talking to some of the other travellers the best place to find accommodation. They repeated the name they had been given on the boat to the people in the street who pointed towards some dilapidated housing in a vaguely southern direction. The port area was run down, but as they walked on further, the houses became much smarter and there were orderly streets, the people were well dressed. Felipe and Maria held each other's hands tightly and could not help feeling rather pleased with themselves. It appeared to be an altogether more prosperous and civilised part of the world than the small, depressed pueblo they had left behind.

It wasn't difficult to find accommodation or work. Felipe at first took employment in agriculture where he studied and learned the business from top to bottom. Maria worked at one of the big houses and in the evenings studied the French language and became familiar with the bureaucracy of trading goods in the port of Oran. She got to know the right officials to bribe, and the men who paid a fair price for the goods they'd take to sell to Europe, Asia and beyond and slowly but surely they progressed and prospered and Algeria became their home.

~

It was two years before they felt they had enough resources to make the first trip back to Spain. They'd purchased a run-down bodega some six months earlier together with several acres of vineyard. The first harvest had been spectacular and whilst they had sold most of the succulent cinsuit grapes, Felipe had also kept several fields produce for wine production. An old Berber native of the area, Mohammed, had befriended Felipe and Maria and been instrumental in advising exactly how to begin the exact process of wine production. He'd suggested mixing other varieties of grapes, Grenache and Carignane in particular to add softness and bouquet to the wine. The old man had said that in seven years the wine would be perfect and Felipe would be a very wealthy man. Felipe laughed at him and said there was no way he'd still be in Algeria in seven years' time. The old man sat under the shade of a pistachio tree smoking from a long clay pipe. He looked at Felipe and smiled nodding his head knowingly.

Maria turned to him. "You're a wise old man Mohammed, but I can assure you there are many things we need to sort out back in Spain. We don't doubt your wisdom, but Algeria is just a temporary measure for us and anyway I'm sure we can put people in place to run the business. We can return a couple of times each year and oversee things."

Mohammed took a long draw on his pipe and blew the smoke up into the late afternoon sky. The sound of the crickets in the trees could be heard as he eased himself from the ground and stood. He snubbed out his pipe, tipped the excess burned tobacco on the ground and slid it in a specially made holder in the side of his hat.

"I must be on my way mes amis." Mohammed said as he started to walk. "There is much to be done and there is no rest even for an old man like me." He reached for Maria's hand and shook it gently. "You do what you need to do pretty one; I will always be here for you." He sighed as he positioned his hat on his head. "I fear you will have many journeys across the sea before you find what it is you are looking for."

Felipe's forehead wrinkled as he let out a forced laugh. "Who said we are looking for something Mohammed?"

Mohammed stopped. He looked at Felipe first then seemed to study Maria before speaking.

"Your faces, they read like a book. Something has been taken from you that is very precious and you want it back." He walked towards Maria. "Your face especially pretty one, it contains many words."

He brushed the side of her face. "It tells me you want your child back."

Eight

Felipe sat in his favourite seat on the veranda studying the stars. He drank from a clay cup, he drank greedily at the wine the Algerian sun had produced and felt a little light headed. Maria walked out from the house and sat down beside him. He stroked at her hair.

"Mohammed suspects we will have many trips to Spain Maria, are you prepared for them?"

She gazed up at him. "I'm prepared if you are my love. In fact I'm prepared for anything as long as I have you by my side."

Felipe smiled. "I feel the same way Maria, I draw strength from you, just like I did when we were small children. I loved you from the day I set eyes on you."

Maria leaned into him and he spoke again.

"There is one thing we must do before our next voyage across the sea."

Maria frowned. "Something we must do?"

"Yes, something we must do to make our union stronger."

Maria sighed. "I was just getting comfortable Felipe, why do you have to spoil things and how can we make our love stronger?" She pointed into the sky. "Mohammed tells me there is a million stars out there. I love you more than all the stars in the night sky and you tell me likewise a dozen times each day."

Felipe reached over and she took his hand and pulled her into him. They faced each other, their lips only inches apart.

"We must be married," he said. "We must marry before the week is out, we must travel together as man and wife."

Maria laughed out loud. "Hah, if that's your idea of a marriage proposal then it's a poor one. Haven't you forgotten our rift with the church?

Felipe pulled her closer as he kissed her strongly. They parted and he spoke. "I don't know my love I just feel the urge to take you as my wife."

Maria caught her breath, pushed herself hard against his growing erection as she reached inside his trousers and gripped his stiffness. "You feel an urge you wicked boy, you feel an urge

73

alright. Forget the proposal of marriage it's a proposal of the bed you are looking for."

Felipe shook his head, "no wait, I mean it, I want to marry you."

He broke free from her, took her by the hands cursing the direction of his blood flow.

"I want you to be my wife. Please Maria marry me."

Maria's mouth fell wide open as she gasped. "Well, well. I swear that is the first time you have ever refused me. You are either sickly or you are serious."

Felipe grinned. "I am serious Maria, marry me. Mohammed knows a preacher from the port who will join us without the need for the Catholic Church."

"A Muslim preacher Felipe?"

Felipe shook his head. "I don't know and I don't care. Our God their God, what does it matter? As long as we commit ourselves together forever, that is all I ask for."

Maria kissed him again. She kissed him passionately and his blood started flowing again. She wore a thin cotton slip and nothing else as she arched her hips and rubbed her swollen clitoris expertly against his ever growing penis.

She moaned quietly as she pressed hard against him. "That feels good Felipe, that feels so good. If you take me inside and to that place they call heaven then the answer is yes."

At noon the following day, Felipe summoned Mohammed and asked him to fetch the preacher man.

"We are to be married Mohammed, just as soon as it can be arranged."

Mohammed bowed and walked away in the direction of the port of Oran. "So that's what all the damned noise was about last night," he mumbled to himself with a smile on his face.

Felipe sat with Mohammed on the veranda of the small house that backed on to the working units of the bodega. Maria carried three cups of mint tea as Felipe studied the parchment spread out on the ground.

"I took this map from Father Cano's study the evening we escaped." Felipe held a long piece of stick as he pointed to various marked places. "In the centre is Abdet and Confrides and the other places are the villages and towns round about."

Felipe explained his theory to Maria. "Our son is somewhere in this area, I'm sure of it. We must work on the likelihood that he was abandoned. Father Cano would simply have ordered someone to take him to another town or village under the cover of darkness and dump him somewhere where they would be sure he would be found.

Maria interjected. "But he was in Alcoy when he was taken. Surely it would be easier to find a home for him in a big town like Alcoy with many people; he'd blend in far more easily."

Felipe shook his head. "I don't think so, too risky. You had already been seen in Alcoy, many people had seen the babies face. Anyway, Cano wouldn't have known anyone trustworthy in Alcoy; my guess is that he used a man closer to home."

His stick trailed across the map. "A man from Confrides, perhaps, Alcoleja or here, Guadalest. From there the man would walk until he felt he'd walked far enough and abandon our son. Over the next few years we must visit all of these places and we will find him."

Maria frowned as she spoke, threw her arms up into the air in frustration. "But look at all the towns and villages Felipe there are too many."

Felipe looked up into the tear filled eyes of his lover as he tried to offer her a glimmer of hope. "Not as many as you think *cariño*, we can rule out the likes of Formaco, Beniarda, Benimantel and Benifarto as they are too close. An abandoned baby in any of these places would surely be news that would filter back to Abdet?"

Mohammed listened carefully in silence, studying the map intently as Maria nodded in agreement.

"So we have to go to these places? Tarbena and Bollula, Polop and La Nucia." She questioned.

"Yes my love, and further afield in the other direction to Penaguila and Relleu and we must look for the boys of the right age because I know he is out there somewhere."

Felipe turned to Mohammed. "Speak to me Mohammed; tell me our journey will not be in vain."

Mohammed traced his finger over an imaginary line on the map between the villages of Polop and Chines and looked up.

"Tell me a little more Felipe, tell me about Father Cano."

"Don't you think I asked him Mohammed, don't you think I begged him to tell me where my son was?"

"And?"

"He knew nothing. At one point I had him by the throat and although he admitted giving the go ahead to take our child he claimed his involvement thereafter finished."

The old Berber sat for some time stroking at his beard deep in thought. Eventually he looked up and spoke. "And you believed this man, Father Cano, the man of the Christian cloth?"

At that point Felipe simply shrugged his shoulders. He didn't know what to believe any more.

Nine

They set off from Oran in the autumn of 1911. Mohammed had agreed to watch over the Bodega until their return. By now they had built up a tried and trusted workforce of twenty five men and women and even a small boy who kept the workers supplied with water and sweet tea throughout the working day.

To all intents and purposes they were on holiday as they visited the towns of Sella and Seguron. They were merchants from Algeria visiting the area where they once lived. They took dinner in the village cafes and attended church several times while they watched and studied the young boys of a certain age. Both Felipe and Maria felt that recognition of their son would be instant. They talked to the townsfolk, mentioned the villages around and fished for any information they felt might be of use to them.

Each time they drew a blank.

They took the same trip every autumn. In 1912 they lodged in Benilup and Malena, in 1913 they stayed longer and ruled out the villages of Balones, Tollos and Facheca. As each year passed Felipe's worst nightmare grew ever stronger. The child had been stolen to order and sent to a different part of Spain altogether, perhaps even to another country. But still they persevered, building their business, steadily growing more experienced and more wealthy and as the final days of September closed in they would sit down and discuss the next towns and villages they would head for, logically trying to establish a reason or two why the boy would be sent to each location.

In October 1914 Maria sat in the cabin of the boat taking them to Spain. It was an expensive luxury hiring a bed for the evening crossing but tongue in cheek Maria had insisted that sitting on the damp deck of a filthy rat and cockroach infested steam ship was not fitting for a woman of her social standing, the wife of one of the most respected merchants in Oran.

Felipe had paid out the extra money without questioning her. If she wanted a cabin for the crossing why not? Alright it seemed a little extravagant and went against her nature to boast of her position in life but perhaps it was time to stop living the life of a peasant.

Maria broke the news early the next day as they sighted the Spanish mainland. Felipe had questioned her and asked if the bed had been to the liking of such a high standing woman.

Maria smoothed her smock over her stomach and for the first time Felipe noticed the subtle difference.

She took his hand and placed it over the slight swelling. "My dear Felipe I suspect something of your making is growing inside me."

Felipe was lost for words at first and then broke out into a wide beaming smile.

"You are sure my love."

Maria nodded her head. "I have been there before remember? This time no one will take our child away."

Ten

Mar was named after the Mediterranean Sea, she was born six months after another disappointing and fruitless search. If Maria thought another child would take away the pain of losing her first born she was very much mistaken. If anything the pain level intensified.

They made the trip again in 1916 and 1917, they visited Relleu and Finestrat and smaller villages further afield but the trips yielded nothing.

On their return, Mohammed sat under the same pistachio tree that was almost like a second home to him. It was a familiar sight as the horse and trap pulled into the bodega compound and Maria stepped onto the dusty ground with Mar draped around her shoulders. It had been a long crossing and the sea rough. They'd had little sleep and the child was exhausted. Once again the faces of Felipe and Maria told their own disappointing story.

Mohammed stood to greet them as he embraced first Felipe and then Maria.

Maria shrugged her shoulders and Mohammed nodded his understanding. He picked up two of their bags and walked into the house, spoke to the maids and gave them their instructions.

"Sit at the table," he said to the weary couple. "We have a little food and drink prepared for you then you can tell me all about your journey."

Felipe shrugged his shoulders. "I fear there is little to tell you Mohammed, it is the same old story."

Felipe almost collapsed onto the long bench as his arms flopped onto the table; the candle's flickered in the gentle evening breeze.

"Fetch me a bottle of your finest reserva Mohammed I fear I need to drown my sorrows yet again."

Mohammed had already reached for a bottle of the wine from a rack in the kitchen. He took out a knife from his pocket and began to loosen the cork.

"You will not find the answer in the bottom of a bottle Felipe; it does you no good to get drunk, it will not help." Mohammed poured the wine into a glass and handed it to Felipe.

Felipe held up the glass to the window as he studied the patterns of light in the wine. He brought the glass to his nose and inhaled deeply.

"That is where you are wrong Mohammed, getting drunk does help, it makes me forget about the son I have never set eyes upon." He swallowed the contents of the glass and banged the empty receptacle on the table. "Another refill my good friend."

Mohammed did as he was told, poured out a small glass for himself and sat at the table.

After picking at a few scraps of food, Maria took Mar to bed and left the two men talking. They talked into the early hours of the morning. They talked until the sun came up.

As Felipe opened the fourth bottle of wine he announced to Mohammed that he was ready to give up.

"I have a good life here and a beautiful daughter who makes me very happy. The wine is good and selling well and we want for nothing. How silly am I taking off to Spain every year on a wild goose chase? I fear I am looking for a needle in a haystack."

Mohammed sat back in his chair and placed his empty glass on the table. Felipe reached for the bottle and attempted to replenish his glass. Mohammed's hand covered the top of the glass.

"No more my friend, I fear we are quite drunk enough and we have lots of work to do today." He stood. "It's time I made myself busy before the sun is at its hottest."

Felipe stood with him and spoke. "Tell me Mohammed should I give up, should I settle down in this place that has been good to me and my family and accept that it is simply not to be?"

Mohammed walked around the table and placed his hands on his friend's shoulders. He shook his head as he stared into Felipe's bleary eyes. "No friend you don't give up, giving up is what kills people. You will never give up because I know you like one of my own sons. You are not of the make-up of a man who gives up. You must continue looking, for I suspect there cannot be many villages left. You are separating the final pieces of hay that are hiding the face of your son. But..."

Mohammed paused.

"What is it Mohammed tell me?"

He looked at the remaining villages that Felipe and Maria had not yet visited. They were circled in red.

He spoke. "Onil, Ibi, Castalla, Monforte, Agost, Vilajoyosa, Xirles, Callosa, Alfas and Benidorm. The towns and villages are many and I fear you could be searching for many years. And look." He pointed at the map. "There are more villagers further beyond."

Felipe took another mouthful of wine. "You tell me something I already know Mohammed but what solution is there?" He pointed to the map. "And La Nucia and Altea, Vallada and Moixent and more. We may get lucky or the good Lord may continue to tease us for many years. The boy could be a grown man before we find him."

Mohammed walked around the table slowly, opened the door to outside and the sun streamed into the darkened room. He turned around to speak to Felipe, his shape silhouetted in the brightness of the open doorway. "There is one man who knows where your son is." He said.

Felipe reached across for the bottle again as he laughed. "Hah, then pray tell me Mohammed for I have been trying to find him for many years. I search for my boy year after year but he does not show his face."

He slugged back another mouthful of wine before dragging his sleeve across his lips.

"Tell me where I will find this man."

Mohammed shook his head and took a deep breath. "I do not know where this man is, indeed I do not even know if he is alive."

Felipe's voice climbed a decibel or two in frustration. "Mohammed... you know I respect you like my own father but why do you fill me with sunshine and then dash me on the rocks? I do not deserve this; you feel how much pain I have."

Felipe walked towards the open doorway as he continued. "You tell me of a man who can find my son then tell me in the same breath he may be dead. What use is this information to me? You have told me nothing Mohammed."

Mohammed didn't reply, didn't apologise. A brief uncomfortable silence ensued as Mohammed brushed past Felipe and walked outside towards the well. He sat on the well wall as Felipe strolled over towards him. Felipe stopped a few metres from where he sat as Mohammed gulped greedily from a rusted old ladle.

And then he spoke. "If he is alive I have a man that will find him."

Felipe gasped in frustration. "Who Mohammed, find who?"

Mohammed placed the ladle back in the bucket.

"Father Cano," he said. "My man will locate Father Cano, for it is he who knows where your son is."

~

Mohammed explained about the man known as *The Carrier*. He wasn't cheap, but through his contacts in Europe, boasted about being able to deliver anything to any man in Spain. Gold, silver, money, hallucinogenic powders, potions and simply messages. *The Carrier* delivered every time.

Mohammed was convinced that the whereabouts of Felipe and Maria's son would be known to the Catholic Priest.

He explained. "The church is aware of all happenings in Spain, they have ears and eyes in every wall," he said. "I will send word to *The Carrier* today. If Cano is alive he will find him."

Felipe spoke. "One other thing Mohammed."

"Yes my friend."

"Will he also take a message to my father, Maria's family too? It is time we spoke. The years have been too many."

Mohammed nodded and smiled. "If you have the money he will deliver anything."

Eleven

Two months later Mohammed brought a small envelope sealed with brown glue into the bodega. It was addressed to Maria. He handed it to her and she tore it open in excited anticipation. The rough print was in her mother's hand.

There was a great disease falling across the area, it read. They had given it the name of the cockroach, *la cucaracha*. People were being struck down in large numbers and the medical men had little idea of what to do. Maria's mother wrote that no family had escaped, everyone had been affected and her father lay in bed gravely ill. As Felipe walked into the room their eyes met and Maria burst into tears as soon as she started to explain. Felipe picked up the letter and read it.

He turned to Mohammed. "I suspect we must make another trip Mohammed, it is time to see our families again. We must go before it is too late."

Mohammed nodded as he spoke. "I will come with you. We must leave as soon as possible for *The Carrier* has also found Father Cano."

The following day Maria made all the necessary arrangements booking their passage out on the next boat from Oran. They had decided to leave young Mar behind, it was much too dangerous to take her. The servants would fuss over her and spoil her and although her small eyes filled with tears when Maria explained what was happening, it was quickly forgotten when Habika, the oldest maid told her she could help bake some cakes and they would prepare a grand fiesta for when Mama and Papa returned.

Their arrival at Alicante port on the same rusting hulk was fairly low key. Felipe had suggested they hire a small horse and trap with driver; they would be at the village of Abdet in less than 24 hours.

The shadows of the valley grew longer. As they set off in the dark the driver grunted behind the scarf wrapped tightly around his face. He suggested they do the same as breathing in the air around an infected person was asking for trouble.

After a few hours they reached the village of Busot. There were many people in the street, most of them had some sort of cloth wrapped around their mouths and piles of dead bodies lay neatly stacked on the street corners awaiting mass burial. The smell of death lingered in the air.

They arrived at Abdet at around 8.30 in the morning, the village was unusually quiet. Normally children would have run out to see the spectacle of a horse and trap, this time nothing.

They parked adjacent the church and Maria hurried over to her house, pausing for a second before going in. Her mother was lying on the bed, a pale grey colour; it appeared that death was not so far away.

Maria's tears started immediately as she made to rush over towards her mother.

The old lady held up a hand. "Don't come near me pretty one." Her voice strained and cracked as she struggled to get the words out. "I have la cucaracha," she whispered. "Your father is gone, your young brother too."

As her eldest brother, Jose walked into the room to greet her she ran into his arms and sobbed her heart out. Jose explained the devastation that had arrived at Abdet.

"We seem to be over the worst of it Maria, thank God. There have been no new cases this month but more than half the village have been struck down and there have been many deaths." He looked over to the open doorway where Felipe stood. "You must go to your family Felipe.

Felipe stood rooted to the spot. He wanted to come over to comfort his wife but something had poured lead in his boots.

"What news of my family Jose? Have they also been touched by this plague?" He said.

Jose stroked the hair of his grief stricken sister as he spoke. "You have been luckier than most my friend. The last I heard only your father has the infection but he is not in any immediate danger."

As Felipe ran out into the street to be with his family, Jose's eyes took in a quite amazing sight. "Why my dear sister I cannot quite believe what I see."

Maria wiped the tears from her eyes. "What brother, what do you see that puzzles you so?"

Jose's face broke out into a broad grin. "Your feet Maria, they are covered. I do believe you prosper in that place called Africa for your feet are hidden. You are wearing shoes."

Maria smiled between tears. "Shoes Jose, yes." She looked over to the bed where her mother lay. "And before my ship sets sail again I will see that my families' feet are protected too. It will be winter soon and when the Lord is bored with cloudless skies and sunny days he will send the snow and rain once more." She stroked at the side of his face. "My dear brother and Mama will never set cold feet on the streets of Abdet ever again."

The 1918 flu pandemic (the Spanish Flu) was an influenza pandemic. It was an unusually severe and deadly pandemic that spread across the world said by some experts to have originated from Spain. Most victims were healthy young adults, in contrast to most influenza outbreaks which predominantly affected juvenile, elderly, or weakened patients. The pandemic known in Spain as La Cucaracha (The Cockroach) lasted from June 1918 to December 1920 spreading even to the Arctic and remote Pacific islands. Between 50 and 100 million died, making it one of the deadliest natural disasters in human history.

The Spanish King Alfonso XIII became gravely ill and was the highest-profile patient. The disease was described as "the most viscous type of pneumonia that had ever been seen" and later when cyanosis appeared in the patients, A Doctor of the time described it thus "it is simply a struggle for air until they suffocate." Another physician recalls that the influenza patients "died struggling to clear their airways of a blood-tinged froth that sometimes gushed from their nose and mouth. Within hours of feeling the first symptoms of extreme fatigue, fever, and headache, victims would start turning blue. Sometimes the blue color became so pronounced that it was difficult to determine a patient's original skin color. The patients would cough with such force that some even tore their abdominal muscles. Foamy blood exited from their mouths and noses. A few bled from their ears. Some vomited; others became incontinent. The Spanish flu struck so suddenly and severely that many of its victims died within hours of coming down with their first symptom. Some died a day or two after realizing they were sick. This huge death toll was caused by an extremely high infection rate of up to 50% and the unusually severe disease killed between up to 20% of those infected.

They had been in Abdet three days when the messenger brought fresh news to Mohammed. He read the note as he took a coffee in the bar in the village. He passed a few coins to the owner and bid him farewell. He found Felipe by his father's bedside. His father looked well; he showed a big improvement from when Felipe had first set eyes on him. Mohammed said he had drawn strength from his young son.

Mohammed rested a hand on Felipe's shoulder. "We must go Felipe, the carrier has news of Cano in a place called Lliber in the Jalon Valley."

Felipe dragged a cool damp cloth over his father's brow. "Tomorrow Mohammed, we can leave tomorrow, I will prepare a mule to take us to Lliber where Cano is."

Mohammed shook his head as he squeezed Felipe's shoulder. "No mon ami we leave now."

"Tomorrow Mohammed. I must stay with my father one more night." He pointed at the old man lying on the bed. "The colour in his face has returned and it has been some hours since he last coughed. La Cucaracha had indeed left his body. See how good he looks. Another few days and he will be back in the fields again."

Mohammed squeezed a little harder and Felipe looked up into his eyes. They glistened wide in a steely stare. "We leave now Felipe for Cano has La Cucaracha also. If his God does not intervene, by nightfall he will be dead."

∿

Felipe and Mohammed were met by an elderly woman on the outskirts of Lliber in the Jalon valley. She introduced herself as Señora Delores and they were taken quickly to a large house on the edge of the village. The woman would not dare to cross the threshold of the house.

"I have three children and a good husband and they are all clear of la cucaracha. You understand I cannot take any chances. Father Cano is being looked after well but even if God himself summons me, I will not go into that disease ridden house."

Felipe gave the woman a few coins and she hurried away. He pushed the door to the house and it opened.

They discovered Father Cano on the third floor of the large house. A young woman sat on the left side of his bed. As they entered the room the girl stood. She was no more than twenty years of age and clearly fit and healthy, la cucaracha had not troubled her.

She spoke in a whisper. "The father is sleeping; I fear it may be that he never wakes."

The girl explained that Father Cano was in the last throws of death and a priest had been brought in from Jalon only that morning to read him the last rites.

"Delores tells me you have travelled many miles to pay your last respects." She walked towards the open doorway. "I will give you your privacy. Call me if you need me I will be downstairs."

Felipe nodded rather uncomfortably. *Last respects* he thought to himself, *God give me strength*. He thought about the many visits he had made trying to locate his son over the years and wondered if perhaps on that fateful night many years ago he could have pushed Cano just a little further. He looked at the pathetic broken form of the priest. *This man deserves no respect at all.*

Mohammed moved closer to the bed and leaned over and placed a hand on his chest.

"His lungs are weak Felipe, he has not got much time."

"Can he talk Mohammed?"

Mohammed slapped gently at his cheek. "We will make him talk. He will tell us where your son is if he uses his last breath to do so."

Mohammed slapped his face a few more times and Cano's eyes flickered slowly open. He showed no sign of emotion as his eyes fell on Mohammed. As he focused around the room and his gaze settled on the form of Felipe there was an unmistakable look of recognition.

"You boy, I know you." He said. "Who are you and why do you come to my death bed?"

Felipe took a few steps forward. "You know why I am here father. I come for my son you took from me fourteen years ago."

"Felipe?"

"Yes Father it is I. Felipe of Abdet."

"Cano immediately became agitated, breathing heavily as the hollow rattle in his throat echoed through the small room.

"I cannot help you Felipe," he said as he struggled for breath. "I know not where the boy is."

"You sent him away Father," said Felipe." You must know where it is they took him, make your peace with God."

Father Cano shook his head from side to side as the perspiration built up on his b

"No Felipe... no. I told you so when you held a gun to my head that I called on a peasant from Confrides. He took the boy. All I know is he walked in the direction of the sea. The boy could have been taken anywhere and the peasant is now dead. Please believe me Felipe I cannot help you. I swear by the good name of my maker whom I will meet very soon."

Felipe's heart sank. The dying priest was of no help to him.

"I'm a dying man Felipe," said the priest, "I would tell you if I knew, believe me."

Felipe took a deep breath and walked out of the room and into the long corridor. He propped himself up against the wall and slid down until his backside hit the floor. He covered his hands with his face and sobbed like a baby.

He was aware of Mohammed standing over him. "Why do you cry friend," he asked. "We are so near."

"So near and yet so far Mohammed," he sobbed. "You heard Cano, he knows nothing; he would tell us if he did. He is on his death bed and to him it matters no more."

Mohammed eased his body down on the floor alongside him and took Felipe's hand. They sat in silence for two or three minutes before Mohammed spoke.

"I come from the tribe of the Berber, Felipe and we have many skills handed down from our fathers and their fathers before them. I know a good man from a bad man." Mohammed cocked his thumb at the door. "That bastard in there is lying."

"He is?" said Felipe with a frown.

Mohammed nodded. He pulled on Felipe's hand. "Help an old man to his feet and give me some time with him." Mohammed smiled. "I will speak to him man to man. I will make him see sense."

Felipe lifted Mohammed from the floor and opened the door to Cano's room. Mohammed paused in the doorway. "You stay here my friend, I will work quicker on my own. Before Felipe could answer the door slammed shut in his face.

Felipe walked the corridor for what seemed like an eternity. He had no concept of the time but was aware of nightfall closing in as he looked from the window at the end of the long passage. He studied the mountains in the distance; they retained a lingering gleam of daylight and wondered if his son was out there somewhere. Mohammed had surely failed, Cano must be dead by now.

He jumped as he felt a hand on his shoulder. "Mohammed you startled me, you have been many hours."

Mohammed sighed. "Yes. Father Cano was a stubborn old mule."

Mohammed picked his old leather bag from the floor and slung it over his shoulder. "Come," he said, "we must make haste."

"We are going?"

"Yes" said, Mohammed. "We are going to a place called Xirles to meet with Juan Francisco Cortes."

"Juan Francisco Cortes?" Felipe stated with a puzzled frown on his face. "And who is Juan Francisco Cortes?"

Mohammed grinned a grin as wide as the Mediterranean Sea. "Why Felipe you do not know? He slapped him on the shoulder. "Juan Francisco Cortes is your son."

Twelve

They were several kilometres from Abdet when Mohammed disclosed that Cano had died. He never explained his method of extracting the truth from the elderly priest only that his life had ebbed away and that Cano felt the time was right to meet his maker.

"It is fitting that his last breath of life was the breath of truth," Mohammed said.

What if it wasn't? Uttered Felipe, suspiciously.

Mohammed almost glared at him. "It was mon ami... believe me it was."

The two men explained the story to Maria as they readied the mule for their journey to Xirles. Maria almost trembled with excitement as she kicked the mule into action and they set off on the road to Guadalest. She couldn't quite believe how close their son had been all this time. It was less than two hours away and incredibly Juan Francisco Cortes had settled in the village nearby where he had been conceived. She daydreamed as she remembered her first time with Felipe in the goat herder's caves in the middle of an electrical storm. It all seemed so long ago.

Was it really fourteen years ago since their son had been taken from them? Maria had to be supported by Felipe as they stumbled into the small village of Xirles. The village felt right, she could feel her son's presence as she gripped Felipe's hand tightly. Felipe reciprocated, he could sense it too. Mohammed had been right; Father Cano had spoken the truth.

They wasted no time taking coffee in a small rundown house in the middle of the village. After a generous tip the owner spoke freely telling them all about the boy they were looking for. The gossiping old lady with only two remaining black stumps of teeth in her bottom jaw said that Juan Francisco Cortes had been touched by the hand of God.

He was a good boy, the son of Vicente Cortes Ortuño and his wife Fatima Ausina Devesa and he spent every waking hour with his head in the bible or helping Father Ismael at the village church.

She cackled as she spoke. "I'd bet a peseta to a pinch of salt that's where he is now."

She offered more food and coffee, glad of the extra business but Maria bid her *adios*, told her they must be on their way.

They walked the narrow, dusty streets finally turning into Calle Major. At the end of the street they looked onto the small church. It was an unimposing building, but spotlessly clean and highly polished. The huge church doors, almost the size of the entire building were open and a young man stood in the entrance sending clouds of dust into the air as he brushed the steps that led to the street.

"Come," said Mohammed. "It is time to meet your son."

As they got within ten metres of the doors Maria froze. She reached for Felipe's hand.

"Why my darling, I swear I cannot take another step, something is holding me back. What do I say to him? How do I -

Felipe placed a finger across her lips and silenced her. "You say whatever you want my love, tell him who you are, tell him you have missed him like he could never have imagined."

Maria nodded and took another few steps.

"Boy," Mohammed called out as young Juan stopped what he was doing and looked up.

"There's someone here to meet you."

Mohammed turned to Maria and Felipe. "I am in need of a little more coffee. The journey has left my throat dry." He placed a hand on Maria's shoulder and a hand on Felipe's as he edged a little closer and whispered. "There is no doubt who that boy is. He even stands like you Maria, there is no mistake he is his mother's son."

Felipe was nodding, wiping at a tear in the corner of his eye. "I see it too Mohammed, I remember Maria at that age. He has the same posture and the same shaped back."

Mohammed squeezed gently. "I will see you in the old gossips house; I will be there if you require my services."

Felipe took Maria's hand. "Come my love; let us take a few more steps."

With all the courage and strength she could muster Maria walked over to the steps. She tried to call out but barely a whisper left her lips. Her eyes met Juan's and his brush clattered onto the old stone steps. The tears she had been fighting all morning eventually gave way and she slumped to her knees. The boy rushed forward.

∼

What was happening? Those eyes, the eyes of the pretty young woman, it was like looking into a mirror. And why had he dropped his brush? What had come over him? Juan looked bemused at the now sobbing woman who was lying at his feet.

"What's wrong lady?" He said, as he bent down and placed his hand on the woman's shoulder. "The church is open if you need to come in and pray. Tell the Lord of your troubles and he will listen to you."

Felipe smiled as he spoke gently. "I do not think the Lord would begin to understand her story Juan Francisco Cortes."

Juan turned to the stranger. "How do you now my name sir, I fear I have never met you or this lady before and what of your troubles?"

"Our troubles are over Juan," Felipe said. "We have had fourteen years of troubles but today they are over." He pointed to Maria. "You have met her before and me too, only you were very young at the time and you can't remember." Felipe looked up at the bell tower of the small church. "Your church has a lot to answer for," he mumbled. He knelt down on the steps of the church and took hold of his wife's arm. He lifted her and cleaned at her face with the cuff of his shirt. He held her chin and lifted it up high. "Who do you see Juan?" he asked the boy. "Who do you see?"

Juan was shaking his head, desperately trying to fight the feelings of confusion welling up inside him.

"I see no one but a stranger," he said, "a stranger in need of help. Come... come into my church and I will clean you up." Felipe helped Maria to her feet and into the welcoming environment of the cool darkened building. Juan helped them both onto a pew at the back of the church as he went to fetch a jug of water. He returned after a few minutes with the water and a clean white cloth. He handed the cloth to Felipe.

Felipe shook his head. "You do it Juan... you wash her face."

The boy bunched up the cloth nervously, poured a little water onto it and began to wipe at her face. He patted gently at the familiar curves and traced the damp cloth along the contours of a face that he felt he had seen a thousand times. But this was foolish; he could not know this woman.

Felipe spoke. "I see it in your eyes that you know Juan. I see it in your eyes that you see it in her eyes.

"I know not what you are talking about stranger. You speak in riddles."

Felipe smiled. "It is no riddle boy." Felipe placed his hand on Juan's arm. "You are washing the face of your mother."

The clay jug fell from the boys grip as if in slow motion and shattered into a thousand pieces on the floor of the church. He turned to Felipe shaking his head as the perspiration stood out on his brow.

"It cannot be. It is impossible. I have a mother."

Felipe nodded. "It's true Juan. This is your Mother Maria, and I'm your father, my name is Felipe."

Felipe held out a hand. "It's nice to meet up with you again my dear son. It's been a long journey."

∼

Felipe explained at great length how a child had been taken from them. He thought it sensible to leave out the role of the Church at that particular moment and thought it rather ironic that Juan Francisco Cortes was so involved with an organisation that had changed the course of his very existence. What on earth was going through the poor boys head?

Juan was finding it hard to take everything in. Maria suggested he ask the question of the man and woman who he believed to be his real parents.

Juan, Felipe and Maria walked the dusty street to the door of his adoptive parent's house. Juan held the door open and beckoned Felipe and Maria in. Vicente sat just inside the door, his wife Fatima was in the coral at the back attending the chickens and he called her into the house to greet their unexpected guests. They were fortunate, Juan explained and had escaped the attention of *La Cucaracha.*

"Praise the Lord, for he protects my family." said Juan.

"Father," he said as he stood in front of the open door. "These people have just arrived in the village; they come to our church to speak to me and they come to me with an incredible tale."

Juan took a deep breath as he reached for Vicente's hand. "They tell me that they are my real parents. How can this be, is it true?"

Vicente stood open mouthed as Fatima covered her face with her hands. He looked at his wife and then Juan and then into the faces of his visitors and wanted to speak, wanted to explain but the words would not form on his lips.The look was not lost on Juan. At that precise moment he knew the truth. The stranger's faces were not the faces of strangers and the look on the faces of the man and woman who for fourteen years had looked after him as their son painted a thousand words although they tried to deny it.

The four adults sat in the tiny room at the front of the house. Maria was calmer now and began to recount their incredible story, only stopping for breath when Felipe interjected to add the details of how they had searched for years to finally find Juan.

Juan shook his head in disbelief at the story that was unfolding before him. The room fell silent many times. Felipe explained that Father Cano had said the boy had been abandoned in a basket tied to a tree just outside Xirles.

Juan turned to Vincent. "Is it true that you found me like that father?"

Vicente ignored the question. "You are our son Juan. No father or mother could have loved a child more."

Juan walked over to Vicente's side and hugged him tightly as he fought the tears brimming in his eyes. Fatima recounted Juan's young life as a baby and a small boy. She proudly detailed the day of his communion at eight years of age and his progression as a young man which led to a deep interest in the church and his religious studies afterwards. She explained to Felipe and Maria that Juan had already committed to a life in the priesthood and ignored any question that related directly to his abandonment.

They talked for two hours. In the end they went round in circles Vicente and Fatima refusing to admit the truth. Juan prayed under his breath and begged the Almighty to answer the many questions racing around his mind. If it were true where would he go? Where would he live and with whom? What of Vicente and Fatima, of his new found parents if that's who they truly were. His head was spinning and he knew that the only eventual outcome was certain heartache for at least two of the people sitting in the house.

"Lord," he mumbled to himself, "I do not deserve to be placed in such a quandary, help me I beg of you."

Maria had been patient with the elderly couple but could hold back no longer.

"We want you back Juan, we are your real parents, you were stolen from us and we have searched for you for fourteen years."

Fatima stood up and walked to the door. "I have listened to you for long enough and it's time for you to leave us all in peace, we have the correct papers, he is our son. Juan belongs with us."

Juan cradled his head in his hands and the tears fell freely. He stood. He spoke to Felipe and Maria. "I think it's best if you go. I need some time alone with my..." He gestured towards Vicente and Fatima. "With my parents... I need some time with my parents."

Felipe and Maria held hands as they walked down the dusty street away from Vicente's house, Maria was doing her best to hold back the tears but was doing a poor job of it.

"What are we to do Felipe, what are we to do if our son does not want us?"

Felipe was deep in thought. "We cannot force him to come and live with us. He is our son and we have found him. We know what he looks like and that he is a good boy. We can come to Xirles every damned day if we need to.

"But-"

Felipe interrupted. "Enough of this Maria, stop torturing yourself. Do you not feel as joyous as I do? We have found our son at last." He turned to face her and took her by the hands. "Do you hear me? We have found the son we have searched a lifetime for; how good does that sound?"

"But Felipe I want to hold him and hug him and see his pretty face each morning when I wake. I have been denied that for too long, deprived of being able to give a mothers love."

"And what of Vicente and his wife?" Felipe said. "They are good people and they clearly love him too."

Maria was crying as she shook his head. "I do not know Felipe and I do not care, my brain is turning summersaults. I thought this would be different, I thought it would be easier than this. We have found him and we should be able to take him home where he belongs, is it not that easy?"

Felipe shook his head. "No my love I fear it is not."

They found the old Berber in the house of the local gossip. He had drunk his fill of coffee and had feasted on bread and cheese, taken a little wine. Maria smiled as she met with his gaze.

Mohammed will have the solution to the problem, she thought. He always did. They told him the fine details of their meeting with their son and his adoptive parents and how they were eventually shown the door.

Mohammed explained that they would need to involve the authorities. They had to do things correctly according to the law of the land. Because of the dispute the Judge would need to make a decision if necessary and because the boy was under age he would have to abide by it.

Maria spoke. "Mohammed, I do not want to drag my son to Abdet, I do not want a court to decide his destiny."

Mohammed took another mouthful of coffee wiped at the corner of his mouth and spoke again. "I agree Maria; it is up to the boy if he wants to return to Abdet but if he does and you do not have the legal paperwork then Vicente and Fatima have every right to drag him back again and you will end up in jail for kidnap."

"I suspect even he does not know what he wants to do at this precise moment in time," said Felipe. "God help the poor boy, I do not envy him one little bit."

Maria stared straight ahead, her gaze lost in time as she whispered gently. "In time he will come to realise that however much he loves his adoptive parents the bond of blood is stronger."

She turned to Felipe. "Mohammed is right. We have searched for our son for fourteen years and after such a long time we must do what is right by the law and have just a little more patience."

Thirteen

Two days later Felipe and Maria stood together outside the town hall of Polop having registered their dispute officially. Maria was determined to take Juan home with her and prepared to fight anyone who stood in her way. The pueblo was the controlling authority for a number of small hamlets and villages in the area, including that of Xirles.

Mohammed had contacted Vicente and Fatima and persuaded them to at least listen to what the authorities had to say. Reluctantly they had agreed and turned up at the *Ayuntamiento* building with Juan and the village priest, Father Ismael.

They were there to see the *Juzgado de la Paz*, the people's judge who would listen to Maria and Felipe's claim to be seen as rightful parents to the boy, Juan Francisco Cortes. He had the authority to make binding decisions in all things to do with family matters. The town hall was a fairly imposing building considering the general state of the village. The judge's office was clean and tidy and quite ornate with a huge picture of King Alfonso XIII on the wall behind the judge's chair. The picture was flanked by two huge flags of Spain.

The judge sat in front of the lags at an elegant mahogany desk, an elderly man in his late fifties, stout, with snow white hair and a beard to match.

Alonso Giraldo Palmer had been in the position for five years. He was the most powerful man in the district and well he knew it. He had position and power and what was the use of position and power if you did not use it to your advantage. His wife kept reminding him that his best years were firmly behind him. *Pah! She knew nothing of where his power had taken him since he came to office.*

Maria and Felipe sat in front of Judge Palmer, and recounted for the second time in two days their incredible story. The judge's eyebrows twitched in time with the twists and turns of their extraordinary tale. Finally they shrank back in their seats, exhausted with the emotional stress of their ordeal.

Then it was Vicente's turn to speak as he documented every single year of the boy's life and the expense and sacrifice his family had made and the payments he had paid to the Church for his study. Finally he produced the legal paperwork the mayor of Xirles had provided for him fourteen years ago and asked the judge how he could possibly verify who these strangers were who had suddenly appeared like ghosts in the night claiming to be the boy's parents. They had no right to be here Vicente explained, and no right to fill the boys head with nonsense.

The judge summoned his clerk, whispered in his ear, and then spoke to the assembled individuals. "I have known Juan since he was a baby, Vicente, Fatima and their family for many years more. They are well respected members of our community; Vicente is a hardworking man and Fatima a splendid wife and mother. They look after the boy well; he is a fine young man with a good future in the priesthood."

He looked at the boy as he continued. "Juan should not be here today, he should not be listening to this. It is not right." He turned to Felipe and Maria. "Can you prove your story; can you prove you are the boy's parents, do you have any paperwork at all?"

Felipe and Maria looked at each other and then faced the judge. The silence was deafening.

"I thought not," he continued.

Felipe put his hand over Maria's and spoke. "We do not want to force Juan to do anything he doesn't want to do your honour. We simply wish to be recognised as his rightful birth parents. At the end of the day it is the boy who will decide where he lives. But no, to answer your question we have no papers."

Maria stood up trembling with emotion as she shouted loudly. "He was stolen from us, he is our son and he belongs with us."

Felipe bit his bottom lip, annoyed at his wife's emotional outburst. They had agreed on the course of action the night before. There was no way the judge would grant in their favour to remove the boy from their adopted parents now, this was merely the first stage of a long process.

"Please do not stand and speak until I permit you to do so. This is a court of law and you will respect my authority." said the judge forcefully.

Palmer was a little frustrated. Normally his cases were decided by the power of the purse, the wealth of the individual, yet this case was slightly different because he knew not the financial position of the strangers from Abdet and was well aware that Vicente and Fatima could pay very little. He laughed inwardly; *perhaps I will need to judge this one on its merit* he thought to himself.

Felipe pulled his wife back into her seat and wrapped an arm around her. It was all going horribly wrong.

Judge Palmer pondered over the situation. The strangers had not came forward and offered any money. He looked them up and down. They looked affluent, well heeled. Perhaps?

His eyes fell on the priest as if by some strange divine intervention. *Why not,* he thought, *let the Church decide. Let the church make the decision. If the boy Cortes is to be removed and we can swell the coffers of the church a little and line my pocket then all is not lost. Ismael can talk to them; explain that the costs of his studies and his parent's sacrifices must be reimbursed.*

The judge waved a hand in the direction of Father Ismael who stood up and walked towards him. They exchanged words between themselves for at least five minutes and the priest sat back down.

The Judge turned to face Juan. "You have only a few more years before you are of age and able to do as you wish. Until then we must make that decision for you. The Holy Father advises me that you are a wise boy, wise beyond your years. You are a good scholar with a good future in the church. That is the most important issue here. I will see that you are not deflected from your destiny by these extraordinary happenings. But if you truly believe that these strangers you see in front of you are your real parents I am prepared to allow you to leave as long as Vicente, Fatima and of course the church are not financially disadvantaged."

Felipe could not believe what he was hearing. The Church, that damned church again. The judge and the church wanted paid off.

The judge pointed at Juan. "Tell me what you are thinking Juan. Tell me what your heart is telling you and perhaps we will be able to solve this situation."

The judge looked at the clock on the wall opposite and let out a long deliberate sigh. His dinner, a normally large bowl of Valencian lamb stew would be waiting for him in the house of Señora Martinez. After lunch and a glass of wine or two, the fifteen year old daughter of Señorita Martinez would be waiting upstairs to entertain him. It was a perfectly acceptable and financially beneficial arrangement for the Martinez family who lost Señor Theodor Martinez to La Cucaracha several months prior.

Lost in his thoughts he pictured the beautiful sight of young Magdalena, standing naked before him ready and willing. Willing to do anything he asked of her. It was only right that she should take the place of her mother. For twenty years Palmer had *looked after* Señora Martinez while her husband Theodor had toiled on the jobs that Palmer had arranged for him as the Clerk of Works at the Ayuntamiento. What a wonderful position to be in. He knew where Theodor was every minute of every working day and made sure that if Señora Martinez didn't go along with their *little arrangement* Theodor would be unemployed again and they would surely starve.

Alas, as wonderful as Mother Nature was, Father Time takes it away. Señora Martinez did not appeal to him anymore. He had told her early last year, proud of his brutal but blunt honesty and explained that Señor Theador would keep his job and his salary if young Magdalena could replace her mother. Señora Martinez was horrified and swore that she would rather die.

When Palmer suspended Theodor for a minor faux pas she quickly changed her tune. A week on stale bread and water had incredible powers of persuasion.

Palmer took Magdalena's virginity on a Friday afternoon while her Father celebrated his reinstatement with his friends in the local bar. Palmer had slipped him a few pesetas as he'd told him the good news and as always, Theador had found what he was looking for in the bottom of a wine bottle.

The judge remained stoic as Juan Francisco Cortes stood lowly and spoke in barely a whisper.

"They are my parents." He said. "Of that there is no doubt. I see it in their eyes and the lines and creases in their faces, the texture of their skin." he paused for breath and looked lovingly over to where Vicente and Fatima sat. "I want to deny it but cannot. Even the way they smell is somehow familiar."

The judge peered over the top of his glasses. "Are you sure?" he said.

Juan nodded. "I'm sure Sir."

Juan walked over to where Vicente and Fatima sat. He rested on the table in front of them.

"For fourteen years these wonderful people have been my parents and I will always think of them so. But I cannot ignore the truth.

He looked over to where the priest sat. "Father Ismael, does it not say in the good book, you will know the truth, and the truth will make you free?"

"It does my son," said the priest. "It does. The words were spoken by Jesus himself documented in the Gospel according to John I believe.

Judge Palmer stared once again at the clock. *Damn it. Young Magdalena would be waiting eagerly. The little whore loved to be on her back, it's what she was made for. What is the boy saying, what does he want? The stupid little peasant.*

Juan spoke again. "Your Honour, according to the constitution we work to, you owe a duty to God to ensure that your court of law complies with the truth."

The judge squeezed at his ever growing erection underneath his thick bulky robes. *Let's get this over with as soon as we can,* he thought. *I'll tell Señora Martinez to keep the lamb warm while I have my way with her daughter. I can eat afterwards.*

Juan explained to the judge that his birth parents had every right to see him whenever they wanted and it should be noted by the Ayuntamiento of Polop that they were his natural parents. In time he would go back to Abdet but would remain in Xirles and continue his journey with the church for the foreseeable future.

Father Ismael nodded his approval and gazed in the direction of Vicente and Fatima. They raised no objections. Everyone was happy... a perfect solution for everyone.

The Judge questioned Felipe whether he had the funds available to cover court costs and expenses and Felipe had no option but to nod his agreement. Palmer banged his gavel on the desk and picked up a pen and began to write in the ledger. "Granted," he declared. "It is duly noted. Now, if everyone is finished we can have a little lunch."

The court stood while Judge Palmer explained to Felipe and Maria that he would have the papers prepared later that day and that there was of course the necessary financial transfer of funds. Once the papers were prepared and rubber stamped Felipe and Maria would be seen as the boy's parents and were free to speak with the boy without interference from anyone else.

The judge then retired to his office at the back of the building.

Soon after, he hurried out of the back door towards the house of Señorita Martinez.

Magdalena did not disappoint him. Her mother had taught her well and what she could do with that mouth of hers was more than any man could wish for. And Señorita Martinez had excelled herself too with a Valencian *cordero* fit to serve a king.

Life was good. Life is what you make it he thought to himself.

Palmer left for his prearranged meeting with Felipe and Maria and Father Ismael. He was a little late and they all stood patiently on the steps of the town hall. Palmer opened up the door and beckoned them inside. He took no more than two minutes to fill in the documentation.

That will be two thousand pesetas Señor Felipe, he announced with a wry smile.

"Two thousand pesetas," exclaimed Felipe. "Why that is equivalent to a year's earnings for a man from these parts?"

Palmer shrugged his shoulders. "Take it or leave it stranger. If you want this documentation that proves you are the boy's parents then it will cost you two thousand pesetas. The church has spent a fortune on the boy's education and if he decides to move to Abdet permanently to make up for lost time it is likely that he may have a change of heart."

Palmer sank back into his seat smugly. As Felipe opened up his bag and counted the money onto the table the judge thought for a second that this was surely the best job in the world. Soon after, Felipe and Maria left, leaving only the Judge and the priest to divide up the spoils. Ismael suggested that a little be handed across to Vicente and Fatima too. They decided that fifty pesetas was more than sufficient.

The old Berber and his employers sat in the small room of the old gossip. Several times Felipe had suggested it was time to be off but Mohammed had reasoned with him that the stress from the previous few days has taken its toll and sharing a little food and drink with friends would do no harm.

The door to the old lady's house opened as Mohammed drained the last of the bottle of brandy, wiped at his lips with his sleeve and smiled.

Felipe and Maria's son stood silhouetted in the bright doorway.

Maria turned to Mohammed. "You knew...You knew he would come here," she said.

Mohammed placed his brandy glass on the table and spoke. "It was his eyes, pretty one, his eyes as I looked into them in the courthouse building. His eyes told me he wanted his mother more than anything in the world. It was only a matter of time."

Juan walked over as Mohammed pushed out a chair and the boy sat down.

He smiled, "Father, Mother he said, I have made my peace with my adoptive parents and they have given me their blessing. If you don't mind I would like to spend a few days with you in Abdet."

Maria and Felipe were lost for words. They wanted to speak but the words simply would not form.

Juan smiled. He leaned over and placed a hand on Maria's knee. "I would like to see the place you call home. It has been many years and such a short distance away."

He stood. "I am ready when you are."

Maria, Felipe and Mohammed gathered up their possessions and stepped out into the late afternoon sun to the sound of a lonely chirping cricket.

Fourteen

Abdet

"This is your grandson mother."

Maria spoke while she held the hand of her son as they stood at the front entrance of the house where she had been born and her mother had been born and her mother had been born before her. But she felt slightly hostile towards her Mother. Juan's right to be born in his home town had been taken away from him and that wasn't right. It was a silly little detail but one that was important to her.

Juan's hand was trembling, Maria's mother stood stunned as her mouth fell open. Maria wondered what thoughts were going round in her mother's head. Had she fought the church's decision to take her child away, had she even begged the question of them or had she just stood meekly and nodded as Father Cano had announced his decision that she should be removed from the village. It was not a question she had ever asked nor would she.

Staring into her mother's tormented eyes at that very moment, she knew the torture and anxiety and guilt she was experiencing and would continue to suffer until the day she died. But that was the way. The church spoke and the villagers listened. The church ordered and the villages obeyed the command.

Inmaculada Aznar could not speak. Her reaction was to open the door a little wider and Maria and Juan walked through into the darkened room where Miguel, Juan's grandfather dozed in a seat trying to escape the heat of the day.

These were Juan's grandparents. Again they were familiar to him. Inmaculada walked over and shook the old man.

"Miguel, Miguel wake-up."

Juan smiled. Even his grandmother's voice was more than a little familiar. It all made sense now, the questions he had asked of his adoptive parents from childhood, questions about his family, questions about his grandparents that Vincent and Fatima had failed to answer satisfactorily. He had posed questions that normal boys asked of their parents but they had always skirted around the issues or given answers that contradicted answers that they had given previously. On more than one occasion Fatima and Vincent had mixed up their tales.

Other boys in the village had grandfathers and grandmothers, elderly people who would come and take the boys out into the village to play or even to church. Fatima's parents had died before he was born but Vicente's mother and father still lived in the village and yet not once was he ever told they were his grandparents. It bothered him a little back then. No, not once had he ever called them his *abuelos*. He simply knew them as Xavier and Nieves.

There had been a gang in the village of Xirles and on a boys eleventh birthday it was a tradition to join, a rite of passage. Juan had passed the initiation tests with flying colours and as the senior gang members sat to decide whether he was to be accepted, one boy had objected, said he *wasn't from these parts*.

Juan had been a popular boy and the other gang members had overruled the one lone dissenter and again, he'd asked Vicente that same evening what the boy had meant. He recalled the look Vicente had given Fatima as he tried to convince young Juan that the boy and his father were the village imbeciles and he wasn't to take a blind bit of notice of what he had said.Why hadn't he asked more questions? Perhaps he would have found out the truth a lot earlier and who knows even taken the necessary steps to trace his real parents? That didn't matter now he'd put it behind him and look upon this day as the first day of the rest of his life. He had found his birth parents and now his real grandparents too. He was luckier than most, one boy in the village had never met his grandparents as they lived in a faraway place called Galicia which was too far to travel to. He would make up for lost time. Starting today.

He walked towards his grandmother and reached out a hand. Inmaculada took it and they came together and held each other tight.

"I'm sorry," she whispered in his ear as her tears stained his shirt.

He placed a hand on the nape of her neck. "There is no need," he said gently.

Inmaculada battled through the tears as she woke her husband from his slumber.

"This is our grandson," she announced proudly. "Juan Francisco Cortes of Xirles."

Later Maria explained recent events to her parents and how they now held the legal paperwork that proved Juan was their son. And as Felipe and Mohammed joined the family for lunch she proudly boasted that the boy was studying hard with the blessing of the church and that one day he would make a great priest.

After they had eaten they took a stroll through the village, Juan formally introduced to everyone they came across. Old friends even an odd stranger stood patiently while Inmaculada proudly showed off her new grandson. Most were polite and asked no questions, those who did were simply given a short rebuff of how the boy had spent his informative years away from the village, studying with the church. They took a glass of wine in one or two of their friend's houses by way of a celebration and showed Juan around the church in the main street. Inmaculada had mixed feelings setting foot inside the church. The respect and fear of God was still there, it was hard to shake off, but part of her was now bitter. Why hadn't she stood up to the church? At least objected in some way? Father Cano and his organisation had deprived her of fourteen years with this wonderful boy. It wasn't right. It simply wasn't right she said to herself as she walked away from the church into the stifling heat of the day. By all accounts her own grandson was well on the way to becoming a Catholic priest, how ironic. He was studying hard and never wasted an opportunity to preach to people how good God was or how wonderful the Church of Rome was and how they helped the poor all over the world.

In time she'd speak to him. Not today but perhaps when she knew him a little better. She'd sit him down and explain as best she could. She'd tell him about Father Cano and how respected he had been but she'd also tell him how the priest had made mistakes, how he'd taken too much money from the pockets of the peasants and how one big mistake had nearly torn their family apart. Oh how she wished she could have turned back the hands of time.

Later that evening Juan's grandfather walked out into the purple haze of the warm summer evening, took a young lamb from its pen and slaughtered it. After even more food at the house of Inmaculada and Miguel, Juan took a walk down to the church. He opened the door and walked slowly to the altar where he knelt to pray.

"Thank you Father... thank you from the bottom of my heart. My mother was wrong; she sinned in the eyes of the church and of God and was rightly punished."

He made the sign of the cross on his chest.

"She took of the fruit thereof, and did eat. Her sins have reached unto heaven, and you hath remembered her iniquities and acted accordingly and you have forgiven her and returned me to the bosom of my family." He paused and drew breath.*"She is fortunate. We are more fortunate than you my Lord and it pains me to remember that your son died on the cross so that we can live free but we must also remember that sin is sin. My mother and father may be sinners but they are also good people. They have searched long and hard and have never given up. If that was a test Father then they have surely passed?"*

Juan sat in silence, contemplating the severity of the punishment the Lord had placed on his parents and fought the feeling that perhaps it was a little over zealous. Juan was in no doubt that it had been the Lords wishes and would not question his wisdom. Father Ismael had instilled within him an unquestionable faith and he had committed his life to the church.

He absorbed like a sponge, the knowledge the good Father and his assistants fed him almost on a daily basis. He could read and write and while other boys of a similar age frolicked in the sun or swam in the river that flowed through Xirles, Juan's' nose would always be found in a book. He studied the planets and the stars and the seas and oceans and marvelled at the sheer scale of God's incredible planet and the universe beyond. He wondered how it was possible to create such wonders in only seven days. God truly was an incredible being.

His boyhood curiosity had occasionally got the better of him and he'd posed a question or two from time to time. When Father Ismael couldn't seem to find an answer he'd tell him to have faith.

There were some things that no one could find an answer for Father Ismael had told him. The villagers had posed occasional questions too, though not so very often. He recalled old Manolo, the *mule man* as they knew him as he never ventured far without his old trusted mule. Even when he came to church the mule was always tethered to a nearby tree. Old Manolo surely had to be the poorest man in the village and one Sunday Father Ismael had noticed he hadn't placed his weekly offering in the church collection plate; instead he'd fiddled nervously with his hat as the plate passed him by.

Father Ismael had invited Manolo to stay behind and share a coffee with him and after several minutes of pleasant conversation Manolo had disclosed that he did not have the money and felt deeply ashamed. Father Ismael had instructed young Juan to advise the priest's housekeeper that an extra plate was needed at the dinner table later that day. Several hours later Manolo had feasted like a King and even enjoyed a glass of Father Ismael's favourite wine. Later Father Ismael explained that the church would always look after the less fortunate.

It was a defining moment and one that Juan would always remember. The old mule herder had tasted meat for the first time that year and couldn't thank Father Ismael enough. After dinner Father Ismael had given an impromptu sermon to Manolo and the old man had expressed his undying devotion to the church promising he would work harder than he ever had before during the following week in order to make up the shortfall in his weekly offerings.

The old man tottered off just after dark with a smile on his face as wide as the River Turia.

Juan had been impressed and talked with Father Ismael late into the night. Juan praised Father Ismael's kindness.

Father Ismael gave a wry smile. "Kindness it may be my son," he said. "It is a day Manolo will never forget for he dined like a king and he will never stray far from the ways of the church ever again."

Father Ismael drained the last of his wine as he took a napkin and dabbed at the side of his lips. Father Ismael let out a deep contented sigh as he gazed up into the night sky.

Father Ismael looked down at the boy. "In time you will understand young Juan. You will come to realise exactly what it is I have done today."

Juan protested. "You have helped him, you have fed Manolo and been kind, Father. I saw nothing else"

The priest nodded. "Yes Juan I have helped him by filling is belly for one day. That much is true, but I have filled his belly for only one day."

Juan was shaking his head. "I still don't understand."

"You will my son," said the priest. "We must help the poor but at times we must almost think for them too. They are simple people and we must control their waking thoughts."

"Why is that Father?" Asked Juan.

Father Ismael reached across and ruffled Juan's hair. "For that is why we are here Juan. It is our role in life, the role determined by God Almighty. We must control their lives because they are unable to form their own opinions. We must give them hope and a belief that there is something better in this world, something better than the way they live their wretched uneducated lives."

"Yes," whispered Juan, "hope and belief."

Juan stood slowly and walked down the centre aisle of the church. By the door stood a large glass case and inside was a jewel encrusted gold cross with a ceramic figurine of Jesus Christ, his head displaying a bloody crown of thorns. The bright red paint ran down the terrain of his face and onto his cheeks, more paint splashed strategically on his chest. His hands and feet were painted red too and Juan stared for a minute or two at the tortured yet dignified expression on the Lords face. The sculptor had done a fine job, a rare talent indeed.

As he pulled the large wooden door that led into the main street he was beginning to understand what Father Ismael had been talking about all those years ago.

Fifteen

Berlin

The telephone line was crackling noisily, a bad line that somewhat annoyed him, not German engineering at its best. It mattered not... the conversation was drawing to a close. He could sense that the message was sinking in.

One last push he thought. "I urge you Mien Fuhrer, to give support to Franco under all circumstances, in order to prevent the further spread of communism in the country and secondly to test my young Luftwaffe. It is an ideal opportunity Mien Fuhrer."

Hitler eventually agreed; his parting words were that they had nothing to lose and everything to gain.

Reichmarshal Hermann Goring congratulated the Fuhrer on his splendid decision, said his goodbyes and replaced the receiver. He sat down. He always stood up when he talked to Herr Fuhrer... a mark of respect. He was satisfied with what he had achieved that evening and reached for his glass of whisky as a broad smile pulled across his face.

Sixteen

Juan stirred in his bed. The noise of the copy of the ABC newspaper being slid under his bedroom door had interrupted his light sleep. He hadn't been sleeping well of late and he'd prayed late into the night once again. He'd prayed for peace and understanding and he'd prayed for solutions he felt certain that the Lord would provide and yes... he grinned to himself, he'd prayed for a good night's sleep too.

None of his prayers had been answered. It was June 1936. The previous evening he had celebrated his 32nd birthday with some fellow priests in the town of Seville, Andalucía, where he had lived for the past two years. They had taken a little wine at a local tavern just off the main street and the owner had killed a young piglet earlier that afternoon. He had roasted the animal over an open fire at the back of the property and served it with potatoes and fresh bread. It had truly been a feast fit for a king.

He stretched himself out before rolling off his bed and wandered over to the door groaning as he reached down to pick up the newspaper. His housekeeper Carmen was good; she never missed a day's work and made sure that all of the priests that she looked after were fully up-to-date with the murmurings of discontent that seemed to be ravishing the country. In a little while she would prepare their breakfasts and they would all sit discussing the previous day's incredible events.

Juan frowned as he read the headlines. More riots and protests, many of them against the church. Politics, always politics. He had tried not to get involved in the subject that did not interest him but this time it was difficult to sit on the fence and say nothing. Jose, the eldest priest, a man in his late 40s said it had not been the same since King Alfonso had been forced to abdicate just over five years ago. Jose said the King had kept everything in order, but then the second republic had replaced the monarchy and made things very difficult. The left wing government that had been elected had even closed down newspapers like the one he was holding because of their rigorous support for the church. Juan shook his head. The church looked after the people did they not? From the moment he woke up each morning to the time he went to bed in the evening he wanted to do nothing but help the poor. And yet he understood many of the grievances the people held against the men of the cloth. Since he joined the priesthood he had not known hunger or thirst which many of the peasants experienced on a daily basis. The grand opulent churches were in marked contrast to some of the hovels which the people called home. He knew, he visited them often enough.

The problems had worsened just after the Archbishop of Toledo, Cardinal Seguro, had declared back in 1932 that, *In Spain, you were Catholic or you were nothing at all.* He hadn't helped their cause and Juan couldn't help feeling it was a stupid thing to say. Live and let live. If people were content with a secular life that was there choice and who was he to look down on them as inferior citizens.

He sighed and shook his head. Alas not all the church held the same view. He was slowly but surely beginning to realise that. The Archbishop's comment caused a wave of church burnings from Madrid to Andalucía, with the socialist government refusing to send in the Guardia Civil to restore order. Some of his fellow priests from Andalucía had said that in parts of the South, churches were almost completely empty of worshippers. The common complaint was that the poor were going hungry whilst the church continued to accumulate vast wealth and of course it caused great division.

The government had tried to appease the working classes and they separated the church from the state. They made all religious orders register and promised the people they would only allow the Church enough money to cover their basic needs. At first this seemed to work, for a short while at least but of course the Catholic Church was already extremely rich and depriving them of a fraction of their income made little difference. The government then introduced a most dramatic measure when they announced they were to allow civil marriages and divorce. The right wing of Spain had regarded this action as an attack on Spain itself and dared to suggest an attempted *red* takeover.

Juan shook his head, folded the paper and carefully placed it on the side of his washbasin.

There were serious problems ahead. There had been uprisings, in fact armed uprisings led by Generals, supported by their own command of soldiers on the promise of better food, wages or conditions, were a fact of life in Spain and had been for many years. Most of them were badly organized affairs, effortlessly quashed by the government forces, but somehow Juan sensed this was a little different.

He washed quickly and made his way downstairs to the breakfasting room. There were six priests sat around the table, Juan groaned as he looked at the table, once again laden with food. It was the same every morning, ham, eggs, bread and cake, a pot of hot coffee and a jug of orange juice. In an instance Juan had lost his appetite.

"Sit brother," said Ignacio, "come and join us and take a little sustenance for we have a long day ahead of us."

Ignacio was holding a cup of orange juice with one hand and the morning paper with the other. He crammed another piece of bread into his mouth as he spoke. "More trouble Juan. Those bloody Communists are getting above themselves."

Juan pulled out a chair and sat down at the roughly hewn table. Carmen handed him a coffee.

"Who can blame them Ignacio?" He said. "Men do desperate things when they have no food in their bellies."

Ignacio stopped chewing and looked up. He raised his voice a little. "Desperate things Juan? They are burning churches and killing priests and nuns. This is not the work of hungry men, these are the acts and deeds of cut throats and murderers and I'll not have you defending them in this house."

Ignacio was the oldest among the priests, just a couple of years short of his 50th birthday. He'd come into the way of the church late in life but was well respected among his fellow priests. Juan kept quiet as Ignacio continued.

"Do we not help the poor, look after the sick and injured? Just what is it they have to complain about?"

Juan's appetite had deserted him. He took a mouthful of coffee and wiped at his mouth with his sleeve. "Look at this table brother. There is a mountain of food, enough to feed two or three families." He turned and pointed at his fellow priests. "And you sit there cramming as much into your fat mouths as possible."

A few of the priests stopped eating and could hardly believe their ears at Juan's uncharacteristic outburst. But he continued with his tirade. It was as if everyone had closed their ears and eyes to the outside world.

"And you will eat the same again this afternoon and again this evening. We do not know what it is like to go hungry."

Another priest, Jose, banged his fist on the table. "How dare you speak to us like this? The Lord has provided the food that fills our table, do you expect us not to eat, do you expect us to throw it back in his face?"

Juan was shaking his head. He grinned as he raised an eyebrow. "The Lord has provided? Is that what you really believe Ignacio?" He looked at Jose. "And you too brother?"

Ignacio and Jose looked at each other for a second as a puzzled look crept across their faces.

Juan turned to Carmen. "Who provided the money for this food Carmen? Was it the Lord who delivered the peseta's from heaven or was it taken from the collection plate after mass?

Ignacio leapt to his feet red with rage. "Enough. Enough of this drivel; be silent man I order you." He wiped at his sweating brow with a handkerchief. "I sometimes wonder whose side you are on."

Juan pulled at a tiny piece of bread and placed it in his mouth. "We have sides? I thought we were all Spanish, all good Catholics."

Juan cast his eyes to the heavens and whispered to himself. "Be not among drunkards or among gluttonous eaters of meat, for the drunkard and the glutton will come to poverty and slumber will clothe them with rags."

Ignacio cocked his head to one side but could not decipher the softly spoken words.

"It isn't the church killing and maiming innocent people," shouted Jose. "The reds are breaking the law, burning and looting churches, they have to be stopped or the church will be no more."

Juan opened his mouth to speak again but was cut short before he could begin.

"Stop it! Stop this now. You are men of God; you shouldn't be fighting like this."

It was Carmen. Tears had glazed her eyes and she was trembling like a leaf. She'd served the Catholic Church for many years as a housekeeper in the large house left to her by her grandfather. He too had been a man of the church and had asked her to dedicate her life to God.

God had looked after her, provided for her every need and over the years she had grown to love and respect many of the priests who had passed through her doors. It would've been nice to get married and raise a family but it had not been possible. She'd served the church and asked for nothing in return, just a peaceful life and an occasional word of thanks.

"I won't listen to you arguing and bickering I won't."

A momentary silence fell around the table.

Young Juan had fire in his belly, she thought. That was for sure. He had spirit and wasn't afraid to speak his mind and had a certain aura when he walked into a room almost as if the room belonged to him. His dark, jet black hair, slightly overlong she thought for a man of the cloth was neatly combed back, smoothed with just enough olive oil to maintain the necessary degree of tidiness. His features were fine, almost to the point of feminine but there was no doubt he was a man in every sense of the word, as the other ladies in the town never tired of pointing out. A real waste, they would say to Carmen whenever she stopped to talk. A crying shame the man would not sire many handsome offspring.

Carmen walked over and stood behind him. His dark eyes glistened with emotion and just a hint of anger. "Can I ask you to leave the table Juan?" She said. "Leave your brothers in peace and take a little breakfast with me in the village."

At first Juan objected. His appetite was long gone he claimed but Carmen insisted and eventually he left the table and walked outside with her. Carmen linked his arm as they walked towards the town square.

The streets were different today. He could sense the tension and couldn't help notice the anguished looks on the faces of the people. Was he just imagining it but were one or two of the villagers purposely crossing the road to avoid him?

Carmen walked with him out into the countryside and they took some water from a stream and oranges and figs from the fruit trees as they sat for an hour or two in the early morning sun and put the world to rights.

A little later Carmen pleaded with him to be calm and not to antagonise his brothers.

"It is my house," she said, "and you must respect it because it is a house of the Lord. It may not be a church but to me it's every bit as holy."

Reluctantly he agreed and as the sun gained its summer strength they walked back to the house calling in at the local *tienda* where Carmen bought more bread and some fresh eggs for lunch.

Juan did not join his fellow priests for lunch nor did he take his evening supper with them. Carmen came to his room with a little milk and bread shortly after midnight. It would be several days before Juan had the stomach to dine with the priests again.

The news just over a month later was far more serious. It was July 17th 1936; a group of generals led by general Seguí had come together and taken over Spanish Morocco, killing all trade union members and anybody else that was not actively supporting their fight against the left. The generals had used the foreign legion troops, a motley crew of prisoners and cut-throats that served in the forces rather than languish in jail. Their battle cry was 'long live death' and they obeyed whatever order they were given without question. The right wing had also recruited Riffian tribesmen, known as *los Moros* to the native population, they were Islamic mercenaries under the command of Spanish officers; they had a terrifying reputation and were, without doubt the most feared of any of the troops that were on Spanish territory. The generals had informed them that the elected government of Spain were looking to outlaw the worship of Allah. They needed no other reason to take up arms.

These incidents were being discussed across the dinner table once again. Some of the priests cautiously welcomed those that were rebelling against the *reds* and the communists.

Juan sat with his head in his hands unable to comprehend the sheer pace of recent developments. Just then the youngest of the priests, Faustino burst into the room.

"The left are on the warpath here in Seville brothers, we must hide. They have heard about the news in Morocco and hope to crush the resistance." The young priest was almost in tears. "There are lorry loads of armed men driving around the streets looking for people they think may be supporting this uprising."

What the young priest said next turned Juan's blood to ice.

"I have been told that they are taking priests as prisoners."

This can't be happening, Juan said to himself. It's just not possible. Several minutes later Carmen burst through the front door. She confirmed what Faustino had told them.

"It is true," she said. "You must flee until it is safe to return. It will blow over I'm sure of it. God will make the people see sense and put an end to this nonsense before long."

Ignacio and Jose stood up from the table as young Faustino fell to his knees and prayed.

Juan walked towards Carmen and took her by the hands. "And what will become of you sweet Carmen? Where is it you will run to? For if it is true that the mob is hostile to the church then they will surely take a little retribution on those who support us. You have fed and clothed the men of the cloth for many years now and there's not a single villager that does not know of you and your work."

Carmen smiled. "I will not leave my house Juan, I made a commitment to my grandfather as a small girl and to God too. Just as you have made a vow to the Almighty so have I. I will not let a bunch of thugs drive me from these four walls. This is where I belong, it will blow over I'm sure of it. I will pray like I've never prayed before and I will be seeing you quicker than you know it."

Carmen leaned forward and kissed Juan twice on each cheek. He fought the feelings of confusion she aroused in him. Although in her early thirties, life had treated her well and she would have passed for a woman some years younger. Her complexion was fair and her skin unblemished and smooth and many years of toil and hard labour had kept her slim and well-toned. She was the perfect figure of womanhood and for a fleeting moment Juan despaired that this girl had not been allowed to enter into a union with another man. What a beautiful wife she would have made for someone, what a perfect mother she would have made for any child.

Juan wanted to tell her just that. He wanted to tell her how special she had made him feel and how enjoyable the last two years had been under her roof. He wondered if she had caressed another man, been held tightly, even kissed someone with a passion. Before Juan could daydream any longer Carmen had disappeared into the kitchen.

Ignacio ordered the men to their rooms advising them to pack what they could in bags that were easy to carry. Ignacio tried to reassure them, agreeing with the sentiments of the housekeeper that it would all blow over in a few days.

Juan returned back to the kitchen not knowing his next move. Where would they go, where would they run too? If the newspaper reports were true there were skirmishes happening all over Spain. They should stay in Seville he reasoned with Ignacio. They had been good priests and had always tried to do the best for the poor in the town and they would be safe here. He appeared a little unsure of what to do next. Naturally, the younger priests looked up to him with a certain respect and they waited for his next command.

Carmen's younger sister had entered the house bringing more news. "I have been into the centre of town where there is much fighting." She said. "The people tell me that there are many soldiers and that they have taken over the barracks." She wiped a tear from her eye. "Many people have been killed already."

Part of Juan wanted to stay with Carmen to protect her. He knew he had done nothing wrong and wanted to place his faith in the Lord. And yet something or someone was telling him to run. He wasn't afraid like some of the priests but suddenly the four walls of Carmen's house didn't seem such a wise place to lay his head that night. Poor Jose looked absolutely petrified and Juan had seen Ignacio looking a lot better than he did at the present time.

"Take these," said Carmen, thrusting a bag at each of the priests. "You have more than enough food to last you several days.

You must cover your priest's clothes and travel to find friends that will shelter you."

Juan walked over to Carmen and spoke. "Come with me Carmen, please. It will only be a matter of time before you receive a visit and what will you tell them?"

Carmen's sister was ushering the priests towards the door. "You must go, hurry."

Carmen was shaking her head. "I gave my answer before Juan, now go. Be quick, I will see you all soon I'm sure of it."

Ignacio had called the priests to prayer as they waited by the door. Juan clasped his hands together and joined them.

"We must take our chances individually," said Ignacio. "It's no use running in a group."

Wise advice thought Juan. For once Ignacio's brain was functioning correctly. The other priests agreed and they shook hands and embraced as they walked towards the door. Carmen ushered them away kissing them all individually and the door closed behind them. Juan noticed his heart beating strongly in his chest as he walked quickly, trying desperately hard not to run down the dimly lit street. There were sounds of gunshots in the distance now and there was an orange glow in the sky from the area of the town hall. Spaniard killing Spaniard. How on earth had it come to this?

There were many people on the street and Juan hid his head as he passed them. They seemed not to notice him, long may it continue he thought. There were many lorries on the streets too, and each time a vehicle approached he would hide in the darkest corner available. One truck passed him with twenty rough dressed people in the back; arms raised with fists clenched high, singing songs of victory. They were heading towards the area of the fires.

It seemed to take forever for Juan to reach the house that was his destination. It belonged to the family of Tomas, a carpenter who had a young son who had almost died of a fever the year before. The family had had no money for a doctor, but Juan had called upon a friend with medical training who owed him a favour. With his help the young child had survived.

Juan was now looking for the young family to repay that favour by sheltering him for a day or two or at least until they could all see how the situation was progressing. He would be safe there, the family had no other connection to him; even the other priests knew nothing of how he had helped them. The house was also out of town, on the campo far away from prying eyes.

He walked for some hours. It was difficult to find the house in the dark, Juan had never been there before other than in the daylight hours. Eventually he recognised the silhouette of the house and noticed a candle flickering in the small window at the front of the house. Even in the dark as he walked through the well maintained gardens he could see that everything had its place. The sun bleached wood that Tomas, the carpenter worked with was meticulously laid out in piles of different sizes and thickness, some bulkier pieces covered with heavy tarpaulin to protect it from the rain. Juan looked up into the night sky and laughed to himself. Rain, there's a thing he thought to himself, when was the last time it rained? He shook his head, couldn't quite remember. He paused at the door of the small cottage and looked around. He held a hand to his ear and strained to catch a noise of a truck or the voices of the people. He could hear nothing, so he took a step forward and rapped quietly on the door. Tomas's wife Julieta opened the door as her face broke into a wide smile.

"Father," she cried. "What a pleasant surprise, to what do we owe this pleasure at such a strange hour?"

Before Juan could answer he heard Tomas's voice from inside asking his wife who it was.

"It's Father Juan," she answered happily as she pulled the door open about to ask him inside. The door appeared to open and then close swiftly. The figure of Julieta was replaced with the unmistakable shape of Tomas. He was not smiling nor did he offer a welcome to the puzzled priest.

"What is it Father Juan, how can we help you?" Tomas asked. "You have caught us unexpectedly and my young son is just about to go to bed."

Juan held out his hand but it lingered in mid-air rather awkwardly as Tomas's hands remained by his side.

"Tomas what is it?" he asked. "Take my hand and ask me inside, let us break a little bread together and share a drink. You act as if I'm stranger. I need your help and I need it tonight. I require a little shelter for a day or two until this madness blows over. Tomas did not move a muscle and the door opened no further.

Tomas shook his head. "I'm sorry Father; you are not welcome in this house anymore. I bid you good night."

Seventeen

Juan stood stunned as the door slammed in his face. He clenched his fist ready to knock again, an anger welling up inside as he thought of everything he had done for them. He decided against it. Tomas and Julieta were warm decent people, what on earth had got into them. He trudged down the path wearily. All of a sudden his legs had turned to lead and his head ached. Madness, he thought. Sheer bloody minded madness, friend against friend. He could think of many people in the surrounding area who would welcome him with a hot coffee or something a little stronger, but now he wasn't sure. If Tomas's head could be turned then so could anyone's. Tomas and his family weren't just friends; he'd saved their son's life.

Juan fought the feelings of bitterness and anger that welled up inside saying a silent prayer begging the Lord to give him strength.

"Father, Father," he whispered softly. "Please put an end to this stupidity I beg you. Give me strength to forgive them."

Juan walked back towards Carmen's house figuring that at least he could count on her to give him a bed for the night. She would never turn him away. If necessary he could hide if anyone called at the house. The old property was large with plenty of nooks and crannies; it even housed an old wine cellar with several secret doors where Carmen's grandfather had kept his special stock of gran reserva.

He made it back without any more dramas. Juan thought it best not to knock on the door and after waiting a few minutes outside, slipped in the back door without making a noise. He found Carmen sitting at the kitchen table. It was clear she had been crying. He coughed announcing his presence and she let out a stifled squeal as she looked up.

"Juan, what are you doing here it's not safe."

Juan stepped forward and placed his fingers on her soft lips. "Be quiet sweet one and I will explain what has happened. I may not be safe here but I can assure you I would be in greater danger wherever I go in this town tonight. Spain is falling apart at the seams and there is nothing I can do to prevent it.

Juan explained what had happened at the house of Tomas and Julieta. Carmen was furious and promised an early morning visit to remonstrate with the couple. Juan pacified her and told her it would do no good.

"It is understandable I'm afraid, they fear for their safety and that of their son. I'm placing you in danger too, just by being here. There is so much anti-cleric feeling in this part of Spain I can feel the hatred coursing through their veins"

Juan gave a chuckle. "It's ironic isn't it? I joined the Church to help people. That's all I ever wanted to do, support the community I've lived in." He reached across and took Carmen's hands. "I'm a good man Carmen, tell me I am. Tell me I'm kind and considerate; tell me I'm the sort of priest God should be proud of."

Carmen reached across the table and stroked tenderly at the side of his face. She smiled lopsidedly. "Yes Juan Francisco Cortes, of course you are and you know it. You don't need my assurances. And..."

Carmen's face took on a feint glow as she slowly pulled her hand away looking down at the table in a clear attempt to avoid eye contact.

"What Carmen? What is it?"

"Nothing Juan, nothing."

Juan edged a little closer and placed a finger under her cheek and with firm but gentle pressure forced her gaze upwards. "Look into my eyes Carmen and tell me what you wanted to say."

Carmen shook her head. "You don't need to know about the feelings of a foolish girl and I won't tell you if you beg me from now until Christmas. Now enough of this nonsense, we have work to do and I need somewhere for you to hide when the reds decide to come knocking on my door."

Before Juan could argue anymore Carmen had swept up the dishes from the table stacked them in the sink and walked over towards the door that led to the wine cellar. She moved with a fluid grace as if not fully tethered to the floor. She turned round and beckoned Juan forward. "There's a bed down here for you Juan, its best that way."

Juan walked towards the door.

"The cellar has several doors behind the racks of wines and one has an old room where grandfather used to get away from it all. He showed me where it was when I was a little girl but I'm convinced he never ever showed it to my grandmother up until the day she died. As Carmen turned, her face was only inches from his and he could smell the delicate natural aroma of her body, her sweet breath as she breathed heavily. He felt oddly exhilarated. Without thinking he placed his right hand on her face and brought it towards his. Their lips were only centimetres apart. He no longer fought the urge. He wanted to kiss Carmen more than anything in the world, taste her lips and embrace her. It was against everything he had ever been taught by the church and Father Ismael but as their lips touched he could not help himself. He recalled over and over again the vows he had taken and wanted to stop as Carmen responded and the act grew ever passionate. He now knew what was it like to kiss a woman? And as they continued for what felt like an eternity he felt Carmen's hands settle in the small of his back and he realised it was her first time too.

Please Lord, forgive me. The consecrated life is my vocation. I will conform my life to Jesus Christ and live as he did in poverty, chastity and obedience. I will dedicate myself to you and to the service of the Church and for the salvation of the world.

He wanted to stop, he wanted to apologise to Carmen and tell her he'd made a mistake. He reached around his back and took her arms, slowly prising them from him. They parted and he gazed into her moist eyes. Her pupils were dilated and dreamy looking and she looked so content. For a second he loved her with all his heart and then came to his senses and realised that the church must come first.

"I'm sorry," was all he could find in his vocabulary to say to her. Suddenly he saw anger in her eyes and was aware of her hand coming towards his face. The blow was powerful and stinging and he fell against the stairwell holding the side of his cheek. A tear rolled onto Carmen's face. He wanted to speak, wanted to say more but the words would not come.

It was Carmen who spoke first. "You disappoint me Juan. For nearly fifteen years I have served the church implicitly and in an instance you have ruined everything."

Carmen pulled a handkerchief from her pocket and dabbed at the side of her eyes. "You are a priest Juan you should not have acted that way, you should be ashamed of yourself."

Juan's hands opened out in a gesture of apology. "I'm sorry Carmen; I don't know what came over me. I tried to fight it, believe me I did."

Carmen walked down the stairs that led to the wine cellar without saying another word. Juan followed her into the dingy underbuilding. They spoke as if nothing had happened; the incident at the top of the stairs was completely ignored. Carmen led him through the maze of wine racks and barrels that seemed to go on for ever.

"My grandfather was always extending this cellar with a small pick axe. He would chip away for hours and hours. I swear it holds a million bottles." Carmen crouched down at the far end of the cellar and crawled under a large barrel on her hands and knees. "Follow me."

Juan eased himself under the barrel. It opened up into a larger space and with the help of a match that Carmen had struck he could make out the shape of a small door. Carmen looked over her shoulder. The light from the fire fell on her face and Juan's heart skipped a beat as the shadows bounced across her delicate features.

"Why must you do this to me Lord," he mumbled to himself.

"My grandfather's secret lair Juan, complete with bed and as much wine as you can drink."

"What more could a priest ask for?" He said.

It was cleverly concealed. What was it the man wanted to hide from? A vision of the future perhaps?

"You can stay here as long as you like, no one will find you."

Juan sighed as realisation set in once again. He'd already accepted that he would have to sleep in this makeshift cave for at least a few nights but why? Why should he hide and run?

As if reading his mind Carmen spoke. "You must hide because at this precise moment in time a man of the cloth is not the most popular person in Spain."

Juan shook his head. He pointed at the small opening. "It's a little cramped, perhaps a bit damp as well."

Carmen reached for a bottle of wine. "Here, fortify yourself with this I'll see you in the morning."

Juan took the bottle and smiled. "You'll be safe upstairs?"

"Yes," she answered. "I'll tell them I've kicked you all out, sent you packing. I'm a good liar when I need to be."

"You are sure?"

"I'm sure. Now you get your head down and place a little faith in the Lord. After all it's you that's supposed to be the priest."

Juan lifted the bottle. "To your good health Carmen and long may it continue."

Carmen was awoken at around three in the morning as the door was kicked in from the front street. An angry mob ran through the house looting a little food and wine before confronting her in her bedroom.

The ringleader, a thickset man with a greying head of hair and moustache spoke. "Where are they?"

Carmen slept naked and hid her modesty with a plain white sheet. "I have kicked them out, every stinking one of them. Check the bastard's bedroom if you don't believe me, I am glad to be rid of them.

A man carrying an old musket spoke. "You should have handed them over to us."

Carmen shrugged her shoulders and grinned. "I wanted them out as soon as possible; they were beginning to irritate me. I have better things to do than to wait around for you shirkers.

"Watch your lip lady," the ringleader announced. "We know of you and your work with the church. You won't be the first and you won't be the last little Nationalist whore we'll put in front of the firing squad."

Carmen jumped from her bed holding the sheet behind her. She drew from reserves deep in the back of her throat and spat a huge ball of saliva at his feet. "How dare you call me that you fat oaf."

The man stepped forward and delivered a powerful back hander to the side of her face. Carmen fell to the floor. He moved forward to kick her but his comrade stepped forward to restrain him. "Leave her Pepe, give her a chance. You insulted her and she responded how we would want her to respond."

The man knelt down to speak to her. "Tell us more comrade. Convince us you are with us and not against us."

Carmen wiped the blood from the side of her mouth and raised her clenched fist. "Viva La Republica," she shouted. "Viva La Republica."

The militia allowed Carmen to dress and took her downstairs.

"You have a wine cellar here we are led to believe," The ringleader said. "Show us where it is so that we may search it. For all we know the place could be crammed top to tail with Priests."

Carmen laughed. "I know what you want from my cellar comrade and it isn't Catholic Priests."

The rest of the men were laughing.

Carmen continued. "You are welcome to as many bottles as you can carry, if it fortifies the fighters of the republic then I will die a happy girl."

Carmen's suspicions were right. The militia looked no further than the thousands of bottles of wine on display. They brought in two trucks and virtually emptied the cellar, graciously allowing the larger barrels to remain under the care of the housekeeper.

Carmen sat for some hours later staring at the empty racks. Her grandfather's lifetime's work had been destroyed and ransacked in just a few hours.

The door to Juan's secret hideaway opened just after eight in the morning. True to his word he'd finished the bottle of wine and rolled out onto the floor a little worse for wear. He spotted Carmen sitting on the floor and bid her good morning. She sat staring into space, sadness in her eyes. Juan looked around at the empty racks and realised what had happened.

"I didn't hear them," he said. "They came?"

Carmen nodded. "They came looking for clergymen and left with enough wine to fill a lake."

"I'm sorry," Juan said.

Carmen eased herself to her feet. "Don't be," she said. "It was a sacrifice worth paying. In time they can be replaced and the best wines remain hidden anyway."

She reached down and helped him to his feet. "My life changed last night Juan. At one point I thought they might take me out and kill me. I was scared. Life is cheap to some men."

She took Juan by the hand and led him through the cellar towards the foot of the stairs.

She spoke again. "And what of God? What is he doing to stop this?

Juan could offer no reply.

"I believe Juan, I really do, but part of my being is asking many questions and I can find no answers."

Her small delicate hand felt good in his as she pulled him gently through the kitchen.

"I'm hungry," he said, "I need to eat."

"Later," she replied. "There is something we must do together."

Carmen climbed the stairs as Juan followed on behind. They stopped outside her bedroom and she turned to face him and spoke.

"Just supposing Juan. Just supposing that religion is all nonsense. Just imagine for one minute that everything we have ever been told by the men of God is a load of lies. The stories, our parents, aunts and uncles, brothers and sisters relayed to us as small children... all rubbish, make believe like the little fairies at the bottom of the garden.

"No, that isn't possible. I know you believe as much as I do.

Carmen placed a finger over his lips. "Shhh...quiet for a moment I'm asking you to imagine it just for one minute, imagine it for me at least."

Juan nodded.

"Imagine lying on your deathbed many years from now and discovering the truth, wouldn't you feel rather cheated?"

"How do you mean?" He replied.

She took him by both hands and edged nearer. "Your vow of chastity Juan, would you lie there and wonder what it might have been like to sleep with a woman? What it would have been like to marry and to have children, a son to take hunting and fishing?"

Juan squeezed her hands. "I think that is almost certain Carmen."

"Good, good," she answered. "I can see that you playing along with me and I have got you thinking." She opened the bedroom door and beckoned him inside.

"I have fought these feelings for many years, taken my own vow of chastity even though I didn't need to and you Juan, have stirred something up inside of me and I don't know how to fight it, I'm not sure if I even want to fight it."

Juan took a step backwards but she reached for his hand and pulled him further into the room.

"I want to experience this wonderful act of love the Lord gave to us, who knows, our deathbeds may only be days, weeks, away."

Her face was flushed as she gripped Juan even tighter. "You have awoken sensations that I never knew existed." She eased her face forward and kissed him gently on the lips. "I'm going to take you into my bed so that we don't die wondering what the pleasure of our flesh was like."

"No," Juan protested, "we can't, we simply can't."

Carmen walked over to the side of her bed reached behind her back, unbuttoned her dress and let it fall to the floor. It was the first time Juan had ever seen a naked woman. The shape and form of Carmen's body fascinated him as he became aware of a stirring in his loins and reminded himself to breathe. Carmen climbed into bed and he closed the door behind him.

He shook his head. "This is so wrong Carmen, this is so wrong."

She smiled as he unfastened his trousers and let them fall to the floor.

"That may very well be the case Juan, but we will make many more mistakes in our lives that's for sure. Now come to me quickly we have much time to make up."

～

Pepe's patience had been rewarded. He knew the church loving bitch had been lying. He'd sensed it all along. She was more than happy to allow them to take away a wine collection that would have graced any castle in Andalucía and Pepe had felt that something about her demeanour wasn't quite right. While his comrades had left with their alcoholic stash and moved on to an early-morning fiesta, Pepe had broken into the old derelict house opposite the building that had housed priests and bishops for more years than he could care to remember. The upstairs roof terrace was a good vantage point with a clear view of the kitchen area below. But better still was the stunning proximity to Carmen's bedroom, no more than spitting distance. He grinned as she entered the room, closely followed by a man. He had been here before, he knew the territory well, had spent many hours watching Carmen undress for his solitary pleasure.

Who was the man who's hand she held, the man who had obviously been hidden somewhere in the house? A Nationalist sympathiser no doubt.

He gasped. No it is not possible he thought to himself. Yes it was him... he was unmistakable. He banged his fist on the old stone ledge. The dirty filthy bastard spouting off at mass every week lecturing the poor about what was right and wrong and all along he's been lying with his housekeeper like a man would his wife. And as Carmen's dress fell to the floor, Pepe was furious. Furious and more than a little aroused at the sight of her beautiful body and the anticipation of watching what would be following. He slipped his sweaty hand inside his trousers.

I really should go and put the cat among the pigeons he thought to himself. Not yet he grinned... not just yet.

Eighteen

Juan dozed fitfully on and off as Carmen's head rested on his breast. He couldn't remember being as calm and relaxed and more content in his entire life. Despite the troubles on the streets of Seville and other Spanish cities he felt as if he was protected in their own private cocoon. Momentarily at least.

He wondered when the guilt would kick in, wondered when he would come to his senses but couldn't help feeling why his God and his church could deprive a priest of that wonderful sensual act and everything that came with it, a wife, children and in time grandchildren. It made no sense whatsoever.

He had some big decisions to make. He'd given the church the best years of his life and now, at this precise moment he wondered whether he was cut out for a life of celibacy, the life of a Catholic Priest. He'd talk with Carmen in the morning and see how she felt, discuss it with her.

Had he had fallen in love? Was it possible to fall in love that quickly and what did being in love feel like anyway? If he was honest with himself he'd always felt an attraction to Carmen. Everything about her made him tingle in a strange way. Her smell, the way she moved, her beautiful piercing green eyes and her smile. Thinking about those things painted a smile on his face yet again and what they had experienced together as one over the last few hours had accentuated his feelings for her a thousand times. Yes he was in love. He was sure of it.

His thoughts drifted away to Father Ismael and his pledges and vows he'd made to countless bishops. The priesthood was his destiny he'd been told more times than he cared to remember. Everyone had said that to him, ever since he was a small boy. Perhaps it was? Perhaps Carmen had been a test set by the Lord. Did he have what it took, was he able to put all thoughts of Carmen out of his mind and pick up the pieces and move on? Is that what he really wanted?

He heard the feint squeaking noise outside the bedroom door and became aware of the immediate tension that beset Carmen's body. She reached for him and sat bolt upright with a look of fear.

"The floorboard," she whispered. "The floorboard outside will not take the weight of a man."

Juan needed no prompting as he threw back the covers and placed a foot tenderly on the cool floor. By the time he started to move the door swung open. Juan stood naked in front of a big man with a familiar face. It came to him immediately, he'd noticed the man several times sitting within the congregation of his church. The man was dirty and unshaven with several days' stubble on his face and as he threw a wicked looking smile, displayed a mouthful of blackened neglected teeth. It was the man known as Pepe Martes.

Juan's eyes were firmly fixed on the rifle muzzle that was levelled at his chest. Instinctively he raised his hands and moved back slowly until his legs came into contact with the bed and as his legs buckled he flopped onto the mattress. Carmen had pulled a sheet from the bed in an attempt to cover her modesty.

The man spoke with a load guffaw. "Do not bother trying to cover yourself my lovely, for I have seen every centimetre of that wonderful body of yours." He gesticulated with the rifle towards the open window. "That terrace upstairs in the widow Ausana's wreck of house gives a great view into your bedroom and I have seen you undress many times."

Pepe kept the rifle trained on Juan while he continued. "Perfectly shaped little titties Señorita Carmen, and the finest most delicate, tightest little bush I've seen in a long time."

He laughed again while he struck a match and lit the cigarette that dangled from his wet salivating mouth. "And you Father. Lucky you eh? The Good Lord made sure you weren't at the back of the queue when he handed the cocks out did he? Your little whore enjoyed every minute didn't she? I confess she would make a great horsewoman the way she straddled and rode you like her life depended on it."

Pepe lowered his rifle slightly as he placed a hand on his groin. "Alas, my dear Señora back home is no longer able to produce the movements of a young girl anymore and I do not experience the pleasures of the flesh to often these days." Pepe flushed as a wave of anger swept visibly over him. "You fucking men of the cloth are all the same aren't you?"

Juan made an attempt to speak but before he could utter a word Pepe thrust the rifle towards him.

"Silence do you hear? For once in your life spare me a fucking sermon. This time I'll do the talking and you will listen." Pepe moved forward and stabbed the gun into Juan's chest. "You listen and listen well. For twenty years I've watched your sort turn up in my town and lecture my people. Your church grows fat while the people go hungry and I've watched as you stand alongside the rich and the privileged, the land owners as they decide who to hire for a day or two's wages."

Pepe's rifle trembled in his hands. Juan was more than aware that he was speaking from the heart, very angry and more than capable of pulling the trigger.

"And you stand in your stupid black frocks with your stupid little hats and enough gold dripping from your necks to feed a family for a year while you tell your little tales on who has been bad and who has missed church on Sunday so that the landowner can decide who to choose."

Juan sighed. It was true. Many priests did exactly what Pepe had described. The farm owners and wine bodega men had asked Juan to help many times but he'd always declined, unwilling to be part of a process that would effectively condemn many families to go hungry.

Juan protested his innocence. "But Pepe, you have never seen me stand with any landowner giving instructions of who to hire and who to fire."

Pepe appeared to mellow a little. "You remember my name Father."

"I do."

Pepe nodded. "Good... Good, that's nice. And what you say is true and that is why I am going allow you to live." The anger flared up in Pepe's eyes again. "If it had been any of the other bastards sitting there they'd being chewing lead by now."

Pepe took a step forward. "You will live." He took the cigarette from his mouth and threw it on the floor. He reached down and threw Juan's clothes at him. "Get them on and get out or I will shoot you like the hypocritical pig you are."

Juan looked at Carmen and wondered what lay in store for her. Pepe caught the look. "I haven't made my mind up about her yet, the priests fucking whore." He turned to face Juan. "But you must run and you must run hard and don't stop until you are a hundred kilometres from Seville."

Pepe laughed. "Ha! I've already seen the mob hack three priests to death tonight." He scratched thoughtfully at his stubble. "You Father Juan, could easily be number four." He pointed to Juan's robe. "Black and red go so nice together don't you think?"

Carmen eventually found her voice. "You must flee Juan while you have the chance."

Pepe grinned. "Listen to your whore Father; she speaks the words of a wise woman."

Juan dressed quickly. "You must come with me Carmen?"

Pepe took a step forward and cuffed Juan across the face as he fell back onto the bed. "The bitch stays with me and if you don't get out of this room before I take my next breath your blood will paint her walls."

"Please go Juan, I will take my chance here, it's where I belong."

Juan stroked at the side of his face which was swelling rapidly. "But Carmen, no, I..."

"You can return when this all blows over it won't be long."

Pepe laughed and his words rattled in his throat. "Won't be long? Don't you believe it? Forces fighting against us are already moving in on the city. It promises to be quite a bloodbath." Pepe cocked the rifle and brought the stock into his shoulder as he levelled the sights to his right eye and trained the gun on the priest. "You've tested my patience enough. On the count of three if you're still here you die." He licked a droplet of spittle from his top lip and grinned as he began counting. "One—"

"Please Juan go. Go now."

" -Two."

Before Pepe could count any further Juan had bolted through the bedroom door and took off down the stairs stopping at the bottom to grab a light cloak from the back of the main door into the street, he didn't look back as he opened the door and ran out into the blackened street not knowing where he was going to run to.

Upstairs Carmen did not appreciate the look of menace that appeared to creep across Pepe's face. He stood and walked towards the window as he looked out onto the street.

"Your bed mate has scurried away like a filthy garden rat." He grinned. "Now it's just the two of us. Me and the priests whore." He turned and walked towards the bed. Carmen drew the sheet up to her face.

Pepe lunged towards her and ripped the sheet from her grip and cast it onto the floor leaving her naked.

"Ah that's better," he said. "It's nice to cast an eye over one's property. And what a delightful little property it is." Pepe sat on the bed, one hand holding the rifle pointed at her midriff. "My father told me I was born too poor, that I would never own anything. But here I am and now I own you. You are my property and my slave and you will do anything I ask."

He leaned forward and gripped her face hard between his forefinger and thumb as he snarled. "Because if you don't the whole of Seville will know exactly what it is you've been up to and you'll be in front of a firing squad quicker than you can blink." Pepe stood again as a leery grin pulled across his face. "If you obey me it will remain our little secret." He laid the rifle against the bottom of the bed. "Is that a deal?"

As the tears began to roll down Carmen's cheeks she nodded slowly.

"Good." he said "Good. I'm glad we've worked that out because the sight of your naked flesh is stirring my blood." Pepe reached for his belt buckle unloosened it and let his trousers fall to the floor. "Let's begin."

He reached for his rapidly stiffening penis. "You get over here and take me in your mouth like a whore of the streets."

Carmen let out a barely audible whimper. "I'd rather go to hell."

Pepe reached for his rifle and aimed the barrel angrily at Carmen's head. "That can easily be arranged."

The dull blast reverberated around the small room.

Nineteen

Juan ran towards the outskirts of the city. He ran for fifteen minutes, walked a while then ran again continuing the sequence until he could go no further. He slumped to the floor beside a tree. He was mentally and physically exhausted. As he rested he tried to gather his thoughts. It was his worst possible nightmare, like something out of a book of fiction or the worst play imaginable. The phrase came to him over and over again like a horrible dream. Spaniard killing Spaniard.

He'd wanted to discount the rumours, imagined that events had been blown out of proportion but after his experiences over the last twenty four hours he doubted it. He drank his fill of water from a nearby spring and walked for many hours before eventually collapsing by the side of the road. He eased his aching body under a small bush. He needed to sleep and it had been some time since a morsel of food had passed his lips. Eating every four or five hours had been something he was used too. He smiled to himself at the irony. Now he knew what it was like to live like a poor man. He pulled his cloak around his head in an attempt to block out the cold night air. As he closed his tear filled eyes a fine drizzle began to fall.

He awoke with a start. A group of young men and women dressed in blue shirts stood over him. A young girl no more than twenty years of age stepped forward and raised an old revolver at him. She pulled back the bolt of the gun and gritted her teeth as she squeezed on the trigger. It was time he thought. The nightmare was coming to an end. Juan instinctively crossed himself and lifted his cloak from his body. He wanted to die as a priest not afraid to meet his maker.

"Stop Adela." someone shouted, "He's one of us."

The young girl put her gun away and one of them laughed as they lifted Juan to his feet.

"We are so sorry Father we thought you were a red."

They helped Juan to a nearby truck and eased him onto one of the rear seats.

The young people explained they were on the way to the Town Hall and brought him up to speed on recent events. They were members of the *Falange,* the Spanish fascist movement founded in 1933 by José Antonio Primo de Rivera. The blue shirts signified that the young people were part of the Falange militia hoping to oust the reds as they continually referred to the opposition.

The scene inside the huge central square of Seville was like something from another age. A pall of acrid black smoke lingered in the sky from the many buildings that had been set on fire. There were lone children crying looking for parents and dead bodies lying on the street and in doorways. One young girl no more than five years of age stood wailing and crying underneath a large acacia tree outside the town hall, pleading with everyone who passed but they all walked on. At her feet lay the bullet riddled body of a middle aged man.

A large group of blue shirted youths were systematically breaking down doors to the houses and offices in an attempt to root out the enemy and the smell of fear and of anguish and pure hatred permeated the early morning air.

A makeshift altar had been set up against the side wall of the town hall and there were hundreds of people in line waiting to be blessed by a small group of priests in attendance. Juan couldn't work out what was going on. It seemed a strange place to hold mass when the church was just a stone's throw away.

Adela, the young girl who had nearly executed him noticed the puzzled look on his face. "Reds, Father."

"Reds?" Juan asked.

"Communists, enemies of Spain." She appeared to bask in pride as she spoke. "Seville is now under Nationalist control." She pointed to the far side of the square. "Over there Father, the Falange recruiting table. Look how many are signing up to join us."

The numbers were indeed huge but then the truth dawned on him. The blue shirt was the equivalent of a lifejacket to the poor people who would otherwise be at risk of execution.

She pointed again to a man dressed in a fine uniform smoking on a cigar chatting to a group of similarly dressed men. "And that is General Quipo de Llano who has secured Seville for the forces of Franco."

"Franco," questioned Juan. "And who is Franco? I have never heard of this man."

Adela turned to face him and smiled. "Oh you will Father. By the grace of God you will."

One of the Falange who had been in the truck tapped him on the arm. "That's where you need to go Father. We need your help." He pointed to the growing crowd of people outside the town hall. "They are waiting to be given the last rites."

He had just reached the building when the heavy doors of the town hall burst open and a group of men and women with their hands wired behind their backs were pushed unceremoniously out of the doors. They were herded to a wall some twenty metres away. Juan noticed with increasing unease the hundreds of pock marks on the wall and the dark colour of the earth underneath. He looked behind him at the line of some twenty Falange members with rifles held up in the air. He realised in an instant that his help was needed to give the last rites to the poor people about to be executed.

One of the Falange was shouting at the people by the wall asking them to repent their sins before they met their maker.

He beckoned Juan towards them. "Do it Father, we need to get on with it quickly, there are many more after these bastards."

Juan had never felt so helpless. He wanted to beg the man to stop, to come to his senses. He wanted everyone to come to their senses but he knew it was a hopeless cause. The Falange had murder on their minds; there was no place for mercy or compassion. In their eyes they were the enemy of Spain even though to a man the blood that would surely flow would be pure Spanish.

Juan walked forward almost in a daze, trying his best to collate his thoughts and remember exactly what it was he was supposed to say. He felt for the small bottle of blessed olive oil that he'd curiously started to carry about his person these last few weeks, a necessary article in administering the last rites. He removed it from his pocket and stared at the first condemned man, a poor wretch battered and bloodied about the face no more than seventeen years of age.

Juan removed the top from the bottle of oil and made eye contact. He spoke in Latin. "Through this holy anointing, may the Lord in his love and mercy help you with the grace of the Holy Spirit. May the Lord who frees you from sin save you and raise you up."

The man snarled as he spat on the ground by Juan's shoes. "Do not bless me priest. I want nothing from your corrupt shit tarnished church." The man gazed skywards and shouted out loud. "Viva la Republica hijos de puta."

Within a split second or two the young man was falling to the floor. One of the soldiers had overheard what he had said and had shot him through the heart. It was the unofficial signal for the rest of the firing squad to open fire as Juan dived for cover.

Juan lay on the ground as the air filled with the sound of gunfire and bodies fell around him. The gunfire seemed to be far more than was needed to kill the small group of men and women. Then it stopped as suddenly as it had started.

Juan rose tentatively to his feet as a pool of blood formed like a huge man-made lake on the ground beside him and the stench of death filled his nostrils. He felt like he was in a trance as the soldiers moved forward, some smiling some even laughing, some with flecks of white around their lips. They walked over and started to kick the bodies making sure there was no sign of life. He heard a groan from behind and looked around at one pretty dark haired young woman as the blood oozed from her chest. As he approached her twisted body one of the soldiers pulled him back and Juan recoiled in horror as he shot her in the face. Her head exploded like an overripe water-melon.

"You can't be pretty if you are a Red," the soldier joked as he lit a cigarette and walked away.

Even though his stomach was empty Juan could not control the retching that started deep inside him. He carried on vomiting until his stomach muscles begged for mercy and his tears stained the parched earth. He was eventually helped to his feet by one of his fellow priests, a short bald headed man with a huge stomach.

He explained that the first time was always the worst and that he would soon get used to it.

"Get used to it? Juan said, astonished at the priest's almost casual manner. "Get used to killing and murder. I think not brother, I think not."

The priest took him by the arm and led him towards the other priests who had congregated near the town hall. He pointed at another line of poor unfortunates who filed out of the doorway.

"They are heathens," the priest said. "They've killed our brothers, nuns too and burned and desecrated our finest churches." The elderly priest was red in the face as he continued. "They want to wipe the Church from the face of the earth. They have incurred the wrath of God and will pay the ultimate price." The priest let out a deep sigh. "They will answer to their maker very soon."

"I don't understand," said Juan. "The Good Lord gave us a commandment, *Though Shalt Not Kill*. Can't we stop them; can't we appeal to their religious conscience? There are many church goers amongst their leaders I'm sure. Surely we can at least talk to them?"

The old priest mopped at his perspiring brow as he shook his head. "They cannot be stopped my son and there is little point talking to them. They will throw back in your face many more wise words from the Good Book. Many of these people have killed our own and they are calling life for life, eye for eye."

"But what of those who have not killed," Juan protested.

"It matters not," said the priest. "If we allow them to live then they will fight against us another day."

The priest appeared to quote from memory. "From the book of Ezekiel, '*show no mercy, have no pity kill them all old and young, girls and women and little children*'." He pulled a small bible from under his cassock and flicked through several pages. He smiled as he found the verse he was looking for. "*And when justice is done it brings joy to the righteous and terror to the evildoers.*"

The priest closed his bible as a grin of satisfaction pulled across his face and replaced the book under his cassock.

Juan raised his voice a decibel or two. "Have you no compassion man."

"No I have not," he cried angrily. "I have no compassion when I am trying to survive; trying to protect the church I have dedicated my life too." The priest smoothed his cassock down and seemed to regain a little composure. He leaned forward and whispered to Juan. "And you my son could do a lot worse than to heed my words and hold that tongue of yours." He straightened his hat and brushed a fleck of dirt from his sleeve. "By the grace of God you could be next in line on that wall."

Before Juan could find the words he wanted to say the priest had walked away.

Over the coming days, Juan worked from dawn to dusk. There was a never ending line of new converts desperately brandishing their crudely constructed crosses or bibles. They grasped at anything that would convince the Falange that the individual was ready to become part of the new Spain, in their fight against the republicans. It was as clear as spring water, the Church and the Nationalists stood as one.

And so it went on, week after week, the same events, lorry after lorry of poor unfortunates who were judged to be against Franco's Nationalist forces. It was enough to have been a teacher, an intellectual, or even just to have voted for the previous left wing party to earn a place at the execution wall. Occasionally the Falange would engage in a little digression to break the monotony. They would stage a two or three minute trial for a prisoner protesting his innocence. They were a sham; mere entertainment for the masses. Very rarely did Juan ever see anyone acquitted.

The firing squad was the favoured method of execution, though occasionally a miscreant was hanged from a public building and placed on display for the people to see. The bodies were taken away by other prisoners and buried in common graves on the outskirts of the city. They in turn were shot and replaced by other prisoners when they became too weak to carry on.

The Falange had no shortage of prisoners as they raided the offices of the town halls for names addresses and details of anyone who were judged to be left wing, or had been in a workers trade union. Every day Juan was called upon to preach to the newly converted or read the last rites to the condemned. It seemed the dark days would never end and yet he wanted to be there, wanted to give a little hope to the men, women and children who were executed on a daily basis, never failing to remind them they were on their way to a better place than the Hell they were leaving.

And he longed for Carmen. On more than one occasion he was ready to turn his back on the duties the Falange had requested of him and return to her house. But these were dangerous times and the hour's walk back through the narrow streets was fraught with danger. He prayed several times a day that she would be safe and comforted himself that if it were God's will they would be together again soon.

Twenty

It was during a lull in the work of the firing squads that Juan sat down with one of the Nationalist soldiers. He felt a mixture of fear, revulsion and more than a little curiosity as to how a man could be shooting young women dead one minute, and while they were still twitching on the floor, sit down to eat bread and cheese his appetite unhindered.

"How did it come to this?" asked Juan. "Tell me why it is you can execute without hesitation and enjoy a meal so soon after?"

The soldier screwed up one eye frowned a little and then spoke. He recounted the story of how the rebel general Quipo had brazenly walked into the barracks in Seville and congratulated the officers and men on their decision to join the uprising.

The Nationalist soldier grinned as he took a mouthful of cheese and without bothering to swallow what was in his mouth continued. "We are trained well father," he said. "We learn from our leaders and must be as brutal as they are."

He detailed how General Quipo had noted which officers had dithered and which had quickly stiffened to attention obeying his orders without question. He quickly called the ditherers outside where they were quietly arrested taken away and later shot. The soldier laughed as he recounted that General Quipo had declared any reds that surrendered without a fight wouldn't be harmed. He wiped at the food residue at the side of his mouth with his blood encrusted sleeve.

"So he has a little compassion this general Quipo?" Said Juan, with a ray of optimism.

The soldier let out a loud guffaw as a morsel of bread shot out of his mouth and landed on Juan's lap.

He was shaking his head, laughing loudly trying hard to compose himself. "Compassion Father? Compassion? Are you as green as you look?"

Juan hesitated. "I, I don't understand."

The soldier reached down for a half empty wine bottle and brought it level with his lips as he eyed Juan cautiously.

"We shot them all regardless Father, every last one of them."

But you said... I don't understand... General –"

"General Quipo Father. He gave the order. Shoot the dogs he said. Shoot them so they can bite us no more."

Sitting with the Nationalist troops not only gave Juan an insight into the mentality of the average foot soldier but they also told him how the war had started and how it was progressing. It appeared that within a few short weeks the entire population of Spain was divided, right or left, Republican or Nationalist. Sitting on the fence was not an option in this war.

The military uprising in North Africa had started on July 17, under the leadership of colonel Seguí, under orders from General Franco and rapidly gathered pace attracting the unwanted attention of the entire world. The Nationalist troops basked with pride as they told Juan that Italy and Nazi Germany had pledged their support for Franco and the Nationalist cause. The Nationalists had captured the main Spanish naval base at Ferrol in northwestern Spain, a port of huge strategic importance especially for Germany who some said were already sowing their own seeds of destruction and longed for a facility where they could try out their latest weapons and aircraft for future hostilities.

In Germany, Adolf Hitler opened up a personal dialogue with Franco rather than the Nationalists in general. To the average Nationalist this was viewed as a vote of confidence in Franco and cemented his leadership in the eyes of the common man.

Juan listened in horror as the men relayed their tales telling how they had resolved long-standing feuds and settled scores. It was clear that the war was the 'excuse' that many men and women had waited for. Juan shook his head in disbelief as one old man dressed in the shirt of the Falange boasted that nearly 50,000 people had already been *taken care of.* Juan sat slumped on a large sack of discarded clothes left in the shade at the side of the town hall building. Surely this horror would end soon? He missed his family back in Abdet and Vicente and Fatima too. He wondered how Father Ismael was coping and if the uprising had reached his small community too. Oh how he longed for normality and to be back in the gloomy atmosphere of the small church at Xirles. Why had they sent him to Seville?

He lay his head back against the cool stone wall and for the hundredth time in as many weeks fought back the tears. He had been giving the last rites to the prisoners for the last ten days now, with only a few hours troubled sleep and an odd meal of beans and rice. Even now he felt starving but had no appetite for food. He could feel his clothes hanging loose around his already slender frame. He moved his hand onto his ribs and squeezed. He barely had the energy but it was fact, the weight was falling from him almost by the day. He reached for a piece of bread he'd stored in his knapsack the previous day. He had to eat. He needed to force himself because if he got the chance he would flee this madness. He didn't know how but he'd head back to Abdet and Xirles. He'd find peace there he sensed it, he knew the villagers, all of them. They wouldn't fight against each other, he felt sure. And then the thoughts returned again. A beautiful image filled his mind, illicit thoughts and stolen passion and a forbidden love, forbidden by the church and the Lord Almighty too. Carmen, where was she?

There had been a few whispers at the town hall of some important visitors arriving. Sure enough the wagging tongues had been proved right when Juan had seen, albeit from a distance, General Quipo De Llano, the man responsible for the uprising in Seville at lunch time the previous day. But now the soldiers of the Falange were nervous and a little excited as the rumour mill gathered pace. They were polishing their boots, some smoothing down their hair with olive oil and to a man most had shaved that morning.

They had been notified by their commanding officers that Francisco Franco, the unofficial leader of the uprising was expected at any time. Juan sat on a small wooden chair at the entrance of the square watching the many lorries passing by. By this time, the arrival of another truck load of prisoners was nothing out of the ordinary and Juan stared as one particular lorry screeched to a halt and the poor human cargo dumped unceremoniously onto the hot dusty earth. His blood froze as he recognised two of the latest arrivals. One of them was the filthy form of Pepe, who snarled through his dirty blackened teeth at one of the Falange soldiers who hammered the butt of his rifle into Pepe's ribcage as he kicked him from the back of the truck into the dust. Pepe lay in a crumpled heap groaning but still shouting out obscenities at anyone who would listen.

But it was the dishevelled and bleeding form of the girl who jumped down beside him that stopped his heart in its tracks. She looked around at the carnage surrounding her and her beautiful blue eyes welled up with tears. Her hair was matted and dirty and her face blood stained and grimy but she was unmistakable. It was the girl who had cared for him and his fellow priests for years, only to become his accidental lover in a moment of madness never to be repeated. He froze to the spot for a second or two unsure of the correct course of action. The Falange soldiers herded the individuals together and ordered them to move. They were guiding them towards another group of republican prisoners as the realty and horror of what was about to become of her eventually sank in. No, thought Juan, there must be some mistake. Carmen is not a republican she is with the Church. The next sentence he whispered to himself would haunt him till his dying day.

He'd thought the thought... the words had crossed his lips and they couldn't be taken back. *She's one of us* he'd mumbled quietly. Father Juan Francisco Cortes, had taken sides. Every moral he'd held dear to his heart had been dashed to pieces when he finally realised that only a few seconds ago he'd became like the rest of them. He hadn't wanted to and flatly refused to engage in any discussions when allegiances and oaths were being pledged. But now his sub conscience had decided for him. It was a shame like no other he'd ever experienced before and he sank to his knees and buried his face in his hands.

Carmen felt a slap to the back of her head. "Move you red bitch," someone squealed at her and she quickly picked up her feet moving to the far side of the square towards the pock marked wall. The earth beneath it appeared wet and yet she couldn't remember rain for many weeks now.

Pepe walked alongside her. He laughed. "You're a little curious aren't you my pretty little whore." Pepe massaged his aching ribs. "Wondering why that wall has so many holes in it and why the ground bleeds?"

Carmen looked again and took a sharp intake of breath as the reality and horror of the situation sank in.

Pepe caught the look and laughed again. "Ahhh... I see you have it."

Carmen faltered and began to shake her head.

"That's right... we're heading for that wall over there and the men in the blue shirts will pump a dozen bullets into your pretty little head and your sweet mouth will never pleasure a man again."

Carmen stopped and looked around not sure what it was she was looking for.

"There's no one here to help you. You're on your own but fear not because you've been a good little Catholic girl helping all those priests over the years and I'm sure the good Lord has a special life for you once you get to wherever it is you think you are going."

Carmen felt a shove in the back and fell to the ground. The boot of a Falange soldier commanded her to rise and Pepe dragged her to her feet.

"Keep walking or they will spare you the wall and keep you for themselves and I swear to you that's a fate worse than anything the wall has to offer."

Carmen blurted out as her tears began to fall. "But I'm not-"

Pepe was nodding. "I know, you're not a red, you're not one of us." He pointed to one of the soldiers walking along side. "Do you want to tell him, do you want to reason with him because I'll tell you something for nothing he won't listen? Men have changed in these few short weeks, changed for the worst. They'd sooner shoot than listen to reason."

Carmen stepped out of line in a desperate attempt to speak to the soldier. She'd tell him she was a simple housekeeper, a girl of the church and she'd been picked up with Pepe because he'd taken her captive. Before she got within a few feet of the soldier she had been knocked to the ground by one of his colleagues because she'd dared to step out of line. He stood over her and pointed his rifle at her head as his finger tightened on the trigger.

Whatever Juan did he had to be quick. He was all too aware that by now the Nationalists had dispensed with the charade of a mock trial and simply lined the prisoners up in front of the bullet pitted wall, no questions asked, no defence, no mercy or forgiveness. Juan acted more on impulse rather than a plan covering the thirty metres distance to the prisoners in a flash. But something was wrong. Where was she? He couldn't see her. His eyes picked through the throng of people as he squeezed and pushed his way through.

"Carmen," he shouted, "I'm looking for Señorita Carmen, she is with the church."

His eyes fell instinctively to the crumpled heap lying on the ground and the soldier standing over her. He recognised her hair which had fallen over her face. She let out a whimper as she brought her hand up to her face and brushed aside her hair.

"Juan," she whispered. "Help me please; they are going to kill me."

He started to drag her away to be met by the rifle muzzle of the soldier. He spun around and screamed at the soldier that this was the woman who had saved his life and that of his fellow priests at the start of the uprising.

"She is with us," he pleaded."

The soldier faltered for a second, unsure what to do. His finger eased from the trigger as he looked around at his colleagues hoping for a little guidance. Juan seized the moment and insisted on speaking with a superior officer realising the soldier was out of his depth. He lifted Carmen to her feet and she leaned into him. The soldier nodded in the direction of the town hall. "I will take you to the commander's office, he will decide."

Pepé had cleared his thoughts and realised that the priest was trying to save the skin of his lover. He started to scream obscenities at both Juan and Carmen shouting at the Falange that the woman was the prostitute of God and she'd prove more than useful to the twenty or so soldiers for a little after dark entertainment.

"Don't waste her on the wall," he shouted. "The nights are long and her body has been blessed by the Lord."

God's whore, he shouted over and over again, vilifying the Church at the same time. The members of the Falange were losing patience with Pepe, as one or two of them stepped forward and ordered him to be quiet. Pepe was having none of it. He screamed out what were to be his last ever words in the direction of the priest. "You know how good she is Father; tell your troops what a good little fuck she is, how she kept your bed warm at nights."

The bullet slammed into Pepe's right temple exiting the other side of his head as Carmen let out a stifled scream. He died instantly as his limp body fell towards the ground. To die quickly and pain free had been Pepe's plan for some time, to die cursing the Church and God was an added bonus.

Juan lifted Carmen from the ground and supported her as they walked to the commander's office. As they entered the room the commander sat at a heavy wooden table covered with papers. He was an immaculately dressed individual who looked towards Juan and Carmen as the soldier explained why they were there. He waved Juan and Carmen into his office and they stood forlornly at the desk while the Commander fiddled with his pencil looking as if he had better things to do.

Juan recounted how Carmen had been the priest's housekeeper, and then weaved an elaborate tale of how she had bravely hidden them from the raging red mob putting her own life in danger. He told of how he had to make himself scarce and described how she been left alone in the house at the mercy of the mob. He was convinced she was dead but spotted her on one of the lorries coming into the square.

"God has spared her," he said as he smiled at the Commander. God has decided that she must live to carry on his good work."

The commander listened intently as Juan pleaded for her, suggesting that she could take care of the priests yet again as they carried out their work for the new regime. The commander sat silently, eased back in his chair and then leant forward as he pulled an official looking paper from his desk. Juan prayed silently under his breath. The commander had made his decision. He looked at Carmen and beckoned her forward.

"This is all true Señorita?"

Carmen nodded. "I have worked for the church for many years, you may check up your official records or indeed ask any of the priests in the square. I am well known for my work with the church.

The commander was shaking his head." There is no need, I have heard enough and trust the word of Father Juan." The commander glanced at Juan then back to Carmen. "I have watched him over the last few weeks and he works well for us. He is committed to the cause." He shuffled the papers on the desk top then looked up. "This is for you Señorita Carmen, new papers. It will ensure you are not mistaken for a *Red* again. You may carry on where you left off, working for the priests. Make sure they have food and water." He paused for a second. "I suspect some of them have gone hungry these last few weeks." He pointed at the paperwork on the desk. "This is my authorisation and you will be well taken care of."

With the thump of his stamp on the sheet of paper he waved them away.

The square was quiet now, the soldiers fed and watered and some were taking siestas under the shade of the many olive trees that lined the warren of small streets. Juan gazed over towards the wall where the prisoners had been herded. The floor was still wet with blood but the bodies had disappeared.

Carmen had been cleaned up by one of the old cooks and clothed with items from the sack Juan had been sitting on earlier. She still had her bruises and a cut or two but looked almost as good as new though her eyes were heavy and sad. He almost expected a smile from her beautiful lips but realised it would be some time before that would happen. It had been many days since she had eaten and Juan insisted she took a little food. Despite her protestations she ate a little bread and cheese. Afterwards he took her to one side and they talked quietly for many hours.

It was the 6th of August 1936 when Franco arrived in Seville.

Juan and Carmen stood quietly with the other priests at the back of the large wildly over enthusiastic crowd who screamed their approval at his every word. The General was a slight figure with a high pitched voice and Juan thought he was rather a strange sight, not at all what he expected, but decided to keep his thoughts to himself. Franco explained how he had organized the first airlift of troops in history and it should be a cause of great celebration. More than 15000 specialist soldiers had been moved by air from their bases in North Africa to Andalucía. There had also been troop movements across the straits of Gibraltar, the fascist ships protected by German destroyers and aided by British communication facilities based on the rock.

Franco detailed in his speech how he was going to divide his troops into two armies; one was to march under the orders of General Yagüe through Extremadura meeting up with the fascist forces of the uprisings in the North, before swinging around to attack Madrid. The other army was to move east and take the rest of Andalucía. Juan wondered what his part in all this was to be and he didn't have to wait long. At the end of the spectacle a group of twenty priests were summoned to the commander's office. Carmen was told to follow on behind.

They were addressed by the Commander who had reprieved Carmen. "I have selected you personally," he said to the group. "Your work here is done but there is so much more we need to achieve together. You are heading North with Yagüe and his men and you have two hours to prepare."

Juan was shocked, they were heading in the wrong direction. He yearned for the simple life back home in Xirles again. Oh how he missed it. He wanted to walk through the narrow streets shaded from the hot sun and take refuge or a glass of water in the small cafe that he knew so well. And he so much wanted to take another mass among the familiar faces of his friends and family that packed the church when he and Father Ismael called the village to prayer. Father Ismael. What of him? How had life changed in the village he knew so well?

On 17 July, Quipo de Llano, who was the chief of the carabineros (the frontier police) came to Seville in a tour of inspection On the morning of 18 July, Quipo de Llano accompanied by three officers entered in the office of the general Villa-Abrille and arrested him. After that he went to the San Hermenigildo barracks and detained the colonel of the 6th regiment, Manuel Allanegi who had rejected his suggestion to join the uprising. The artillery regiment also joined to the rising and the rebel troops surrounded and bombed the building of the civil government held by loyalist assault guards. The civil governor surrendered after Quipo promised to save their lives but then went back on his word and executed the chief of the police and the assault guards. At that point the Guardia Civil also joined the rebellion.

A general strike was ordered by the trade Unions and the workers withdrew into their own districts of Triana and La Macarena. They built barricades, but had a limited supply of weapons. The rebel troops numbering approximately 4,000 men seized the nerve centres of the city, occupying the telephone exchange, the town hall and the radio station.

On 20 July, the rebels bombed the working-class districts of Seville and more rebel troops supported by the troops of the Spanish Foreign Legion arrived from Africa using women and children as human shields as they entered the loyalist areas murdering every man they found often with knives and bayonets.

By July 25, the Nationalists occupied all of Seville. According to the Quipo's press assistant: "In the working-class districts the Foreign Legion and the Moors patrolled the streets throwing grenades in the windows before entering with bayonets and knives. The Moors took the opportunity to loot and rape at will. General Quipo de Llano, in his night-time talks at the Radio Seville microphone urged on his troops to rape women and recounted with crude sarcasm brutal scenes of this sort.

After the coup, all persons with Republican and Left sympathies were rounded up by the Nationalists and imprisoned or killed. The repression in Seville was organized by Captain Díaz Criado, who was reported as signing death sentences at a rate of 'about sixty per day'. Three thousand Republican supporters were shot in the first weeks after the coup. After the coup Quipo de Llano sent mixed columns made up of Civil Guards, Falangists and soldiers financed by wealthy landowners in order to occupy other towns in the province. Large numbers of prisoners were sent to Seville and executed.

Twenty One

It was an argument he had heard a hundred times before. Vicente's wife was protesting he was too old to attempt to walk to his brother's house in Finestrat.

"You are too old Vincent and well you know it." She said. "The last time you arrived back you complained about your knees and ankles for a week."

"It was more like a day or two my sweet one. And anyway what do you want me to do, sit on the back step, smoking and sharing gossip with the other old men until I collapse and die. It's good healthy exercise I tell you."

Fatima knew Vicente was right. The exercise would never harm him but she worried that the stubborn old goat would carry on walking until the day he died just to prove a point. She pictured him stumbling into a ditch by the side of the road lying for many hours in agony until he breathed his last breath. That was not the way she wanted him to go. Death was nothing to worry about he kept reminding her.

"When the good lord wants you he will take you. Walk, run, work, and play it makes no difference." When your time is up your time is up he would tell her.

Fatima sighed. She handed him a small bag containing a little bread and cheese and told him to take care of himself, she would see him in a day or two. She reminded him to be extra careful this time. It wasn't every day they would share an audience with an Archbishop.

And so he set off looking forward to the adventure ahead of him but more than a little nervous at the news the Archbishop would hand over on his return. That's what it was he told himself, it was an adventure and at the end of the road his brother would be waiting, his brother and his wife, his nephews and nieces...his family. They would greet him like a long lost child and welcome him in into the humble family home and spoil him with the finest foods and always, yes always a bottle of decent wine too. He would sleepover for a night or two, be treated like a king and then he would be on his way back home again.

It was almost like a ritual, something he had always done since his brother had decided to leave the village of Xirles in his early twenties.

Vicente sighed. Could it really be forty years ago, he mumbled to himself. As he set off he contemplated how life had changed. *Politics* he mumbled to himself. *Damned bloody politics. Why couldn't the politicians leave well alone and let the people get on with their lives?*

He'd trekked the road a thousand times, knew every centimetre of the route. He passed the road end at Polop and headed south towards La Nucia. The church at Polop was almost overbearing, standing high on the hill to his left. He said a silent prayer to himself that the violence dished out to the clergy in other parts of Spain would not come to these peaceful parts. Live and let live, that was his life's philosophy. Break a little bread and share a little wine with your family. Nothing else mattered.

Six or seven kilometres into the walk and the therapy was working. He'd forgotten about the unrest that was filtering through Spain and the problems at the town Hall. He laughed to himself as he realised it had been at least an hour or two since he'd thought about his son. It had been over two months since his last letter sent from a district of Seville.

Juan wrote that life was good. He had a pleasant attractive housekeeper called Carmen who cooked well, not unlike the wonderful food that Fatima could concoct from a few basic ingredients. *Attractive...* yes that's what Juan had said. God forgive the boy, had he forgotten he was a priest. Priests shouldn't think that way.

Vicente rested at his favourite spot on the Finestrat side of La Nucia. It was the half-way point in the journey and he allowed himself a break under the lone olive tree just after the painted white stone announcing to the traveller heading from the opposite direction that they were only two kilometres from the pretty little village.

Vicente drank voraciously from the water flask, well aware of a hidden stream that ran from the mountain of Puig Campana. He would top his flask up there, praying to himself the stream had not dried up after the recent hot spell.

Vicente's older brother Carlos, greeted him like a long lost son, smothering him with kisses and hugging him tightly until Vicente pushed hard to break his grip.

"Be away with you Carlos, it's only a few weeks since we last shared a bottle together. Save that sort of thing for your wife."

Carlos planted another kiss onto Vicente's cheek and took him by the arm as he led him inside. "I wish brother, those days are long gone."

Vicente frowned at his brother as a smile crept across his face. "Gone Carlos... gone? Don't bring me news like that on this fine day. Once those days are gone it's time to build your coffin. Elena is fifteen years younger than you; tell me you are still active."

Carlos slapped his brothers back. "I will tell you nothing young one but it will happen to you soon. Elena is more than willing to take me into her bed at nights but although my mind is strong and willing the flesh is weak."

Carlos let out a shrieking laugh and opened the door to his modest home. The two brothers stepped inside and Elena breezed from the kitchen with two glasses of red wine in her hands.

The brothers drank late into the night sharing tales of their everyday struggle to exist and of course their opinions on the ever worsening civil war. Neither brother shared a strong opinion on where their political loyalties lay but each agreed that an elected government should be allowed to govern and war and violence was not the answer.

Vicente expressed his concern at the killings of priests and nuns further north and couldn't help shedding a few tears when talking about Juan. Carlos assured him that God would look over him and they toasted his health with yet another full glass.

They raised their glasses. "To Juan." they announced in unison.

"May God watch over him," announced Carlos.

∾

It had been a long time since Father Ismael could remember being part of such a high ranking delegation. He had to cast his mind back several years, to Barcelona when a group of parish priests from the Valencia province had travelled over quite some weeks to take an audience with an Archbishop at the Sagrada Familia Church in the heart of the city. They'd been specially selected and he recalled trembling with excitement when he'd been presented to the high ranking official. Father Ismael scratched his head and furrowed his brow. He could not even remember the Archbishops name it was such a long time ago. He recalled the church and even name of the street but not the dignitary he met. It mattered not. He had to focus on tomorrow and the many tasks that still had to be completed. God forbid if anything went wrong. What would they say on their return about the hospitality afforded to them in the small hamlet of his home town? Old Sebastian, the pig farmer had offered his fattest piglet to the feast on condition his wife and he could be present at the special dinner. Father Ismael had readily agreed. There would be a special table set for the villagers who had given the most after his appeal two Sunday's back. It was a very generous gesture from Sebastian and his wife, a fat piglet generally sustained them right through the winter months and he had no doubt there would be many days ahead without ham and bacon on the pig farmers table.

He'd also been supplied with several bottles of fine reserva from the bodega of Gomez Marques. One bottle, Gomez insisted, was over one hundred years old having been bottled by his father who had passed away many years ago. There were tears in his eyes as the wine producer handed the bottles over to the priest.

Many had handed over their hard earned wages to provide for a feast the likes they'd never seen before. Father Ismael had wished he could have sat them all at a huge table and had the Archbishop thank them all personally but he'd had his instructions from Valencia, a dozen... no more. The Archbishop and his bishops and priests would be tired from the day's exertions and needed to eat and sleep in preparation for another tough day ahead.

The Archbishop and his entourage travelled incognito. These were dangerous times for men of the cloth. Thankfully the violence breaking out in other parts of Spain had not quite reached this part of Spain, but they could take no chances.

The Archbishop's party consisted of three armed soldiers; the very best Spain had to offer. They were fighting men, battle hardened and armed to the teeth, though to look at them sitting astride their mules you would think they were working men taken straight from the fields. Such was the plan. The Archbishop himself had chosen the men personally and although they were no guarantee of survival it would take a significant band of heavily armed men to outwit these body guards, particularly as they looked as harmless as a day old child. The rest of the party consisted of two bishops, four priests, a trainee priest and two young servant girls who would pander to the Archbishop's every need and make him as comfortable as possible on his four month mission. These two females had also been handpicked by the Archbishop as he explained to their families the great honour he had bestowed upon them.

In the provinces of Valencia and Alicante, life seemed to go on with little change. The farmers tended their crops and the main worry continued to be whether there was going to be sufficient rain to ensure a good harvest. Gradually though, news began to filter through of the uprisings and of the increasing pace of the fascist advance and with it came the first tales of the terrible atrocities carried out by both sides. Father Ismael crossed his heart and looked skywards. Surely they must be over exaggerated he thought to himself as his lips moved ever so slightly while he said a silent prayer to the Almighty. The first he'd heard of any activity in the region came only last week. Señor Gonzalez had disclosed in the confession box last Sunday that he'd heard of a revolutionary committee that had formed in the Town hall of Polop. He said they'd spent hours huddled in the meeting room, amid foul smelling clouds of acrid tobacco smoke making elaborate combat plans that always ended up being finalized in the bar. Ismael laughed to himself. Such was the way of Spain, everything settled in the bar. He sighed and mumbled to himself. "And the confession box. The things they say in that strangest of dark places."

Archbishop Alfonso had consulted with the hierarchy of the Catholic Church of Spain. Their instructions had come direct from the Vatican. It wasn't so much an opportunity as a life line. Church men, priests and nuns had been murdered by the republicans and the church in Spain had never looked so vulnerable. But then the good Lord had intervened.

He always did. Have faith they had told him, have faith and the Lord will put things right, it was simply a test of faith. And he had put things right or at least he had sewed the first few seeds in the shape of the nationalist uprising led by General Franco. The church had to act, work alongside the troops and sympathisers of the uprising and re-establish a power base from which to work from.

Archbishop Alfonso didn't like war or violence but it was a means to an end. It was a battle of survival and if it was up to those damned republicans they would do away with God and the Church altogether. They had to be stopped, it was as simple as that. The Nationalists would win the war. Defeat was unthinkable. God was on their side. Archbishop Alfonso and his party had spent the day in Altea with the officials of several churches in the area. Priests had travelled from Calpe, Benissa, Alfaz and Benidorm. They told the Archbishop of their fears; one or two even disclosed that they disguised themselves in order to make it to Altea in one piece. The archbishop had told them they were overreacting and the good Lord would protect them. His own entourage had travelled well over one hundred kilometres since their journey had begun and encountered no hostility whatsoever. They had nothing to be ashamed of and they should wear the clothes of their ministry with pride.

Archbishop Alfonso was rather pleased at the way he delivered his two hour address, pleased with the way the priests and other officials had listened and yes... changed. He had sent them on their way with a new sense of purpose, a renewed optimism and hope in the organisation they had dedicated their lives to.

He quoted from the book of Jeremiah. *I know the plans I have for you, declared the Lord, plans to prosper you and not to harm you, plans to give you hope and a future.*

The church would survive and God would be worshipped in every village, town and city in Spain. The church had been threatened before, by Islam and the Moors but they'd fought passionately and won, sending them back to where they belonged in the 15th Century.

Archbishop Alfonso had given a lecture on history as his flock looked up to the pulpit with obvious admiration. When the history lesson was over he'd schooled them on faith and their duty, their duty to God.

The Archbishop stood on the stone steps of the ancient church of the Virgin de Consuelo overlooking a glassy, early evening sea. He peered up into the storm ready sky, studying the ever thickening cloud line way out on the horizon. He pulled up his coat collar as a shiver ran the length of his spine. His work here was nearly complete and it was time for something to eat.

The faithful of Altea had laid on a feast for the Archbishop and his team. They'd handed him a small menu as he walked from the church and advised that everything was just about ready. The specialties of the region, paella with octopus and Valencian lamb stew would all be washed down with a fine local wine and a brandy or two to follow. Yes... the Archbishop always felt that a brandy was the most exquisite way to round off a fine meal. He'd no doubt some of the villagers would go hungry tonight but that was hardly his fault. It wouldn't do them any harm he told himself. One day of fasting for the Lord wasn't too much to ask of anyone.

The Archbishop patted at his ample stomach as he licked at his lips in readiness of what he was about to receive. It was more than a little satisfying spending a hard day working in the service of the Lord then appreciating the good food and drink he would surely provide afterwards?

"Archbishop."

He looked back to the steps of the church where an elderly woman stood, head almost bowed. The Archbishop nodded and with a slight movement of his hand beckoned her to continue.

"Everything is ready your Holiness. The table is set if you would like to follow me."

The woman turned to her left and began walking down the old stone steps that led to the edge of the town. Behind her followed a procession of middle aged and elderly women all dressed in the very best clothes their wardrobes contained. Each of them gave a little curtsey and bowed their heads as they passed him. The

Archbishop couldn't help a wry smile to himself. He doubted the Holy Father the Pope would be treated any better.

Tomorrow they would head inland to a small pueblo called Xirles. He pulled out his paperwork from a small leather purse attached to a belt round his waist and studied his list. The priests from La Nucia, Polop, Finestrat and Callosa were all expecting him and the four parents of a priest lodged in Seville was waiting for news of their son.

The Archbishop furrowed his brow. *Four parents?* Damn the stupid scribe, he'd made a mistake, how could the priest have four parents? The Archbishop made a mental note of the names on his list took out a pencil and placed a mark beside all four.

"Four parents he muttered to himself. How can anyone have four parents?"

~

In Abdet, Maria and Felipe were almost ready to leave for Xirles. The trap was packed ready for the journey down towards the coast. As they opened the door the forlorn figure of Maria's brother José waited under the shade of the olive tree the horse was tied to. Maria knew instinctively that something was wrong. She walked over rather hesitantly faltering as she spoke. José... why aren't you working? What is wrong? You cannot be hungry so quickly?"

Jose had a tear in his eyes as he recounted how he had received notice to make his way to Albacete, the site of the nearest Republican training base.

Her brother put on a brave face and said he was sad to be leaving home yet excited by the idea of fighting for their democratically elected government against the fascists and Moors. Jose said the furthest he had ever travelled was Alicante city on the train and the idea of fighting against troops from Africa was very exotic.

Maria fought back her tears as she bid José goodbye. Felipe helped her onto the back of the trap. This couldn't be happening. She didn't want her brother fighting fascists and Moors she wanted him here, in Abdet, tending the farm, providing for the family as their father had done and his father before him. In that instant the tiny, tranquil village of Abdet had plunged into the reality of war.

~

Father Ismael was nervous, pacing the centuries old stone floor of the church like a cornered wild beast. The elderly stooped form of Señora Adela bent over her brush pushing and pulling it back and forth as she tried to reassure him the Archbishop wouldn't let him down.

"Be calm Father, he will be here soon, when the good Lord wants him here. Take a glass of something strong and take some fresh air."

Father Ismael shook his head. The last thing I need or want is alcohol Señora, have you forgotten where we are?"

The old lady grinned. "Then be off with you to the bar around the corner and take a brandy there. You'll know soon enough when the bishops arrive."

The priest shook his head. "The Archbishop Señora, an Archbishop no less."

He brushed down his cassock as he had done a hundred times that day and picked a grain of dirt from his sleeve flicking it onto the floor.

The old lady tutted. "Be off with you then and take some fresh air. You're getting under my feet and making more mess than I can sweep up."

The priest looked up at the clock suspended from the wall above the door. "Fresh air, yes. That will do I'll take a little air I think."

"And a drink too, I'll call you if I get any news," said Señora Adela.

Father Ismael had walked to the edge of the village. The sun had fallen down below the horizon and the sky had turned to a deep red. He whispered a silent prayer. *Please Lord let them come soon, we have worked so hard for this day.* He looked up into the rapidly dwindling light. Swallows swooped and dived into a copse of huge pine trees skilfully catching insects in the rapidly cooling evening air. Father Ismael was just about to turn back to the village when he heard a voice on the wind. He peered up the road and noticed the shape of a small boy tearing towards him. As he got closer he smiled. It was Aitor, his runner, the boy he'd posted several kilometres up the road earlier in the day with a more than generous lunch parcel and the promise of a few pesetas if he carried out his duty.

"They come Father, they come," he shouted as he came ever nearer. The boy was almost on his knees, sweat pouring down his face as he explained the delegation was no more than a few kilometres away.

"I ran as fast as I could Father, they are nearly with us."

The boy held out his hand in anticipation. Father Ismael ran his fingers through his unkempt hair then patted his head.

"You've done splendidly Aitor, absolutely magnificent."

He reached into his pocket and pulled out a few coins placing them into the boy's outstretched hand. "There you go Aitor, now see and spend it wisely."

"Thank you Father, thank you, I will."

Father Ismael turned and hurried back to the village taking two minutes out to settle his nerves with a large brandy in the small bar adjacent the church.

It was a stirring address full of passion. Archbishop Alfonso spoke with fluidity and emotion during the forty minutes he stood in front of the priests from the local parish's surrounding the Xirles community. Afterwards he spoke with Father Ismael in private, re-emphasising the many years work he had ahead of him if the Nationalists were to succeed in their mission to overthrow the Republican government. At first Father Ismael had been confused, well aware that many of the young men in the village had already left to sign up and defend the republic. Their mothers fathers brothers and sisters worshipped in his church every week.

"You must be forceful Father Ismael," the Archbishop explained. "I am very aware that the majority of the region is republican but the people must be re-educated. We have a job to do and you must explain that they cannot worship the Lord and fight for the republican cause also."

The Archbishop lifted his finger. "But be careful Ismael, be sensible. It will take time and you may want to tread carefully. Explain to your flock that the Nationalists aren't as bad as the propaganda paints them out. They are God fearing men sent by our Father. Remind them of the atrocities the reds have carried out against his church."

The Archbishop sighed and removed his hat. He scratched heavily at his balding pate.

"Teach them Ismael and teach them well. They may not want to hear what you have to say but if you say it loud enough and often enough then eventually it will sink in."

The Archbishop took a gentle grip on Father Ismael's sleeve. "Now my son, point me in the direction of the dinner table because even Archbishop's have to eat."

Ismael led the Archbishop and his delegation through the streets of Xirles to the house of Señora Pamela. Her house was very large and easily accommodated the half dozen tables that had been set in preparation for the grand dinner. Señora Pamela welcomed the party to her home and held out a tray of cool white wine which the religious men accepted gratefully. In a small table by the door Father Ismael noted the anxious, expectant faces of Maria and Felipe and Vicente and Fatima.

The news was not good. Felipe knew by the Archbishops face as he sat at their table after the dinner had ended. The Archbishop was red in the face and Felipe noticed that his words were a little slurred. Nevertheless he pulled no punches.

"The republicans broke down the doors and dragged the priests and their housekeeper away. Your boy Juan Francisco was one of them." The Archbishop took another mouthful of wine and swirled the liquid around his mouth. "Seville was in turmoil that night and much blood was spilled onto the streets."

"But where did they take them your holiness, surely you have some sort of record?" Maria asked.

The Archbishop shook his head. He reached across for Maria's hand and held it firmly. "I'm afraid my child you must prepare yourself for the worst."

Twenty Two

It was 4am in the morning on the 6th of August 1936 when Juan and Carmen climbed up the steep steps of the large grimy truck that was to take them and their clerical colleagues on their journey north. There were twenty priests on the truck, four armed guards, Carmen and another two middle aged ladies in waiting, devoted churchgoers and lifelong followers of the Church who had left their husbands and families behind to wait hand and foot on the men they held in such high esteem. They would talk for many hours during the long journey northwards and explain that this was their calling and they had received their instructions from God. One woman had left behind two teenage children who stood by the side of the road to wave their mother on her way. They carried small home-made flags and waved pale blue and white bunting. There were a few tears but their mother sat proud towards the rear of the truck and reminded the children how special she was to have been chosen and their family would be the toast of the town. Her husband, not so convinced, looked on from the relative shade of a nearby bar nursing a harsh local brandy in the biggest glass the bartender could give him and he wondered what on earth would become of his family unit. He wondered when, if ever, he would meet up with his wife again, took a large mouthful of brandy winced as the powerful liquid burned at the back of his throat and realised that it probably didn't matter to him as much as he thought it might. She had gained a lot more weight than he thought she would since childbirth despite the shortages of food. In fact she was beginning to look a little like her mother. Perhaps it was for the best and as she constantly reminded him, the Lord works in mysterious ways.

The Nationalist troops had been gathering for the past two days, a mix of legionnaires and Moroccan regulars, experienced men with little fear of death. It was just before first light when they started to move off, the sun still low in the sky behind them turning the city of Seville amber with its powerful shimmering rays.

After a few hours they heard the sound of the first aircraft. Little did they know at the time but it was an Italian piloted Savoia 81, and a short while later the deeper sound of the heavier German Junkers 52´s. The planes flew low in towards the convoy taking in the cheers and salutes of their comrades in arms. Juan looked up the strange logo on the side of one the planes. He had seen it before but he struggled to remember where and when. A strange symbol that sent an involuntary shiver the length of his spine, an equilateral cross with its arms bent at right angles. It was not something he had ever seen on a flag of Spain. The pilot was dressed in a Spanish Nationalist uniforms but somehow Juan knew the man had never set foot on Spanish soil in his life.

Then it came to him, he recalled his studies with the church on Buddhism and Hinduism. It was in a book that he had first set eyes on that strange symbol and hadn't somebody said that the Germans had claimed the symbol for themselves? He had heard both German and Italian voices whilst they had been in Seville. It seemed that the whole damned world wanted to take part in their war.

The move north was a rapid affair, the noise in the trucks was deafening as they advanced without opposition up the deserted dusty road, the main artery northwards. The soldiers on board the trucks explained that aircraft had been bombing the towns that were thought to be offering red resistance and they may need to 'clean' a few towns up as they ventured towards their final destination near to the Portuguese border.

The convoy snaking behind them was immense. Juan had tried to count the vehicles behind him but the back end had been lost in the dust that rose from the parched road. The soldiers seemed in good spirits, particularly the Moors whose trucks echoed to the sounds of ghostly fighting songs.

Without warning the soldiers in the trucks became edgy, some smiling nervously and the Moors haunting tunes gradually turned into a series of loud repetitive chants.

A middle aged soldier sitting opposite Juan smiled as he pointed to the truck behind them. "They are going into battle Father. That's an old Moorish war song. The Moors smell blood."

After an hour the convoy stopped at the end of a road which led to a small pueblo.

The same soldier explained that the town had been bombed and then subjected to two hours of artillery to make sure that the spirit of the town was crushed. He pointed to the Moors.

"The generals have decided to send them in to finish the village off. The Spanish soldiers or Legionnaires do not need to get involved, not unless we have to."

Juan climbed down from the truck together with a few other priests and walked over to a large group of Moors who were preparing to move off.

"Where are you going Father?" The same soldier shouted from the truck.

I am going to do my job," Juan said, "I will enable the spiritual conversion of the defeated."

The soldier laughed. "Best of luck to you Father, but I don't think you've seen these savages in action. There will be no survivors."

It was an ominous prediction and one that Juan would witness first hand. He followed the Moors into the battered village. Corpses lay by the remains of the shattered buildings, grieving family members draped over them.

Then the slaughter began. The Moors ran from house to house, a grenade through an open window before entering with their bayonets to finish of any wounded. There was no distinction between civilian or soldier, woman or child. Juan was sickened to the stomach and begged them to stop. They ignored him as the Spanish Generals looked on and did nothing.

He turned to face a group of officers. "In the name of God control them, at least tell them to spare the children."

It was as if they'd been deafened by the explosions that had rained down on the village some hours before. Two Moor soldiers were stripping the trousers from a dead male and one of them held up a large hooked knife.

"Holy Mother of God what are they doing?"

Juan started to run over to stop them but his path was blocked by a thick set Legionnaire.

"Don't get involved Father," he said. "They must have their sport and their trophies of victory."

The Moor kneeling between the legs of the corpse made a swift slash with his knife and squealed with joy as he held up a fistful of bloody matter.

The Legionnaire grimaced. "God rest his soul, the Holy Father has spared him the pain and indignity by allowing him to die. He is indeed merciful after all."

Juan wore a puzzled frown on his face. "What is it? What on earth have they done?"

"His balls," said the soldier. "They remove the testicles of their male victims."

Although Juan hadn't eaten for some time he couldn't control the involuntary spasms of his stomach as his head jerked forward and he vomited into the dust.

After the Moors had cleaned the village, the Legionnaires moved in and then it was the Priests turn to pray for the dead. It seemed everyone was dead.

Juan noticed that many of the elderly dead had smashed in mouths. He would later find out that this was the Legionnaires trademark, a consequence of inspecting for gold teeth and then removing them with the blows from a rifle butt.

As nightfall closed in the order was given to clear out.

The tail end of the convoy set up camp a few kilometres outside the village. The officers, Spanish soldiers, Moors and Legionnaires were in good spirits and a feast of victory had been prepared with several young lambs taken and slaughtered from the surrounding smallholdings and the village ransacked for wine and brandy. The troops ate and drank heavily.

Carmen walked over to the back of the truck where Juan sat silently. "You have to eat Juan; it has been many days now."

She handed him a plate with a shoulder of lamb and a large portion of bread. The smell of cooked flesh reminded him of the burning bodies in the blazing houses and yet he knew he had to eat to carry on his work and do whatever he could to stem the evil tide. He looked up at Carmen but before he could speak a ghostly apparition of a small boy seemed to appear from the smoke of the burning camp fires.

The boy spoke directly. "How could God let this take place Father?"

The boy's clothes were tattered and torn and hung to his skeletal like figure, he was no more than six years old. There were traces of blood on his bare arms and face and his dark hair matted and caked with blood.

The small child repeated his question. "How could God let my Father be killed, how could the black men do that to my mother and my sister?"

Carmen's hand covered her mouth as she took a step forward to comfort the boy realising he must be from the village.

"You look hungry child," she said. "When did you last eat?"

The boy shrugged his shoulders but remained silent staring at the priest. A lump formed in Juan's throat. Carmen pulled the boy forward and wrapped an arm around him.

"Let the Father be little boy, he needs to eat and rest."

Juan questioned the logic himself. He had witnessed the same horrors the boy had. They had acted like animals, they were worse than animals.

"Come and sit beside me," Juan said. "But if you are looking for answers I can give you none."

The child took a step forward and Juan offered a hand which he took and pulled himself up onto the truck. Juan edged along in the seat and the boy sat down.

"Share some bread and meat with me."

The boy shook his head. "I have no hunger."

Juan slid the plate away from them. "Me either."

"My mother was a good woman," said the boy. "She helped at the church and went to Mass each week. Me too, and I helped with Father Roberto's vegetable garden and took confession regularly and I am a good boy and Father Roberto told my all the time—"

The first tears fell to the floor. "I liked Father Roberto but the townsfolk made him leave, they said he wasn't welcome anymore."

"Did they harm him?" Asked Juan.

"No, they just asked him to go; my mother gave him a parcel of food for his journey."

Juan shook his head. He suspected Father Roberto had fared better than some priests; at least he'd escaped with his life.

"Were we punished for running Father Roberto out of town? Did God punish us for that?"

Juan was shaking his head. "No child." He played the priests ultimate trump card.

"The Lord acts in mysterious ways but he is not evil, he wouldn't -

The boy interrupted. "But father Roberto said he would, father Roberto said he would send us to hell if we—"

Juan pulled the boy into him and slipped an arm round his shoulder to comfort him.

"What is your name boy?"

"They call me Kiko."

"And how old are you?"

"I have six years."

"You must have faith Kiko, God is a man of love and good deeds and wonderful things."

Even as he uttered the words he knew how empty and meaningless they must have sounded to the boy. He'd prided himself on his ability to convince from the pulpit and he'd believed everything he'd ever said until this dreadful day. What on earth had the poor child witnessed? What horrors would be with him until the day he died and yes, he had to ask the question himself, why had God let it happen? Why had God let those men torture and mutilate and rape?

Kiko buried his head into Juan's chest and cried again. He sobbed like a baby, he sobbed like a small boy who had witnessed the blazing inferno of hell and came face to face with the devil. After an hour of uncontrollable crying he fell into a fitful sleep. Juan and Carmen talked while the boy slept.

"We have to take him with us, he has no one left," Carmen said. "If the Moors find out he's a survivor from the village, they'll surely kill him."

Juan was in full agreement but how would they explain his presence to the officers. Juan placed his hands together and looked up to the heavens. He closed his eyes and prayed. After a few moments he spoke.

"We'll move to a different truck and if anyone questions us we'll claim he's been with us since we left Seville. We'll tell them he's your nephew and his parents were killed by the Republicans."

Carmen frowned. "Do you think it will work?"

Juan shrugged his shoulders. "I don't know, but it's the only hope he's got. If we leave him here the tail-enders will finish him off. Either that or he'll starve to death. Our convoy has destroyed his village. They've ransacked and looted everything, poisoned every well and dead bodies have been left rotting in the street. Before long his village will be riddled with disease."

Carmen stroked the boys head. "Let him sleep." She opened up the bread and filled it with meat. "And you Juan, you must eat and get strong. Tomorrow you have a lot of things to think about and you won't be able to do that on an empty stomach."

Reluctantly, Juan took the bread and bit into the crust. Carmen was right... as always. He managed three or four mouthfuls before pushing the unfinished sandwich into his satchel. He lifted young Kiko into his arms, kissed him on the crown of the head and turned to Carmen. "Come, let us find another truck."

It was four days later when they arrived at the approaches of the city of Mérida. They had been challenged about the boy only once, by one of the older priests. Juan had joked with him that his old brain was wearing out and that the boy had been with Carmen all along. The old Priest had relented and even said he'd remembered talking to the boy back in Seville. "My memory is deserting me Father Juan, I'm sorry." he said, tapping at the side of his temple.

~

"I will not give up hope, no matter what the Archbishop thinks."

Maria and Felipe were back in Abdet making plans for the wedding of Mar but as much as Maria had thrown herself into the preparations her mind was only on one thing- her son and his whereabouts.

"I need to write him a letter, Felipe. I need to tell him we still believe. I need to write to him as if there is nothing wrong as if we hadn't heard the words that came from the Archbishop's mouth."

Felipe was studying the latest accounts from the bodega in Algeria and Mohammed's report. He pushed them to one side as he spoke. "It's not quite as easy as that Maria. Even before the war the Postal Service was at best, very bad. We were lucky if one in three letters ever reached Juan and now the military has more or less taken over the postal infrastructure and they have more important things to busy themselves with. Personal letters from a mother to her son are cast to one side and it has been at least three months since we have had anything from Juan."

Maria stood and walked through to the kitchen picking up a cloth in a half-hearted attempt to clean up. Felipe followed her.

"There is however one person who may be able to get a letter into Seville."

Maria turned around and looked at her husband, a puzzled look etched across her face.

"You have forgotten about *The Carrier* my dear haven't you?"

Maria's face lit up as she beamed a huge smile and took a step forward. "I had Felipe, I had forgotten all about him. Do you think he still lives?"

Felipe kissed his wife tenderly on the lips. "Of course he still lives silly, who do you think delivers this correspondence between me and Mohammed?"

Felipe scratched at the side of his head. "The man is not cheap I can assure you and I confess his work has slowed up considerably because of the war." He walked back through into the sitting room and began scribbling on a piece of paper. "But if anyone can get a letter to our son then it is him."

∼

The convoy set up another temporary camp. The news coming from the advance party was that the republicans had had enough of retreating and for once had set up a strongly defended position south of the city. Within a few hours Juan heard the distant drone of aircraft.

He looked at Carmen and spoke. "Something tells me this war is a little one sided. The Republicans are on a hiding to nothing."

Soon after the bombers and fighters started their onslaught of Mérida. For hours they pounded the ancient Roman city that came into existence twenty five years before the birth of Christ. The 75mm guns added to the hell that the defenders suffered. Hopelessly outnumbered and woefully under equipped they fought on, suffering horrendous losses. Gradually though they fell back, losing ground to the more experienced troops of the Nationalists. The fighting raged on for most of the day and then the city fell silent. Juan and the other priests were led into a narrow street at the entrance of the city by one of the Nationalist officers and allocated an abandoned house.

"Pick your room," said one of the priests. "Hopefully we will be able to rest here for a few days."

Juan wanted to take comfort from the fact he had a room with a wash basin and a large bed. It would make a welcome change to be able to wash and sleep in a proper bed but all he could think of was the poor souls in Mérida, dead and dying and now suffering at the hands of the Nationalist troops, Moors and Legionnaires.

He placed his bible on the bed, dropped his bag onto the floor and went to look for Carmen and Kiko.

He found them sitting on the back of a truck. Juan had already prepared his story, a huge lie, in order to take Carmen and Kiko into the relative safety of the abandoned house. He frowned as he started to formulate the words in his head. For twenty five years he'd worked hard on his spiritual self, played the promise and truth games with God and refrained from telling lies no matter how insignificant or small they'd been. Over the last few days he'd lied like there was no tomorrow, as if his life depended on it. Ironic he thought... it probably did.

Two nationalist soldiers stood at the rear of the truck with their rifles slung across their shoulders. As Juan approached they came to attention as a mark of respect. Juan bit his lip and spoke a little bit louder than he was normally used to.

"I've come for the girl and the boy, they are needed at the priest's house. One of the soldiers looked a little puzzled and Juan spoke before he could gather his thoughts.

"Are you both stupid? She is the priest's keeper and we need her to prepare our food. Now help her down and the boy too, we all very hungry."

Without hesitation one of the soldiers unfastened the tailgate on the back of the truck and helped Carmen out. The other soldier beckoned the boy to come forward and lifted him onto the ground. On the way to the outskirts of the city Juan explained his plan to Carmen.

He was determined that Carmen and the boy would spend the next few evenings with him so he could watch over them. Carmen had seemed a little unsure as she entered the house, conscious perhaps of what had happened the last time that they had been under the same roof together. Kiko held her hand in a vice like grip as Juan showed them to his room. A large table sat in the corner of the room and Juan pointed to it.

"I will bring some provisions and you can prepare some food. As long as the priests' bellies are full they will not question me. I will try and find some wine too and with a bit of luck they will all be sleeping before we are."

Carmen seemed to shake her head in surprise as she suddenly realised what Juan had in mind. Before she could object he spoke.

"I will not have you and Kiko sleeping out there when there is so much murder, rape and torture in the minds of every man who walks the streets. You will be safe here and I won't hear another word."

"But Juan," Carmen objected, "I can't sleep in the same room as a priest, word will get out and they'll excommunicate you and then where will we go?"

"I've already thought of that." He said. "I will tell the other priests that you are my cousin, we are related by blood. I will make up another bed in the corner of the room and I will sleep there. You and Kiko can have the big bed."

Despite Carmen's protestations, Juan made his way into the city just as nightfall settled in. It was in ruins, hardly a building had escaped the onslaught of the bombers and artillery and many were still on fire. The men under the Nationalists charge had finished their gruesome deeds and stood in groups talking and boasting about their exploits in ridding the city of its red population.

They ate and drank the stolen spoils of Mérida. It was yet another victory feast and it seemed there was no one strong enough or well organised enough to stop them. Juan asked one of the soldiers where the delegations of priests were and where he could get food for them. The soldier pointed him in the direction of the church.

"The Priests are nearly finished their work Father, there aren't many reds left. A few of them have joined the cause and are being blessed as we speak."

Another soldier wheeled a small handcart in front of Juan. "Take this Father and pile it up with whatever you require. Two streets behind the church there is a storeroom with shoulders of ham and pots of beans. That should fill your bellies tonight."

"Thank you. One other thing."

"Yes Father."

"Do you know where I can find any wine?"

The soldier grinned. "I must say Father, you men of the cloth have a taste for the fine things in life."

Juan winked. "If it was good enough for Jesus my son, it's good enough for his servants."

The soldier told Juan to wait awhile and five minutes later he returned with a wooden crate which he loaded onto the handcart. "That should keep you going for a few nights Father, Mérida's finest."

Juan collected the food for the priests within twenty minutes, his priests clothing gained him access to all areas. He passed groups of legionnaires loading dead bodies onto trucks and one of them informed him they were taking them to the outskirts of the city where they would be buried in mass graves. The scale of killing was on a different level to that of the small village they'd ransacked a few days earlier. This was well-organised and planned.

Juan trudged silently up the main street and made his way back to the church. The other priests were pleased to see him and welcomed him with handshakes. Some of them were actually smiling and seemed to rejoice in their increased level of importance. A priest he recognised from a district of Seville rushed forward to greet him as he spotted the cart laden with goods.

"Ah I see you have been hard at work young Juan. God bless you my son.

Juan bit his tongue and started to act. "I'm sorry I couldn't help you today. I thought I would be more useful helping my cousin prepare the evening meal.

"Your cousin Juan?"

"Yes. The girl Carmen. You remember her, the housekeeper from Seville?"

"Ah yes, the pretty one."

Juan wagged his finger. "Father please... as a priest you should not think like that."

The priest placed his hands together and bowed his head. "You are right Juan, I should remember my place and my vows but I confess, surely it is the Lord's work that we priests can look and marvel at such perfection which our maker has created."

A few of the other priests laughed as they turned to Juan awaiting his reply.

"As long as you just look, I can find no harm in that. Now, enough of this nonsense I have a dinner to prepare, you must all be famished?"

"That we are Juan," said the priest, "that we are."

Juan walked over to the handcart and grasped it. He turned to face the priests.

"I forgot to tell you," he said, digging into the box that held the wine. He slowly teased a bottle into view. "I managed to salvage a little grape juice too. That should help to wash things down."

The priests returned to the house within a couple of hours. They looked exhausted and bore the traces of a harrowing days' work. They ate and talked long into the night. They talked nonsense at times but always with a sincere belief that what they were doing was right and Juan refrained from voicing his opinions. Carmen fussed around the table as she'd always done and the other priests slowly but surely accepted her presence as she refilled their cups and plates at regular intervals. Shortly after midnight Juan's drink loosened companions started to drift or stagger to their rooms and soon their gentle snores echoed through the bare building. Before long, just Juan and Carmen sat at the table.

Carmen sighed. "I suppose I'd better tidy this up. They'll be out of their beds in a few hours and will be wanting their bellies filled again."

Juan stood to help but she waved him away.

"Go and see how Kiko is and I'll be through soon."

Juan nodded. He'd almost forgotten about the little boy who'd been asleep for several hours. As Juan walked through to the bedroom the little boy stirred. He opened his eyes for a split second, caught sight of Juan then closed them again. Juan was amazed. It was only a few days ago that he'd seen his family massacred and yet he'd taken to Juan and Carmen as if he'd known them all his life. What was going on in his little head, what scars would he carry through into adulthood and how would that affect him for the rest of his life?

Juan sat on the bed and stroked his hair. He leaned forward and kissed him gently on the cheek. "You will survive and you will prosper boy," he said. "I will see to it. I promise you."

The door to the bedroom creaked behind him and Carmen walked through. Juan turned to face her, drank in her natural body scent, her face, her beautiful form and for a second he longed to take her in his arms. He fought the temptation. She had been lucky to survive this dreadful war once and if anyone had believed Pepe in the square back in Seville she may not have been the only one to have been placed in front of the firing squad.

It was a test he convinced himself. "Yet another test from the Lord," he muttered under his breath. "Why do you have to test me so much? I have witnessed the rape and the torture and killings and the evil things men do and surely I have responded the way you would have wished? Let it come to an end dear Lord. End it soon I beg of you."

"What?" Carmen asked.

"Nothing," Juan replied. "I was just praying."

"Again?"

"Yes... again Carmen."

She removed her shawl and placed it on the end of the bed. "And you think he hears you, this God of ours."

Juan stood and approached her. He placed his hands on her shoulders. "I know he hears me Carmen, I know it. You must believe, you must retain your faith."

Carmen nodded. "I do Juan, I do, but I confess I have some bad days."

"Me too Carmen, believe me, me too."

Carmen looked over to young Kiko lying on the bed fast asleep once again.

"And his parents Juan?" She said. "They believed too. You heard the boy with your own ears, they were good churchgoing people. How can you tell him now that our God is the great protector?"

Juan opened his mouth to defend his belief but Carmen took a step forward and pressed her fingers to his mouth. "Enough priest, I have heard enough claptrap these last few days to last me a lifetime." She pointed to the roughly made up bed in the corner of the room.

"Take to your bed and stay there. Don't even think of coming anywhere near me. I will lie with the child and God forbid I hope he allows us to see the morn."

Juan had another restless night. He was almost getting used to them, sleeping for an hour or two, waking, thinking and then drifting off again. It was the first stirrings of the birds that woke him. Juan stood and stretched, groaning as his vertebrae protested loudly. He walked over to the bed and looked at Carmen and Kiko in the semi darkness. The chill of the early morning air encircled the room and he replaced a blanket that had fallen to the floor in the middle of the night. Carmen let out an appreciative moan as she gripped it unconsciously and pulled it to her chin. For a minute or two Juan froze, unable to prise his eyes from her elegant face. What had he done to her? What was going on in that beautiful head of hers, a head that he had corrupted? Her rebuff of him last night had been clear. Stay away from me she had said.

She couldn't have been clearer. His actions had nearly cost Carmen, her life. And even now, right at this moment in time he wanted to reach out to her and hold her, caress her, make love to her. He was disturbed by a gentle knock at the door.

It was Father Satur, the eldest of the priests in the house. "I wondered if you were awake Juan? You were looking a little troubled last night, I wondered if you wanted to take an early stroll and tell me what's on your mind."

The old man lingered in the doorway, occasionally peering over Juan's shoulder, looking into the room.

Juan pushed the door wide open. "Is your curiosity getting the better of you Satur, you are wondering if my cousin has taken to my bed?"

"No, no, the priest protested. I...I..."

"There," Juan pointed. "There is my bed in the corner and the girl sleeps with her nephew."

"No Juan I just—"

"Walk in, feel my bed, you will see that it is still warm."

Juan reached for his collar and pulled the priest through the doorway but he resisted.

"No Juan you read me wrong, unhand me at once. You are paranoid man, paranoid." The priest dusted himself down and Juan wondered whether he had read the situation wrongly.

The priest reached out and took Juan's sleeve. "Come," he said forcefully. "Come with me now and walk I beg you."

It was sometime before Father Satur spoke. They had walked to the boundary walls of the city but not ventured in. Father Satur guided Juan to a seat under a mimosa tree and they sat down.

"You were right Juan, I was more than a little curious. I confess I'm a nosy old pig these days."

Juan's jaw almost hit the ground as Father Satur continued. "I've seen the way the girl looks at you. She may be your cousin but her feelings are deeper than family blood and you will do well to resist her."

Juan protested Carmen's innocence at once. "You are wrong Satur, you are wrong, there is nothing further from the truth I would have sensed it by now, we have known each other since we were children."

Satur wagged his finger and laughed. "God made all men equal Juan, even priests. You don't think for one minute he made us different to the next man or the animals in the forest. God made man so that he would reproduce and the act of love is sent from heaven itself."

"You have experienced it Father?" Juan said with a cheeky grin.

Satur hesitated, stuttered a little. "Not at all Juan, not at all but I'm not going to tell you that I haven't been tempted. You will undergo many temptations of a sexual nature during your priesthood but you must be strong and resist, the Lord needs you Juan, you are a good priest, an honourable man and you have much work to do."

"Is that why you brought me here Father?"

Satur was nodding. "Among other things. I'm telling you that you're putting temptation in the way by sleeping in the same room as the girl and tongues are wagging."

Juan shook his head. "I've slept in the same room as Carmen since we were a few weeks old and I won't stop doing so, I won't put her in danger because a few tongues are on the loose. These are dangerous times and I need to protect her."

"Fear not, said the old priest. "I will set the record straight with our companions and make sure their mouths do not run away with themselves. I have seen enough to know you tell the truth. These are dangerous times indeed, it seems a man needs little reason to accuse and kill." Satur stood. "Anyway you do not have to worry for the next few days because we are on the road again."

"I don't understand," said Juan, "I thought we were resting for a few days before we head for Madrid."

"Not now Juan. We leave after breakfast for a place called Badajoz."

"Badajoz. Where's that?" He asked.

Satur tipped his head to one side as he puckered his lips. "I'm not sure exactly but the General said it's quite close to the Portuguese border.

Twenty Three

Juan explained the Nationalist strategy to Carmen that evening after dinner.

"Badajoz?" She asked. "Why Badajoz?"

Juan shrugged his shoulders as young Kiko snuggled into him and closed his eyes. Juan stroked the boy's hair as more emotions coursed through him, this time emotions of a paternal nature and curiosity. In just a few days he had grown so fond of the child, and although he tried to fight his ever stronger feelings for Carmen he knew it was a battle he was destined to lose. At times he loathed the hypocrites within his church and wanted to be free of the shackles that almost mapped his life out for him. *Be a free thinker*, his father had once said to him when they were discussing the ways of the church and their teaching. At the time he didn't know what his father meant but now it was becoming ever clearer.

"Badajoz?" Carmen repeated bringing him back to the present. "What of Badajoz and what will we be doing there?"

"The area is a Nationalist stronghold now I'm told," he said. "All territory to the west of Merida is now isolated from the rest of Spain but there are many Republican sympathisers in Badajoz and they are holding on to their city well. One of the priests told me we have much work to do there."

"Pah!" Carmen said with a look of disgust. "You mean we must rid the city of them, bless them before they are shot against the wall like the countless others in the villages and towns we have passed through?"

Juan nodded his head. He had no answer. He simply repeated what one of the officers had told him the previous night.

"The area a few hundred kilometres above Badajoz is the place where General Mola´s troops started the uprising in the North of Spain. He has met up with the troops led by General Yagüe from the South and it's just a matter of time before Badajoz falls." He wiped a tear from the corner of his eye. "There is no doubt that our country is now split in two Carmen and there's nothing we can do about it."

Juan inched his chair forward so that he was no more than a few feet from where Carmen sat. He spoke in a whisper. "Remember back in Seville when you said this madness would blow over quickly?"

Carmen nodded.

"Forget it Carmen, this war is here to stay, for months, maybe even for years." He stood, handed the sleeping child to Carmen as he began to pace the room. "It could have been stopped I'm sure of it but it's as if some outside force wanted it to continue and escalate."

"The Church?" Carmen gasped almost apologetically.

Juan looked over and gave a half smile. "No Carmen, it was not the Church who started this bloody outrage." He pinched hard at the bridge of his nose and screwed his eyes tight shut. It was at least a minute before he opened his eyes and spoke to her. "But let's just say they didn't exactly bend over backwards to try and stop it."

"Cortes, Juan Cortes. Yes young man I am speaking to you. When I speak you listen, when I speak the whole world listens."

"Yes Father."

"I made the sun and the moon and the oceans and seas, I built the mountains and gave you light and the heat from the sun so you can grow your crops and eat and I put animals in the fields to give you milk and meat and fur so that you may stay warm in the winter.

"Yes Father."

"And you doubt me? Still you doubt my power."

"No father I don't it's just-"

"Silence do you hear?"

"Yes Father."

"I control the winds and the rain and the snow and lightning too, I can send hurricane's and floods and famine, disease and misery on any nation I want. I control it all and I can even control your thoughts. I am looking at you Juan Francisco Cortes and you displease me. You displease me greatly because you doubt me."

"No father I don't."

"Don't lie to me Juan Francisco Cortes, I can read your mind and you must be punished."

His head was fully visible through the clouds now, he had a huge beard and piercing blue eyes and as he spoke tiny flames licked from his mouth. A hand appeared holding a huge cross which he threw from the cloud and it landed on the ground beside him.

"Do you know what it is like to be nailed to a cross Cortes and left to die? My son does.

He died for you priest do you know that?"

"Yes father, I believe I truly do."

"You are lying Francisco Cortes."

Before Juan could answer the soldiers appeared grabbing him roughly. One of them struck him violently in the face and he begged for mercy. Another of them produced a large hammer and pushed him backwards onto the cross. There were soldiers everywhere now they were like giant ants as they grabbed his arms and legs and placed them into position. The soldier with the hammer hovered over him. In the other hand he held three rusty nails dripping with blood. "Forgive me Father," he said to Juan. "I know not what it is I do."

Juan awoke bathed in sweat.

There was a deathly silence in the truck as Juan's party of priests joined the force of Nationalists on the 60km trip west to Badajoz.

The following morning the priest's truck stopped on a vantage point overlooking the medieval city two kilometres away. It was the morning of the 14th of August 1936 and Juan and Carmen watched in horror as wave after wave of aeroplanes started their bombardment.

"Viva Italia," one of the other priests shouted with glee and when Juan asked him what he meant he explained that the Italian aircraft were part of an International effort supporting the Nationalist forces.

"It seems God and the entire world is on our side," he whispered quietly.

The town had a medieval wall and gates and were no match for the bombs and artillery of the attackers as they opened up holes as though the stonework was made of cardboard.

After several hours the combined Nationalist forces poured through the breaches in an advancing tide of death and destruction. Soon after the priests were moved towards the broken city walls and told to prepare for duty. At least Carmen and Kiko were out of danger Juan thought. They were back at the area known as *la comedor*, the dining room. Carmen and her colleagues were to prepare a feast for the soldiers on their return.

Juan and the other priests were instructed to make their way to the town and immediately took stock of the horrendous slaughter that had taken place there. He could hear gunshots and explosions deep within the city as still more soldiers streamed in. Machine gun fire and screaming filled the air; it was like a hell on earth as he stepped over the bodies of dead Republicans and their families. There were even dead on the steps around the altar of the Cathedral in the ironically named Plaza de la Republica. Large groups of people with their hands held in the air were being herded by Legionnaires and Guardia Civil forces, towards the centre of the town. Juan took the sleeve of a Guardia Civil officer. "Where are you taking them, what is happening?"

The officer's tunic was stained with blood, his face encrusted with dirt. "Father," he said, "we are taking them to the bull ring."

"Why," Juan asked in desperation. "Why are you taking them there?"

The officer just shrugged his shoulders. "I know not Father, I am simply following orders and they are to be held there until further notice."

Two Legionaries were stripping the shirt from a young man no more than eighteen years of age. He had a white handkerchief tied to his arm. Juan rushed over to where they stood.

"What are you doing?" He asked. "He carries the white flag of surrender, let him go."

The tallest of the Legionnaires shouted at Juan that it was none of his business but his colleague offered an explanation.

"See here Father." The Legionnaire pointed at the youths shoulder. "He claims he was not one of the shooters positioned on the city walls but we know different. His gun has left a black mark, a bruise on his shoulder. He is lying."

The youths face showed he was resigned to his fate, a terrified and hopeless look, drained of all colour.

"Be off with you priest or you will be next," shouted the tall Legionnaire. The youth was pushed into the throng of wretched souls being forced along the street and Juan rushed ahead to the bullring to see what he could do. As he rushed along some of the people desperately tried to grab at his robes as though they would provide some sort of talisman against death. It was not to be.

As they reached the outer walls of the bullring the sound of gunfire was almost deafening. Upon entering the Plaza de Toros he realised it was being used not as an area to hold prisoners but to execute them. There were piles of bodies everywhere and people being machine gunned en masse. As the prisoners entered the bull ring they realised what was happening. Some tried to run, others pleaded and some prayed. A few died with their heads held high insulting everyone from Franco to the Virgin Mary but it didn't matter, they all died the same.

The gun barrels of the Guardia Civil began to glow red as more and more groups of people continued to arrive. Juan ran around pleading with anyone who he thought would listen and sought out high ranking officers and begged them to stop the massacre. It was futile. Even his fellow priests seemed to ignore him. He ran to one man giving the command to open fire.

"Please, I beg you, please stop this madness they do not deserve this.

The officer held his hand up and the soldiers lowered their rifles temporarily in a moment of confusion. He took Juan by the arm and led him into a quiet corner beside the bull pens which were crammed with even more prisoners.

"Oh they deserve it father don't you worry about that. They will be killed but at least it will be quick. In July at the height of the rebellion these same bastards locked fifty six Nationalist in a church not far from here and set it on fire"

"But I... don't believe..."

"Oh you had better believe it Father and you'd better believe the other atrocities you'll hear about too." The officer turned to walk away and paused for a second. "So don't come in here and try to tell me my job. Take your bible and say a few prayers for them because that's all they're going to get by way of sympathy or mercy."

Before Juan could offer a response the officer was gone. Several seconds later he heard his voice bark out a command and another volley of gunfire echoed around the bullring.

Juan trudged out of the bullring in the direction of the Cathedral and as he sought out the relative sanctity of the imposing religious building he sank to his knees and prayed. He prayed long and hard. He prayed like he'd never prayed before.

Eventually darkness came and the guns fell silent.

Juan raised himself to his feet. As he walked from the Cathedral the clean-up operation was under way. Prisoners were pushing carts piled high with bodies. Behind them a small truck laden with petrol cans followed on behind. The air was permeated with a stench like he'd never smelled before as plumes of smoke drifted across the city. He pulled a handkerchief up to his face and hurried back to the *comedor* anxious to find Carmen and the boy.

The *comedor* was a rough field mess set up on the banks of the river close to the Roman Bridge. Once again the spoils of battle supplied the victors with ample food and drink. There were two dozen so priests sat around a rough wooden table, the centre point a large suckling pig which they carved individually. Carmen and another lady brought bread and fresh vegetables, fruit and of course copious supplies of wine.

Juan lowered himself into a seat but was unable to pass a morsel over his lips.

Satur spoke. "What is it Juan, aren't you hungry?"

Another priest spoke up. "You had better get used to it Juan, there are many more Reds to do away with before our job is done."

Juan looked down at the table and rested his head in his hands shaking his head and sighing.

The other priest continued. "I do not like your attitude father Juan. You are turning your nose up at the good food the Lord has provided and at times you are almost hostile towards us."

Juan looked across the table at where he sat. "Hostile? No brother. I have no hostility towards my fellow man but I wish the same could be said for others."

"What do you mean?" The priest asked.

Juan looked around the table then back to the priest who had confronted him.

"Did you have your eyes closed today brother, did you not see the massacre taking place within these city walls, men women and children systematically murdered in cold blood?" He let out a loud laugh. "Hah I fear the good Lord has struck you blind Brother Simone or was it a mirage you witnessed today?"

The table had fallen silent apart from Brother Simone who raised himself to his feet and slammed a cup on the table. "We are getting tired of you Juan, just who do you think you are? They deserved it; you have heard of the massacre in the church of Fuente de Cantos in July?"

"Oh yes," said Juan. I have heard that a score of people were burned in the church by the Republicans but does that give us the right to slaughter thousands in return including women and children, young boys and girls who have known nothing of life or understand any politics? I saw the Moors dragging away a young girl, she was just a child and judging by the looks on their faces there was only one thing they had in mind. It sickens and saddens me that God made some men this way."

Satur sliced a corner of pork from the pig and ripped off a mouthful as he chewed.

"You do not need to worry about those savages and heathens now Juan, they are gone. General Yagüe has sent them on their way. But just be glad they are on our side because I wouldn't want to cross them."

Juan stood and made to leave the table. He reached for a cup of wine and took a large mouthful.

"Are you not sitting with us?" asked Simone.

Juan replenished his glass from a bottle. "No Simone, I am not hungry. The scorched flesh of the pig reminds me of the burning bodies I smelled earlier today. I have not the stomach to eat tonight."

"Then take a little bread with your wine because I fear it will go to your head."

"I certainly hope so Brother Simone, I certainly hope so and if it does perhaps I will sleep without nightmares."

Juan reached for the bottle on the table, placed the cork in the neck and pushed it deep into his pocket. "I bid you good night." He looked at the table. "You have plenty of bottles to drink your fill so I hope you don't mind if I take this one to my bed?"

Satur raised his glass. "Not at all Juan."

As Juan walked away, Carmen followed closely behind.

When he was out of earshot Simone turned. "Your friend needs to watch his tongue Satur. His big mouth will no doubt get him into some serious trouble." He took a large mouthful of wine. "And the girl Carmen, I fear she could cause him a little problem too."

Carmen was furious. "They are killing people for far less, you must not criticise their deeds so openly."

"You approve of them Carmen?"

"No of course I don't, but I know when to seal my lips."

Juan threw his cup into the bushes and took a mouthful of wine straight from the bottle, wiped his lips and spoke. "You didn't see what I saw today Carmen. There are times when a man cannot keep his mouth closed."

Juan's eyes filled with tears as he drank again. "They murder in cold blood. There were no trials and no mercy, they shot them where they stood and when they were finished they took their corpses to the Cemetery covered them in petrol and burned the flesh from their bones."

Juan flopped to the floor and wrapped his rough woolen blanket around his shoulders. He leaned over and stroked the hair of Kiko who lay fast asleep on the ground.

"Small boys and small girls, Carmen, it mattered not, they shot and burned them just the same."

Carmen lowered herself on to the ground and took his hand. "I cannot imagine what it is you have seen today Juan, but now it's all about survival."

The first of Juan's tears fell onto his cheeks. "I'm not sure I want to survive this hell Carmen, I'm not sure I want to be a priest and be a part of this anymore. For many weeks now they've asked me to comfort those wretched souls and send them to meet their maker with peace in their hearts. But I look into their eyes Carmen and I see their fear, I feel their fear and my church stands by and does nothing."

Carmen squeezed his hand and wiped the tears that were now streaming down his face. "They are going to a better place Juan."

He was nodding. "I agree. I do not care for this life anymore; I fear there is nothing left to live for."

Carmen gave a wry smile.

The look did not go unnoticed with Juan. "What is it? Why do you mock me?

"I do not mock you Juan but I fear you are deluding yourself." She said.

"How... why?"

"You say you have nothing to live for and yet you stroke the hair of a boy who looks on you as his father. You see that he has a warm bed each night and food in his belly each day and I have seen the way you look at him."

Juan took a handkerchief from his pocket and wiped at his face for several seconds.

"That much is true, I have grown very fond of the boy."

"Then you owe it to him to protect him and see him through this nightmare. Whatever you have seen is bad but it is nothing compared to what his little eyes have witnessed."

Juan sat in silence staring at the small bundle wrapped up in his blanket, snoring softly while Carmen continued.

"And what of me Juan, do I count for nothing? Have the feelings you expressed for me as we made love disappeared now?"

Juan looked up. "What do you mean?"

"You declared that you loved me many times when we were in the throes of passion. Did you mean it Juan, did you truly mean it?

Juan lowered his head and spoke in a whisper. "I did Carmen, I truly did but that night as we slept in the same room you told me to take to my bed and not come near you. Your words tore away yet another piece of my heart."

Carmen edged near to him so that their lips were centimeters apart. "You stupid, stupid man. Did you think I didn't want you, do you know what your touch does to me and how it makes me feel?"

"But I.. We—"

"If we'd been caught we would have surely been shot and I have noticed the way that Father Satur has been watching us. He is not to be trusted Juan nor is Simone."

Juan nodded. "I know, I know for sure." He leaned forward and gave Carmen a gentle kiss on the lips. She responded before breaking the embrace and looking around.

"I know it is dark Juan but we must be careful. My darling, I wish I could give you more but the day will come when I will be able to take you into my bed each night and not worry about who is watching."

Juan shrugged his shoulders. "But how can that happen Carmen?"

"Because we will make it happen my love. You have many difficult decisions ahead of you and I suspect that one day you will even consider leaving the church. But it matters not if you don't because I will become your housekeeper and we will live as man and wife regardless... in secret if need be."

Juan was shaking his head. "But that is not right, is not possible."

Carmen was laughing now. "Oh you are so naïve Juan. Look how many priests have a housekeeper. Do you think that they all just bake cakes and clean the house?"

"You cannot be serious?"

"Oh I am serious Juan. We women gossip and I know for sure that Father Satur took in the daughter of the local mayor back in Seville. Her family was so proud that she'd been chosen to serve the church."

"Go on." Said Juan.

"Her grandmother came to confession one day and couldn't find the priest. She took it on herself to wander through the vestry and into the kitchen of Satur's house. She entered without knocking and the poor girl was bent over the kitchen table with her skirts around her hips."

Carmen could hardly stop giggling. "Father Satur was behind her with his cassock lifted up over his head thrusting at her for all he was worth. He didn't even see the grandmother and didn't know she was there until she took her stick to his bare arse."

Carmen's laughter was infectious as Juan pictured the extraordinary scene in his head.

"What happened?" He asked in fits of laughter.

Carmen composed herself. "She told the Mayor and Father Satur was ran out of town as fast as his legs would carry him."

"But this is so wrong," said Juan. "Father Satur is still a priest, why?

Carmen edged a little closer to Juan and whispered. "The Church simply moved him on."

"He wasn't defrocked?"

Carmen shook her head. "Of course not, the church isn't stupid and they are well aware of the natural urges of mankind. Just because you wear a collar and a black frock doesn't mean you can change nature. Satur is a good priest and the church knows that. He'd have had a stern lecture and told to be more careful that's all."

Juan was absolutely speechless. Carmen gave him a little kiss on the cheek, her voice grew lower and more intimate. "So my lover, you have some decisions to make. But know this. Whatever conclusion you come to I'll be by your side forever. That is if you want me."

Juan turned and kissed her. "I want you Carmen I truly do. I've never been more certain of anything in my entire life."

Twenty Four

"Why do you look at me with that stupid grin on your face? Asked Father Satur. "I swear you have the look of an imbecile this morning."

"It's nothing," said Juan, "I've just been sharing a small joke with Carmen."

Satur frowned. "Well, it's nice to see you with a smile on your face for a change Juan. I haven't seen that for a while."

"No Satur."

Satur pulled out a seat at the table and beckoned Juan to sit down. "Take a little breakfast Juan, you have a long hard day ahead of you."

"I have?"

Satur nodded. Juan did not like the look on his face, an apologetic almost sympathetic look. He did not have to wait long to find out why.

"A messenger of General Yagüe has been over here first thing this morning. He wishes to take mass this morning."

"To clear his conscience no doubt."

Satur looked up as he tore a piece of bread and pushed it into his mouth. He chewed slowly as he glared at Juan. "That may be the case but you'd be well placed to bite your tongue young man."

"And why would that be?"

"Because my friend, General Yagüe has asked Juan Francisco Cortes to take the service."

Carmen was more than a little concerned. "General Yagüe has a fearsome reputation Juan. He was directly responsible for giving the orders to kill the Republicans in the bull ring."

Juan sat on the grass beside the river bank as the warm summer sun made an appearance through the battlements of the ancient city walls. He mopped his brow as the first beads of sweat formed.

"What do you think he wants?" Asked Carmen.

Juan raised an eyebrow. "Who knows? Absolution? Forgiveness?" And then he grinned. "But he is more likely to want to pick a fight. As you said last night my big mouth tends to run away with me at times."

Carmen frowned, her brow furrowed as a look of worry pulled across her face.

"You must be careful Juan, tell him what he wants to hear, tell him you are sorry, tell him anything but be careful please I beg you."

Juan stretched out on the grass and pulled his hands behind his head as he lay back. "I will be careful my love. I owe it to you and Kiko to get us all through this horror we have stumbled upon, but I will not tell him what he wants to hear. I will remind him of the Ten Commandments and of the teachings of Jesus Christ. He needs to know what he is doing is wrong and he must repent and change his ways."

Carmen jumped to her feet. "You will not Juan, do not be so stupid, a man like him will never—"

"He will Carmen, he will change or this war could go on forever. Of course man can change, of course we can evolve and improve and stop behaving like animals and I will ensure he sees sense or at the very least gets a piece of my mind."

Carmen took his hands in hers. "Don't desert me Juan Cortes, I command you, don't desert me at this time. I have waited many years to find love and I don't want to lose you. You are a strong willed man I know, but there are times when a tongue needs to be bitten. After your meeting with the general come back to me. Come back to me Juan Cortes, come back in one piece I beg this of you."

Juan stood and held her. He kissed her on the lips.

Carmen looked around. "Juan, it is daylight, be careful what you are doing with me."

He spoke. "I will come back to you Carmen for I feel it is the will of God, it is written in the stars that we will be together for a long long time."

Juan looked around. He noticed Satur standing by the river back casting an occasional look over his shoulder.

"As for worrying about what people think or what they say behind my back then I'm afraid I am beyond caring."

He kissed her again. Long and hard and she responded to him as they wrapped their arms around each other. As he walked away he made a beeline towards Father Satur. He grinned as he passed him. "A wonderful thing a housekeeper Satur, don't you think? I'm going to take Carmen as my housekeeper when we return home."

Juan laughed. "I'll have a housekeeper just like the one you did in Seville."

Satur's mouth fell open.

"The prettier the better." Juan said. "Just as long as we just look and don't touch."

Satur nodded his head slowly without replying.

Juan raised his hand in the air as he walked away. "I must tell General Yagüe that we priests should all have one."

General Yagüe sat patiently in the Cathedral as Juan walked in through the huge but rather battered and broken 17th century oak doors. He recognised the general immediately, a thick set man with a greying moustache perhaps no more than 45 years old.

Juan made the sign of the cross and spoke. He pointed to the left hand door in the entrance way; it hung loosely, suspended by two twisted brass hinges several centimetres in diameter.

"Even the Good Lord cannot ward off the bombs and bullets of the Nationalists," he said.

General Yagüe looked up and smiled.

"I'm sorry about that Father, but they can be made good again and I will see that the work is carried out before we leave Badajoz.

"That is most kind of you General."

General Yagüe stood and offered his hand. Juan took it and shook it gently.

"You believe that Our Father stands with us Father Juan?" He asked. "Our movement is integral with the church spirit is it not?"

Juan sat down in a pew close to General Yagüe. Juan stretched out his legs in front of him and shook his head. "I do not know what to believe anymore, General Yagüe. I swear my faith has been tested more times these last few months than any priest should have to endure in a lifetime."

General Yagüe loosened a few buttons at the top of his tunic. "Me too Father Juan, I have been a good Catholic for more years than I care to remember but I have taken decisions lately that would make my dear old mother turn in her grave."

Juan turned his head towards the general. "Is that why I am here General Yagüe, so that you can repent and ask for God's forgiveness or do you need a shoulder to cry on?"

The general stood. He spoke a little louder as he paced slowly in the aisle. "None of those Father Juan, I am here," he pointed to Juan, "...you are here because I wish to talk to you but I certainly do not need a shoulder to cry on nor do I regret any of my actions these last few days. Strong men need to make tough decisions in war and I have had to make my fair share of late."

Juan fought the urge to interrupt as the General continued.

"I do not think you realise how much you are respected among your fellow priests and how much influence your words have on others less intelligent than you. People are talking about you Juan Francisco, and people are listening and I have brought you here to reason with you and beg for your cooperation. These are difficult times and I want you to remain strong and stand with me and my troops. If we all pull together we can turn this country around quickly. If not this damned war will drag on for years, for there are many that want it to do just that."

Juan was momentarily lost for words. He'd feared the worst from his meeting with the general but here he was speaking man to man, almost asking for help and it suddenly came to him that this war was just as difficult for a soldier and a general as it was for the average man in the street. Outside forces were in evidence everywhere, outside forces that were prolonging the Spanish man's agony. The Italian aircraft that had bombed Badajoz, those strange markings on the other planes he now knew were called Swastika's and the Moors and the Legionnaires and the other soldiers made up from countries from around the globe. It seemed that every country in the world wanted to get involved in the so called *Spanish Civil War.*

Juan felt nauseous, as if a big gaping hole had been opened up in the pit of his stomach and despite his feelings for a general who had given an order that sent so many to their deaths he also felt a degree of sympathy for him too.

Juan patted the seat next to him. "Sit with me General Yagüe and talk to me."

The General looked a little surprised but nevertheless walked over and sat with Juan.

Juan spoke. "They are calling this the Spanish Civil War are they not?"

General Yagüe shrugged his shoulders. "Can it be called anything else Father?"

Juan smiled. "Indeed it can. I have heard it called the war of God because of the Republican stance against my church."

"I can understand that Father, the Reds have killed and tortured many members of your church. Our forces and the Church stand as one, don't you agree?"

Juan was shaking his head. "The Church shouldn't take sides General. That is not what we are here for. Most Republicans are good Christians, God fearing people and will attend weekly mass just like me and you."

"They've killed priests and nuns," said the general, "burnt churches and cathedrals to the ground and in Barcelona they dug up the remains from graves of holy men long gone and pissed on their bones in the street."

Juan raised an eyebrow and shrugged his shoulders. "I have heard that general, but they were not the men, women and children you sent to their deaths yesterday."

General Yagüe stood once again. "I brought you here to talk reason and to stand with us and to use your influence in a way that will help our cause. You need to support us, for people listen to you, I see it in their eyes."

"I will not condone or support a massacre," Juan said.

The general was shaking his head. "It was a necessary evil, it was my duty, my country demanded—"

"Your country General Yagüe?" Juan interrupted. "It is no longer your country because it's being overrun by Germans and Italians and Moors and the French and the English. I've heard that even the Russians are getting involved. This isn't a Spanish war, it's much more than that and it's the poor Spanish man that is suffering the most."

General Yagüe picked up his cap and stood. "I have changed my mind Juan Francisco. All of a sudden Mass does not appeal to me. I have much work to do."

The general, fully aware that piety was no guarantee, nevertheless made the sign of the cross on his chest as he turned his back on the altar and walked quickly towards the cathedral door.

Juan spoke as he reached the huge doorway. "Tell me one thing General."

General Yagüe turned and paused.

"They say you shot four thousand." Juan said. "Tell me that is not true."

General Yagüe placed his cap onto his head; his shape silhouetted in the early morning sunshine and appeared to take a deep breath.

"Of course we shot them." He announced. "What do you expect? Am I supposed to take 4,000 reds with me as my column advances, racing against time? Am I expected to turn them loose in my rear and let them make Badajoz red again?"

Juan's legs turned to jelly and he was unable to support himself as he sank slowly to his knees. General Yagüe adjusted his cap and walked out into the sunshine with a look of determination etched across his face. As the broken door slammed shut Juan held his head in his hands and his tears flowed freely.

The occupation of Badajoz occurred during the advance of the rebel army from Andalucía to the north of the peninsula. The assault on the city was vital for the Nationalists as it would mean the joining of the Army of the south with that of Felipe Mola which dominated the north.

Badajoz found itself isolated after the fall of Merida several days before. The siege of the town was carried out by 2,250 Spanish legionnaires, 750 Moroccan regulars and five batteries of artillery under the command of Lieutenant Colonel Yagüe.

The final assault was made on the evening of August 14 after the city was bombarded from both land and air for most of the day.

Badajoz's recently re-occupied 18th century walls were defended by 2,000 Republican militiamen and 500 regular soldiers led by Colonel Idelfonso. After opening a breach in the walls to the east at the Puerte de la Trinidad and Puerte de Carros, the Nationalist troops entered the city and after bloody hand to hand fighting Badajoz fell.

That day saw many killings of civilians in the streets of the city including of women and children especially by the Moroccan troops.

On the same day, General Yagüe ordered the confinement of all prisoners (most of them civilians) in the town's bull ring and that night he began the executions. According to articles published, many newspapers including the Chicago Tribune said mass executions took place and the streets of Badajoz became littered with bodies and soaked with blood. The American journalist Jay Allen in his report in the Chicago Tribune, spoke of 1,800 men and women killed on the first night alone.

On August 15, Le Temps reporter Jaques Berthet sent the following report:

"Around 200 people have been shot by firing squad, we have seen the sidewalks of the Comandancia Militar soaked in blood. The arrests and mass executions continue in the Bull Ring. The streets are swept by bullets, covered in glass, tiles and abandoned bodies. In the Calle San Juan alone there are 300 corpses."

The method of execution used was firing squad or machine-gunning of those who had defended the city or who were suspected to be sympathisers of the Republic. They were seized by the legionnaires, Moors and officers of the Guardia Civil or local members of the fascist Falange party. Afterwards their bodies were burned at the walls of the San Juan cemetery.

According to the testimony of survivors, the executions were carried out in groups and the bodies were then taken by truck to the old cemetery where the bodies were burned and then deposited in mass graves.

One employee of the city council, interviewed by Francisco Pilo recalled:

"The Guardia Civil came looking for us at three in the morning. One of them said he would get the truck from the yard and that we had to go to the bull ring. At half past three we arrived. Inside the

ring on the left there were many dead laid out in a line and they told us to load them into the truck and take them to the cemetery. When we returned from the cemetery there were more dead bodies, but not all together, a pile here, another over there. Then I realised that they were taking them out in batches and shooting them. That day, we made at least seven trips from the bull ring to the cemetery.

There were also firing squads in other areas of the city. Among those executed were men and women who supported the Republic, workers, peasants, soldiers who took part in the battle and those merely suspected of belonging to one of those categories.

Twenty Five

Many weeks had passed since the hell that was Badajoz. Most of the large armaments and troops had moved onwards to their next objectives, to the north and west in the direction of Madrid. Juan had also heard that the Nationalist troops were sent to relieve a garrison of Guardia Civil that had been besieged in a place called the Alcázar at Toledo.

Most of the priests had gone with the troops, but Juan had been instructed to stay behind until receiving further instructions.

The relative quiet, now that most of the troops had gone was surreal; the evidence of their stay, the bullet marked ruined buildings and the surviving people walking around thin and bedraggled, pasty faced, walking the broken streets of a once proud city. The people of Badajoz had no time for war or politics. They simply wanted to live their life, to work and to provide a roof over their head and food on the table for their families. And incredibly, like a Phoenix rising from the ashes, the city was slowly but surely rebuilding itself again.

It suited Juan to be away from the main scenes of death and destruction, he and Carmen had started to try and help some of the survivors especially the hundreds of desperate orphans. The house they now lived in had been converted into a soup kitchen. Juan spent most of the day begging and looking for food, bringing it home for Carmen who seemed to work wonders with what little offerings he provided.

The word was carried on the wind by the countless refugees who walked the cobbled streets which meant a never-ending queue outside their humble abode. The house was a never ending cacophony of sound, tales of woe abounded and yet a childlike innocence of optimism was never far away and occasionally, just occasionally a smile and a laugh would permeate the depression that hung like a huge cloud over the city. The adult population of Badajoz took a great deal more convincing that the intentions of a priest and his church were honourable and genuine. Most shunned him, regarding his holy robes as proof that he wore the uniform of the enemy. It was both frustrating and Juan thought wholly unfair. Juan prayed in the huge cathedral most days. He prayed for peace and acceptance and of course forgiveness and wondered when the Lord would hear him.

Juan had spoken to Carmen of his meeting with general Yagüe, she felt sure that getting left behind was a direct result of his discussion, citing that his words had been too close to the truth for the general, maybe for that reason they were to see out the war here, in relative obscurity. The city streets were still patrolled by the Nationalist soldiers who had been left behind. There were several hundred at the most, many of them who had been injured and unfit enough to make the tiresome journey on to greater things. Several months after the massacre of Badajoz a nationalist soldier who had been injured in the carnage and had been hospitalized as a result, limped up to Juan with an instruction to report to the field command centre.

Juan felt the familiar sickness in his stomach as he waited to enter the officer's quarters. He was ushered in without a word and was met by a smartly dressed young officer in his early twenties. As Juan entered the room, the officer eased himself back in his chair, a heavy machine pistol lay on his desk and Juan noticed the safety was in the off position.

He tossed a letter across his desk. Juan instinctively caught it.

Without taking his eyes from Juan's, he sneered. "You are to make your way to Burgos, and report to the Archbishop there." He pointed at the letter. "This gives you permission to travel and also to use any military transport available. You will leave immediately but the journey may take several weeks."

Juan stumbled as he went to leave, the officer's hand had moved nearer to the gun, his final words were softer, but made Juan's blood run cold.

"If I had my way I would shoot you on the spot. We are all aware how you disrespected the General." He fondled with the gun in front of him as a finger traced across the trigger. "Get out of my sight priest, pack your bags and take your whore with you."

As Juan moved swiftly towards the door the officer called him back. "I almost forgot." He was holding what looked like another letter. "This came for you, a truck heading north brought it up from Seville."

Even in the gloom of the room as Juan's eyes focussed on the handwriting his heart skipped a beat.

"I believe it is from your mother." The officer smiled as he stroked at his heavy moustache. "An intellectual women I see. A woman of substance and passion."

Juan stepped forward and for a brief moment he was about to offer a protest.

"Yes Father I have read your letter. We read all letters for we need to find out whether we are dealing with friends or enemies. Thankfully there isn't an awful lot of reading to be done because most do not have the education." The officer stood and walked around the desk handing the letter to Juan. "To be honest with you priest that's the way I prefer it." He stepped closer. "Isn't that the way your church prefers it too?" He laughed. "It doesn't do us any favours if we allow the people to think for themselves."

It took every ounce of self-control Juan could muster to keep quiet. He took the letter from the officer and walked slowly from the room.

The officer looked down at his instructions clearly written by *The Carrier*. He wanted to know whether the letter had been presented personally to Juan Francisco Cortes and if so if the priest wanted to reply. The officer shook his head. The poor woman he thought. It wasn't much to ask was it? She just wanted to know if her son was still alive. He held that power in his hand. He fingered the pen and fed it through his fingers as he pondered. *Unable to locate recipient* he wrote as he sealed the return envelope and smiled.

Less than an hour later Juan, Carmen and Kiko were on an ammunition truck heading north. Juan kept the correspondence from his mother and the travel pass in a small leather pouch inside his jacket, patting at the pocket far too often.

It was going to be a long trip. Burgos was situated around 200 kilometres north of Madrid around 120 kilometres from the coastal resort of Santander. On the truck, Juan learned that the whole area around Burgos had given in to the Nationalist cause without a fight. But even that hadn't stopped the bloodletting; the soldiers were desensitised and hungry for blood. Whole swathes of the population had been slaughtered after the town halls and police stations were ransacked and records seized. As in Badajoz and Seville they were used to judge in which direction a person's political leanings lay. And the soldiers on the truck basked in glory as they told their gory stories.

One soldier told of his encounter with a General Mizzian: "I was with the general when his troops threw two girls of less than 20 years to his feet. He discovered in the pocket of one of them a trade union card. I walked with him as he took her to the public school of the village where forty Moorish soldiers were resting."

The soldier gripped at his groin and grinned widely. "He threw her to them. A huge cry of joy came from the building as her screams filled the air," said the soldier.

"There was an American journalist present who was none too happy at what he was witnessing. The general smiled and dismissed his protests telling him that she would not survive more than four hours."

The soldier's belly laugh lasted for some time as his colleagues on the truck joined in. Carmen shed a silent tear as Juan wrapped a thick cloak around her. He wondered if the time was right to tell he about the letter from his mother, his dear sister's wedding and his plans to escape. He looked around the truck. Many of the soldiers were still awake and very, very close. He decided to bide his time.

The truck pulled up in the town of Caceres for the night. They had travelled only around 50 kilometres, but their bodies were aching from the vibrations and jolting of the heavily laden vehicle. They had been perched on top of green boxes, words written on them that Juan recognised as German. They were big and bold, almost harsh letters daubed white against the boxes and if it were possible they spat out their fury and their aggression to all who viewed them.

The driver of the truck was urinating against the wheel as they stumbled down to the ground.

"We are going as far as Avila tomorrow," he said. "We leave at 7 o'clock. There are no houses to sleep in tonight, they're all occupied, and you'll need to make yourself as comfortable as you can wherever you can. Don't be late or we'll leave without you."

Juan reached for his pack which held their entire worldly goods including a couple of blankets. Carmen handed him Kiko, who despite all the noise was sleeping soundly.

Juan helped her down from the truck. "We'll need to keep warm tonight; I fear we may even see a little frost on the ground tomorrow morning."

Carmen answered him. "I suspect you may be right, I swear I am frozen to the bone and you will need to stay close tonight Juan Cortes, to keep me from freezing to death."

The thought warmed Juan. They would sleep with the child in between them. He was past caring what anyone saw or thought and was now more than aware that it was almost acceptable for a priest to take a mistress as long as it wasn't displayed openly. He led Carmen by the hand to corner of the field away from the rest of the soldiers and priests.

He pressed at the ground with his bare hands then spread one of the blankets on the ground. "It's dry here," he said. "The trees and bushes have taken up most of the moisture and if it does rain tonight the overhanging branches will protect us a little."

Carmen looked up into the night sky. There were a few clouds hanging ominously but there were many stars shining brightly.

She spoke. "Make sure you say your prayers tonight Señor Cortes and tell your maker to hold the rain. Kiko is still very weak. He has had no appetite these last few days and I dread to think what will become of him if the heavens open up tonight."

Carmen knelt on the blanket and Juan handed her the child which she buried in her bosom. She lay down. "It is so very cold Juan, I don't know how many nights like this he will survive."

Juan lay down on the blanket next to her, the child in the middle and he reached for the other blanket which he draped over them. They came together and Juan pulled them close in. "We will survive my darling, I know it. Now, before you go to sleep I have a little tale to tell you." He reached into his leather pouch and pulled out his mother's letter. "I want to tell you about my mother back home in Abdet and how there is peace in my home region."

"Yes?" Carmen asked looking rather puzzled.

"That's what the letter says," he said excitedly. "I know it was written several weeks ago but there is no conflict there. Neighbour is not fighting neighbour or brother fighting brother. Can't you see Carmen we have a little hope?"

Carmen sat up. "We have hope?"

"We do Carmen." Juan was smiling, his toothy grin visible in the moonlight.

"Forgive me Juan if I don't sound as joyful as you are and that may be the case down in Valencia but we are stuck in the field several hundred kilometres from there without any means of transport. I like walking as you well know, but the thought of a route march with Kiko on my back with no food and a pair of shoes that are just about hanging on to the bones of my feet is not something that appeals to me at this very moment."

Juan sat up and reached back inside his leather pouch. He produced the second letter.

"This is our pass Carmen, our travel warrant to get us onto any military vehicle we wish. Of course there will be many kilometres to walk but if we plan our route well we can make it." He whispered.

Carmen positioned herself so that their lips were barely apart. She pushed herself forward and kissed him. "Whatever you say my sweetheart; I can see you have fire in your eyes and there is a belief there too. It's the fire in your eyes that keeps me going. Just tell me what to do and I will walk with you to the ends of the earth."

She kissed him again and he responded. She closed her eyes as she whispered. "Even without shoes."

In a few short moments they were all asleep.

The next day they headed for Avila, bypassing Madrid to the right by less than 100 kilometres. As they neared the town, Juan noticed many divisions of troops loitering by the side of the road and sitting around crudely constructed camps. The build-up of troops to the west of Madrid was impressive, they were obviously preparing for an assault on the capital.

How could the poor people possibly defend themselves against such vicious battle hardened troops? They boasted of the best weapons money could buy, supplied, it was rumoured by Italy and Germany. Avila was a freezing cold place in winter owing to its altitude of over 1300 metres. It was the first week in November as they pulled into the town and they noticed the change in temperature from the cities down to the south. Juan, Carmen and Kiko shivered and huddled together in the back of the truck. Juan looked up and couldn't help but be impressed by the town, surrounded with its huge thick stone walls and elegant architecture which went back to Roman times and before. It appeared to be intact, with little sign of any fighting; Juan thought it was almost a step back into normality.

The driver told them to embark. There was nowhere to stay, he said but suggested the cathedral might offer a little shelter to a working priest. It took them 40 minutes to carry their belongings along the flagstone streets and they arrived at the steps of the cathedral.

Juan stood still for a moment and gazed up at the superb Gothic Architecture.

"I suspect this is the sort of place that God presides over." He said. "I feel something special here Carmen, I feel protected."

"You do?"

Juan nodded without averting his gaze.

"Then I'm glad to hear it." She said.

"It was built between the 12th and 15th century, the summer residence of the Catholic Monarchs." Sais Juan

"It was?" Carmen enquired. "At times you know too much my dear."

Juan picked up Kiko and reached for Carmen's hand. "You can never know too much Carmen remember that."

They were met just inside the main doors by one of the church wardens who despite Juan wearing his clerical clothes couldn't help turning his nose up at the sight of the three of them. Juan pulled out the travel document order to report to Burgos, and offered it for inspection. He raised his voice a decibel or two.

"We need a place to sleep until we can go onwards"

It came across more of an order than a request, but Juan was too tired to care.

However, it seemed to do the trick.

After a moment's hesitation, the man shrugged his shoulders. "Follow me Father." He said.

A sense of peace washed over Juan as they stepped through the centuries old doors. The warden led them into the depths of the cathedral, several floors down and to a small room no bigger than a cupboard.

He turned to face them and laughed. "There is no room at the inn, so to speak. You are welcome to lay your head here as long as you want father." He pointed to Carmen. "Though I don't know where your companion will sleep, we have nothing else available and the Archbishop will not have anyone dossing around the Cathedral. This is a Holy place not a home for waifs and strays."

Juan placed a hand on the man's shoulder and whispered in his ear. "She will sleep with me my friend; a man needs to keep warm at night." Juan gave him a little wink and the man smiled.

"Et tu, Brute." He said, as he walked away smiling, shaking his head.

On the 11th of November 1936, Avila was bombed by Republican aircraft. Juan, Carmen and Kiko took refuge in their makeshift home in the bowels of the cathedral. The bombardment lasted for several hours. When Juan thought it was safe to leave he unbolted the brass bolt that held the door.

"You are to stay here with the boy Carmen, at least until we are given the all clear."

Carmen offered no resistance. "I'm quite happy down here for the time being Juan, besides, Kiko is tired and he needs to get some sleep now that the bombing has stopped."

Juan stroked at the boys brow, his eyes were heavy with sleep. "I'll try and find some food, he must be hungry too."

He kissed Carmen and pulled Kiko's threadbare woollen jumper up tight around his neck. "Sleep little one I won't be gone long."

The city of Avila had fared well during the bombing, a military airfield just outside the city being the main target of the

Republicans. Juan was told that many planes had been destroyed. Of course a few buildings had been hit by bombs and this time Juan could see first-hand the sheer devastation man's latest military invention could wreak upon humanity. Some buildings had fallen like a pack of cards, still on fire, the familiar smell of burning flesh hung on the still evening air. He walked for many hours attending to the wounded or offering a prayer to those without hope or who were already dead. Juan also collected a little food from the people's broken houses. They would no longer have any use for it he reassured himself. He felt no guilt anymore. Was he becoming as desensitised as the troops he had travelled north with?

He made his way back towards the cathedral. He stopped outside another shattered dwelling, its roof no longer there and only one wall remaining intact. He stepped through the space where the door frame had once been and saw the blood spattered remains of the young woman, a pretty girl, no more than eighteen years of age, her face unblemished but white as snow. A huge blast had almost torn her in half as she lay sprawled at a grotesque ninety degree angle where her energy had finally expired.

He took off his hat and crossed his heart. "We beseech Thee O Lord in thy mercy to have pity on the soul of thy handmaid. Thou hast freed her from the perils of this mortal life; restore to her the portion of everlasting salvation."

He placed a limp hand on her brow. It was freezing to the touch. "My child you did not expect death today did you?" He stood, more than aware there was nothing he could do for her. He looked around the remains of the property and pulled a blanket from a twisted bed frame in the corner. He'd cover her; at least afford her a small piece of dignity until the burial squads arrived later that day.

It was then he noticed her feet. A pair of leather boots was more than unusual, even in a city and even in the depths of a cold winter. They were new. They looked a similar size to the feet of Carmen and before he could even think of the morality of his actions he was undoing the laces. He slipped the boots under his cloak and covered the girl with the blanket.

He repeated the sign of the cross. "With your bright and open heart, forgive me for showing darkness to the light. I have sinned against you, forgive me merciful one because I have relished my wrong and I am sorry for what I have done."

Twenty Six

The snow began to fall in Avila in early December, cutting off the city from the surrounding countryside and stalling the troop movements north. The church warden had informed Juan that they would be staying in Avila until well after Christmas. The weather had scuppered Juan's escape plans and he had agreed with Carmen that it would be better to see out the winter where it was relatively safe instead of making the long trek in adverse weather conditions.

Kiko was growing stronger each day and it made sense to build his strength up as they had no idea what difficulties they may encounter en route.

Carmen was preparing for Christmas. They had been moved to a bigger room at the back of the huge cathedral. It was more than comfortable with two beds and a small dining table with two chairs. She had cleaned it out thoroughly and even brought a small pine tree in which she had decorated with the young boy. They had found some ribbons and Carmen had managed to bake a few biscuits in the cathedral kitchens which she tied on the branches of the tree.

On 24th December 1936, as night closed in around them, the makeshift family sat down to their first Christmas dinner. Juan had managed to snare a rabbit some days before which Carmen had cooked with some onions and potatoes and they'd also gone without any bread for several days saving what little flour and yeast they could lay their hands on so that Carmen had sufficient to bake a full sized loaf. For afters they had oranges and of course the biscuits that hung from the tree.

For once their bellies were full and the world outside appeared to be at peace. All was quiet on this, the most special day of the year. There were no bombs or shootings, nor were there any screams of anguish or terror. Juan thought he had heard enough of those to last a lifetime.

A little before six in the evening of the 25th, Juan prepared to take mass with the Bishop. Christmas Day was always well attended and Carmen and Kiko sat just a few rows from the front watching over Juan as he carried out his duties for the Bishop.

The snow lay on the cobbled streets of Avila until mid-February.

It was still bitterly cold but as Juan stood on the stone steps of the cathedral ready to take his early morning stroll he sensed a change in climate. He felt a strange spring in his step that morning as he walked his normal route within the perimeter of the old city walls. He offered up prayers and advice and of course a little charity for those who needed it the most and those who did come into contact with him that morning would have said that the smile on his face was a little broader than normal.

He couldn't wait to get back to the cathedral and talk with Carmen. He found her in one of the common rooms at the back of the choir vaults teaching Kiko the alphabet. He carefully closed the door behind him making sure that there was nobody in the near vicinity. He explained to Carmen how he felt and that the weather was definitely on the turn.

"I sense that we will not be here much longer my darling, don't ask me how I know but I feel it so strongly."

Carmen looked a little annoyed that Juan had interrupted Kiko's lessons. This was not normally like him as he attached great importance to the young boys learning. Carmen collected together a few pencils and a pad of paper and took the boy by the hand.

"Come little one, I suspect father Juan has something to tell us today. He has that look on his face," she said with a wry grin. "The look that says I will listen to everyone but hear no one."

Juan exhaled a deep sigh. "Carmen you know that is not true."

But it was true. Carmen had long since given up trying to change him. If Juan Francisco Cortes had a notion of an idea then it had to be shouted from the rooftops and everything and everybody else simply had to wait. And as Carmen took his hand and they walked into the main body of the cathedral, that look was etched, as if in stone, right across the priests face.

They stood outside. Carmen looked up into the grey cumulus.

"Pah, it feels just as cold as yesterday and the day before and look, the snow is still lying on the rooftops."

Juan pointed to a building opposite. "No you are wrong, look it is melting."

Carmen nodded. "So what are you telling me priest? Come on spit it out man."

Juan looked around the busy street then back through the open doorways of the huge cathedral. He pulled Carmen a little closer as he whispered into her ear. "Not today and not tomorrow, not even the day after, but I suspect our days here are numbered Carmen. We have talked long and hard about the journey we must make and I fear the time is near."

"You fear Juan? Why do you fear? Is this not a journey we were destined to make, it is written in the stars you tell me and that God will be your protector, why now are you frightened to make the trip, are you losing your faith?"

Juan wanted to say that it was simply a bad choice of words. But it wasn't. He was frightened... he was absolutely terrified and couldn't shake the feeling that his confidence in the grand architect of the universe had waned slightly since the Spanish Civil War had wreaked such devastation on his homeland.

But there was no point infecting Carmen or Kiko with such feelings. He needed to stand strong and try to regain his faith once again. He needed to see good things and experience the humanity of man once again. He was sure he would find what he was looking for during the long trek south.

"We will leave the first week of March." He said. "On a Thursday the cathedral sleeps till midday. The Warden takes his day off then and its late afternoon before any priest takes a confession. I will tell the warden the previous day that I am feeling a little ill and he will think nothing of it when he does not see me. With a little luck it will be Friday at least before we are missed."

"And we will be many kilometres away by then." Suggested Carmen.

"I sincerely hope so. We will not be able to get a truck south from this city, so we must walk for the first week until we reach Toledo. Our travel warrant should take us almost anywhere after that. We'll need to be careful and keep to only Nationalist areas."

"And throw away your priests robes." Carmen said.

Juan shook his head. "It matters not about my robes, if any republican finds this warrant then you can be sure I will receive a bullet as quick as they will look at me."

Carmen fell into his arms. "Oh Juan I am so scared. It's not easy here but at least it's safe."

It was not what Juan wanted to hear. It was a strong feeling pulling him towards his home town, a feeling that he felt sure the Lord had planted in him but he knew it was not without risk. He pulled Carmen close and held her tight.

"We must keep our faith my darling and I must follow my instincts. There is still much fighting to be done around this region, we both know that. Look at the troops and the supplies and tanks and trucks we have seen and they are all heading north or towards Madrid. In the south it is safe, in the south there is peace."

Carmen wiped at a tear that rolled involuntary down her cheek. "And what then? What then when they have finished fighting and killing in the north won't they turn their attention to other regions?"

Juan was shaking his head. "No my dear they will not."

"Oh, what makes you so sure? Are you a military strategist all of a sudden?"

"No Carmen I am not a military strategist but I know the Good Lord will intervene to stop man's humanity against man."

"You are sure?"

"I am sure Carmen... I know it."

Carmen leaned into him and kissed him passionately. After a few seconds she broke away from him. "It is time to go. I must find Kiko, he will be hungry. The little rascal has gone walkabout again."

She opened the door into the nave of the cathedral and walked away. As she did so she muttered under her breath.

"I hope this God of yours is listening Juan Cortes. I hope he does not let you down."

It was the evening before their planned escape when the soldiers came into the cathedral. The warden was playing idly with a broom stick in a half-hearted attempt to sweep the stone floor clean.

The first soldier spoke. "Where is Father Juan Cortes?"

The coarse black hairs of the soldier's moustache hung past his upper lip concealing his emotion. The warden could not tell whether he was angry or not but his eyes displayed more than a little impatience.

The warden pointed to the back of the cathedral. "That door over there, the one painted shiny green is where he lays his head at night."

Twenty Seven

Burgos

Commanding officer of the Condor Legion, Oberstleutnant Wolfram Freiherr von Richthofen sat with one of his more senior officers studying a map of the Basque Country.

The officer looked more than a little perplexed. "This order comes from above?"

Von Richthofen nodded. "It does."

"We are to deliberately target the civilians?"

The Oberstleutnant stood. "We must. It is a doctrine known as terror bombing in which we attempt to break the hearts and the resolve of the enemy. It started as an experiment in Madrid and in Malaga too and the results are most promising, it breaks the resolve of the people. You must instruct your men to shoot at anything that moves, men women and children, even cattle and dogs."

The officer was dumbfounded. "You are serious Oberstleutnant?"

Oberstleutnant Wolfram Freiherr von Richthofen smiled. "I am Herr Schafer, I am. The first attack is some weeks off but it promises to be quite an occasion."

"It does?"

The Oberstleutnant traced a finger over the map as he pushed his glasses onto the bridge of his nose and lit another cigarette.

"It does Herr Schafer, it does. Our friends the Italians are lending a hand too and we are deploying Heinkels, Dornier Do 17s and Stuka's too."

The Oberstleutnant blew a long plume of smoke up towards the ceiling. "It will be quite a display, I can tell you."

The young officer moved forward and stood beside the Oberstleutnant as he overlooked the map and pointed to a large red circle the Oberstleutnant had drawn.

"And this place, this town is our target?"

"It is Herr Schafer."

The Oberstleutnant placed a hand on the officer's shoulder. "We are lucky men Herr Schafer, our names will go down in German history. Our children and grandchildren and great grandchildren will proudly shout the word *Guernica* for generations to come."

Twenty Eight

"You will fly to Burgos before the night is out."

Juan Cortes stood before the officer a little puzzled but slightly relieved. As he was frog marched from his living quarters in the cathedral of St Teresa, Avila he was convinced he was about to become another statistic of this insane conflict. Convinced he had been overheard discussing his escape plans in the cloisters of the Gothic cathedral he had prepared to meet his maker and said a few silent prayers during the short walk to the building of the Ayuntamiento where the military had made its headquarters.

He stood with another three priests as the officer explained that a lorry carrying 12 priests and their companions had suffered a direct hit from a Republican mortar bomb.

"There were no survivors, twenty people killed almost instantly," the officer said. "It seems we are in need of some more men of the cloth in Burgos. The German soldiers and airmen are very religious it seems."

"The Germans?" one of the priests enquired.

"The Germans and Italians are very much behind our cause father, so much so that they have supplied us with armaments and planes and some of the finest pilots in Europe."

The officer stood as he walked around the room waving a hand in the direction of the assembled priests.

"It is not important for you to know about the politics in this conflict. You are religious men and we are simply asking you to do your job. Italy is a Catholic country as you know and the German soldiers go into battle with their helmets or belt buckles reading *Gott Mit Uns.*"

"God is with us." Juan stated.

The officer smiled. "You speak German Father Cortes?"

"I studied it the language back home. Father Ismael, my teacher spoke it almost fluently."

The officer walked over and slapped Juan on the shoulder. "Splendid. Then you will be even more help than we first envisaged."

The officer briefed the priests further on what was expected of them. "The aircraft leaves at midnight. We see no reason to put you aboard a truck when an aircraft is heading to Burgos anyway. It will be quicker and of course a lot warmer, I hope you all enjoy the flight. And now," he said, "I will need to check your travel documents."

The priests stood in line and handed the officer their documents and identification. When it came to Juan he placed his travel warrant on the desk. The officer studied it for a few seconds for speaking. "This travel document is for three persons."

Juan nodded.

"It is not possible. My instructions were for four priests only."

Juan picked the papers from the desk. "Then I will stay here."

The officer stood, anger etched across his face. "You will go where I order you to go."

Juan nodded. "With pleasure lieutenant, but I travel with my companions for that is what the warrant states."

The officer leaned across the desk almost spitting, venting his fury. "You must remember your place priest and do as I say."

"Whatever you say lieutenant."

Juan remained calm. He opened up the papers and held them so that the officer could see them. "A simple telephone call to General Yagüe will clear it up."

"General Yagüe?" The officer enquired.

"Yes," Juan replied. "He signed these papers himself. I'm sure if you tell him he has made a mistake he'd give you his blessing and allow you to override his authority."

The officer glanced down at the paperwork as his eyes focused on the signature. There was no doubt it was General Yagüe's signature and the stamp on the bottom bore his name too.

As if by divine intervention another of the priests spoke. "Señora Carmen is a good woman and works hard lieutenant, she cleans and cooks like my own mother and looks after us well. She will keep our bellies full so that we may continue with the Lord's work and that of the Nationalist cause."

It was exactly the type of face saver the young officer was looking for. He threw the paperwork back across the desk at Juan and with a wave of the hand dismissed them all.

The signs on the aircraft were familiar. Swastikas.

They walked swiftly across the runway as a light flurry of snow swirled around them. The interior of the plane was warm and dry and a young German navigator welcomed them aboard showing them to two rows of seats at the rear of the plane. "Sitzen Sie meine Freunde, genießen Sie den Flug."

"What did he say?" said one of the priests.

Juan spoke. "He is telling us where to sit and hopes we enjoy the flight." Juan turned to the young man. "Vielen Dank."

The flight to Burgos took just over an hour. It was relatively uneventful apart from a little turbulence twenty minutes into the flight. Although the other priests looked more than a little concerned it was a case of the bumpier the better for young Kiko who enjoyed every minute of his new experience sat on Carmen's lap.

At Burgos they boarded a truck and drove the short journey to an empty town house and were told to make themselves comfortable. Juan sensed they would be there a while but escape was still paramount in his mind.

The priests were allocated a room each while Carmen and Kiko were dispatched to a large attic in the roof of the house.

Carmen came to him in the early hours of the morning while Juan dozed fitfully. The door opened slowly and despite the cold of the night and the ice forming on the inside of the window pane Carmen stripped off her clothes before sliding into the bed beside him.

"I come to confess father," she joked. "I confess there is something I need and only a man like you can give it to me."

The following morning at eight o'clock they were rudely awoken. Two Nationalist troops let themselves into the house and barked out their orders that the priests were to report to the Ayuntamiento on the edge of the town. There was no transport, the priests would need to walk they said. The eldest of the soldiers give rough directions but said it could not be missed as the flags of the Falange hung proudly outside.

It took them twenty minutes to reach the town hall and once there, they were quickly assigned to their projects. Because Juan could speak German he was told to report to the military airfield several kilometres on the outskirts of the city. Once again he was reminded by the officers present what a deeply religious, God-fearing people their German Allies were.

One officer went on to say there was a makeshift chapel alongside the control tower and the German pilots and aircrew had requested a resident priest so they could take mass and confession. Juan was told to collect his belongings and that rooms had been made available for them. Within the hour he was back at the Ayuntamiento with Carmen and Kiko and their possessions.

As they drove towards the airfield, Spanish and German troops guarded the entrances and it took some time for their paperwork to be inspected and cleared. They were shown to their rooms and then Juan was given the guided tour of the airfield, shown the chapel, the dining area and also a sitting area that was occupied by German aircrew. A large billiard table took pride of place in the centre of the room where four German officers stood smiling, each one stopping what they were doing to show their respects to the priest. Juan acknowledged them and was told by his German guide that he was welcome there any time he wished.

"You may take the rest of the day off father and familiarise yourself with our surroundings. Lunch is served between one and two and your housekeeper and her boy are more than welcome too."

He took Juan's hand and shook it firmly. "I'm not sure how long you'll be here and of course war isn't the ideal theatre to practice devotions but you are much needed here and I hope that we can make things as comfortable as possible for you. If there's anything you require please let me know."

Juan was speechless as he watched the young airman walk away. It was thousand miles from what he had experienced in the last few months. It was comfortable and dry and despite the chill in the air, each room was heated to a perfect temperature. He had to hand it to the Germans, they were organised and efficient and if any of their countrymen were displeased to be fighting in the Spanish war their faces did not show it.

For several weeks all thoughts of escape had been erased from Juan's head. Juan took mass several times each day and confession whenever it was requested of him. They ate three hot meals each day and wanted for nothing, one of the German pilots even made a rocking horse for young Kiko, who was gradually coming out of his shell.

It was his pride and joy and gleamed as if it were polished every hour of every day. Even von Richthofen enjoyed polishing the machine, though when it came back from a particularly dirty run he made sure it was one of the junior airmen who got his hands oily and dirty getting into the places that were almost impossible to reach. The BMW motorcycle and side car wasn't even in full production but as a keen enthusiast he'd been asked to give his opinion on the bike as a sort of test pilot. He'd had the bike shipped in a Heinkel bomber from Dusseldorf airfield and hadn't regretted his decision for one moment.

It was a little risky of course, taking the bike out into the Spanish countryside but he checked with intelligence every day and knew to keep to the Nationalist areas and steer well away from that damned Basque country.

Life was good, he considered himself a lucky man. Oberstleutnant von Richthofen was born in 1895, the son of a Prussian nobleman and grew up more than familiar with the good side of life, joining the German army at 18 years of age. Some would call him a little arrogant; they would say he thought he was better than the next man. An Iron cross winner fighting on the Western front in World War I and the cousin of Manfred von Richthofen, the famous Red Baron, the criticisms did not concern him. Von Richthofen knew all about the whispers in the airmen's mess rooms and the officers dining area too and when a fellow officer, slightly inebriated one particular evening call him an arrogant bastard to his face, Von Richthofen simply shrugged his shoulders and said.

"Early in life I had to choose between honest arrogance and hypocritical humility. I chose the former and have seen no reason to change."

It was towards the middle of April when Oberstleutnant von Richthofen formally introduced himself to Juan Cortez as he sat in the small chapel waiting for the priest who arrived each day at around eleven o'clock in preparation for a midday mass for anyone who wanted to take it.

Juan had heard all about the Oberstleutnant from the camp gossip mongers who he'd became quite familiar with. As Juan walked in, the thin, wiry German stood, removed his cap and clicked his heels together before formally introducing himself. He then sat in a front row pew and placed his cap on his knee.

"I come not for mass father," he said.

The Oberstleutnant walked to the front of the church and placed a small notepad on the altar which he opened up at a specific page. He took out a pair of glasses as his finger traced down the page of the book.

"We are flying a special mission early on the morning of April 26th and I will be briefing my men the evening before."

"A special mission?" Juan enquired.

"It is none of you concern father," he said, "suffice to say many of my men are deeply religious and want to hear that their God flies with them. My remit is to give them what they want."

The Oberstleutnant explained that Juan would be present at the briefing, prayers before and prayers after, a show from the Catholic Church that they supported and endorsed the actions of The Luftwaffe.

"It is not a request Herr Cortes, it is an order. After the briefing you will be invited back to my office to share a brandy or two with some of my officers."

Von Richthofen replaced his cap and walked towards the door. "It isn't exactly a difficult task Herr Cortes." He laughed out loud. "And I believe you priests have a taste for fine brandy anyway."

Without another word, Von Richthofen left.

The briefing room was a small aircraft hangar on the far side of the airfield and security was tight. Juan had to produce his paperwork on three separate occasions, making his way past both Spanish and German soldiers armed to the teeth. He sensed this was big, more than just *another mission*.

As he walked into the 'briefing room' he noticed a huge map of Northern Spain suspended at the front of the room. The men were drinking beer, in good spirits and a table to the left of the room was laden with food. His eyes scoured the seated uniforms. Pasty faced Germans with an occasional swarthy skinned colleague in a different uniform with an Italian flag emblazoned on the left breast pocket.

There was not a Spaniard in sight.

He did not notice Von Richthofen until the Field Commander of The German Condor Legion took him by the arm.

"Father. I'm glad you could join us."

I didn't have a choice Juan wanted to say but he bit his lip.

"Here take this."

He handed him a glass. "Specially selected from my private supply."

Juan took the glass. "Thank you."

"You are first up father. Nothing special, just a few prayers, the usual sort of thing and tell the men that God is with them."

"But I cannot guarantee that the Lord flies with them Herr Richthofen, It would—"

"Just say it father. You don't have to guarantee it," he snapped. "Just tell my men what they want to hear and your little family unit will be preserved a little longer. If you displease me the girl and the boy will be on the next plane to Morocco and they can take their chances with those black savages I hear so much about."

Juan's blood had turned to ice. Without being able to field a response Von Richthofen took him by the arm and guided him towards the lectern, introducing him to his colleagues and then asking them to bow their heads in prayer.

Juan led the German troops through a few basic prayers and some verses from the Bible. He looked over towards Von Richthofen who stood glaring, almost scowling at him waiting for the blessing he had insisted Juan bestowed on his countrymen.

And as Juan looked deep into the eyes of a man he knew had no compassion or mercy he sensed that the Field Commander would have no hesitation in dispatching Carmen to whatever corner of the globe that took his fancy. He had no choice. Blessing these men and their obvious mission of destruction and death went against everything he was ever taught by the church.

Juan bit his lip and swallowed. "It is not my place to ask why we have been plunged into this conflict or why you men sitting here today have been asked to fight on a foreign soil many miles from your homeland. All I will say is that the Lord works in mysterious ways." *How many more time must I say that?* He thought to himself.

He continued. "The Lord doth watch over us in his constant never-ending fight of good over evil and he will judge us all in time. We must all fight in what we believe in and keep remembering the good Lord as your constant companion. If you do that then he will not fail you... if you want him with you then he will be there to guide you on the ground and in the air."

Juan made the side of the cross and nodded in Von Richthofen's direction signaling that his address was over.

Juan stood down and walked over to where Von Richthofen had been standing. The German clutched a notebook as he made his way to the lectern, passing over the final few sentences of his most important message to the Condor Legion.

"A fine speech Father," he said. "You have done me proud," he whispered as he passed the priest.

For Juan Francisco Cortes, the next thirty minutes was the most excruciatingly painful of his entire life. He listened in horror as Von Richthofen delivered exact technical details on how the Luftwaffe would raze the Basque town of Guernica to the ground.

Von Richthofen explained the strategic importance of the bridge in the Renteria suburb, apparently the primary objective of the raid. The mission would coincide with Nationalist troop movements against Republican forces near to Marquina. It was made clear on more than one occasion that the Condor Legion would meet with no resistance.

Juan listened in horror as the German pilots and their crew laughed and joked and smiled throughout a briefing that instructed them to terrorise the population of Guernica to the point that they would bring the entire Basque region to its knees. Anything that moved was a legitimate target, Von Richthofen instructed, growing more and more animated.

A young pilot in the front row quipped, "Even sheep and cattle Oberstleutnant?"

Von Richthofen's demeanor did not change. He did not smile or joke as he said. "If we can't kill them on the day then we can starve them to death at a later date."

He turned to the pilot. "Leave nothing alive, leave them without hope, and yes... leave them without meat for their tables."

He turned to face the mass of assembled men once again. "The operation will last no more than a few hours but its effects will last for years." he said proudly.

Towards the end of Von Richthofen's briefing , Juan left the hangar and stepped outside.

He walked over to a grassy area and vomited the insides of his stomach.

"But Juan it is safe here," Carmen protested. "The boy sleeps."

She had never seen him as agitated as he took time to explain the German assault on Guernica and how they must do something to help.

"But what can we do Juan, Guernica is many kilometres away."

"We will go there by motorcycle."

Carmen wiped the sleep from her eyes and ran her hands through her hair. "I feel you are truly mad priest, and just where are we going to get a motorcycle from?"

"Von Richthofen keeps the keys to a motorcycle on his desk, it has a sidecar too and you and Kiko will be protected from the weather." Without pausing for breath he continued.

"My Uncle Eduardo taught me to ride a motorcycle when I was a young boy and after we have warned them at Guernica we can head south for Valencia. We will keep to Nationalist areas and our travel warrant will take us most of the way."

Carmen sat up in bed. "You have it all planned Juan." She took his hand and stroked at his face. "And what if you are caught stealing this bike, what if the guards-"

"They have stepped down security for the evening, Von Richthofen has thrown a party for them and he now entertains his officers and his favoured pilots as we speak. I have been instructed to attend, he leaves the keys to his motorcycle on the desk Carmen, I can get them and we can escape it's what we promised ourselves we would do."

The moment Juan entered the room, his gaze fixed on Von Richthofen's desk. His heart sank and he did his best to hide his disappointment. It was covered with a table cloth and glasses and several bottles of spirits and there were certainly no keys in the immediate vicinity. The field commander of the Condor Legion welcomed Juan as he introduced him to several of the assembled party. They welcomed him warmly and several congratulated the priest on his fine words at the briefing in the hangar, one or two even patted him on the back which made him very uncomfortable.

"Take some food and a little wine or perhaps something a little stronger," Von Richthofen suggested pointing at a table by the window stacked up with sandwiches, smoked sausages on sticks and various pastries.

Juan politely declined a drink but walked over to the table laden with food and ate while speaking to several of the officers.

Von Richthofen walked over and stood adjacent Juan. "I can see what you are thinking, Herr Cortes, you are thinking that my men drink too much alcohol."

Juan smiled. "I confess colonel that thought had crossed my mind, it's not the ideal way to prepare for an early morning flight."

Von Richthofen raised his glass. "Don't worry, they will all be in bed by midnight with a good eight hours sleep inside them before they ever set foot near to one of my aircraft."

One of the young airmen spoke. "We don't have an early start father; the marketplace does not get busy until well after midday."

Juan look at Von Richthofen's by way of an explanation, he was more than a little confused.

"My pilot is correct Herr Cortes; the marketplace in Guernica opens up around ten in the morning but is at its busiest in the afternoon. The Basque's are a lazy race of people, they sleep late and mornings are a mere inconvenience to them. To maximise the terror aspect of the mission we must hit the town then."

"But it will be full of women shopping and children playing in the streets," Juan objected.

"Not my problem father, I am a soldier with an order and civilian casualties do not concern me, they are a necessary part of war."

Juan was horrified but managed to stifle any more objections. He too had a mission. He couldn't stop the pilots of the Condor Legion but there was just a chance that he could warn the residents of Guernica before was too late. At least they'd have a chance. If he could get there in time he could tell them to flee to the hills and forests and hide until the horror had passed over them. It was at that split second as he glanced over Von Richthofen's left shoulder that he noticed the motorcycle keys hanging from a small hook by the door.

Von Richthofen and his pilots grew progressively drunk but true to his word right on midnight Von Richthofen glanced at his watch and called time on proceedings. One by one the officers and pilots left until only Juan and Von Richthofen remained.

"I must be getting along too," said Juan, as he thanked Von Richthofen for his hospitality. "This is somewhat later than I am used to."

Von Richthofen glanced at his watch again. "Yes me too, a good night's sleep is essential." As Von Richthofen turned and walked towards a coat stand, Juan strode briskly towards the door, reached for the keys and slipped them into his pocket."

"Hey priest," Von Richthofen barked out.

Juan froze to the spot his blood turning to ice. He turned around to face the German.

Von Richthofen was smiling. He pointed to the table.

"There is plenty of food left over, do you want to take a little back with you it will only go to waste."

Juan thought ahead. He thought of his journey to Guernica and beyond, of the many kilometres they would need to cover in order to make it back to the Valencia region. It was a total unknown where they would even lay their head each night let alone where they would find food. They had little money and no provisions at all.

"That would be good," he said. "The boy eats as if he has worms I'm sure he will appreciate it."

Von Richthofen thought it a little strange the amount of smoked sausage the priest pushed into his pockets before he eventually left.

Twenty Nine

It was 2.30 in the morning as they left the rooms that had been home for the last few months. During his tenure at the airbase Juan had discovered one or two doors or gateways to the outside areas that were not manned and they made their way to one on the south of the base that led from the huge kitchens. It was a simple doorway that led to a refuse area which was cleared daily. The cooks and assistants disposed of all the waste through the doorway and it was secured by two simple bolts at the top and bottom of the doorway. Juan collected more food and water from the kitchen before he loosened the two bolts and they exited through the doorway.

It was a long walk to Von Richthofen's bike which was parked fifty yards from the main entrance which of course was always manned.

As he approached he could see the chromed spokes of the wheels sparkling in the light of the moon. He told Carmen to wait with Kiko and crouched down as he neared the bike. He waited for some minutes not knowing exactly what it was he was waiting for. And then he heard the sound he was waiting for. Snoring. The sound of the sleeping sentry carried gently on the wind and he thought it was the most beautiful sound he had ever heard.

He kicked the gear lever into neutral and began to push. It was a struggle. The motorcycle although brilliantly engineered was as heavy as two fattened calves and by the time he reached Carmen he was out of breath and sweating profusely.

"We must push it further Carmen, he said, at least another kilometre before I dare start it up or we will wake the devil himself."

Carmen licked a finger and held it in the night air as she smiled. "The Lord is on your side Juan Francisco Cortes, he has given you a favourable wind. Any sound will be carried away from the base but yes I agree let us not taking any chances."

Carmen placed Kiko into the sidecar and they began to push.

It was three hours before they eventually stopped by the side of a road sign that told them it was 30 kilometre's to Guernica.

"We are making good time," Juan said, "and the good Colonel has provided us with more than enough fuel to take us many kilometres south." Juan stretched his legs and rubbed at the muscles above his hips. "I fear we may need to ditch this beautiful machine in the next twenty four hours though, because Von Richthofen will put two and two together and make five. He'll have every road block in Spain looking for a priest on a bike and God help us if he catches us."

They stopped for some minutes to rest and watched as the sun came up over the Arizgoiti mountains. Kiko slept in the sidecar as Carmen and Juan sat together on a fallen tree trunk watching Mother Nature at her most spectacular as the sun kissed the tips of the pine trees and the shadows rippled down the hillside.

"It is hard to believe we are in a country of war is it not? Said Carmen.

Juan nodded as he slipped an arm around her shoulder. "It is. Just what is it that man desires, why can't they be happy with the beautiful things the Lord provides them? He brings them food and water and light and warmth, the flowers and the trees and still they want more."

"Such is life Juan, some will never be content"

He reached for her hand. "And you Carmen, are you content my angel."

Carmen laughed. "That's a strange question priest." She punched him playfully in the stomach. "Let me see." She placed a finger against her lips and gazed into the sky. "I am in a forbidden love with a man of the cloth on the run from the Germans. I have no house and no family, no money and we are about to venture into an area that half the Luftwaffe will be bombing in a few hours." She gripped her chin with her thumb and forefinger. "Hmmm... let me think that over."

Juan pulled her towards him and kissed her. "But those are just minor distractions my love."

"Pah! Minor distractions. I fear you are crazy priest. C'mon let's get going before Kiko wakes up."

It was true. Everything that Carmen had said was true and yet Juan felt strangely invigorated and yes... a free man once again and that felt good. It was a dangerous game they were playing but sitting on the stolen German bike as the wind flowed through his hair and they ate up kilometre after kilometre was something he would never forget and although their time at Burgos was more than comfortable and relatively safe he hadn't regretted the decision for a moment.

As they approached the town of Guernica they encountered the first Republican road block. It was not unexpected, something Juan knew would happen sooner rather than later. He braked slowly and brought the machine to a stop as several rifles leveled on him. The soldiers manning the road block looked weary, underfed and dirty.

"He's a German one of the younger soldiers shouted. "That's a German motorbike."

"I am not, I am Spanish," Juan said. "I am a priest from Valencia and I bring you grave news."

A soldier stepped forward. He wore three stripes of a sergeant on his sleeve. He spoke.

"My comrade is right, that machine is German how did you come by it?"

"I stole it. I have been based at the airbase in Burgos for some weeks now and it's full of Germans and their planes, perhaps twenty five to thirty, even more."

Carmen spoke. "And they plan to bomb Guernica this afternoon."

"Silence woman, no one gave you permission to speak, let this man tell me."

"It's true, Juan said. I was in the briefing meeting yesterday; they are going to bomb the market place."

"He's a spy," another soldier shouted. "Don't listen to him he's not a priest at all."

Juan was pleading now, pleading harder than he could ever remember. "Please, it's true, I am a priest and believe me Guernica will be razed to the ground, we must warn them."

By now the motorcycle was overran by several republican troops. They ignored Kiko sleeping in the sidecar and eventually found what they were looking for.

A soldier held the bag aloft. "It is true the man is a priest because he has enough food here to feed the five thousand."

The men who had not eaten properly for many days almost fought with each other over each handful.

"I am sorry about your food," the leader said, "but my men have not eaten anything decent for many weeks."

Juan was nodding. "I understand; times are hard."

"Times are more than hard they are impossible."

"Please reason with your men," Juan said. "There will be many hundreds killed."

He was met with a deafening silence as the sergeant shrugged his shoulders and walked away.

If Juan thought that a little food in the Republicans bellies would have a calming effect he was to be sadly disappointed. The soldiers grew more aggressive demanding more food and searching the motorbike and their bags on more than one occasion. The man who at first acted a little reasonable seemed to grow weary of the interrogation by the roadside and at one point sat on the grass watching as proceedings developed.

Carmen begged them to listen to Juan but they would not. After a few minutes one of the soldiers produced a length of rope and tied Juan's hands roughly behind his back. At this point Kiko awoke and startled by the raised voices started to cry. Carmen was unceremoniously marched away with the child and Juan pushed into the sidecar of the bike and told not to move. He sat looking over the brow of the hill, the town of Guernica tantalisingly close sprawled out below them. It was within spitting distance and yet a million kilometres away.

They were now ridiculing Juan as he persisted in telling them what he had heard in the briefing room.

"Why would the German's get involved in our war?" one of them asked. "The whole idea is preposterous."

The man sitting on the grass didn't have the will to intervene. He had heard the rumours about the bombing of Durango some days before and the villagers told of strange markings on the side of the planes. Could this man who claimed to be a priest be telling the truth?

They would find out soon enough he supposed. God help him should his story prove to be false. He stood and gazed down the valley towards Guernica. "And God help the poor bastards down there if his tale turned out to be true," he mumbled under his breath.

They heard the aeroplane engine before they saw it. The noise came from the direction of Mount Oiz in the west. The men looked a little apprehensive as they spotted the small vanguard plane with strange markings on the side but then as it appeared to circle above them and head back in the direction which it had come from, they taunted Juan.

"Thirty planes you say priest, pah, you talk in riddles."

"He is a church man right enough, full of false promises and shit."

Thirty

In Guernica the market place was in full swing. It was a perfect day, hardly a cloud in the sky and possibly the warmest of the spring so far. Food was scarce and bargains hard to come by but although trading was poor the villagers had turned out in force. The old men of the village sat in and around the many bars and café's watching life pass them by. They looked on at their grandchildren's antics as they played games or complained that mother or father walked too fast.

In one such café under a rough willow wood awning to shade their old skin from the sun sat Josepe Otxoa and his friend of nearly seventy years, Alain Ubriq. Josepe had been born and bred in Guernica. In fact he'd never set foot more than a few kilometres outside the town save for a three day trip to Bordeaux for a close relatives wedding. Even then at the age of sixty one he had longed to return home and cut short the festivities in order to do so. He needed the comfort of his own bed he had said and home is where the heart is and he couldn't wait to get back despite the pleasantries and celebrations he left behind in France.

Alain was a Frenchman and proud of his country which he would tell anyone who was prepared to listen. It was rumoured his father fell into bad company with some Arab immigrants in his home town of Montpellier and had to flee with his family under the threat of death. Alain was six when his family came to live in Guernica and yet even now he refused to kowtow to the Basque's and admit he was one of their own. He was fiercely patriotic and liked nothing more than a good argument on superiority and national pride where the insults flowed freely.

And despite everything Josepe and Alain were the best of friends. A few drunken punches had been thrown in the past but their hostilities never lasted longer than the time it took to finish a glass of red wine.

"The market is desperate these days, Josepe," Alain commented. "I don't think I've ever seen it so bad."

Josepe nodded as he finished the last of his ration of red wine. Two glasses a day was all he could afford these days and even then he had to forego his supper. It was a price he was prepared to pay.

"I fear you are not wrong Frenchman but we Basques will recover like we always do."

Alain pointed at a stall holder. "I see the biscuit seller seems to have plenty of stock, I wonder where she finds the ingredients."

Josepe looked over. "Ah yes but I hear her *barquillo's* are not as sweet as they used to be and they do not melt in the mouth like they once did. And what of the strangers Alain? I once knew every line of every face around here but now I see only strangers."

"Refugees Josepe," he replied. "Men and women from Durango, without a home or any hope with which to furnish it."

The old men continued their conversation in the bar of Marinelarena. The one time sailing family had served the villagers of Guernica with their cerveza, vino and pintxos for five generations. The old lady Marinelarena, even older than Josepe and Alain shuffled through with two more glasses of vino tinto for the two old friends.

They would be *'on the house'* she told them, something she didn't do very often especially in these troubled times. As she delivered the wine to the two appreciative gentlemen she bent down and massaged her troublesome arthritic knee. It always played up in wet weather or when some sort of mischief was afoot. As she stood in the threshold of the ancient doorway she looked up into the clear blue sky and shook her head. As she wandered back through to the kitchen she crossed her chest and mumbled to herself as she gazed skywards. "Dios – God, do not bring any trouble to my door today I simply do not have the energy."

∽

As the first wave of Heinkel bombers flew above their heads towards Guernica, the republican soldiers and their clerical captive fell silent. It was no more than a few seconds before the dull thuds resonated through the soles of their boots and the dust started to rise from the valley several kilometres in the distance. The soldiers took cover in a small copse adjacent the side of the road and a few minutes later Carmen appeared with Kiko, the men who were holding her had joined their comrades in the woods. She untied Juan without uttering a word as plane after plane flew overhead. They watched as the scene unfolded below them.

Messerschmitt´s followed the Heinkels. Juan did not have to wait long to see what their role was in the operation as they flew around the periphery of the town in no particular order firing off bursts of machine gun fire in the surrounding fields and roads. From where Juan and Carmen watched, the terrified refugees and villagers looked like long lines of worker ants. And then the ants started to fall.

The pilots of the planes showed no mercy, no respect for age or gender. Their targets had no guns, no defense and no chance. If the pilots missed their intended targets the first time they simply banked their machines around and came again. Some had made it into a large wooded area which seemed to infuriate the Messerschmitt pilots even more who strafed the area time after time before a large incendiary bomb dropped from a Heinkel scored a direct hit and the entire area was incinerated from the heat of the explosion as it erupted into a huge fireball.

Kiko buried his face in Carmen's skirts as Juan held them both tight. A new noise now. A screaming shrilling whistle and Juan realised the noise was coming from the nose of the bombs as they fell to earth. What was the purpose? No. He shook his head. Surely the whistle was just a trick of the wind, an accident, a natural result of poor aerodynamics.

What were those poor people going through down there?

Josepe and Alain were too old to run. They had viewed the panicking masses in the street and taken the decision to stay put and say a few prayers to the almighty. They moved inside with the old lady Marinelarena and Josepe looked at the thick wooden beams and centuries old stone work that surrounded them.

The old lady caught the look. "You are right Josepe, it will take a big bomb to bring this lot down. We are safe here, the good Lord will see over us."

The whistling sound was getting louder now as the three of them cowered under the thick oak table that ran the length of the entire bar. Josepe covered his ears as Alain shouted something to him that was not audible.

The phosphorus bomb sliced through the terracotta tile roof and vaporised everything and everyone inside the bar of Marinelarena as the four walls blew out over reducing the ancient house to a pile of dust and rubble.

And still the German planes bombed and bombed and bombed again over a three hour period and the Messerschmitt´s shot at soldiers and refugees, women and fleeing, frightened children, the injured and the dying, cattle, sheep, pigs, even cats, dogs. They shot at anything that moved and those that no longer could who lay in streets or fields incapacitated through missing limbs or shattered bones.

And then it was silent.

Juan could only imagine the sheer devastation of the town now clouded in smoke and dust. He clenched his hands together. "Tell me what they have done Almighty God to be punished in such a way?"

Although initially frozen to the spot, Carmen was altogether more practical strapping Kiko into the sidecar telling Juan it was time to make their escape.

"Come on Juan we do not have long, the soldiers will break cover soon and God knows what sort of revenge they will want."

Juan was still praying. He struggled hard to recall a positive message from the Bible, verses he had studied and learned since he was a small child. He opened his eyes and looked down into the valley at hell itself.

"Come Juan, hurry." Carmen shouted.

He fell to his knees. "This is how it will be at the end of the age. The angels will come and separate the wicked from the righteous and throw them into the fiery furnace, where there will be weeping and gnashing of teeth."

"Juan we must go."

At that moment a figure appeared to drift towards them from the woods. It was the sergeant.

"I should have listened to you priest. I sincerely believed you, I really did but I was too much of a coward to act."

The sergeant was ashen white, a forlorn figure who seemed to stare right through them as if they weren't there.

He continued as he pulled his rifle from the shoulder and cocked it. "Your words rang true. Don't ask me why but they did and I should have acted upon them." As he looked out over his devastated home town the tears began to fall. "My mother and father are down there and my wife and my son too. I have friends and many relatives and only the good Lord knows how many he has spared." He wiped at his tears with the cuff of his sleeve. "I have their blood on my hands."

The soldier fell to his knees as he broke down and wept. "I should have warned them... I could have warned them, we had plenty of time."

Juan stepped over to him placing an arm around his shoulder. "You must not blame yourself friend, it is the pilots of those planes to blame and their generals and colonels in Burgos and in Berlin."

The man was shaking his head and appeared not to hear Juan's words of comfort. He turned to face the priest and pushed him away roughly as he clenched his teeth and spoke angrily. "Get away from me, leave me alone. Make your escape while you still can."

The sergeant placed a hand on the stock of the rifle as he turned it towards himself. He gripped the top of the butt as he slipped his thumb behind the trigger and brought the rifle barrel towards his face.

Juan realised his intention and threw himself forward. "No," he cried.

He was too late. The sergeant opened his mouth, pushed the barrel inside and pulled the trigger. There was a muffled dull thud as the back of his head exploded and Carmen screamed as she turned Kiko's head away. The man slumped to the ground as Juan reached him.

There was nothing he could do but say a prayer. The man was clearly dead. Panic stricken voices filled the air. The sounds came from the woods. Carmen was pleading now, begging between the tears that were rolling down her face. Figures were emerging from the wood 100 metres up the road. At that instant Juan's life flashed before him. He knew the soldiers would not listen. He'd experienced that before and now they would see that their leader lay dead in the grass.

Juan reached for the dead man's rifle and ammunition and ran towards the motorcycle. He thanked God for the contours of the hill as the Republican soldiers let off a few loose shots which flew harmlessly over their heads. Within seconds they were out of sight as they sped down the hill towards Guernica.

It was over. His mission had failed and despite his best intentions Guernica had been razed to the ground and its defenceless citizens massacred. He stopped the motorcycle at the Renteria Bridge over the Oka River. He wondered if he could have done more.

"You tried Juan. No one can say you didn't try," said Carmen.

She climbed from the motorcycle. "And I know exactly what it is you are now thinking and I won't let you." She walked round to the front of the bike and removed the keys. "You are not going into that town. You want to help but I won't allow it. You will be killed you stupid man, you are on a German motorcycle and dressed as a priest. You might as well go in there with a target painted on your chest."

Carmen walked calmly towards the river and dangled the keys over the bridge parapet. "So tell me now what you want to do priest." She said. "Tell me if you want to sacrifice yourself or tell me if you want to run so that you can continue your work another day in a different place?"

At the time of the raid, Guernica represented a focal strategic point for the Republican forces. It stood between the Nationalists and the capture of Bilbao. Bilbao was seen as key to bringing the war to a conclusion in the north of Spain.

Guernica was also seen as the path of retreat for the Republicans from the northeast of Biscay.

Prior to the Condor Legion raid, the town had not been directly involved in any fighting although Republican forces were known to be in the area; 23 battalions of Basque army troops were at the front east of Guernica. The town also housed two Basque army battalions, although it had no static air defences, and it was thought that no air cover could be provided due to the recent losses of the Republican Air Force.

Guernica had a nominal population of around five thousand as well as numerous refugees who were fleeing into Republican controlled territory. The raid took place on a Monday, market day in Guernica. Generally speaking a market day would have attracted people from the surrounding areas to Guernica to conduct business.

The Luftwaffe and its Blitzkrieg operations were known to have a doctrine of terror bombing in which civilians were deliberately targeted in order to break the will or aid the collapse of an enemy. This was denied by the Luftwaffe who claimed the air arms were used in battlefield support. Despite that official position, the Luftwaffe practiced 'terror bombing' over Madrid in the autumn of 1936 as well as against Malaga civilian refugees in February 1937.

German legal scholars of the 1930s carefully worked out guidelines for what type of bombing was permissible under international law. While direct attacks against civilians were ruled out as 'terror bombing', the concept of attacking vital war industries with probable heavy civilian casualties and breakdown of civilian morale-was ruled as acceptable.

It has been said[that Von Richthofen, understanding the strategic importance of the town in the advance on Bilbao and restricting Republican retreat, ordered an attack against the roads and bridge in the Renteria suburb. Destruction of the bridge was considered the primary objective since the raid was to operate in conjunction with Nationalist troop movements against Republicans around Marquina. Secondary objectives were restriction of Republican traffic and equipment movements and the prevention of bridge repair via the creation of rubble around the bridge.

The first two waves of bombing was devastating. If the aerial attacks had stopped at that moment, for a town that until then had maintained its distance from the convulsions of war, it would have been a totally disproportionate and insufferable punishment. However, the biggest operation was yet to come.

Several Junkers Ju 52s of the Condor Legion then took off to complete the raid on Guernica. The attack would run from north to south, coming in from the Bay of Biscay.

The 1st and 2nd Squadrons of the Condor Legion took off at about 1630 hrs with the 3rd Squadron taking off from Burgos a few minutes later. They were escorted from Vitoria by a squadron of Fiat fighters and Messerschmitt Bf 109Bs, a total of twenty-nine planes.

From 1830 to 1845 each of the three bomber squadrons attacked in a formation of three Ju 52s abreast – an attack front of about 150 metres. At the same time, and continuing for around fifteen minutes after the bombing wave, the Bf 109Bs and Heinkel biplanes strafed the roads leading out of town, adding to the civilian casualties.

The bombing shattered the city's defenders will to resist, allowing the Nationalists to overrun it. The attacks destroyed the majority of Guernica. Three quarters of the city's buildings were reported completely destroyed, and most others sustained damage. Strangely enough Richthofen recorded that the bridge (the main target) was not destroyed or even hit during the raid.

The number of the resultant dead will be argued about forever more. After Nationalist forces led by General Mola's forces took the town three days later, the Nationalist side claimed that no effort to establish an accurate number of dead had been made by the opposite side.

The Basque government, in the confused aftermath of the raids, reported 1,654 dead and 889 wounded. It roughly agrees with the testimony of British journalist George Steer, correspondent of the Times, which estimated that 800 to 3,000 people perished in Guernica. These figures were adopted over the years by some commentators outside of the conflict as accurate.

Thirty One

Von Richthofen was more than happy with the first intelligence reports. Two German paratroopers had been dropped under the cover of darkness and sat on a hill overlooking the devastation just two kilometres from the town. Their high powered binoculars told them everything they needed to know.

Three quarters of the town's buildings had been laid to ruin and surrounding hillside farms had been singled out for target practice. As far as the eye could see lone farm buildings smouldered silently and hay lofts and agricultural machinery still burned, such was the ferociousness of the flames during the attack.

The paratroopers had maps marked with significant targets they naturally assumed their colleagues in the air would have prioritised. And for five minutes they discussed the reasons why the arms factories *Unceta and Company* and *Talleres de Guernica* along with the Assembly House *Casa de Juntas* remained intact. It was more than a little puzzling and even the bridge across the Oka River continued to carry traffic. The younger of the paratroopers, Fritz Klinsmen surveyed the ancient stone walls of the bridge and could not see a single bullet hole let alone any damage caused by a bomb or incendiary device. Was the mission a failure he wondered to himself?

Back in headquarters as the intelligence reports filtered through, Von Richthofen thought the mission was anything but a failure. They'd dropped nearly 40 tons of bombs during the three-hour period and the casualties were horrific.

The town of Guernica would take years to recover Von Richthofen announced proudly to the assembled hangar of pilots, and the spirit of the town had been well and truly smashed to pieces. Von Richthofen had been on his feet for thirty minutes, his speech was drawing to its climax.

"Every single person within the town boundaries will have had a family member killed or seriously injured." He smiled. "They will see them no more; there will be no coffee or beers in the town square for some time but you must shed no tears for them for they are the enemy and therefore expendable."

It was what the pilots wanted to hear and there was a light ripple of applause before Von Richthofen held up his hand to acknowledge their appreciation.

"The effect on the morale of the men and women of Guernica is immeasurable. My glorious soldiers of the Third Reich," he announced proudly as he smiled and paused for impact, "we terrorised the population into surrender. Today is a great day for Spain and for Germany and for Europe."

Von Richthofen took a drink of water from the lectern he stood behind and surveyed the happy smiling faces sat before him. "There will be other wars," he continued. "There will be war in Europe and possibly all around the world and one day the great German Army and fascism will take control of the entire globe. Friends, be proud but prepare. Prepare for more of the same. I thank you from the bottom of my heart... I could not have asked for more."

He nodded his head and saluted. It was a signal that he was finished and the signal for the applause and the cheering to begin.

The men slapped his back and congratulated him as he walked among them towards his office. He'd thrown another celebration for the men and ordered his next in command to commence the festivities. Von Richthofen though did not feel like celebrating and would not join them. He had unfinished business to attend to.

He wanted his motorcycle back and he wanted the hide of the man who called himself a priest.

Thirty Two

The motorcycle ran out of petrol just south of Logroño. Juan removed his bag and told Kiko to climb out of the sidecar. He threw his priests clothing in the sidecar and heaved the big machine towards the side of the road as he pushed it over the side of the hill.

"We can't take any chances," he said. "We may be in a republican area now and if they see this clothing most of them will want to put me against the wall."

As it bounced down the hill and came to rest at the base of a large tree he looked at Carmen. "From now on we must walk and beg for rides. We will keep to what we think is the Nationalist areas as much as we can, we still have my warrant remember?"

Juan climbed down the hill and covered the visible parts of the bike with broken branches. They ate the last of what food they had and set off on foot in the direction of Saragossa.

Never had he been more grateful to old Vicente, his first father who had taught the young Juan the ways of the countryside. Vicente had taken him into the Sierra Bernia Mountains from the age of five and passed on his knowledge his father had passed on to him. He taught him how to look and forage for nuts, roots and the seeds that would not cause him to double up in pain. He singled out the mushrooms on the forest floor that would satisfy his hunger then pointed out the strange markings and bright colours of the ones that would kill him.

Old man Vicente taught him how to cook and most important of all he told him how to hunt and to snare and how to butcher the meat. And the good Lord did provide he reminded Carmen. She confessed they were eating like kings as they kept to the countryside and Juan used up his supply of German bullets on rabbits and birds and even a young wild boar. The supplemented their mostly meat diet with wild vegetables and fruit from the trees and washed it all down with a never ending supply of spring water. They slept where they dropped and Juan would construct shelters from the branches of trees or sleep in goat herder's huts or caves.

Occasionally they would stay in one place for many days. High in the hills of the Aramon Mountains they came across an abandoned shepherds hut with a bed and a table and even two chairs. The weather had turned pleasantly warm and a tributary of the river Ebro flowed close by. The war could have been happening on another planet as Carmen turned the dilapidated shack into a home. Juan repaired the gaping holes in the roof and the walls and even constructed a sun shade under which they idled away many hours. He took Kiko hunting and taught him how to catch rabbits and hares without the need for a bullet. He taught the boy to fish with a bent pin and a piece of old net which he'd found in a store room behind the shepherds shed. The fish supply was plentiful and Juan even built a small smoking shed in the forest where he smoked the flesh of the fish in order to preserve it longer.

Occasionally a military aircraft or two flew overhead but it was as near as they got to the war.

Carmen walked the hills and the forest trails for many hours collecting the seeds and fruits which she would dry and retain for such times as they may be needed. In the meantime they enjoyed their almost idyllic existence as days turned into weeks and weeks turned into months.

It was early October 1937 when the weather began to change.

"I suspect we must be moving on soon," said Juan.

It was not something Carmen wanted to hear but she knew that they were much too high in the mountains to exist over the winter months.

"We have much meat," he said, "and smoked fish and seeds and nuts too. My bag is full and will last us many weeks. We must make our way south and into the valleys where the weather is less harsh and we must head for Teruel then Valencia."

Carmen agreed. "It makes sense Juan I know it does but I can't pretend I have not been happy here."

"We have planned well Carmen and the boy is strong as an ox."

"He's a good boy isn't he Juan?"

"He is Carmen, he does his parents proud, I only wish they were here to see what a fine boy he is turning into."

They talked long into the night as Kiko slept. They talked about family and Abdet and Xirles and Carmen's life in Seville. Juan discovered that Carmen had never set eyes on the sea. Juan described a town called Altea on the coast and how he would bring her to the beach there and they would swim to an island called L'Olla.

"But I don't swim Juan," she confessed. "I have never needed to."

"Then I will teach you and we can swim together to the island and when I get you there I will make love to you on the deserted beach."

Carmen grabbed at his leg. "I will keep you to your promise priest and you'd better be sure that it is indeed deserted for if it's not and you have a witness to your debauchery I fear you will be up before the Pope himself who will excommunicate you."

It was beginning to get light and still they talked. Carmen wondered if the war might be at an end.

"Who knows?" said Juan. "We will find out sooner or later."

Two weeks later they packed up all of their belongings and left.

Thirty Three

Mar and Sebastian were married in 1936 just as the winter came to the mountains around Abdet. They had not wanted to wait so long, preferring to be married late summer or in the autumn, but providing a feast for the fifty or so close friends and family had proved more than a little difficult.

But they'd done without and they'd saved and Sebastian had supplemented his meager wages as a farm hand, hunting for game in the mountains with an old rifle which had been handed down by his father. And when successful he'd sell the produce around Abdet and the few pesetas he'd receive went into a jar in the kitchen of his mother's house and when it was full he promised Mar that their wedding would be a splendid affair... the best Abdet had seen for many years.

Although the jar hadn't been quite full the decision to arrange the wedding had been made for them when Sebastian had shot a young boar early one morning in November. Carrying it the six kilometres home strapped over his back was just about the hardest thing he'd ever done but he willed himself on every step he took down the mountainside with the vision in his head of Mar's beautiful face when he told her the good news.

At last, with the money they'd saved and enough meat now to feed at least a few dozen they'd be able to go ahead with their plans.

Mar was ecstatic, her father said the wild boar population around the Sierra Bernia Mountains had all but been hunted into extinction given the tough economic climate and the scarcity of meat and Sebastian had worked miracles seeing one let alone getting one in the sights of his rifle.

Sebastian basked in the adulation as Felipe took the beast away to clean.

The civil war that had raged around Spain had affected the entire country, even in the rural backwaters of Xirles and Abdet. Juan's family and their fellow villages had not escaped the horror of the conflict.

Thankfully in Abdet there hadn't been any violence. Although the village was in the heart of republican territory, its geographical position and its scattered run down houses and outlying farmlands did not constitute any worthwhile target. But the effect of the war had never been far from people's minds particularly within the close knit family of Felipe and Maria who had been told their only son was missing in Seville, presumed dead.

The wedding, on the 1st of December was a fun filled affair in the village barn which had been specially decorated for the occasion with sprays of wild flowers and sprigs of greenery from nearby trees. During the speeches, Felipe had made a point of toasting his son Juan, several times who he said was many miles away and unable to attend.

Sebastian knew the truth. The man was dead and why didn't they just accept it and get on with their lives. He was more than a little annoyed that the festivities had grown a little solemn thereafter but after more wine and several brandies as night closed in, the damned priest was conveniently forgotten once more as the songs and dancing commenced.

The war, thought Sebastian. He let out a deep sigh as he took another large mouthful of brandy. To begin with he had tried to carry on as though nothing was happening; it was after all a long way off.

Gradually though, as the years had gone by, Sebastian had become almost obsessed with the idea of the fascists coming and what they would do if they ever reached this quiet backwater. Even now, at his own wedding feast he eyed some of the guests with suspicion.

Two years ago Sebastian didn't have a political bone in his body but was now heavily involved in the republican and left wing ideals. In the larger towns like Altea, there were regular meetings of all the different left wing parties where young men volunteered the services to the Republican cause. At first Sebastian had drawn attention to himself for not volunteering to go and fight the fascists but he was fascinated by what he heard at these meetings, absorbed the knowledge and wanted to learn more.

He joined in the heated political debates in the café's and bars at nights and ultimately he had assumed a position of importance in the PCE, the Communist Party of Spain. He was content in his role of recruiter for the cause, and instructor in the ideals of the left.

Mar bore his political ranting with patience; he was after all a good, hardworking man, who had always put his wife first. She couldn't forget the sacrifices he'd made in the year preceding the wedding.

Gradually however his political indoctrinations had begun to take hold and he became obsessed with the idea of 5th columnists around every corner. He motioned at the next meeting to arrange patrols to 'keep an eye' on the wealthier neighbours in the area.

In the most part these people were landowners with estates handed down over generations. Some would say most of them had treated their labourers well; the wages were small but sufficient to put food on the table.

Sebastian knew differently. Watching them became an obsession.

News from the front line areas was slow to come through to the community in the mountains and was so distorted by the time it reached them, it was practically worthless. One of the neighbours had a son who was fighting in Madrid. He wrote to his parents regularly but the letters took many weeks to filter through. In one such letter the news appeared to be encouraging. Sebastian listened in awe in the small café that evening as the boy's father spoke proudly, reading the letter verbatim. The capital was surrounded on three sides, but the fascists had been held back suffering terrible casualties.

Sebastian had never been to Madrid, but he told himself that with victory almost reassured they would make the journey north for the victory celebrations and all stand united in one of the magnificent plazas that he had heard mentioned in the letter.

Mar tried to carry on with life as normal, much the same as the other women in the village. Most of the families had sent a son or two to fight the fascists and sadly some had been killed. It seemed like almost every day another mother or a widow appeared on the streets dressed from head to toe in black.

Agriculturally there were new rules in place. Every single square metre of earth that could be tilled was turned over to the production of food. The farmers were allowed to keep a certain amount depending on the numbers in their family, but the majority of the crop had to be turned into the town hall to be warehoused and sent on to feed the republican troops.

There were some families who tried to hide that little bit extra for themselves, but Sebastian was placed in charge of that job ensuring everyone complied with the rules. He prided himself that nothing escaped his attention.

He regarded his job as a vital key to the success of the war and he was determined to play his part well. He had his eye on another damned priest, Father Ismael's latest recruit. There was something about him he didn't like. The church, so long the centre of village life, was strangely silent. The young priest who was now in residence kept the doors locked for much of the week opening them on Sunday, more in hope than anything else and always looked more than a little nervous.

Few people entered the church to worship; stories of the church's involvement in the Nationalist cause were voiced in some of the letters from Madrid. The elder ladies of the village would still not have a bad word said against the church or the young priest but Sebastian knew exactly what he was up to. And the mood was slowly changing, people no longer trusted the clergy, he could sense it and one day this young man would get what was due to him.

Sebastian formed a town hall revolutionary committee in Altea where he attended twice a week. It consisted of brave but poorly armed men from the surrounding areas. Sebastian gave grand speeches on how they were going to kill any fascists that dared enter their territory and they would give the savage Moors a taste of their own medicine and send them back to Africa as stiff as the wood from an almond tree while their testicles remained on Spanish soil. The crowd cheered and laughed and Sebastian wondered why he couldn't live this life seven days a week instead of having to work in those damned fields for that bastard of a boss who seemed to control his life from the moment he woke up until the moment he fell asleep at night.

It would get better, life would change. It was only a matter of time before his wife's parents took him into the bosom of the family and brought him into their wine business in Algeria. They had built it up from nothing and it paid well. He too would have a big house overlooking Abdet with outbuildings and sheep and goats and even a car like Felipe.

Thirty Four

"We have no choice Juan, our food is running low and we must take our chances on the roads," said Carmen.

They had been walking for three weeks, sticking to tracks and trails away from the main roads that ran the length of Spain. They had trekked over two hundred kilometres living off the land but now their supplies were exhausted. The last of the German bullets had been used up, the final two on a wild boar that Juan had failed to hit, and now the rabbits and squirrels and voles were beginning their winter hibernation save for a few stragglers. The fruits and nuts and seeds they had supplemented their diet with for many months were finished too.

Juan threw the rifle in a ditch adjacent to the main road to Teruel and they resigned themselves to their fate. They could live of the land no longer and as they started walking on the tarmac road Juan thought it was a little hard on the soles of his feet, feeling every stone through the thin soles of his boots and he said a silent prayer that they would come across someone soon who could help them.

That night they slept by the side of the road under a lone laurustinus tree. The bare branches gave them little shelter and a thunderstorm interrupted their sleep in the early hours of the morning. They had no option but to start walking south again hoping to find better shelter. They walked until it was daylight. Kiko was crying almost constantly, he was fatigued, cold, wet and hungry.

"I can walk no more Juan," he said. "My feet have holes in them and I can feel my ribs again."

Juan grinned. It had been Kiko's favourite expression whenever he'd felt a little hungry but he was far from starving. Juan thought perhaps Kiko had eaten a little too well lately and reassured himself that a few days of hunger wouldn't do him any harm. They walked on until the sun was at its highest, directly overhead and despite the lateness of the year and the chill in the air it was one of those freak winter days in southern Spain where it was almost too uncomfortable to walk in.

"It's too hot Juan," Carmen said.

Juan nodded. "I know, we need to find a little shade but at least our clothes are now dry."

Half a kilometre ahead, a long abandoned building gave them exactly what they needed.

Juan forced the door and they entered. Carmen fell into an old seat and Kiko collapsed onto the floor. Juan walked through to the kitchen wondering if he could salvage anything. After ten minutes he gave up. The cupboards were bare, everything of any use had been taken long ago.

"There is nothing here Carmen. I fear we may need to wait a little longer before we can eat."

Carmen waived a hand in the air. "I'm past hunger I think, it's Kiko who needs to consume a horse every day."

Kiko turned up his nose missing the obvious joke. He looked at one adult then the other and lay back on the floor. Within a few minutes he was asleep. Carmen stood and placed a blanket over him.

"We can stay here tonight, said Juan. "I'll rest an hour or two and then have a wander around to see what I can find."

Juan dozed; when he woke Carmen was sleeping too.

It was a pleasant evening, relatively warm and Juan knew they were heading closer to their final destination because of the noticeable change in climate. He stood outside the house not really knowing what to do next. He looked down the road in the direction they would be heading and started to walk. He'd walk an hour, no more and see if there was any sign of life nearby.

He could hardly believe the change in temperature as the sky grew dark. After only a few kilometres he was frozen to the bone, turned around and headed back to the abandoned shack

The following morning they set off. They'd walked nearly ten kilometres when the first wave of planes flew overhead.

"Who's do you think they are? Asked Carmen, "and where are they headed?"

Juan stood for a moment listening to the drone of the aircraft. "They have the sound of the German planes at Guernica, at least some of them do. And they are high in the sky so they aren't coming in to land or bomb just yet." He eased the bag from his aching back.

"I'm hungry," said Kiko.

Juan ignored him. He'd stopped trying to convince the boy they'd find food around every corner.

"Teruel I suspect, possibly even Valencia."

"Teruel and Valencia are still Republican?" asked Carmen.

"Yes, there was a map on Von Richthofen's desk. The area around Teruel and Valencia was coloured red."

They heard the rumbling of the trucks from some distance. Instinct told them to run into the forests and hide and yet they needed food desperately.

"We have no choice Carmen; we must stay here and take our chances. If the troops are Nationalist then my warrant will carry us through."

"And if they are Republican?"

"Then I will keep it from them and shout viva la Republic!" he said with a grin in a vain attempt to try and reassure Carmen and the child.

The troops turned out to be Nationalist. Juan presented his papers; the troops were in good spirits and helped them on board. Despite Juan's concerns, food did not seem to be scarce, at least not on this truck. They ate bread and cured ham, cheese and they even gave them a few biscuits. The troops sang songs as they drove for most of the day.

They were heading for Teruel, for what the soldiers said would be the battle that would win the war. Juan hoped they were right. A truce, a ceasefire or surrender, it didn't matter to the man in the street who won just as long as the bloody conflict came to an end.

Did anyone really win in war anyway? Family members maimed and killed, children orphaned on both sides. What of the Nationalist soldier who had lost his brother or his son or both? If his side had taken the spoils could he sit down in a bar many years from now and honestly say his side had won? He would say it for sure but would he truly believe it?

What one of the soldiers said next wasn't so reassuring. He said they had been told to prepare for several months of fighting. The Nationalist planes had already started the bombardments of the Republican held areas and heavy artillery was being moved into place on the surrounding hills. The Nationalist troops would number more than a quarter of a million he said, victory may take some time but it was assured.

"We are only a dozen hours from Teruel, father," the driver of the truck announced. "It is not the sort of place you should consider going to, especially with the small boy."

Juan looked across at Carmen. Although bitterly cold during the few days they'd spent on the truck the Nationalist soldiers had supplied them with decent food. They had been well fed and one of the sergeants had even provided a small tent and extra blankets for the cold nights when they'd stopped en route.

"You think as I do. I should head for home." He said.

Another soldier spoke. "And you must be careful, Valencia is still Republican and a man of the cloth is not the most popular person in Spain."

Juan smiled. "Don't worry, I dispensed with my robes a long time ago and I now walk in the clothes of a simple peasant man."

The soldier pointed to Juan's bag. "Then I would get rid of your travel warrant too, for your paperwork states your profession and the reds will slit your throat as soon as look at you."

"You are very reassuring my son."

Carmen laughed too. "Yes, I think you have put the priests mind at rest."

The soldier gave a puzzled frown. The joke appeared to be lost on him and he eventually walked away.

Juan looked at Carmen. "He is right Carmen, Valencia is a dangerous place I hear."

Carmen frowned. "No more dangerous than Teruel, from what we have heard."

Juan paused for a second or two before speaking. His voice had dropped a decibel or two. "I must get home Carmen, something is pulling me there and I can't explain it but I must be there soon."

Carmen sat down beside him. "What? What is it that is pulling you there my love?"

He looked up. There were tears in his eyes. "Death is pulling me there Carmen, I must get home because I have a feeling I can't shake that someone close to me is about to die."

They bid goodbye to the Nationalist soldiers as they headed south towards Valencia.

Juan had conducted a mass for them prior to leaving and many of the soldiers had given up their rations to sustain them on the long journey. Another soldier had drawn a route that would skirt through the hills keeping them away from the main roads and on the bottom of the valleys. It would still be cold but the tent and the blankets would see them through. As they left the hills of Teruel behind the climate became a little less forgiving.

Two days into their journey they stole a mule from a deserted outlying farm. Juan lifted Carmen and Kiko onto the beast and they began their long trek towards home. He explained to Carmen that there was a war on and even priests must steal if needs must.

The Battle of Teruel was fought in and around the city of Teruel from December 1937 to February 1938. The combatants fought the battle during the worst Spanish winter in twenty years. It was one of the bloodier actions of the war. The city changed hands several times, first falling to the Republicans and eventually being re-taken by the Nationalists. In the course of the fighting Teruel was subjected to heavy artillery and aerial bombing. Both sides suffered over 140,000 casualties between them in the two month battle. It became one of the decisive battles of the war.

The Republican Army was under the command of Juan Hernandez Saravia who had reorganised his army almost from scratch. Among the leaders under his command was the trustworthy and able Communist commander, Enrique Lister. Lister's division was chosen to lead the first attack. The coup de main against Teruel would be an all Spanish operation without the assistance of any of the International Brigades. The Republican Army of the Levante was to conduct the main part of the assault supported by the Army of the East. The total Republican force had 100,000 men.

Colonel Domingo Rey d'Harcourt was the Nationalist commander at Teruel when the battle began. The Teruel salient had a Nationalist defending force of about 9,500 men and that would include civilians. After the attack began, Rey d'Harcourt eventually consolidated his remaining defenders into a garrison to defend the town. The Teruel Nationalist garrison numbered between 2,000 and 6,000 according to various estimates.

Lister's Republican division attacked Teruel in falling snow on December 15 1937, without preliminary aerial or artillery preparation. Lister and fellow commander Colonel Enrique Fernández Heredia moved to surround the town. They immediately took a position on Teruel's Tooth, and by evening encircled the city. Rey d'Harcourt pulled his defenses into the town, and by December 17 gave up trying to keep a foothold on Teruel's Tooth. Nationalist Commander Franco finally decided on December 23, to aid the defenders at Teruel. Franco decided as a matter of policy that no provincial capital must fall to the Republicans. That would be a political failure, and Franco was determined to make no concession to the enemy. Franco had just started a major offensive at Guadalajara and to relieve Teruel meant he had to abandon that offensive much to the disgust of his Italian and German allies. The Nationalist relief of Teruel also signified that Franco was giving up the idea of a knockout blow to end the war, and was accepting a long war of attrition to be won by weight of arms and foreign aid.

By December 21, the Republican forces were in the town. Rey d'Harcourt, the Nationalist commander, however, pulled his remaining defenders back to an area where he could make a last stand in the south part of the town.

By Christmas Day the Nationalists still occupied a cluster of four key points, the Civil Governor's Building, the bank of Spain, the Convent of Santa Clara and the Seminary. Republican Radio Barcelona announced that Teruel had fallen, but Rey d'Harcourt and the remnants of the 4,000 man garrison still held out. The siege continued with fighting hand to hand and building to building.

Although Franco canceled the Guadalajara offense on December 23, the relief force could not begin its attack until December 29. All Franco could do was send messages to Rey d'Harcourt to hold out at all costs. In the meantime the Republicans pressed home their attack in atrocious weather. The Nationalist attack began on schedule on December 29 with the experienced Nationalist Generals, Antonio Aranda and Joe Enrique Varela in command. By New Year's Eve with a supreme effort, the Nationalists were on Teruel's Tooth and actually broke into the town to take the bull ring and the railway station. The Nationalists could not hold the gains within the town, however. Then the weather actually turned for the worse with the start of a four day blizzard, four feet of snow falling and temperatures of minus 18 C.

Fighting ground to a halt as guns and machines froze and the troops suffered terribly from frostbite. The Nationalists suffered the worse from the cold as they did not have warm clothing. Many amputations were performed to remove frozen limbs.

Franco continued to pour in men and machines and the tide slowly started to turn. The Republicans pressed home the siege however, and by New Year's Day 1938, the defenders of the Convent were dead. The Civil Governor's Building fell on January 3, but Rey d'Harcourt fought on. The attackers and defenders were on different stories of the building and fired at each other through holes in the floors. The defenders, by now had no water, few medical supplies and little food. Their defenses were piles of ruins, but still they held out. The Nationalist advances were stalled because of the weather, and finally Rey d'Harcourt gave up on January 8.

The Republicans, in one of their last acts of the Civil War, killed d'Harcourt along with forty-two other prisoners including the Bishop of Teruel. After Rey d'Harcourt's surrender, the civilian population of Teruel was evacuated and the Republicans became the besieged and the Nationalists the besiegers.

The Nationalist buildup began to tell on the Republican forces. With the weather clearing, the Nationalists started a new advance on January 17, 1938. The Republican leadership finally gave up its scruples about the Battle of Teruel being an all Spanish operation and ordered the International Brigades to join the struggle on the 19th. Many of these units had been in the area but in reserve.

Both high commands were in heated trains near the battlefield directing their troops in the final part of the battle. Slowly but surely, the Nationalists advanced. Teruel's Tooth fell to them. The Republican forces launched fierce counterattacks on January 25 and the next two days, but gains were temporary. Finally on February 7, the Nationalists attacked towards the north of the city. This was a weak area since most Republican forces had been concentrated to the south around Teruel itself. A massive attack broke the Republican defenses and scattered them. Aranda and Yagüe swiftly advanced and the victory was complete. Thousands of prisoners were taken and thousands of tons of supplies and munitions fell to the Nationalists. Those Republicans who could, ran for their lives.

The final battle began on February 18. Aranda and Yagüe cut off the town from the north and then surrounded it similar to what the Republicans accomplished in December. On February 20, Teruel was cut off from the former Republican capital in Valencia and with the Nationalists entering the town, Hernández Saravia gave the order of withdrawal. Most of the army escaped before the route was cut off, but about 14,500 were trapped. Teruel was recaptured by the Nationalists on February 22. The Nationalists found 10,000 Republican corpses in the city alone. The battle was over.

Thirty Five

They dropped down the hillside and walked into Callosa den Sarria. It was the middle of January and an unusually warm day. Juan felt at home now. He'd visited Callosa den Sarria many times as a boy and a youth and spoke the Valencian language fluently.

It was the Valencian language he now spoke as they ambled through the busy streets and he was accepted as one of their own. He used up the very last reserves of what money they had left on an extravagant meal in a small café in town and a room for the night. He knew it was no more than ten kilometres to Guadalest and a similar distance on to Abdet. They'd complete the final leg of their journey tomorrow after they'd rested and eaten.

Young Kiko was in fine form as they feasted on a specially prepared Valencian lamb casserole and Juan and Carmen allowed themselves the luxury of a bottle of wine.

"I swear priest, she whispered. "This is the happiest I have ever seen you."

Juan glanced around the room. "Shhh... you must get out of the habit of using that word or you may wake up and find me with my throat cut." He forked a piece of meat into his mouth and took a mouthful of wine. He chewed as he spoke. "But yes, I am a happy man. I sit here with a full stomach with the woman I love and I swear the war has not reached these parts. Tomorrow we will be home."

He stroked Kiko's head. "All of us. And we will never leave and we will set up home together and I will take you for my wife and take Kiko as our son and—"

"Stop Juan," Carmen interrupted. "Aren't you forgetting one thing? The church. What will they have to say about this?"

Juan sat back in his seat. He had prepared for this moment for some time. Now Carmen sat in the confessional box and it was he who was the confessor.

"I can live without the church."

"Are you sure Juan?" Carmen said. "Do you really believe that is what you want?"

Juan took her hand. "You mean more to me than the church, I have lived without it for many months and it has not bothered me. I have not set foot in a church since Badajoz and it has not harmed me. I have done a lot of thinking of late and it is the way I want to go. I do not need the church; I have grown weary of it. I will work for my parents in Abdet or travel to their Bodega in Algiers, it will give me work and I can support my family."

Carmen laid her fork on the table and breathed out deeply. She was momentarily stunned. Eventually she spoke. "By the grace of God you have it all worked out. When did this all come about?"

"Many months ago but I've been waiting for the right time to tell you." He took her hand. "You approve Carmen? Will you be by my side wherever life takes us?"

She leaned forward and kissed him gently. "I have been by your side for more months than I care to remember. I have been beside you when we have been on the run, when we have starved and nearly frozen to death and I was with you at the horror that was Guernica and Badajoz. What makes you think I will desert you when good times are just around the corner?"

He stroked at the side of her face and she leaned into him. "You feel it too Carmen, you feel this war is drawing to a close?"

"I hope so Juan Cortes, I sincerely hope so."

Thirty Six

Maria opened the shutters on the window of the house, grateful to let a little sun into the house. The warmer wind that had blown down the valley had been more than welcome after the many weeks of cold weather. She sighed, another six or seven weeks and surely spring would return to this part of the world.

She looked out of the window towards the hilltops of Guadalest. The peaks were still covered with a dusting of snow but perhaps if this unusual warm spell continued it would soon disappear.

Felipe worked outside on his pride and joy, a car, an Abadal Buick with a 4 cylinder 3104 cc engine. He'd insisted on buying it early last year from a wealthy landowner who had grown weary of its unreliability. Maria confessed it was better than a mule or even a horse and trap but then again it was prone to the odd breakdown. Felipe didn't seem to mind, always up to his elbows in dirt and grease.

It was Saturday, Maria's favourite day of the week as Mar and Sebastian came for dinner. Maria always prepared something a little special and of course a little wine. Times were tough for the newlyweds, she knew that, but Felipe helped them out occasionally with a little cash injection if the Bodega in Oran had produced a particularly profitable quarter.

Felipe had driven down to Altea yesterday and bought two large dorada which Maria would cook with lemons and fresh garlic. As she hooked back the window the dogs started to bark and she looked instinctively down the hill for her daughter and her husband. She looked at the old clock on the wall, just gone one o'clock. They were a little sharp today, but perhaps Sebastian's boss had let him away early so that he could enjoy the sunshine. She could just about make out the shapes in the distance as the dogs ran down to greet them.

Maria was frowning at the window, straining her eyes to get a better look as they came closer. Felipe appeared in the doorway and walked over to the sink to wash.

"They have come on the mule Felipe. They don't normally come on the mule I hope nothing is wrong."

Felipe dried his hands and they walked out into the garden to meet them.

"Mar is carrying something on her lap," said Felipe. "It looks like a child."

"That is because it is not Mar," said Maria. "She is slightly taller than Mar and the man walks different to Sebastian."

She took as sharp intake of breath as she felt her knees begin to weaken. "He walks like..."

Felipe had also noticed the familiar gait. "Yes I see it too. The man looks like..."

Maria reached for her husband's arm as a crutch on which to steady herself. "... It cannot be, surely not."

Felipe had started walking quickly towards the couple and the child, dragging his wife along with him. The man waved and they heard *Hola Mama, Papa!*

Maria broke free and sank to her knees crying as the reality of what was happening sank in. Felipe broke into a full run and reached his son within a few seconds embracing him as he too broke down and sobbed. He held Juan's face for some time as if not quite believing who it was standing in front of him. Soon they were all crying, Maria and Juan and Carmen too, even young Kiko sobbed though he didn't quite know why.

As Juan took his mother's hand she found the strength to stand. "My son," she said, "I knew you would return one day. I did not believe them. I knew they were wrong."

Juan was puzzled. "Who was wrong Mama?"

She held his hand. "The church was wrong son, they said you were dead."

Juan shook his head. "No, surely not?" He looked at his father. "Is this right Papa?"

"Yes," Felipe said. "They told us you had been taken by Republicans in Seville."

Maria spoke. "And we wrote you a letter and a man delivered it to where they thought you were but they said they were unable to locate you."

Juan reached into his pocket. "This letter Mama?" He held it out and she took it from him.

"I have carried it next to my heart for many months," Juan said, "but I was unable to get any news back to you, it was impossible."

Maria opened her mouth to speak but Felipe cut his wife short fearing a long drawn out enquiry that they could do without. "Later my dear. Give our son a little space, we can go over this another day."

Juan took Carmen's hand and pulled her forward so that she almost fell into him. He looked at his father and then his mother. "I have much to tell you my dear parents. This is Carmen. She will soon be my wife."

Maria felt the familiar sensation oozing back into her trembling legs again and reached for Felipe once again. "Madre Mia," she said. "Holy mother of God, he cannot be serious the man has forgotten he is a priest."

She took him by the hand and led him towards the house. "Come... you can tell me while I cook. I need to prepare some food for your sister, she will be here soon and you can meet her husband for the first time."

Juan was smiling. "He's a good boy?"

"A fine boy," Maria said. "He worships the ground Mar walks on."

"And so he should," said Felipe. "He would have me to answer to if he didn't"

Juan slapped his father on the back. "Quite right Papa, quite right."

Maria cooked more rice and vegetables and sent Felipe down to the village for more bread and a bottle of their best wine. Two hours later Mar and Sebastian arrived and the family sat down and ate and drank and urged Juan to tell their incredible tale. It was a celebration that would last well into the night.

Thirty Seven

The Spanish Civil War could have been a million miles away. Felipe and Maria insisted Juan, Carmen and Kiko stayed with them for the immediate future and would not allow them anywhere near the church in the village. Much to Juan's surprise Maria allowed him to take the room in the basement of the large house with his wife to be.

Kiko was more than happy with his small room close to that of Maria and Felipe. They fussed over him and treated him as if he was one of their own and he basked in the attention.

Spring was coming to the hills of Abdet and Guadalest and the weather was getting warmer. Mar visited them often and their relationship as brother and sister blossomed and they bonded as if he'd never been away. He didn't see quite as much of Sebastian but then again Mar explained it was the busiest time of the year and there was much work to be done in the fields.

"I must make the trip to Xirles, in the next few days," Juan announced over dinner one evening. "I need to catch up with Vicente and Fatima and tell Father Ismael of my decision sooner rather than later. Word has filtered down to the village I am back and he will be expecting me to turn up in my holy robes to take a confession or conduct a mass. He has been good to me, he has been my mentor and my tutor and I fear I have let him down."

Felipe spoke. "You have not let him down son, there must be hundreds of priests who see the light and turn their backs on the church. We are at war and given what you have seen no one can blame you for this."

Juan shrugged his shoulders. "That may be the case papa, but I am still dreading the moment when I have to tell him. He has spent many hours with me and whatever way you look at it I am turning my back on him and his church."

Carmen took his hand. "Would you like me to come with you?"

"No," Juan answered without hesitation. "It will be bad enough without announcing I am to take a wife as well." He laughed out loud. "The man is getting on in years and I don't want to give him a heart attack. I will tell him about you when the time is right."

"Let him take your wedding service," Felipe quipped. "That would be something to savour, a priest conducting the wedding of another priest. Even I might venture into the church to see that."

Felipe had also turned his back on the church many years ago. There had been many weddings in the local church at Abdet over the last few years and even a funeral or two but Felipe had not attended any of them.

"I doubt that very much," said Maria. It would need half a dozen oxen to pull you across the threshold of a church."

"You must take the car Juan, it will be so much quicker." Said Felipe.

"But I can't drive," said Juan, I'll be over the first hill and you'll never see your precious vehicle again."

But Felipe was already on his feet reaching for the key that hung on a hook by the door.

"I will teach you, it's about time you learned."

"No I couldn't, I don't know one end of a car from the other."

Felipe was shaking his head. "You tell me you want to help with the family business then you will need to learn to drive. You haven't got the option son, you drive or you go back to the priesthood."

Felipe was laughing as he walked towards the door. "And your first lesson starts now."

Juan sighed. He knew it was a pointless exercise arguing and yes he did want to be involved in the business and make the trips to Oran so that his father could stay at home.

They had talked briefly since he had returned home but perhaps now was the right time to get involved. He would need to learn the business from top to bottom and yes, being able to drive a car would make everything so much easier.

His father drove to him to Alcoy, more than forty kilometres away explaining the controls and the pedals and the fundamentals of what makes and engine work and how it turns the wheels. At Alcoy they changed places and Felipe made Juan drive back.

He was a bundle of nerves at first but by the time they arrived back in Abdet some hours later, Juan thought he'd been driving all his life. He climbed from the driver's seat proudly as Kiko ran to greet him and thought to himself he would leave first thing tomorrow at the crack of dawn. Father Ismael wasn't one for sleeping in late and was generally in the church most days by eight o'clock. If he could negotiate the car down one or two steep hills he would be at the church doors waiting for him. He'd get the meeting over with as soon as possible and would spend the rest of the day with Vicente and Fatima.

Thirty Eight

The embrace was long, warm and sincere and as the two men parted Juan noticed the tears in Father Ismael's eyes. They held each other at arm's length for some minutes while it all sank in.

"The prodigal son returns," said Ismael. "I knew you would. God is great and he has looked after you."

He took Juan by the arm. "Come, you must be hungry and thirsty it's a long way from Abdet on a mule."

Juan shook his head. "It took me little over two hours because I have my father's car."

Father Ismael raised an eyebrow. "You have? You drive?"

Juan nodded. "Only since yesterday and I would warn you if you see me coming keep out of the way. But yes, I managed to get here safely and quickly thanks to modern engineering."

They took a little breakfast in the café down the street from the church and they talked for some time. Juan wondered just how much Father Ismael had heard. He had talked openly about leaving the church in front of Mar and Sebastian and wondered if any of his words had been carried this far. Sebastian sometimes worked in La Nucia, just a kilometre away and something told him that his new brother-in-law was not one to keep a secret too long.

It was time to find out.

"Father Ismael... I..."

Father Ismael looked up as he swallowed a mouthful of bread. He knew, something told Juan he knew.

Why was he so nervous? Why couldn't he just come out with it? He'd thought long and hard about this moment, chosen and composed his words carefully during the long trek from Guernica. That's where he lost his faith, that's where he questioned the very existence of something that had been part of his life for as long as he could remember.

"Guernica." Juan said.

"A terrible business," said Father Ismael. "Is it true you were there?"

"Guernica," he repeated staring into space. "That's where I lost it."

Father Ismael looked up, a puzzled look spread across his face. "I don't understand Juan, lost what?"

Juan reached for his coffee and drained the cup. The caffeine kicked in almost immediately.

He spoke. "I lost my faith Father Ismael."

"Your faith?"

"Yes my faith."

"But I..."

"My faith in mankind, in the church, my faith in my fellow priests I'd traveled with since Seville and I lost my faith in the Lord for he allowed it all to happen."

Father Ismael gave a little laugh, placed his hand on Juan's knee. "You are not thinking straight Juan, you have witnessed many things but must understand the Lord-"

"Works in mysterious ways." Juan interrupted.

"No I was-"

"That's what you were going to say wasn't it?"

Father Ismael looked over his shoulder. "Keep your voice down Juan."

One or two people looked over in their direction.

Juan lowered his voice a little. "The excuse the church uses when they comfort the grieving."

"What else do we tell them?" Ismael said forcefully. "God is our judge and whatever happens there is a reason for it."

"A reason for it?" Juan said incredulously.

"Yes, there is a good reason for everything in life no matter how unpleasant it may be, we just have to accept it."

"You are telling me that the Lord is quite happy to oversee the massacre of defenseless villagers shopping in a marketplace. You're telling me that the Lord approved of what happened in Guernica?" He raised his voice a little. "And what about Badajoz Ismael? Did the Lord sit on his cloud and watch as they brought groups of men women and children into the bullring and lined them up against the wall so that the Guardia Civil could use them as target practice."

Father Ismael looked around. He looked more than a little angry.

"Juan, please, control your tongue and keep your voice down. And if you have quite finished?"

Juan's fist connected with the table as the cups and plates jumped an inch into the air before crashing back down onto the table.

"I haven't even started." He clenched his teeth as he leaned forward. "Our damned church stands and watches while all this takes place and we do nothing." Juan ranted on. "And the Germans who bombed Guernica... they made me tell the pilots that our so called God was flying with them. Do you know how that made me feel?"

Before he could offer an opinion Juan continued. The spittle foamed up around the corners of his mouth. "They worship the same god as we do. Did you know that Ismael? They have inscriptions to him on their belt buckles and their caps. They kill and maim and convince themselves He approves and stands with them."

Juan was breathing hard; Father Ismael took the opportunity to speak. "We cannot choose who worships our God Juan; they have as much right as we do."

Juan looked up. A feint smile crept across his face as he began to wag his finger in Father Ismael's face.

"Not me Ismael, not me. I worship him no longer for I fear he doesn't exist."

Father Ismael leaned forward as he gritted his teeth angrily. "Hold your tongue boy. I order you to hold your tongue and keep your voice down. What will people think if they hear those words coming from the mouth of a priest?"

"Hah! You order me Ismael." He barked. "On whose authority do you order me? Not the church because I do not belong... and God? You've just heard me." He raised his voice as he stood and called out to the people assembled in the bar.

"He doesn't exist. God doesn't exist do you hear."

Father Ismael had a hand on his sleeve begging him to sit down and be quiet. Two elderly ladies were shaking their heads and others were voicing their disapproval.

"It's the war," someone whispered. "It has sent the poor boy crazy."

Juan caught the comment and looked over towards where it had come from.

"You think I'm crazy?"

He walked towards the centre of the room. "I'll tell you what's crazy shall I? Crazy is giving every spare peseta to an organisation that washes your brain with soap just as soon as you can string two words together. It tells you there's an invisible man who watches over you every minute of every day and that invisible man can speak many languages and hears everything you ask of him and he will grant your requests but only if you are good and true and faithful to him."

"Juan sit, please, you do not know what you are saying." Said Ismael.

Juan turned his attention to his old mentor. "And our beloved God sends floods and droughts and famines and disease does he not? And he brings wars and massacres and genocide does he not Father?"

Juan began to laugh. "He works in mysterious ways does our beloved Father and these people are programmed to simply accept it."

Father Ismael covered his mouth with his hand as he looked down at the table.

Juan raised both hands to the ceiling. "He loves us. The invisible man in the sky loves us all."

The silence in the small room was deafening.

He sat down slowly, reached across and placed his hand on Father Ismael's knee as he leaned across the table.

"I am sorry Ismael, I truly am, but I can take no more. You treated me like a son and I worshipped you like a father. You did your job and you almost fooled me."

Father Ismael brushed his hand away aggressively. "Fool you? How dare you suggest such a thing."

Juan nodded. "Ah... now I see Ismael, how could I doubt you? You truly are a believer aren't you? Everything you force fed me you believed in."

"Juan, you are not thinking straight, why do you say these things to me? I did not force feed you anything I preached the gospel of Jesus Christ and his teachings."

"You did Ismael. You did… and you preached it with passion and sincerity I'll give you that but I've had many months to think and there are too many things that do not make sense."

"Like what Juan? What does not make sense?"

Juan raised his eyebrows as he took a deep sigh. "I have traveled the length of Spain," he said, "and without exception the church is the focal point of every village, every town and city, more often than not situated on an elevated position overlooking the people. The churches are clean, the priests and their companions fed and watered well. They are more than prosperous and grow richer almost by the day. Each month we send millions of peseta's to Rome while the people in Spain starve and still we beg them for more. I sat in the church house in Seville while my fellow priests ate and drank till they could eat and drink no more and they gorged themselves in Badajoz while the streets ran red with blood."

"But Juan, there are bad apples in every box."

"There are too many bad apples in this box Ismael and I have had my fill. Nothing you can say will make me change my mind. I am finished with the church and with God. I will live the life of an honest man from now on."

"But Juan, no you must—"

Juan stood. He kissed Ismael on both cheeks. "Thank you for listening to me Ismael and I am sorry for raising my voice. I have said what it was I wanted to say and it was not easy, but I have said it and I feel so much better."

"Juan sit, please, we can talk about this."

He took Ismael's hand and shook it warmly. "I must be going. Fatima and Vicente will be waiting for me."

"Juan no… please don't go."

Thirty Nine

"The bastard was at Badajoz and Guernica and we all know what happened there. I'm telling you he's a damned church spy, a fifth columnist."

"You don't know that and we can't be certain."

Another man stood and spoke. "I'm not so sure, he was in the bar in Xirles last week criticising the church in no uncertain terms."

"It's a front man! I'm telling you it was all for show. As soon as he hears someone else calling the damned church he will be straight to the fascists with a name."

"We can't take any chances," he said.

There was more than a little animosity and jealousy mixed in with the passion as Sebastian pleaded with his comrades to at least question the former priest. Sebastian's plans and aspirations for the future were all in shreds as he'd listened one evening last week as Felipe and Maria described the wonderful business they'd set up all those years ago and how there would always be a position there for their only son. Juan announced he had given up the priesthood and accepted his father's invitation to join the company without hesitation.

And it got worse. The news from Teruel was not good. In fact it was disastrous. The Republican army had been routed; the Nationalists now in control of vast swathes of the country and some estimates said that 150,000 Republicans had been killed.

Paco had sat in the corner and listened throughout the passionate debate. He was an elected councilor and had been for many years. Now the wrong side of sixty he spoke seldom but when he did people tended to listen. He was well liked and respected. He asked the self-appointed chairman for permission to speak.

"Granted," Said Sebastian.

He stood and spoke. "I have listened long and hard to both sides of this debate and tensions are running high. We must not jump to conclusions or be too hasty."

Sebastian was losing patience. "What is your point old man?"

"My point is that it surely can't do any harm if we take the priest away for a little interrogation."

Sebastian smiled. Why didn't I let this man speak earlier he thought to himself.

Forty

They had studied Juan's recent movements, watching him constantly over a three week period. On market day each Tuesday, without fail he made the trip to Altea in his father's car staying in the town until early evening. Sometimes he brought Carmen and the boy but now and again he made the trip on his own.

Sebastian informed the *welcoming committee* that he had casually mentioned his wife and adopted son would not be attending the market that particular week and he would be traveling alone.

The first week in May was particularly hot and the market place busy, though the produce noticeably scarce. As soon as Juan walked among the throngs of people the heart palpitations started in earnest. He hoped they would lessen over time but no matter how hard he tried, he always thought back to that fateful day in Guernica and could not help but look up into the sky at the scavenging seagulls hovering overhead.

More than once his imagination played tricks on him and the birds mysteriously transformed into the shapes of aircraft. Even their shrieks and squeals sounded ominously like the bombs that he'd heard falling on Guernica sending shivers up his spine.

He managed to secure the purchase of two sea bass. Felipe would never forgive him if he returned home empty handed after such a long journey.

He'd had enough, it was time to go. For some reason the heart palpitations were particularly bad today. He gazed into the sky several times as he approached the spot where he had parked Felipe's car. What was it about today? Something just didn't feel right.

As he pushed the car into gear and drove away he was glad to leave the market place behind. After three kilometres he passed the road end which turned left into Alfas Del Pi and headed directly towards La Nucia and once there he turned right in the direction of Polop and Xirles.

He always called in to see Vicente and Fatima on a Tuesday and today would be no different. As he approached the road that led to Xirles he looked over the top of the windscreen at a man waving frantically as if something was wrong. He slowed down. The man was familiar to him. It was Sebastian.

"Hola Sebastian, what are you doing here?"

Sebastian climbed straight into the car uninvited. "I have a little problem Juan; I need to get to a house on the other side of La Nucia urgently. Can you help me?"

"Sure Sebastian, where in La Nucia?"

"On the road to Finestrat, it's my bosses land and he needs me there pronto!"

Juan was already turning the car. "You point the way Sebastian and I'll get you there," he said smiling.

Juan tried many times to strike up a conversation on the way to their destination but it was as painful as pulling teeth. It was clear to see Sebastian was a worried man and after a time Juan thought it best just to stay quiet. Two kilometres outside the village of La Nucia, Sebastian spoke.

"Here Juan." He pointed. "By this tree... stop here."

Sebastian pulled a pistol from his pocket. "Out of the car Juan, now."

Juan looked down at the gun pointing at his midriff. At first he thought it was some kind of prank until he looked into his brother-in-laws eyes. Juan froze, unable to contemplate what was happening.

"Out now priest," he screamed thrusting the barrel of the pistol into his kidney.

Juan made a grab for the door handle and almost fell out of the car.

"Sebastian what are you doing are you crazy?"

The four men appeared from nowhere. They wore large handkerchiefs over their faces and they all carried guns. Juan was ordered to place his hands behind his back and they were tied roughly while some sort of hood was pulled over his head.

As they walked to an unknown destination the questions started. He was aware of walking into some sort of out building, perhaps a barn or a wood store. He was accused of being a spy and a puppet of the church. He recognised his brother in laws voice as that of the chief instigator.

voices were growing more aggressive and the first blow registered on the back of his head as he hit the floor and suddenly he felt very afraid.

The interrogation of Juan Francisco Cortes lasted for nearly two hours. His questioners vilified the Church and accused them of collaboration with the Nationalist rebels.

At dusk they walked him back to the side of the road at La Nucia. They questioned him some more and then they beat him with rifle butts. Juan curled up into a little ball as he begged them to stop.

Nothing made sense, there had to have been some sort of mistake. He'd done nothing but help people since the war started. And then a thought flashed through his mind... did He exist after all? Was this his punishment for abandoning his faith in the Lord?

Sebastian was screaming at him saying something about Badajoz and how he'd helped round up the Republicans and took them to the bull ring.

Juan was exhausted and found it difficult to speak through his broken teeth. His protestations were barely audible. "No Sebastian you are wrong." He took several deep breaths before continuing. "You were not there... you cannot know... I prayed for their souls, there was nothing more I could do."

Sebastian was growing angrier by the second and whipped him across the face with his pistol. Juan felt the blood trickle into his mouth. And then he tasted something different. Something was forced roughly between his teeth. He winced in pain as another part of his front tooth broke but still the object went in deeper.

And then he realised what it was.

Sebastian gritted his teeth and pulled the trigger of his Star pistol. He was aware of his brother in laws body stiffen and then relax all within a split second as the back of his skull shattered into a thousand pieces.

Forty One

"Fatima," he said. "Just let me go and stop fussing."

"But it's hot and you need to carry more water."

Vicente sighed. Why did it always have to be like this? He would tell her that he knew every cold water spring between here and Finestrat and even in summer there were a few that never dried up and he would tell her that carrying more water meant more weight to carry and slower progress.

"Then be off with you, you old scoundrel, you never listen to me anyway."

"Goodbye cariño see you soon."

Vicente was still chuckling to himself as he left the outskirts of the village and walked over the bridge that spanned the river Algar. Fatima had not been in a good mood since Juan had failed to show up on market day. It had been a regular occurrence for some weeks now but Vicente had told her that the produce in the market place was almost nonexistent and he probably just hadn't bothered that day.

He would turn up next week, he was sure of it. He took a slightly different route this time, a deviation that would take him northwards up onto his fruit orchards. With a little luck there would still be a few oranges to pick from the trees which he could push into his pockets for the journey. He had another reason to go up there too. He never tired of gazing into the tree where he first spotted the young baby suspended in a basket. And Juan was back in their lives once again. Despite the war, life was more than bearable

Yes, it was time to pay homage and say a little prayer of thanks to the tree that had brought them so much joy.

His side pockets were full as he walked down the dusty track towards Polop, whistling a tune. He passed a few friends along the way, called in quickly to a bar in the village and took a small beer that would set him up nicely for the hot trek to La Nucia.

He was perspiring freely by the time he reached La Nucia and suddenly the road to Finestrat seemed a lot further away than it had in days gone by. Was it his imagination or did he have to rest a lot more often on the excursions of late?

As he left La Nucia, the views to Benidorm and the deep azure sea in the distance opened up and as always it gave Vicente a little spring in his step. He would never tire of these views Mother Nature had created for him but wondered when Father Time would call it a day on his old knees. The time would surely come, not this year or even next but who knows, possibly the year after.

He was still looking out to sea as something caught his attention out of the corner of his eye. He looked up ahead and strained to get a better look, subconsciously slowing down. Something inside told him this was not something he actively wanted to hurry towards. Another involuntary action, a shiver ran the length of his spine. What was it exactly? It looked like a dead donkey. That was it; an old mule had fallen into the ditch. He picked up the pace. He was only fifty metres away when he made out the shape of a man's leg twisted at a grotesque angle from the body. He stopped, looked skywards and crossed his chest as he reluctantly inched ever closer.

"Holy Mother of God," he mumbled to himself as the huge slick of semi congealed blood revealed itself to him.

"A man, the dead body of a man, oh sweet Jesus."

Had the civil war reached these peaceful parts at last?

As he neared the body a huge carpet of blue-bodied flies took fright and ascended from the cor pse.

"My God tell me what I should do I'm no medical man."

He looked back down the road towards La Nucia. The road was deserted. He stepped into the middle of the road and gazed in the opposite direction towards Benidorm willing for someone to appear. Why would anyone be walking the road at this time of day? There were no markets at Benidorm or Finestrat today; there was no reason for anyone to be on the road.

He looked back towards the body lying face down, the head tucked into the chest and he could see the bloody gory mess on the back of the man's skull. The man had been shot or had had his head caved in with something sharp.

He had to do something, there was a chance the man still might be alive and if not the very least he could do was say a prayer. He knew how to check for a pulse, his uncle had showed him many years ago. He walked towards the body. A pulse, that was it, he would check for a pulse.

As soon as he reached for a hand the body was cold to the touch and stiff and he knew it was a hopeless cause. The poor devil was dead.

He didn't know what possessed him but he suddenly got the urge to see the man's face. He kneeled down, leaned over the body reaching for the sleeve of the arm furthest away from him. He took it with two hands and heaved the body over. The face was bloodless and pale but recognition was instant.

Vicente released the arm and fell back onto his backside his hand covering his mouth as the tears began to well up in his eyes.

"No sweet Jesus, this cannot be." He whispered. "This is not possible, not right."

Vicente lost control of his emotions as he began to wail. He shuffled towards the body again stroking Juan's cold lifeless body. "Please wake up son, please wake up and tell me I'm dreaming. "Wake up Juan... wake up..."

Vicente was still sitting by the dead body when a truck of Guardia Civil found him as it was getting dark. They had to physically prise him from the body and promise him that they would fetch the local priest from Xirles. They explained it was the right thing to do and his son would expect a decent burial.

Father Ismael was brought in the truck within the hour. Fatima was with him. She had been told the news, her face was stained with tears and she trembled uncontrollably. Father Ismael took out a small bible from his pocket and stood over the body as he spoke. "Lord now lettest thy servant depart in peace according to thy word."

Vicente felt a little better. It's what Juan would have wanted he thought.

An hour later the Guardia Civil still couldn't persuade him to move away from the body.

"Who would have done such a thing?" He asked.

"Fanatical republicans," the Guardia Civil officer answered without hesitation. "The reds are everywhere and the church is fair game."

"But he was a good boy, he had no enemies." Vicente answered.

"It matters not. The church and their priests and the Brides of Jesus are the enemies of the Republic and the sooner we have routed the bastards the better and Spain can return to normal and build again."

The officer turned to Father Ismael. "Isn't that right Father?"

Vicente looked over towards Father Ismael. He didn't answer the officer. The priest wondered when the time would be right to explain to Vicente and Fatima what Juan had said that day in the café.

Not today. Perhaps not ever.

And Ismael disagreed with the officer. This was not the work of the republicans because word had clearly filtered out that Juan had denounced the church and even God. This was personal, nearer to home. He was sure of it.

Father Ismael conducted the funeral of Juan Francisco Cortes the following day. Nearly one hundred people had walked the best part of the day from Abdet to attend. Felipe and Maria, Carmen and Kiko had traveled by car.

Felipe had reluctantly agreed to a church service, for Maria's sake he assured himself and of course Vicente and Fatima too who despite everything had not lost their faith, but Felipe absolutely refused to set foot inside the church.

He waited outside while the funeral service took place.

Father Ismael climbed wearily into the pulpit, the wooden casket laid out in front of him. There was lead in his boots today, the six wooden steps felt like the mountain path to the summit of Puig Campana.

He had presided over many hundreds of funerals. During La Cucaracha there was sometimes two or three a day. And as he held his hands up to the heavens and gazed over the coffin towards the mourners this was normally the point in time when a sense of peace washed over him.

Not today.

He sighed inwardly watching the altar candles reflecting off the ancient stonework. He took a deep breath and began.

The words he'd use in an attempt to calm and comfort the friends and family of Juan Francisco Cortes seemed almost fraudulent.

God was watching over them. There were many difficult trials and tests of faith in the bible. And then he said it. *God works in mysterious ways.* He couldn't help it. What else could he say to comfort them? There were no other words. There were no better words he could think of.

And it worked. He looked at several of the tear drenched bleary eyed faces and they visited the sign of the cross, kissed their finger nails and pointed to heaven at the exact moment he'd said it.

He watched as the path of sunlight streamed through the pristine, stained glass window as it crept across their faces highlighting their tears and beyond. A few tears of joy now as the people took strength and solace in their grief comforted by his words.

No Juan, he thought, you were wrong. God is everywhere and although he may indeed work in mysterious ways he is here with us now and I see it in their sad eyes, I see how he lifts their spirits as I talk to them in this his special place.

"God our Father, your power brings us to birth, your providence guides our lives and by your command we return to dust. Juan Francisco Cortes is in company with Christ who died and now lives. May he rejoice in your kingdom where all his tears shall be wiped away. The soul of this righteous man is now in the hands of God and no torment will ever touch him again."

Father Ismael paused for a second. A few of the mourners looked up. For some strange reason he made eye contact with Sebastian, the brother in law of Juan Cortes but the man quickly diverted his gaze and looked down at the floor.

"In the eyes of the foolish he seems to have died but he is at peace. For though in the sight of others he has been punished he will receive great good because God tested him and found him worthy of himself."

Father Ismael found an inner strength and even began to smile.

"There is no greater honour than to join Our Father in his house and sit beside him for all eternity."

One or two of the mourners had regained the colour in their cheeks; a few were even smiling back at him. The priest made the sign of the cross.

"Amen."

"Amen." They replied in unison.

Afterwards, Juan Francisco Cortes was placed in a simple niche in a section of the cemetery of Polop. The priest mingled with the mourners as they took refreshments under a sun shade suspended between the fir trees that surrounded the holy ground.

Maria stood with her husband and Fatima and Vicente.

"A lovely service Father," Fatima said.

"Very much appreciated," Vicente said with a smile.

Maria nodded her appreciation.

The priest turned to Felipe. "It's a sad thing to say Felipe, but I think Juan would have taken great joy from his service."

Felipe took a drink from his glass.

There was an uncomfortable silence as he smiled at the priest but did not answer.

Maria pulled at his shirt and whispered. Felipe where are your manners? Answer the Father.

It was the priest who spoke again.

"Felipe. Juan would have approved, no?"

All eyes were on Felipe as he drained his glass and spoke in a whisper. "If I'm honest I doubt it Father, I truly doubt it."

Fatima's glass fell from her grip and shattered on the ground causing the people in the immediate vicinity to look over.

Maria looked around as her face turned red. "Felipe, please, there is a time and place."

He took her hand. "You are right my love." He gestured to the priest. "I do apologise Ismael, please forgive me."

Granted Felipe," he said. "It is a difficult time for you, I understand."

"Take a small walk with me won't you Father?"

A little taken aback Ismael had no choice but to agree. He walked with Felipe through the fir trees until they were out of sight of the mourners.

At last Felipe spoke. "I am sorry to shatter your perception of my son Ismael, but Juan lost his faith during the time he was away. He did not believe in a God who allows his people to suffer like this."

Felipe continued. "He confided in me when he returned. He said he'd read the bible several times during his year on the road and it was full of inconsistencies and double standards. The more he read it the more it lacked credibility." Felipe laughed out loud. "He said Jesus found out the truth too Ismael. At the end Jesus said, 'My God, my God why have you forsaken me?' Is it true Ismael? Is that what Jesus said? Did your God forsake Jesus, has your Lord forsaken all of us?"

Ismael instinctively began to shake his head and yet try as he might he couldn't find the words to offer up any sort of defence. He wanted to say that Juan had had the same conversation with him a few days before he died.

"Did Jesus truly say that Father?"

The priest did not answer.

"Your church tries to tell me how to live my life, you told my only son how to live his and this is how he is rewarded. I confess it took me all my time not to storm into your church this morning and stop the farce you were conducting."

"But Felipe," Ismael protested, "Juan's friends and family took great comfort from the service. We cannot bring him back but we laid him to rest with dignity and respect."

Felipe was nodding. "You did Ismael, I'll grant you that and I thank you from the bottom of my heart because your soul is good and I know you truly believe. It's just..."

Father Ismael placed a hand on Felipe's shoulder. "What is it Felipe? Tell me."

Felipe looked into the priests eyes and smiled. "I do not need to tell you Ismael. You know the story only too well. The church ruined my life from the moment they stole my son in the middle of the night."

"But Felipe there was good reason, the church-"

"There was no reason." Felipe snapped. "There was never a reason to take my boy like a robber takes a purse; the church had no right to do that to me and Maria."

"Felipe please calm down."

"And your beloved church sent me away and by the time I found my boy again you'd sank your poisoned claws into his head and took him from me a second time."

"But Felipe I—"

"And you wonder why I'm so bitter."

Felipe looked skywards and began to breathe deeply. He wiped a tear from the corner of his eye.

He placed his arm around the priest. "It is time for me to go Ismael, I have said my piece."

He kissed him on the cheek. "Goodbye Ismael. You take care and do what it is you believe you have to do."

He walked a few steps down towards the party of mourners and then he turned. "I will say one thing though Ismael."

"What's that Felipe?"

"He died a free man Ismael. My son died a free man."

He stuck a hand up in the air as he waved and walked away. "You tell your bishop that Father Ismael, Juan Francisco Cortes is free at last."

Epilogue

Juan Francisco Cortez died in March of 1938.

There remained more than 13 long months of fighting, which for most Republicans was increasingly futile. They had been fed a continuous stream of propaganda for some time promising their supporters an 'ultimate victory.'

An increasing number however realised the real truth of the situation including Sebastian and his comrades in La Nucia and the surrounding areas who did their level best to blend into the background and keep their political ideals to themselves in the hope that the locals would conveniently forget about their previous passions for the Republican cause.

After the Nationalist troops reached the Mediterranean there was little doubt that Barcelona could have been taken fairly quickly, however Franco was content to take his time, pushing his troops slowly toward Valencia, and maintaining and strengthening the front line that faced the powerhouse of Barcelona to the North.

By now Barcelona was a disaster zone. The capital city of Cataluña was crowded with refugees from all parts of Spain including around 25,000 orphans of Republicans, herded together like animals in this increasingly small section of the country. It was not a time for sympathy or mercy and the commander of the Italian air force stationed in Mallorca decided to try out huge new bombs on this defenceless mostly civilian population. It was not dissimilar to the German objective in Guernica two years prior. The huge blasts killed up to 1000 people a day and caused widespread condemnation on an international level but there was satisfaction for the Italian commanders who regarded it as an important and successful experiment.

Ultimately though, the delay in attacking Barcelona was a mistake, allowing sections of Republican troops to regroup and undertake the last big battle of the war, the battle of the Ebro, when over 80,000 men swarmed across the river taking the Nationalists by surprise and retaking a section of territory.

The Nationalist answer was to open the dam gates of the big reservoirs upstream unleashing walls of water that swept away the bridges that had allowed the Republicans across the river. The Republican troops were now trapped with the Nationalists to the front and the huge river to the rear.

This was the scene of the biggest air battle of the war with up to 300 bombers and fighters in the air at once bombing and strafing the hapless troops below. As the waters eventually subsided the Republicans retreated back across the river but left over 70,000 dead behind. The damage done to the Republican cause was now terminal and when Franco did decide the time was right to push for Barcelona the defenders had few working weapons with which to fight him with. They were easily pushed back with just small pockets of resistance. The resulting refugees, over 500,000 by some estimates streamed towards the French border some carrying a solitary pocket of Spanish soil to remind them of their homeland.

They were mercilessly bombed and machine gunned from the air as they attempted to complete their perilous journey. The survivors managed to force themselves across the border and into the makeshift tented camps that had been set up there.

A precedent had been set, the losers in this war were not a consideration and of course expendable. As Franco's victorious troops entered Barcelona they were allowed several days of complete freedom to do as they liked. The scenes of slaughter were horrific before the church eventually took control and shamed the slaughterers into showing a little compassion. However, the church decided that the city still had to be cleansed of sinners and set up makeshift alters on street corners.

The priests and their assistants invited non- believers to take mass and thereafter convert to the status of God fearing obedient Catholics. The identities of those refusing to kowtow to the church were passed to the blood thirsty Nationalist troops, their fate obvious.

Franco had by now introduced a Law of Political Responsibilities which in effect made every single Republican whether they had fought or not, guilty of a crime. The centre of

Spain was isolated and Franco's troops began their push to finish the war gradually moving westward towards Valencia.

Some of the villages that were now being overrun by Nationalist troops had been almost deserted by the occupants. Those with a little money had fled to the nearest ports to try and get away by boat. Most of those who succeeded chose Algeria as their final destination.

An equal number of residents, realising that they had no chance of escape chose to remain and accept their fate. The tiny villages of Abdet, La Nucia and Polop like many others saw a solitary vehicle with heavily armed Guardia Civil enter and position themselves in the town square or in front of the church.

In Xirles, the terrified residents were lined up outside their homes while Father Ismael was summoned. It was normally down to the priest to inform the troops if there was anyone in particular to be taken away and *questioned*. Father Ismael did not offer up the name of any resident of Xirles but he mentioned the name of a certain Sebastian Jimenez of Abdet who had verbally abused him and the church on more than one occasion.

He also informed them of village whispers suggesting the man may have been partly to blame for the murder of a former resident of Xirles and a man of the cloth, Juan Francisco Cortes.

Some priests who had lived the war quietly with their heads down with churches empty of worshipers were to be catapulted into positions of enormous power, the like of which the church had not seen in Spain for centuries.

The church attendance rate went to 100% overnight as priests were given authority on everything from education, moral behaviour and even the issuing of church attendance certificates guaranteeing spiritual goodness which were now necessary to get a job. Women in particularly were severely restricted in their activities, forbidden to travel without written authorisation from their husband and prohibited from owning property.

Control of people's freedoms extended into every aspect of their lives. Property of former republicans was often confiscated without compensation and reunions or associations of any type were completely forbidden, as was freedom of expression.

Regional languages such as Catalan were banned; everyone was obliged to speak Castellano or *correct* Spanish. A period of re-Christianisation was implemented and people with so called *exotic* or unusual names were given 60 days to formally change them for that of a prominent saint.

Censorship applied to everything, the cinema was filled with films showing miracles that happened to people who followed wholesome, God fearing lives and books were only sold if they had been passed as suitable by the church authorities. There were even guidelines published as to what clothes were deemed as suitable for certain seasons of the year. Men were to wear jackets, even in summer, while on the beaches swimwear had to be of a regulation size and people had to cover themselves up as soon as they left the water so as to avoid immoral temptation in others.

Fines were issued for swimmers who did not conform and their names were published in *lists of shame* in newspapers. It was ordered that in the register of births, children had to be identified as illegitimate if they had been born out of wedlock, something that would prejudice them all their lives under the totalitarian regime.

This particular law did not go down well with Felipe and Maria and their early memories of their enforced separation came back to haunt them. Felipe's bitterness at the growing power of the church spilled over in several bar fights as he fronted up to anyone who dared to support or praise the church reforms. Felipe was heard on many occasions to say that the clock had been turned back to medieval times and living in Spain was like living with the Inquisitors.

The small villages and their inhabitants who made their living almost entirely from the growing of crops had to take a good percentage of their produce and deliver it to the town halls where it was to be *distributed equally*. Poverty and hunger was widespread with people eating anything they could to survive and any attempt to hide food was reported, the offenders risking fines, imprisonment or even worse.

In Abdet, word had reached Sebastian that his name had been given to the Guardia Civil and he fled in the middle of the night as Mar slept. He left her a note blaming her brother and his beloved church and said he would not be back.

Mar was devastated when she found the note just before seven the next morning and at 8.30 a truck load of gun wielding Guardia Civil turned up at the house looking for Sebastian Jimenez who they said was wanted for the murder of her brother, Juan Francisco Cortes.

Sebastian was taking no chances with the Guardia Civil and fled to the Alicante dock area, the last port to be reached by the Nationalists. The port was filled with over 40,000 Republicans many of them realising they faced certain torture and even death. They were determined to get away but there were simply not enough ships and boats. The boats captains were asking for goods as payment for passage, almonds or saffron were favoured currency as the Republican peseta was now almost worthless.

Certain towns such as Benidorm, led by socialist mayor José Pagés Barceló had arranged its own emergency transport in the manner of small fishing boats which carried himself and a good number of his town hall colleagues to the relative safety of Africa.

The desperation back on the port of Alicante led to some people committing suicide by falling on bayonets or hanging themselves from cranes on the dockside rather than face capture.

Some boats and ships were even sabotaged by Nationalist sympathisers to ensure that the evacuees had to remain to face the music. The most notable evacuation was carried out by the cargo ship Stanbrook, commanded by Welsh Captain Archibald Dickson. The ship of just 1382 tons had entered the port on March 19th at 18.00 to load a cargo of tobacco; by March 27th the captain had only loaded a small amount of cargo before he was approached by port authorities asking him to take refugees instead. He agreed to the request.

As darkness fell, many more people tried to push their way onto the Stanbrook and Dickson said the gangway had become choked with people as customs officials began to lose control of the situation. At this point the Captain contemplated leaving the quayside but thought better of it as the poor unfortunates begged him for mercy. He somehow sensed if he left them behind he would be condemning them to a certain death. As darkness approached, a near stampede ensued to board the ship after rumours began to circulate that a Nationalist bombing strike was imminent.

He took a total of 2683 men, women and children, slipping his moorings on the evening of the 29th March. The ship was so loaded with refugees the Plimsoll line was dangerously under the water as it struggled out of port.

As it made its way ever so slowly out into the Mediterranean Sea, a wave of Nationalist bombers approached from the north.

Dickson wrote in his ships log. *"We had only just got clear of the port when the air raid rumour proved to be true and within 10 minutes of leaving the port a most terrific bombardment of the town and port was made and the flash of the explosions could be seen quite clearly from on board my vessel and the shock of the exploding shells could almost be felt."*

The ship made its way to Oran.

By now Sebastian realised he was not going to make it onto any of the ships and fled into the streets of Alicante. It was a scene of sheer carnage as bombs rained down on the city.

Sebastian ran and ran until he could run no more. He collapsed, exhausted in a ditch on the outskirts of the village of El Campello, several kilometres north of Alicante City.

Sebastian lived the life of a vagrant for just over a week, living on scraps of food he salvaged from rubbish bins and drinking water from rain butts.

One morning he awoke staring down the barrel of a rifle held by a grinning Civil Guardia. He was severely beaten before being thrown onto an overcrowded truck.

In less than an hour Sebastian found himself in hell. He had been taken to a short term holding station called Los Almendros, so called because the camp was set within fields of Almond trees on the outskirts of the city.

Within a few days the 30,000 prisoners held in the 100 metre by 200 metre area had stripped the trees of the almonds, leaves and even the bark. It would be the only food they would get and there was only one water tap to quench the thirst of the entire camp population. Many fights broke out and more than a dozen people were beaten to death for the price of a cup of water.

Sebastian was beginning to wish he had stayed in Abdet and took his chances with the local Guardia Civil back home. He sat in the dust, starving and thirsty cursing himself, Juan Cortes, Father Ismael and anyone else he could put a name to.

On the eighth day he was transferred to the bigger working camp of Albatera and put to work in a forced labour gang on reconstruction projects. That night as he sat with up to fifty prisoners in a small, crudely constructed shed he suggested to one of the men that if the Nationalists wanted them to work at least they'd need to fill their bellies. Sebastian could not have realised how wide of the mark he'd be and over the coming weeks thousands starved to death.

There were also indiscriminate removals of prisoners from the camp by Falangists. More than 2000 people were simply hauled out and shot in the first few days alone. More than one man went mad through starvation and witnessing the sheer inhumanity and brutality of their fellow man. Several made a bolt for the perimeter fence during broad daylight in a half-hearted attempt to scale it but in reality it was no more than a simple act of suicide as the nearest machine gun posts responded accordingly, cutting the hapless escapee down.

Sebastian knew he had to escape. He had to get out and make his way back to Abdet. He began to plot, studying in particular the barred windows of the huts the prisoners slept in.

The war was officially declared over on April 1st 1939. It had lasted 2 years 8 months 2 weeks and one day.

As the spring weather turned hotter, conditions in the camp became intolerable with little shade and no let-up in the working day. At nights the prisoners were simply locked in the huge wooden huts and the Italian and Moroccan Guards stood down. The escape rate had slowed considerably, because not only were escapees shot on the spot, but two fellow prisoners with identification numbers above and below that of the escapee were shot too.

In hut 42, Sebastian's sleeping quarter in Albatera, the comrades had sworn an oath that any individual should not attempt to escape and instead they would bide their time until a mass breakout could be masterminded. Each man pledged his oath with his personal mark carved on the back of the hut door. It was 14th May 1939.

On the 27th May 1939 Sebastian Jimenez crept from his bunk in the early hours of the morning, removed the architrave from the bottom of the unglazed windows, loosened the bolts that held the bars in place and removed them. He removed only three which allowed him to squeeze through the space, run across the dusty compound to the perimeter fence, scale it and escape.

The following morning two of the prisoners of hut 42 were pulled from their beds, forced against a tree with their hands tethered and shot dead.

Three weeks later Sebastian arrived in Abdet full of remorse and denying any responsibility relating to the murder of Juan Cortes.

He was accepted back into the family fold as he spun an intricate tale how he'd been kidnapped in the middle of the night by 5th Columnists and forced to write the note left for Mar. He explained how he'd been interned in Albatera for nearly three months. His body was wasted, his eyes sunken into his skull and his skin a mass of sores and lesions. On appearance alone his story was more than plausible.

Within the week he was in church begging the priest for forgiveness claiming to have seen the error of his ways and swearing that he would never turn his back on God again. He had found Jesus Christ in Albatera he claimed, and prayed morning noon and night. He knew the man of the cloth could influence those who still wanted to turn him over to the Guardia Civil.

The priest called the elders of Abdet together the following day and informed them of his decision. They would not report Sebastian to the authorities and he would lie low and live a peaceful life from now on.

The priest's request was obeyed without question.

～

June 1940

Felipe had taught Sebastian how to drive and now asked his senior transport manager to make a business trip to Alicante Port where he would meet the next ship from Oran and supervise the cargo of wine onwards to Madrid and Santander.

Sebastian was more than a little nervous to be going back to Alicante but in accepting the well paid promotion some months back knew that this day was inevitable.

The trip to Alicante took just over three hours as he arrived just after nine o'clock at night to meet the 10.30 boat.

He made his way over to the harbour masters office to check on the progress of the boat.

"Damn, how stupid was Felipe?" he mumbled to himself when he was informed the boat wasn't due until the early hours of the morning.

Alicante port was a dark and desolate place, only now just beginning to rebuild its trade after the long war. Sebastian looked up into the night sky on more than one occasion as he made his way over to the port bar to take a little food and wine.

As he walked in he took a seat at an empty table by the window that gave a view of the port. No use complaining about the delay he thought to himself. Might as well make the most of it and eat and drink his fill. He smiled. Felipe did say he'd cover any additional expenses. He might even stay over at one of the dockside hotels and take one of the local whores for a few hours. A change was as good as a rest after all.

His thoughts were interrupted as a stranger sat down opposite him.

"I hope you don't mind amigo, I've been two days on my own with just the company of an old mule and it would do me good to exercise my jaw again."

Felipe shrugged his shoulders and nodded.

The stranger hadn't been joking, he could certainly talk, and Sebastian was more than interested in the tales of this much travelled man and warmed to him as he insisted on paying for bottle after bottle of wine.

By midnight they were both more than a little drunk. Not long afterwards the door to the bar opened and an elderly priest walked in. He looked around for somewhere to sit and to his dismay Sebastian noticed him walking over towards them. He placed a hand on the empty chair. "Do you mind if a servant of the Lord sits with you until the ship from Oran docks?"

Before Sebastian could open his mouth his new friend had spoken. "Sorry Father the seat's taken."

The priest smiled and raised his hat. "Not to worry gentlemen I see another one over by the door."

It was clear that there was more than a little hatred in the stranger's eyes as Sebastian looked across the table and the priest ambled away.

"Not a great lover of priests are you?" He questioned.

"Nor the fucking organisation he works for," he snarled.

Sebastian was smiling now as the stranger continued his vitriol.

"I'd cut his fucking throat if I had the balls, him and his sort have ruined Spain and it will only get worse."

Sebastian found himself nodding in agreement and had subconsciously lowered his voice to a whisper.

There was now only one topic of conversation and a dangerous one at that. The priest was long gone and the bar quite empty as the clock ticked around towards three o'clock.

More wine flowed and the two republican comrades put the world to rights like two friends who had known each other all their lives. At 2.57 Sebastian took it upon himself to tell Giuseppe all about how he'd taken the life of the priest Juan Francisco Cortes at La Nucia in the spring of last year. He was more than a little pleased at the way Giuseppe pumped his hand in congratulation and insisted on buying a bottle of cava by way of a toast to *Spanish men with balls.*

It was 3.34 when the bar tender gave a shout to his assembled clients that the boat from Oran was approaching the harbour. Sebastian's legs gave way from under him as soon as he stood and Giuseppe lifted him to his feet in fits of drunken laughter.

"Amigo, I fear I will need to carry you to the boat as your legs are filled with too much wine."

Sebastian was grateful for the support as his new acquaintance wrapped a firm arm around his waist and almost dragged him to the door. The outside atmosphere was even worse for Sebastian as the cool early morning air flowed into his lungs giving him yet another alcoholic rush causing him to stumble and almost fall again.

Giuseppe was still laughing as he led the way. "We will need to sober you up a little, or you'll be sending bloody wine to the four corners of the globe."

"Thanks Giuseppe, thank you so much. Where are you taking me?"

Giuseppe explained that the ship would be there for at least 24 hours and he'd have plenty time to return once he'd slept, bathed and sobered up.

"Thanks Giuseppe, I don't know what I'd do without you."

Giuseppe, not his real name, walked Sebastian out of the port and into Alicante town centre. He walked for no more than five minutes before turning into a small back lane.

He propped Sebastian up against a gate slapping him hard a few times.

"Open your eyes amigo you can't sleep here."

Sebastian wanted to sleep, it was all he wanted to do but he would sleep better in a nice bed, he knew that.

"Just get me to a lodging house Giuseppe, as soon as you can."

Another slap to the face, this time a little harder. "Open your eyes amigo."

A glint of shining silver and a hard sober glare. Giuseppe wasn't laughing now; there was no smile on his face and yes... Sebastian focussed on what he was holding."

"Giuseppe... a knife. What the -?"

The man known as the Carrier placed the tip of the blade just under Sebastian's right ear.

The last words Sebastian ever heard was that Juan Francisco Cortes died a free man. The Carrier pushed hard and drew the weapon swiftly across his throat. The razor sharp blade sliced through skin, vein, windpipe and sinew as easily as soft goat's cheese and stopped suddenly as it ground into vertebrae. Sebastian's eyes opened wide for a split second before closing again. He was aware of a dull but numb pain and a warm sensation flowing like a waterfall down his neck and covering his chest.

The Carrier allowed the dying body to fall to the ground and quickly hurried away.

As he drove his vehicle onto the road towards Albacete he thought back on a job well done.

My man from Abdet will be more than a little satisfied, he thought to himself as he lit a cigarette and blew a long plume of smoke through the open window.

The End

About the Authors

Ken Scott

Is the Author of: Jack of Hearts, A Million Would Be Nice, The Sun Will Still Shine Tomorrow. Ghost-writer of: Race Against Me - Dwain Chambers, Do The Birds Still Sing In Hell? - Horace Greasley, This Heart Within Me Burns - Crissy Rock, The Blue Door - Lise Kristensen, Sherlock's Squadron - Steve Holmes, The Shawshank Prevention – Kevin Lane, Revenge is Sweeter than Flowing Honey – Crissy Rock. He has also written two screenplays and assisted with the screenplay to DO THE BIRDS STILL SING IN HELL? soon to be a major film. Pre-production is scheduled for October 2013, to be filmed in the USA and Poland. Ken is represented by The Diane Banks Literary Agency and his publicist is Paul Gough. Follow Ken on Twitter @Kentheghost

Dave Rowland

Dave Rowland is a historian who specialises in the Spanish civil war and wrote and presented a highly acclaimed nine part radio series on the subject in the mid 2000´s for Spanish and English speaking radio. He is a Spanish National currently living in a small inland village on the Costa Blanca working as a radio broadcaster, presenting programs dedicated to Spanish news and current affairs and free-lances to other radio stations worldwide including the BBC. He has appeared regularly on Spanish television and is a journalist working for English language newspapers on the Costa Blanca, reporting on items of interest to both Spanish and English speaking residents. He has a daughter Eva, aged twelve who was born in Spain.

Lightning Source UK Ltd.
Milton Keynes UK
UKOW04f1933040915

258080UK00001B/7/P